from Jan and Jessica, 25/10/2001

PENGUIN CLASSICS

PENGUIN PO...
GENERAL EDITO...

MARTIAL

MARCUS VALERIUS MARTIALIS ...a 40 CE in Spain, but left there in 64 CE to live in Rome, whe... he came into contact with all classes, from members of the imperial court downwards. During over thirty years in Roman society, he made friends with Juvenal, Quintilian and the younger Pliny, and was an extremely keen observer of contemporary life. He published some fifteen volumes of epigrams, the first written to commemorate the opening of the Colosseum in 80 CE, the last sent from retirement in Spain, where he died more embittered than mellow *circa* 103 CE.

JOHN PATRICK SULLIVAN held appointments in Classics or Arts and Letters at the Universities of Oxford, Cambridge, Texas, Buffalo, Minnesota and Hawaii, before taking up his final position as Professor of Classics at the University of California, Santa Barbara. He was the author of *The Satyricon of Petronius: A Literary Study*, *Propertius: A Critical Introduction*, *Literature and Politics in the Age of Nero* and *Martial, The Unexpected Classic*. He also edited *Roman Poets of the Early Empire* (with A. J. Boyle) and Petronius's *Satyricon* and Seneca's *Apocolocyntosis* (in one volume) for Penguin Classics. John Sullivan died in April 1993.

ANTHONY JAMES BOYLE was born in 1942 and educated at St Francis Xavier's College, Liverpool, and Cambridge University, where he later taught. He served twenty years at Monash University, Melbourne, before moving to the USA in 1989, where he is Professor of Classics at the University of Southern California, Los Angeles. He is editor of the classical literary journal *Ramus* and his publications include *Ancient Pastoral*, *Seneca Tragicus*, *The Chaonian Dove*, *Seneca's Phaedra* and *Troades*, *The Imperial Muse* and *Roman Epic*.

MARTIAL IN ENGLISH

Edited by J. P. SULLIVAN *and* A. J. BOYLE

PENGUIN BOOKS

PENGUIN BOOKS

Published by the Penguin Group
Penguin Books Ltd, 27 Wrights Lane, London w8 5tz, England
Penguin Books USA Inc., 375 Hudson Street, New York, New York 10014, USA
Penguin Books Australia Ltd, Ringwood, Victoria, Australia
Penguin Books Canada Ltd, 10 Alcorn Avenue, Toronto, Ontario, Canada m4v 3b2
Penguin Books (NZ) Ltd, 182–190 Wairau Road, Auckland 10, New Zealand

Penguin Books Ltd, Registered Offices: Harmondsworth, Middlesex, England

First published 1996
10 9 8 7 6 5 4 3 2 1

Introductions, selection, notes, glossary and bibliographies copyright © The Estate of
J. P. Sullivan and A. J. Boyle 1996
All rights reserved

The moral right of the editors has been asserted

Set in 10/12.5pt Monotype Bembo
Typeset by Datix International Limited, Bungay, Suffolk
Printed in England by Clays Ltd, St Ives plc

Except in the United States of America, this book is sold subject
to the condition that it shall not, by way of trade or otherwise, be lent,
re-sold, hired out, or otherwise circulated without the publisher's
prior consent in any form of binding or cover other than that in
which it is published and without a similar condition including this
condition being imposed on the subsequent purchaser

For JUDY GODFREY and FAYE NENNIG

and to the memory of
JOHN PATRICK SULLIVAN (1930–1993)
who brought the dance into Italy

CONTENTS

II. THE RESTORATION TO THE AUGUSTANS: 1660–*c.*1700

III. THE EIGHTEENTH CENTURY: AUGUSTANS AND NEOCLASSICISTS

PREFACE

In July 1992 John Sullivan signed a contract with Penguin Books to edit *Martial in English*. He died in April 1993, the task incomplete. John left behind a preliminary draft of the general introduction plus mountains of Martial *materialia*, which have been indispensable to the production of this book. In the months before he died, as the cancer worked its cruel devastation, John's remaining energies and thought were ever on this project, and he and I discussed it constantly. Since his death, John's own publications on Martial, especially the three books he edited or wrote between 1987 and 1993 (see p. 404), have guided and instructed my work. Although the final responsibility rests with me, I should like to think that this *Martial in English* is one with which John would have been pleased.

I thank the following people and institutions for help of various kinds: Dr Don Fowler of Jesus College, Oxford, Dr John Henderson of King's College, Cambridge, the Librarians of Peterhouse and Trinity College, Cambridge, the Bodleian Library, Oxford, the University and Classical Faculty Library of Cambridge, the British Library and the House of Commons Library, London, the Eton College Library, Windsor, the Huntington Library, San Marino, the libraries of USC, UCSB, and of Melbourne and Monash Universities, Australia. Joseph Smith of USC gave invaluable assistance in the preparation of the hard copy and the proofs. The keen editorial eye of Christopher Ricks removed many infelicities. Judy Godfrey, John Sullivan's widow, supported the project throughout, as she had sustained her husband to the end.

USC, Los Angeles   A. J. Boyle
Christmas 1994

ACKNOWLEDGEMENTS

Grateful thanks are due to Jessie Cunningham for permission to reprint selected epigrams from *Collected Poems and Epigrams* by J. V. Cunningham (Swallow Press, 1971); to Carol Publishing Group for epigrams from *Selected Epigrams of Martial* by Donald C. Goertz (1971); to Harcourt Brace & Company for poems from *Sixty Poems of Martial in Translation*, copyright © 1967 by Dudley Fitts and renewed 1995 by Deborah W. Fitts, Cornelia H. Fitts and Daniel H. Fitts; to Bloodaxe Books Limited for epigrams from *U.S. Martial* by Tony Harrison (Bloodaxe Books, 1981); to Timothy d'Arch Smith for Brian Hill's translations from *An Eye for Ganymede*; to James Michie for selected epigrams from his *Martial: The Epigrams* (Penguin Books, 1978); to Richard O'Connell for translations from *New Epigrams from Martial*; to Fiona and Olive Pitt-Kethley, and University of California Press, for selections by Fiona Pitt-Kethley, Olive Pitt-Kethley, J. P. Sullivan and Peter Whigham from *Epigrams of Martial Englished by Divers Hands*, copyright © 1987 The Regents of the University of California; to Fiona Pitt-Kethley for translations from *The Literary Companion to Sex*; to Oxford University Press for selections from *After Martial* by Peter Porter (1972), copyright © Oxford University Press, 1972; to Faber & Faber Limited and New Directions Publishing Corporation for Ezra Pound's 'Epitaph', 'Arides', 'The Temperaments', 'Phyllidula', 'The Patterns' and 'Society' from *Personae: Collected Poems of Ezra Pound*, copyright © 1926 by Ezra Pound, and 'Thais Habet Nigros' ('Epitaph 5.43') from *Imagi* (1950); to Cambridge University Press for permission to incorporate material from J. P. Sullivan's *Martial, the Unexpected Classic: A Literary and Historical Study* (Cambridge, 1991), chapter 7, in the General Introduction to this book; to Southern Illinois University Press for selected epigrams from *Roman Poetry: From the Republic to the Silver Age* by Dorothea Wender (1980); to Anvil Press Poetry for selections from Peter Whigham's *Letter to Juvenal: 101 Epigrams from Martial* (Anvil Press Poetry, 1985).

Every effort has been made to trace or contact all copyright holders. The publishers will be glad to make good any omissions brought to our attention.

GENERAL INTRODUCTION

I. Martial's Life and Works

Marcus Valerius Martial is regarded by Spanish historians and critics of literature as one of the first eminent poets of their literary tradition, along with the younger Seneca and Lucan. The number of Spanish translators, particularly in the *siglo de oro*, who have found him congenial bears eloquent witness to his popularity and *Españolismo*.[1]

Born in Bilbilis, in northern Aragon, around 40 CE, he was one of the many writers who came to Rome from Spain in the early imperial period to take advantage of the rewarding literary climate there. He was unfortunate, however, in that his potential patrons and friends, notably the Senecan family, had fallen into disfavour with the emperor Nero around the time of his arrival in 64 CE. He had therefore to wait until the opening of the Colosseum in 80 CE by the emperor Titus to become a literary success with his first volume of epigrams, *De Spectaculis* ('On the Games'), which celebrated the magnificence of the building and the munificence of the imperial games put on to inaugurate its formal opening. At least one of the epigrams from this mutilated book, *Spec.* 25 (28/29 in Shackleton Bailey's Teubner text), on Leander's swim to his tryst with Hero, became almost a cult among seventeenth-century translators and poets, not only in Spain but elsewhere in Europe.

Beyond the two collections of distichs to accompany gifts and the book of epigrams on the amphitheatre, Martial issued twelve volumes

---

1. For a generous selection of their versions, see D. Víctor Suárez Capelleja, *Marco Valerio Marcial, Epigramas Traducidos en parte por Jáuregui, Argensola, Juan Iriarte, Salinas, el P. Morell y otros*, 3 vols. (Madrid, 1890–91; repr. 1919–23).

of miscellaneous short poems, which varied in length and metre as well as subject, between 80 CE and his death around 103. The total number of the surviving epigrams (1,556) could be raised to over 1,600, if allowance were made for the epigrams that had to be omitted from the censored Book 10 and those lost from the obviously curtailed Book 12. This last volume was hastily dispatched from his home town of Bilbilis, to which he had retired in adverse circumstances a few years earlier. Despite the generosity of a rich woman patron, Marcella, he did not find his reception and life there entirely congenial.[2] Beyond these formal occasions of publication, however, much of his work had been circulated in smaller instalments among his circles of distinguished patrons in Rome. Many of the occasional poems in these smaller collections were addressed to them and reveal something of the original arrangement.

Martial's poetic programme, although it looked back to aspects of Catullus' short poems, was innovative both in its formal consistency, its adhesion to one genre and its determination to elevate the short poem, generally called an epigram, to a lofty place in the artistic firmament. Beneath a mock-modest affectation of playfulness, his aim was to subvert the traditionally respected genres of epic and tragedy in favour of the short lyric and the witty epigram. In later ages, when the 'slighter' literary forms were much in vogue, Martial's reputation progressively increased. His contemporary popularity, however, was also impressive, even though his subsequent reputation has varied enormously, reaching its peak in the European Renaissance and in England in the sixteenth and seventeenth centuries.[3] His lack of esteem in the late eighteenth, the nineteenth and the early twentieth centuries is to be attributed in part to the large number of evidently flattering poems directed to his patrons and to the high proportion of obscene material in his verses, which has always constituted a stumbling-block for moralistic and aesthetic critics. (He himself

2. For further information on Martial's life and publications, see J. P. Sullivan, *Martial, The Unexpected Classic: A Literary and Historical Study* (Cambridge, 1991), chapters 1 and 2.

3. For a survey of his reputation through the ages, see J. P. Sullivan, *The Classical Heritage: Martial* (New York and London, 1993), esp. pp. 1–66.

xvii] GENERAL INTRODUCTION

defended this element in his work on grounds of realism and 'social significance', and by analogy with fertility rituals and apotropaic magic.)

His main poetic talent was for 'wit' (in its broadest sense), which accounts both for the gnomic concision of his quotable reflections on life, society and human foibles, and for the vivid, concrete imagery in his descriptions of people and places. But his range was enormous: translations of Greek epigrams about the professions, fictitious and genuine epitaphs, scarifying satiric descriptions of court characters and literary poseurs, the sights of the streets, and elegant trifles on works of art and books are found in company with lavish descriptions of the architectural wonders of Rome, the building programme, the moral reforms and the military victories of Domitian, the joys of country life and the mansions of his patrons, or, by no means least, polished Epicurean reflections on the happy life, friendship and the true use of riches. Strong claims have been made for his superiority as a thoughtful Epicurean commentator on friendship and the Happy Life – his poem on this subject (*Ep.* 10.47) being perhaps the most frequently translated poem in English literature – or as a writer of poignant memorial poems on dead friends and servants. But his forte was the satiric epigram. His accomplishment here inspired his friend Juvenal and a host of English imitators in the Elizabethan, Jacobean and Restoration periods. Sir John Harington, Ben Jonson, Robert Herrick, Abraham Cowley and Sir Charles Sedley are the most obvious examples of his devotees and admirers in this area.

The picture of the world of Rome that Martial offers us is remarkable for its pointillist detail, but the satirical lens he directs on it has a conservative focus. Martial's vision of his society, a society based on imperialist expansion and a slave economy, is hierarchical and the poet does not openly question its underpinnings. At the summit is the present emperor, whoever he may be. Good emperors are to be praised (Augustus, Titus, Domitian, Nerva, Trajan), the bad to be damned (Nero and, after his death, Domitian). Members of the senatorial and equestrian classes who fulfil their proper functions in terms of service to the emperor and generous patronage towards their clients, not least their literary protégés, must be duly honoured.

If, however, they fall into such vices as avarice, stinginess, extravagance or effeminate sexual perversions, they must be castigated. Upstart rich freedmen must not ape their betters or cross social boundaries. And, from the other side, upper-class ladies must not violate the engendered social codes by adultery, by liaisons with slaves (*Ep*. 5.17; 7.14) or by even more disreputable activities, which usurp the sexual privileges of the active Roman male. This last class may of course take sexual advantage, in a gentlemanly way, of prostitutes and slaves, both male and female. If these know their proper place (cf. *Ep*. 3.65; 4.7; 11.26; 11.39), they will be properly complimented.

Martial, however, like his fellow satirists, describes a world where these social barriers have crumbled. And the veneer of hypocrisy and pretence which overlays the countless moral, sexual and civic transgressions of aristocrats of both sexes, philosophers, miscreant oldsters, social climbers and impudent slaves stimulates still further the poet's mordant and obscene wit. The poet professes to be shocked and he tries to shock his audience in return.

To secure these calculated effects Martial has at his disposal a wide variety of metres, an inward grasp of the Graeco-Roman literary tradition, not least of satire and invective, a keen eye for telling metaphors and images, disreputable analogies and, in general, a superb command of the Latin language and its armoury of rhetorical and poetic techniques.

We are left then an impressive body of work of enormous range from the lyric and elegiac to the satiric and pornographic, from which emerges a well-defined and critical personality (or persona) moving confidently in a fully realized if sometimes sombre world, which alternately fascinates and disquiets. The problem for the modern reader and for the editors of this volume is how to explain, and so appreciate, the reasons for the enormous popularity and influence that Martial enjoyed in the Renaissance and the sixteenth century among European poets and critics. Humour and wit are his most obvious characteristics, but these are not easily transmitted to later generations, whose taste for jokes and in particular amusing verbal play will differ radically from that of Romans in the early empire. And of course there is more to this great Spanish poet than those qualities. Besides the marmoreal and serious poems on death and friendship, there is also the brilliant imagery so admired by Lord Macaulay as well as the imaginative conceits borrowed and stolen by the Elizabethan masters of the epigram such as Sir John Harington and Ben Jonson, not to mention the French poets of the *Pléiade* and such Spanish wits as Baltasar Gracián and Francisco Quevedo in the *siglo de oro* in Spain.

A clue to his fascination for later translators and poets may be found in the younger Pliny's obituary written around 104 CE, on learning of the poet's recent death. Pliny wrote (*Epistles* 3.21): 'I hear that Valerius Martial is dead and I am very distressed. He was a man of great talent, sharpness and perception. His writing shows a high degree of wit and sarcasm (*sal, fel*) and just as much charm (*candor*).' The ambiguity Pliny notices in Martial's work is certainly there and accounts for the intriguing juxtaposition of extravagant praise for his patrons and savage satire on the institution of patronage itself; of lavish compliments to selected high-class Roman matrons and ob-scene disparagement of the female sex in general; of laudations of imperial moral edicts and subtle allusions to their failure and to the hypocrisy behind the power. Humour and wit were recognized, long before Freud pointed it out, as the classic verbal modes for expressing disguised, even unconscious, hostility. No one played better on the humorous inconsistencies and pretentious folly gener-ated by social hypocrisy than Martial, all the while taking his audience into his confidence and disarming all outraged reaction by his deferen-tial apologies to the reader and the modest stance of the poor, but intermittently independent, poet.

The ambivalence, even plasticity, in Martial's work has led, in more recent eras, to serious misjudgements about his *oeuvre*, ranging from tepid and selective praise to moral vilification and even censor-ship. But literary periods which have relished the double-edge of wit and serio-comic comments on society and sexuality have been more than ready to give Martial his due, as the abundance of versions from which to choose for this volume has amply indicated. Perhaps this last decade of the twentieth century with its attunement to the com-plexities of the written word is more suited than many to the semiotic

richness of the Martial poems, their moral and intellectual provoc-
ativeness, and capacity always to make us think. The reader should be
especially aware of the theatrical image underscoring Martial's poetic
productions. He plays with the reader as he does with his world.

II. Martial in the English Tradition

The avocation of adapting or translating Martial into later Latin
verse began early. Godfrey of Winchester (c.1050–1107), the first and
perhaps best of the Anglo-Norman writers of Latin verse, wrote
epigrams in Martial's style, being sometimes mistaken for the Latin
poet himself. Godfrey takes over Martial's fictitious names, and, like
him, varies the length of his epigrams from distichs to quatrains and
six- or eight-liners, and even to poems of around thirty lines. He is
far more moralistic than Martial and deals with more historical and
religious material. Martial was plundered for quotations, and even
vicious turns of phrase, by such learned English and Norman wits as
John of Salisbury (1115–80), Walter Map (c.1133–1213), Peter of
Blois (d. 1200), Henry of Huntingdon, Archdeacon of that ilk and
Herefordshire (d. c.1155), and Gerald de Barri, better known as
Giraldus Cambrensis (1147–1222). Walter Map, in his amusing and
rebarbative *De Nugis Curialium* (c.1182), alludes to Martial (1.3.8),
quoting him simply as 'The Cook' (5.10.7–8).

The further history of Martial's reception in Great Britain is more
complicated. 'A great age of literature is perhaps always a great age of
translations; or follows it,' as Ezra Pound remarked.[4] A strong case can
be made that Martial exercised a profound effect not only on the
practice and style of English poetry but also on the development of
English verse as it culminated in the wit and polish of the heroic couplets
of Dryden, Pope and the Augustan age of English poetry as a whole.[5]

4. 'Notes on Elizabethan Classicists', in T. S. Eliot (ed.), *Literary Essays of Ezra Pound*
(London, 1954), p. 232. Pound's essay originally appeared in *The Egoist* (1917–18).
5. See, for example, P. Nixon, *Martial and the Modern Epigram* (Boston and New
York, 1927) and J. P. Sullivan, 'Is Martial a Classic? A Reply', *Cambridge Quarterly* 18
(1989), pp. 303ff.

The beginnings of Martial's influence in the English Renaissance go back to the neo-Latin epigram writing of Desiderius Erasmus (1466–1536) and, more importantly, Sir Thomas More (1478–1535). More tended to look to the Greek epigram rather than to Martial, but a large number of his short satirical comments on contemporary social and religious subjects are reminiscent of the Roman poet. Verse translations of More's epigrams into English begin with those made by Timothe Kendall for his *Flovvers of Epigrammes* (London, 1577), a collection of classical, neo-Latin and modern epigrams, including the anthologist's own. A larger collection of More's epigrams was included, along with some of John Owen's and Martial's epigrams (from *De Spectaculis*), by Thomas Pecke in his *Parnassi Puerperium* (London, 1659). This practice of englishing Latin epigrams increased Martial's popularity between the late sixteenth and early eighteenth centuries in England despite the carping about his obscenity from such tender-minded translators as Kendall. Around 1540, Henry Howard, Earl of Surrey, the brilliant translator of *Aeneid* 2 and 4, turned into felicitous English Martial's poem on the Happy Life (*Ep.* 10.47). As though to attest to Martial's celebrity beyond English borders, the same poem in 1571 was done into British (or Welsh, as it is called today) by Simwnt Fychan.[6]

The cultivation of exercises in Latin epigram by English public schools such as Eton and Winchester did much for Martial's growing reputation. Epigrams were almost *de rigueur* to preface new books, to please patrons and to commemorate the deaths of scholars and sundry personages at court or in the church. Epigrams were also tempting vehicles to express *odium scholasticum* or to puff one's own educational and critical views. The best Latin epigrammatist of the earliest part of the century was John Parkhurst, Bishop of Norwich (d. 1575). His complete epigrams, with some other poems, were published in 1573. Like Martial, whom he cites, he often employs iambic metres in his short poems. Almost every kind of epigram is represented and his satirical epigrams against human frailties, or against Popish priests

---

6. It may be found in W. E. A. Axon, *Simwnt Fychan's Welsh Translation of Martial's Epigram of the Happy Life, 1571* (Manchester, 1900).

and bishops, rely heavily on Martial's manner. Parkhurst too appeared in translation in Kendall's anthology, and was allotted more space than any other author except Martial himself. The Scot, George Buchanan (1506–82), tutor of King James VI of Scotland ('the prince of poets' to his contemporaries), produced a number of Latin epigrams (about 250), which appeared in his three books of *Epigrammata* (Heidelberg, 1584) and other volumes. His debt to Martial is most pronounced in the frank and sometimes obscene language, in the vivid images, and in the rhetorical structures of some of his more virulent pasquinades. Wit and concision, however, are not Buchanan's most obvious virtues.

Surrey's englishing of Martial's most famous poem had appeared in that revolutionary manifesto of the 'new' English poetry, Tottel and Grimaldi's *Songes and Sonnettes*, better known as *Tottel's Miscellany*, published in 1557. The English Renaissance was a time of unprecedented and self-conscious experimentation in poetic rhythm and verse form. *Tottel's Miscellany* was the fruit of an attempt by Surrey and Sir Thomas Wyatt to profit from their exposure to Italian Renaissance poetic technique and to remedy the lack of metrical strictness and effective rhythm then apparent in English verse. It was in this endeavour that Martial was to be a great ally. The *Miscellany* emphasized the Latin classics, but included translations of the Latin epigrams of later writers. Martial henceforward attracted not only translators but also imitators and emulators. The neo-Latin epigrammatist from Wales, John Owen (1564–*c*.1628), brought out three books of epigrams in Latin in 1607 and was promptly hailed as 'the English Martial'. Most modern critics would find this title excessively flattering for Owen, but he was much admired and widely imitated on the continent, not least in Germany, where his Protestant pieties and contemporary allusions found a receptive audience. Although his religious themes, attacks on simony, the Pope and papist practices, introduced a different strain from Martial, his reflections on moral, classical and literary topics, his jokey epigrams on weather, time, lice, lamps and looking-glasses, his concern with marriage, adultery and sex, his tirades against doctors, lawyers and divines, are self-consciously indebted to the ancient epigrammatist. He became

Martialis rediuiuus, the coveted title vied for by Martial's admirers. Of all this great age's contenders John Owen deserved the title the most. He wrote in all about 1500 poems, almost equal in number to Martial's, but his corpus, because of the large number of single elegiac couplets, totals a mere 4,500 lines as against Martial's 10,000.

During the reign of Queen Elizabeth I (1558–1603) poetic volumes consisting wholly or partly of epigrams in English flooded from the presses. Their authors were in Martial's debt to varying degrees, and one reason for his high reputation among them was that, from the Elizabethan period to the late eighteenth century, poets were tolerably comfortable with the concept of patronage and the self-seeking flattery it seemed to demand. One whole area of Martial's writing, patronal and imperial panegyric, offered grist for English sycophantic mills. Ben Jonson in addressing King James compares himself to Martial addressing the emperor Domitian (*To the Ghost of Martial*; see p. 40), and even Dryden, in his *Discourse concerning Satire*, adopts an adulatory theme of Martial's (*Ep.* 8.18; see p. 115) to compliment the Earl of Dorset. Much of this betokens a somewhat superficial reading of the epigrams, since Martial's laudations of Domitian and others are often qualified, some would say undermined, by the poems with which they are juxtaposed and by their own historical and literary allusions.[7] The reading, however, clearly suited the patron–poet context of the times and was received and exploited enthusiastically.

Another factor that favoured Martial at this time, despite his mock modesty about the limitations of the genre in which he worked, was that the sixteenth century was the great age (before our own) of the amateur poet. It was the time when monarchs, courtiers and country gentlemen, having little enough to do in their leisure, paraded their culture by writing verses, whether religious, reflective or amatory. The amateur poet, however, has a limited breath and an even more limited inspiration. Consequently, the short lyric, and in particular the epigram, flourished. Monumental productions such as Chapman's *Homer* or Golding's *Metamorphoses* are overwhelmed by the plethora

---

7. See J. Garthwaite, 'The Panegyrics of Domitian in Martial Book 9', *Ramus* 22 (1993), pp. 78–102.

of writers whose chosen genre was the short, ingenious, witty poem, whether dedicatory or derisory, sentimental or sententious, directed at the quick or the dead, the real or the fictitious.

The number of collections of epigrams that appeared from 1550 onwards is remarkable and merits its own explanation.[8] To the devotee of these short poems and epigrams, Martial was the ancient epigrammatist *par excellence*; the treasures of the *Palatine Anthology* were not as yet unlocked. Martial became to epigram what Ovid was to love poetry, Seneca to drama and Virgil to epic. The Roman epigrammatist's influence was especially strong between the last decade of the sixteenth century and the first decades of the seventeenth. Typical is the way the Revd Thomas Bastard (1566–1618), one of the more accomplished practitioners of the genre, waxes eloquent on Martial's stature as pinnacle and model for his Elizabethan epigoni (*Chrestoleros* 1.17, *de poeta Martiali*):

> Martiall, in sooth none should presume to write,
>> Since time hath brought thy Epigrams to light:
> For through our writing, thine so prais'de before
> Haue this obteinde, to be commended more:
>> Yet to our selues although we winne no fame,
>> Wee please, which get our maister a good name.

In addition, the complete freedom from the post-Romantic stress on originality and deeply personal experience as material for poetic expression ensured the close relationship of poetry and translation. At the same time, the metrical and linguistic conciseness of Martial's Latin forced his English emulators to strive to reproduce in English a similar sharp precision and verbal economy. The closed form found most suitable was the heroic couplet, which functioned well over the short and the long stretch. This began to dominate in both imitation and translation as Martial's neatness of line and phrase became naturalized in the hands of the best practitioners.

There was a further attraction: unlike other Roman poets then

8. See J. P. Sullivan, 'Martial and English Poetry', *Classical Antiquity* 9 (1990), pp. 149ff.

popular who leaned heavily on mythological topics, Martial drew his subjects largely from everyday life in a metropolis not unlike London. The types to be found there, the Covent Garden abbesses, the Domini Do Littles, the gulls and the fussocks, had their equivalents in the Rome of the Flavians. Only a few changes had to be made.

Given Martial's multifarious styles and interests, different aspects of his work would attract different admirers. Just as the Earl of Surrey had used Martial's lapidary sententiousness in his version of 'The Happy Life', so the Elizabethan and post-Elizabethan satirists found his 'pointed' style extremely effective against their own victims. Most English epigrammatists, of course, toned down Martial's obscenity, even in heterosexual matters. Few indeed translated or adapted, except in the most delicate ways, Martial's references to lesbian or oral sexuality. For the pederastic and otherwise perverse Roman motifs Elizabethans such as the Latin epigrammatist, Dr Thomas Campion, could substitute the imagery of the dreaded pox, that ever-present fear, according to D. H. Lawrence, in the literature of the period.[9]

The techniques of the epigram would suit other, equally contemporary topics. Thomas Bastard, for instance, uses them to tackle such issues as the worship of relics, while boasting in his *Epistle Dedicatory*: 'I haue taught Epigrams to speake chastlie . . . barring them of their olde libertie.' It would have been impossible, without Martial's example, to find such masterpieces of compression and pathos as the famous epitaph 'Upon the Death of Sir Albert Morton's Wife' by Sir Henry Wotton (1568–1639):

> He first deceas'd; She for a little tri'd
> To live without Him: lik'd it not, and di'd.

The epitaph's later expansion into Crabbe's cynical triplet (*Tales of the Hall*) confirms the debt to Martial:[10]

---

9. See E. D. McDonald (ed.), *Phoenix, The Posthumous Papers of D. H. Lawrence* (London, 1936), p. 551.
10. We owe the reference to Professor Ricks.

His father early lost, his mother tried
To live without him, liked it not, and – sigh'd,
When, for her widow'd hand, an amorous youth applied.

Martial's impact on the literary consciousness of Elizabethan England was of the utmost significance for the progress of English poetry, not just its matter. The seed fell at the right time and in the right ground. There was a native Anglo-Saxon tradition of brief poems incorporating satire, realism and humour which tended to rely on sub-literary farce, proverbs and folk anecdote. With these are associated such names as Sir Thomas More, John Skelton, Robert Crowley and the courtier John Heywood. The thinking was simple and direct, but early Elizabethan writing was expansive and rambunctious. The classical formalism of Martial pared down this expansiveness, partly by stimulating the taste for quick and amusing turns of thought. The formal neatness of the epigram was soon to show itself in the emblem books. As well as encouraging brevity and concision, epigram also encouraged pointed and surprising ideas.

The insistence on *aprosdoketon* and startling, often coarse, metaphors and similes was a compelling characteristic of Martial's style. The embodiment by Donne, Cowley, Herbert and others of Metaphysical wit in the seventeenth century was the indigenous flowering of the Mannerism of Italy, Spain and France. Donne's knowledge of, and respect for, Martial is expressed in one of his very few epigrams ('Raderus', see p. 38), and Abraham Cowley did some ingenious *Imitations*, which were appended to William Hay's translations of select epigrams in 1755.

The potentialities of epigram in English literature were best realized, however, in the poetry of Sir John Harington (c.1560–1612) and Ben Jonson (1572–1637), where Martial's lessons are taken to heart and critically absorbed. Harington died in 1612, and there was no substantial edition of his epigrams until 1618. Like Martial, however, he circulated his poems in manuscript among friends (and at court) during his lifetime. At least eighty of his 428 epigrams are based on Martial, some of them being very faithful translations. He expressed the sentiments of many when he wrote (*The Metamorphosis of Ajax*):[11] 'It is certaine, that of all poems, the Epigram is the plesawntest, & of all that writes Epigrams, Martiall is counted the wittyest.' His literary indebtedness to Martial he described as 'honest Theft' (*Epigram to Samuel Daniel*, 9–10):

> You'le spoile the Spaniards, by your writ of Mart:
> And I the Romanes rob, by wit, and Art.

Harington's verses took the fancy of the literary public immediately – deservedly, since he had developed the English epigram to its highest point so far. He would find a place in collections and anthologies over several decades.

Ben Jonson became, somewhat belatedly, Harington's rival as chief exponent of the art of the epigram. The influence of Martial is reflected in his high regard for his own *Epigrammes*, which he called 'the ripest of my studies' in the volume's dedication to the Earl of Pembroke. Again, like Harington, he took the form seriously, not just as an opportunity to show off his abilities as a translator over the short stretch. He dropped the strategic denial of the artistic seriousness and importance of epigram with which Martial, followed by Harington, had intermittently, if ironically, disarmed his readers. Jonson went even further than Harington in imitating his Roman exemplar. He intended to be a radical, as well as a serious, innovator in the now established tradition of English epigram, or rather, since epigram as a genre was developing its predominantly satiric paradigm, the short poem. He shed direct translations, Latinate names for standard characters and Latin titles; he revived the eulogistic epigrams Martial had sent his patrons, and adopted the thematic cycles of interconnected epigrams which were a feature of Martial's books. He took even greater liberties than Martial in the length of his poems. (The coda to his *Epigrammes*, for instance, has two hundred lines; Martial's longest poem, *Ep.* 3.58, a 'model' for Jonson's *To Penshurst*, has fifty-one.)

Before Jonson the epigram was in danger of becoming little more

---

11. *The Metamorphosis of Ajax* (London, 1596), ed. E. S. Donno (New York and London, 1962), p. 97.

than mere 'laughter and a jest', a short witty poem satirizing folly, often with obscene undertones. Jonson, glancing perhaps at the tradition of the *Greek Anthology*, or, more likely, at Martial's broader practice, worked into his *Epigrammes* not only the expected satirical examples, but also dignified epistles, epitaphs and reflections on life and death, covering the whole range of human experience. He insisted that his apparently novel epigrammatic style 'is the old way, and the true' (*Epigrammes* xviii).

The restoration of eulogy in epigram cannot hide the fact that a small preponderance of Jonson's poems are bitingly or comically satiric. His sallies against avarice, gluttony and lechery, even if just a deferential bow to Martial's obscene epigrams, had a disproportionate effect on his friend, the Revd Robert Herrick (1591–1674), whose *Hesperides* (1648) contains even more direct translations of Martial and more offensive poems (150 out of 1100). Herrick's better-known lyrics, on the other hand, reflect the more sentimental and complimentary aspect of Martial's epigrams and the more tender side of the *Greek Anthology*.

Martial's satiric talent was his forte. This Sir John Harington and his fellows wished to refine into a contemporary serio-humorous weapon to criticize, or defend, the great, if troubled, institutions of Church, State, and Family. These epigrammatists accordingly furnished the prototypes of English satire as it would be practised by John Oldham, John Dryden and their aristocratic coevals, and later by Alexander Pope and his successors. In this way, the literary friendship between Martial and his younger contemporary, Juvenal, was reproduced in the relationship in English poetry between epigram and satire.

Elizabethan satire did not initially work towards the polished heroic couplet of Augustan satire. Its enthusiasts looked to Horace's supposedly pedestrian *Sermones*, to Persius' crabbed and obscure diction, and to Juvenal's torrential hexameters for their deliberately flat or rugged style. It was the struggle to imitate the qualities of Martial's (and Ovid's) neat distichs, not the emulation of the Roman hexameter, that refined the English heroic couplet.

There are social, as well as literary factors, that affect our consideration of Martial as a literary model in this period. Satiric epigram, like satire itself, was not a poetaster's pastime to be lightly indulged in, at least in an age of growing absolutism and the repression of dissidents. Martial's social satire, along with his conventional and moralistic sexual jibes, is interwoven with praise of powerful patrons and the current emperor in a way which sometimes seems to subvert those very laudations. Martial, cleverly translated or adapted, could be an excellent camouflage for the expression of unpopular views on Church and State, current politics, the state of poetry or society, or even one's personal piques. Satire would serve much the same purpose in the next generation, when writers of greater staying power met with patrons of greater paying power. As Tudor absolutism and Stuart caprice waned before the growing power of the middle classes and their instrument, Parliament, satiric epigram flourished. With the Restoration, literary hell broke loose: the satiric epigram was freed from any fetters it had felt in Tudor times. The dissolute but gifted Earl of Rochester threw off a number of poems in the spirit of Martial, and Sir Charles Sedley (also gifted and dissolute) freely adapted a number of Martial's satiric epigrams for his own *Court Characters*.

The satiric possibilities which Martial offered his English successors, along with the encomiastic epigrams with which his books were crammed and his chameleon adaptability to climes and times, suggest some explanations for his attractiveness as a pattern for poets. But Martial's unexpected power flows also from that other quality, less political, less social, more verbal and formal, the quality that was, if intermittent, certainly pervasive, in his better books: that is his 'wit', which was accentuated by the natural brevity of the Latin language. That sharpened both the tenor and the vehicle of his invective. All of this aided the makers of English poetry in their struggle towards the formal perfection presented them, for good or ill, by the poetry of Greece and Rome. Martial, like Seneca, seemed to present an achievable goal: compact format and sure control, metrically and linguistically, with a decisive climax. As with a sonnet or a sestina, the 'sense of an ending' was dictated by the form, unlike the unbuttoned dramatic poetry of the age. Elizabethan poetry ached for Italian or classical order, whether this was construed as form or, for the admirers of Martial, climax, a time to stop.

Edmund Waller (1605–87) may have refined English 'numbers', in Dr Johnson's mind,[12] but when certain adventitious circumstances of state and civil liberty encouraged satire and epigram to enter the political arena, Martial and Juvenal trained the English pugilists to punch. Hence the justice of the claim that the lineal descendants of Martial's biting elegiac distichs are the couplets of John Dryden and Alexander Pope, themselves among the best coiners of poetic epigram in the language. The line of descent is there. Just as Martial had inspired Juvenal to become a supremely witty satirist in Latin, abandoning the serpentine postures of Horace and Persius, so in turn the Elizabethan and Jacobean enthusiasm for Martialian epigram led to the more extended, but equally witty, satires of the great Augustans. These could imitate Juvenal himself, but the sure englishing of formal satiric wit would have been scarcely possible without the earlier work of Martial's keen admirers, such as Harington and Jonson. The original satiric moulds could not be taken over directly, because Juvenal's units were the paragraph and the line, but Martial's elegiac distichs, along with Ovid's, had paved the way to the heroic couplet.[13]

As for the avowed verse translators of Martial, the first was Thomas May (1595–1650), the Cambridge-educated parliamentarian, a translator of Virgil and Lucan, who published *Select Epigrams of Martial Englished* in 1629. Perhaps his 'Most servile wit and Mercenary pen' (Marvell's words) found Martial congenial. The next significant set of versions were the work of Robert Fletcher, *Ex Otio Negotium: Or, Martiall his Epigrams Translated* (London, 1656). This was followed by Thomas Pecke's translations of *Liber de Spectaculis* in *Parnassi*

12. *Lives of the English Poets* (London, 1783). 'Waller', §143: 'He [Waller] certainly very much excelled in smoothness most of the writers who were living when his poetry commenced.'

13. On this whole question, see W. B. Piper's magisterial study, *The Heroic Couplet* (Cleveland and London, 1969). Piper comments on p. 5: 'The closed couplet evolved by and large from the efforts of many Elizabethan poets . . . to reproduce in English the effects of the Latin elegiac distich, especially as it had been employed by Ovid in his *Amores* and *Heroides* and by Martial in his *Epigrammaton*.'

Puerperium (1659), and then by Henry Killigrew's anonymously published *Select Epigrams of Martial Englished* (London, 1689; reprinted 1695), in which the author sometimes adapted the versions of his predecessors. This paucity of publicly proclaimed translations of Martial is no true gauge of Martial's popularity. His work was being 'translated' in more creative ways by leading poets and wits, even if, as a somewhat disreputable author, a regard for him had to be also somewhat circumspect.

Even in the next century, witty epigrams borrowing heavily from Martial were still in vogue. Versions or imitations of him might appear in *The Spectator, The Rambler* or *The Gentleman's Magazine*. A number of minor poets drew on him for inspiration, most notably John Byrom (1692–1763), author of the famous ambiguously loyal toast, 'God bless the King! I mean the Faith's Defender . . .' But some of the best writers of the period would quote him (or try their hands at a version or two), Congreve, Walpole, Steele, Johnson, Prior, Young, Addison and Fielding among them. Matthew Prior (1664–1721) in particular reminds one of Martial in his willingness to poke fun at physical infirmities and social contretemps.

Translation of Martial on a larger scale is represented in *Select Epigrams of Martial* (London, 1755) by William Hay, MP (1695–1755), if the versions of J. Hughes (London, 1737) and E. B. Greene (London, 1774) are set aside as too minimal to count. Hay professes that the production 'is a translation or imitation of Martial; or both'. He adds hastily, anticipating the censorious Victorian reaction to the poet: 'Not of all his epigrams; that would be unpardonable. Many are full of obscenity, beneath a man: others of adulation, unbecoming a Roman . . .' The modest selection derives its value from an Appendix incorporating the expansive *Imitations* by Abraham Cowley and some anonymous attempts from the pages of Addison's *Spectator*.

A later assault on Martial was more grotesque: he was taken to be a moralist. James Elphinston (1721–1809), a schoolmaster, devised a plan to publish his verse translations of Martial by subscription in 1782, having submitted a specimen of them to the public in 1778. On this eccentric translation, *The Epigrams of M. Val. Martial, in Twelve*

Books: with a Comment by James Elphinston, two resounding verdicts were passed. The first was by Robert Burns, who wrote (1787):

> O thou, whom Poesy abhors,
> Whom Prose has turned out of doors;
> Heard'st thou yon groan? – proceed no further!
> 'Twas laurell'd Martial calling, Murther!

The other verdict, of Dr Samuel Johnson, is recorded by Mrs Hester Thrale Piozzi, who was at the time collecting versions of the much translated epigram on Arria Paeta (*Ep.* 1.13); he pronounced that the Elphinston translations had in them 'too much folly for madness, I think, and too much madness for folly'.

The last translator deserving attention in this period was Nathaniel Brassey Halhed (1751–1830), a controversial figure and a polemical satirist in his own right. In 1793 and 1794 he published anonymously some versions and imitations of Martial, adapting the originals not only to honour his friend and patron, Warren Hastings, but also to attack such disparate political figures as Tom Paine, Edmund Burke and Charles James Fox. The imitations also made fun of such intimates as Samuel Parr and Richard Brinsley Sheridan. The friends were not amused and the reviews were savage, castigating the model as much as the imitator. The Victorian Age had arrived.

The latter part of the eighteenth century had read the writings of Rousseau and Tom Paine and seen the revolutions in the thirteen colonies and France. A new spirit was abroad, a spirit alien to Martial's genius – Romanticism, with its revolt against the established social and literary order and its exaltation of the individual and the undefiled lyric impulse. Its largest effects on Martial's reputation would be felt later when Victorian moralistic attitudes would further contribute to his unpopularity in England. No matter, the Romantic estimation of epigram is already evident in the remark attributed to the classical scholar and textual critic, Richard Porson (1759–1808), in Landor's *Imaginary Conversations*: 'Certainly the dignity of a great poet is thought to be lowered by the writing of epigrams.'[14] British scholar-

14. *The Works and Life of Walter Savage Landor* (London, 1876), vol. iv, p. 27.

ship therefore in the nineteenth century, by contrast with the activity centring upon Martial's work in Germany, produced only a few sanitized school editions of selected epigrams by H. M. Stephenson (1880), Paley and Stone (1881), and Sellar and Ramsay (Edinburgh, 1884). All of their introductions allude apologetically to Martial's flattery and those 'epigrams bearing most undisguisedly on the fashionable vices'. As one editor put it: 'No writings more imperatively demand censorship.'

Even scholarship may be subject to contemporary prejudice and ideological pressures, particularly when it reaches out to a larger public or assumes a pedagogic role in society. The Romantic poets and their Victorian successors had long been parading their greater affinity to Greek rather than Latin literature. The critical devaluation of Martial had been ironically summarized in Byron's lines in *Don Juan* (1.xliii), published in 1819:

> And then what proper person could be partial
> To all those nauseous epigrams of Martial?[15]

Emblematic of the period, despite its reservations, is Lord Macaulay's magisterial judgement:

I have now gone through the first seven books of Martial, and have learned about 360 of the best lines. His merit seems to me to lie, not in wit, but in the rapid succession of vivid images. I wish he were less nauseous. He is as great a beast as Aristophanes. He is certainly a very clever, pleasant writer. Sometimes he runs Catullus himself hard. But, besides his indecency, his servility and his mendicancy disgust me.[16]

Andrew Amos, with *Martial and the Moderns* (Cambridge, 1858), had little success in changing popular opinion by rehearsing the many allusions to his work found in famous prose and verse authors. His effort to show how Martial had contributed to forming the character and advancing the progress of English literature is

---

15. This does not of course represent Byron's own viewpoint. See the passage from *Don Juan* quoted on pp. 245f., where the practice of removing Martial's obscene poems to an appendix at the back of school editions is lampooned.
16. G. O. Trevelyan, *The Life and Letters of Lord Macaulay* (London, 1878), p. 478.

subverted by his admission that Martial's works were now seldom read, partly because of his references to 'odious vices ... which render his work unfit to be placed in the hands of youth' (p. iv). It must therefore have taken some courage for that admirable publisher of the classics in translation, Henry George Bohn (1796–1884), who had appeared at least once as defence witness in an obscenity trial, to superintend personally the translation of Martial published in 1860 in the Bohn Classical Library. Bohn is naturally defensive in his preface, but one great merit of the collection was the reprinting of various metrical versions from different periods, including those from 'a very interesting MS of the age of Elizabeth'.[17] With the prose versions, he felt impelled 'in those instances where an English translation given faithfully would not be tolerable' to give the Latin only, sometimes accompanied by the Italian versions of Giuspanio Graglia.

This enterprise did not satisfy some 'Other Victorians', who had a somewhat *louche* interest in Martial, among them George Augustus Sala (1828–96), journalist and wit. With some Oxford friends, he published anonymously in 1868 the privately printed *Index Expurgatorius of Martial, Literally Translated, Comprising All the Epigrams hitherto Omitted by English Translators*. This curious volume consisted of a prose translation with copious, and often fanciful, notes on the sexual matters, accompanied by original metrical versions in a bouncy late-Victorian style, somewhat reminiscent of Swinburne. Martial's reputation as an underground classic was going up just as his esteem in academe was declining.

One writer of distinction did take up cudgels for Martial. This was Robert Louis Stevenson (1850–94), who, with the encouragement of a French crib, fashioned some admirable, if occasionally truncated, translations. In an essay on 'Books which have Influenced Me' in *The British Weekly* of 13 May 1887, Stevenson wrote:

Martial is a poet of no good repute, and it gives a man new thoughts to read his works dispassionately, and find in this unseemly jester's serious passages

---

17. This is in fact the British Library's Egerton MS 2982.

the image of a kind, wise, and self-respecting gentleman. It is customary, I suppose, in reading Martial, to leave out these pleasant verses; I never heard of them, at least, until I found them for myself; and this partiality is one among a thousand things that help to build up our distorted and hysterical conception of the great Roman Empire.

But the prevailing opinion of Martial in the nineteenth century, despite some discreet versions by W. F. Shaw (London, 1882) and Goldwin Smith (Toronto, 1890), was not Stevenson's but rather that represented by the Revd John Booth in his preface (p. viii) to *Epigrams, Ancient and Modern* (London, 1863):

Martial has left us a vast number of epigrams ... Many of these refer to odious vices ... which in modern days are unfit to be mentioned ... whilst his adulation of one of the most execrable of the Roman Emperors is perfectly nauseating ...

Equally emphatic is the Revd Henry Philip Dodd (who revives the old contrast between Martial and the Greek epigrammatists) in *The Epigrammatists* (London, 1870), p. xviii:

Martial wrote for bread, and he consequently formed his style in accordance with the tastes of those whose patronage was in a pecuniary sense the most valuable. Flattery of the Emperor Domitian and of the wealthy men of Rome, satirical abuse of those who were out of favour at court and indecent pandering to the vile lusts of an unchaste people form the staple of his writings.

Such sentiments would be repeated even in more modern English handbooks. When these views were regarded as too blatantly moralizing, the alternatives were either to see Martial as a camera, simply recording what went on around him, or to trivialize his work, by making him out to be an amusing clown whose sole aim was the entertainment of his patrons.[18]

After the Victorian period poets found little enough to appeal to them in Martial; he offended their beliefs in artistic independence

---

18. For Martial 'the court jester', see J. Bramble, 'Martial and Juvenal', *Cambridge History of Classical Literature II: Latin Literature* (Cambridge, 1982), p. 611.

and social respectability. The prudish aversion to certain areas of the classics by scholars, the different premises of contemporary writing and the abandoning of serious (or creative) translation to academics or amateurs ushered in a further period of neglect. No one would take their copy of Martial to the trenches. It was left to the critical sense of a twentieth-century poet who prided himself on craftsmanship to try to restore Martial to his just place in the *musée imaginaire* of European literature. Ezra Pound (1885-1972) thought he detected in Martial's verses not only incisive satire, but also the economy of phrase and the fitting of word to thing, which had so impressed Baltasar Gracián and which were among the objectives of Imagism. Pound actually translated only one epigram (*Ep.* 5.43), and that not among the best. Nevertheless he classed him with Catullus, Propertius, Horace and Ovid as one of the Latin classics who matter: 'Catullus most. Martial somewhat.'[19]

With his critical credentials restored to him, and with the rejection of censorship after the First World War, Martial was reanimated. Translating him became popular once more, almost essential. The somewhat academic versions of the twenties have been supplemented in the last few decades by more adventurous translators, such as Rolfe Humphries, Donald Goertz, Dorothea Wender, Olive Pitt-Kethley and Brian Hill, and by practising poets such as Dudley Fitts, Philip Murray, J. V. Cunningham, Peter Porter, James Michie, Tony Harrison, Peter Whigham, Richard O'Connell and Fiona Pitt-Kethley, all of whom are well represented in this collection. In the finest of these the translations are in a real sense palimpsestic, a re-writing of Martial which not only creates a counterpoint with the Latin epigrams themselves but with intervening translations that have themselves helped shape the English literary tradition and the

19. *The Letters of Ezra Pound 1907–1941*, ed. D. D. Paige (London, 1951), p. 138. The impact of Martial on Pound's early work may be seen in the scattered sequence *Xenia*, but also in many of the short early poems. The Roman poet was supposedly an accomplice in Pound's 'escaping from Swinburne to Cathay'. T. S. Eliot in *Ezra Pound: His Metric and Poetry* (London, 1917), p. 22, rightly specified Martial as one of the influences that 'have liberated the poet from his former restricted sphere. There is Catullus and Martial, Gautier, Laforgue and Tristan Corbière.'

Anglo-American literary sensibility. These are large claims. This book exists in part to support these claims and to provide the reader with an intellectual journey of historical and literary importance and extraordinary interest.

TEXTUAL NOTE

The order in which translations are arranged under each individual translator is that of the original Martial poems on which they are based. The epigrams are numbered in accordance with the 1990 Teubner text of Shackleton Bailey. The relevant epigram number heads the translation, whether or not any was supplied by the translator.

As regards the text of the English versions, we have with one exception reproduced the spelling, typographical conventions and punctuation of the texts from which the translations and imitations are taken. The exception is the replacement of the old long s (= f without the cross-stroke) with the modern s. On a few occasions an obvious printer's error has been removed. The texts used in this collection have generally been the earliest printed available, or, if not the earliest, the most complete or the one bearing the poet's final imprint. Occasionally a text is derived from an unmodernized recent edition. The decision not to modernize early printed texts is based on the belief that spelling and punctuation (which are based on different principles at different periods and with different authors) are integral parts of a poet's work, and the process of modernizing such features is not only subjective (each 'modernization' differs from the last) but falsely familiarizes the poems themselves, distorting their visual impact, their historicity, often their semiotic richness and ambiguity, as well as the whole process of linguistic change. The aim has been to present a series of texts as close as possible in form and appearance to those encountered by their contemporary readers. The resulting difficulties for the modern reader are simply indices of the otherness of those texts, the ideological as well as chronological distance between the last decade of the twentieth century and Renaissance, Restoration and eighteenth-century England. Most of the translations in this anthology were not written in this century, and should not look as though they were. They need to be read historically, by twentieth-century readers aware not only of the daunting chasm between past and present but of the rewarding, complex interchange between them which such reading necessarily involves.

A list of the texts used may be found on pp. 397-401.

I. TUDOR ENGLAND TO THE RESTORATION: 1540–1660

INTRODUCTION

Martial was fortunate inasmuch as he attracted early a very talented translator in Henry Howard, Earl of Surrey, who would also translate part of Virgil's *Aeneid*. This innovative metrician turned into felicitous English verse Martial's equally felicitous poem on the Happy Life (*Ep.* 10.47), a poem which would become one of the most famous and most frequently translated of the *oeuvre*. The version appeared in *Tottel's Miscellany* in 1557. This influential volume, which was meant by its real editors, Surrey and Sir Thomas Wyatt, to introduce the stricter Italian Renaissance metrical techniques into English verse, made its appearance during the reign of Mary Tudor. But it was the age of Elizabeth that saw not only a great literary flowering, in drama, didactic, epic, satire, epigram, but also a revolution in translation itself, especially in translation of the classics. Phaër's *Aeneid* (1558–84), Golding's *Metamorphoses* (1565–7), Newton's *Seneca* (1581), Marlowe's *Amores* (1590?) and Lucan 1 (1593), Harington's *Orlando Furioso* (1591) and Chapman's *Homer* (1598–1616) combine with such masterworks of prose translation as North's Plutarch, Adlington's Apuleius and Florio's Montaigne to index the Elizabethan period as the greatest age of English translation. Beginning with Henry Howard, the translation of Martial into English took early and fertile root.

After Surrey the list of Elizabethan and Jacobean translators or imitators of Martial becomes long indeed. And it would be longer still if a number of versifiers had not chosen to conceal their identities with various pseudonyms. Hence the frequent attribution in anthologies to 'Anon.'. A large number of such translations are to be found in two long partially overlapping manuscripts in the British Library, which provide alternative versions of some epigrams (and even of some lines and couplets), as well as having some translations in common. The first of these manuscripts is Egerton MS 2982 (p. 19), initially brought to public attention by the classical publisher Henry George Bohn in 1860, when he used some of its metrical versions in his edition of Martial in prose and verse translation. The other is Add. 27343, a rich collection of unpublished seventeenth-century translations, selections from which appear at the end of Section II in this volume (p. 152). A glance at the contents of these two manuscript anthologies reveals that one cannot point to a particular type of epigram that attracted or repelled the poets of these two centuries. Sage advice, Epicurean philosophy, misogynistic satire, tender epitaph, all asserted a successful claim on the hearts and pens of these writers. Neither the flattery of rich patrons nor blatant demands for money struck discordant notes. There were, it is true, some complaints about his obscenity, but these would be voiced in every period except perhaps the most recent, and translation of the erotic and even the indecent epigrams still continued, as the tender-minded translator, Timothe Kendall, witnesses, after his protest 'to the Reader' that:

> *Martial* is muche mislikt, and lothde,
>> of modest mynded men:
> For leude, lascivious wanton woorks
>> and woords whiche he doeth pen.

Of the poets and versifiers who are to be included in this first wave of translators (Tudor and early Jacobean) Ben Jonson and Sir John Harington are clearly the most talented and important, but lesser or more obscure talents, such as Kendall, are well represented. None of them, it should be noted, are professional university men, but active literary figures, adventurers, courtiers, clerics or denizens of the Inns of Court.

As the seventeenth century went its troubled way through religious and civil strife, Martial's poetry retained its attractiveness to English translators. He was already established as a prime model for practitioners of neo-Latin verse, who continued to find in him ample scope for imitation and emulation, when he was not overshadowed by the more Christian John Owen, whose own Latin epigrams made no attempt to hide their Roman inspiration. Indeed, just about the time that Owen was beginning to publish his poems, the English scholarly world was finally presented in 1615 with its own critical edition of Martial's text thanks to the labours of the politically harassed schoolmaster, Thomas Farnaby (1575–1647). It appeared late, well over a century after the *editio princeps* (*c.*1470 in Italy), and was in no way a monumental work, but it served its purposes and ran into several editions.

More important for our interests, however, is the continuing presence and popularity of Martial in epigram, satire and other minor poetic forms, such as airs and lyrics, and the effect he had (with the Ovidian couplet) upon English verse. The phenomenon was clear enough even in later Jacobean epigram, but it receives confirmation as the seventeenth century proceeds. It has to be admitted too, without descending to the banalities of the Cavalier image, that the Stuart courts were good breeding grounds for wits and amateur poets, to whom Martial's brevity and concision appealed as much as his verse's intellectual twists and arresting imagery. Martial's appeal to the Metaphysical poets was mentioned above (p. xxvi). But poets such as Cowley (1618–67) were also impressed with the epigrammatist's apparent simplicity and charm. At the same time the number of authors who translated large sections of Martial's total *oeuvre* and published them separately or as part of their own poetic work grew: Thomas May (1629), Robert Herrick (1648), Robert Fletcher (1656), Thomas Pecke (1659). Translation styles and levels of accuracy varied, but, as the century reached its middle, there was an increasing reaction against literal fidelity, what Denham called 'That servile path . . . Of tracing word by word and line by line . . . the labour'd births of slavish brains' (Preface to Fanshawe's Guarini). The poetic culmination of this movement was Cowley's development – some would say 'invention' – of the *Imitation* as a literary form in itself. Jonson, despite criticism of his learned fidelity by the likes of Samuel Johnson, had led the way (see especially *To Penshurst*). Indeed in Herrick's case emulation of Martial was an extension of his admiration of Jonson, and as in Jonson's case the independent and translated epigrams are so alike in spirit that the reverend clergyman preferred them intermingled.

To many the seventeenth century has seemed the golden age of Martial 'englished', a period when translators of the calibre of Jonson, Herrick and Cowley (see Section II, pp. 94ff.) possessed the command of language, the sensibility and the social context demanded of the task. The lesser figures too reveal a sympathy with Martial's interests and thematic range, and a feeling for his linguistic compression, rarely apparent later.

TRANSLATIONS AND IMITATIONS

HENRY HOWARD, EARL OF SURREY (?1517–47)

Tudor courtier, poet and soldier, who served bravely at Montreuil (1544) and commanded at Boulogne, where he was defeated and succeeded by the Earl of Hertford. Close friend in his early years of Henry VIII's bastard son, the Earl of Richmond, his political fortunes fluctuated as families rose and fell at the Tudor court. He was beheaded for high treason in 1547 (on the charge of quartering the royal arms). Together with Sir Thomas Wyatt he was a leading figure in the English literary renaissance, influencing the development of English blank verse through his brilliant translations of parts of Virgil's *Aeneid* (Books 2 and 4). Like Wyatt he drew upon Petrarch, and the two of them developed the English form of the sonnet later made canonic by Shakespeare. The following was probably written about 1540 during a period of political confinement at Windsor.

From *Tottel's Miscellany* (1557, first edition 5 June).

Ep. 10.47 *The Meanes to Attain Happy Life*

Martiall,* the thinges that do attayn
The happy life, be these, I finde.
The richesse left, not got with pain:
The frutefull ground: the quiet mynde:
The egall frend, no grudge, no strife:
No charge of rule, nor gouernance:
Without disease the healthfull lyfe:
The houshold of continuance:
The meane diet, no delicate fare:
Trew wisdom ioyned with simplenesse:
The night discharged of all care,
Where wine the wit may not oppresse:
The faithful wife, without debate:
Suche slepes, as may begyle the night:
Contented with thine owne estate,
Ne wish for death, ne feare his might.

Martiall: the name not only of the poet but of his closest friend, the lawyer Julius Martialis, to whom the poem seems to be addressed

TIMOTHE KENDALL (fl. 1577)

Timothe Kendall, 'late of the Universitie of Oxford, now student of Staple Inne in London', was educated at Eton College before proceeding to Magdalen Hall, Oxford, of which he was a member in 1572, but which he left without a degree. He became a student at Staple Inn, where he published his influential *Flovvers of Epigrammes, out of Sundrie the Moste Singular Authours Selected, as well Auncient as Late Writers* (London, 1577). The book contains translations by Kendall of epigrams by Martial, Pictorius, Ausonius, Thomas More, Roger Ascham and several others, including 'Epigrammes out of Greek', and concludes with epigrams ('Trifles') by Kendall himself. The volume is prefaced with a formal and fulsome dedication to Robert Dudley, Earl of Leicester. No other work by Timothe Kendall is known.

From *Flovvers of Epigrammes* (1577).

Spec. 28/29* *Of Leander*

What tyme Leander lustie ladde,
    his Ladie* went to see:
When as with waltryng waues out worne,
    and wearied quight was he:
He saied: Now spight me not (ye seas,)
    Leander spare to spill?
When I haue seen my Ladie once,
    then droune me if you will.

28/29: Originally numbered 25 and thought of as a single epigram.
Ladie: Hero

Ep. I.10 *Of Gemellus, and Maronilla*

Gemellus, Maronilla faine,
    would haue vnto his wife:
He longs, he likes, he loues, he craues,
    with her to leade his life.
What? is she of suche beautie braue?
    naie none more foule maie be:
What then is in her to be likte
    or lovd? still cougheth she.

Ep. I.13 *Of Arria, and Paetus*

Chast Arria when she gaue the blade,
    vnto her Paeto true:
All painted and begoard with bloud,
    whiche from her side she drue.
Trust me (saied she) my goared gutts
    doe put me to no paine:
But that whiche thou my P must doe,
    that greues and greues againe.

Ep. I.64 *To Fabulla, Vainglorious*

Of beautie braue we knowe thou art,
    and eke a maide beside:
Aboundyng eke in wealthe and store,
    this ne maie bee denied.
But while to muche you praise your self,
    and boste you all surmount:
Ne riche, ne faire, Fabulla, nor
    a maide we can you counte.

Ep. 4.49 *To Flaccus*

Flaccus thou knowest not Epigrams,
    no more then babes or boyes:
Whiche deemst them to be nothyng els,
    but sports and triflyng toyes:
He rather toyes, and sports it out,
    whiche doeth in Verse recite
Fell Tereus dinner, or whiche doeth,
    Thyestes supper write:
Or he whiche telles how Dedalus,
    did teache his sonne to flie:
Whiche telleth eke of Polyphem,
    the Shepheard with one eye.
From bookes of myne, are quight exempt,
    all rancour, rage and gall:
No plaier in his peuishe weeds,
    heare prankyng see you shall:
Yet these men doe adore (thou sayst)
    laude, like and loue: in deed,
I graunt you sir those they do laude,
    perdie but these thei reed.

Ep. 5.42 *That We should Benefite Our Frendes*

The crafty thefe from battered chest,
    doth filch thy coine awaie:
The debter nor the interest,
    nor principall will pay.
The fearefull flame destroies the goods,
    and letteth nought remaine:
The barren ground for seede receud,
    restoreth naught againe.
The subtile harlot naked strips,

her louer to the skin:
If thou commit thy self to seas,
 great daunger art thou in.
Not that thou geuest to thy frend,
 can fortune take away:
That onely that thou giust thy frend,
 thou shalt posses for ay.

Ep. 6.60 *Against the Enuious*

Rome lauds, & loues, & reades my works,
 and singes them euery where:
Each fist doth hold me clutched fast,
 eache bosome me doth beare.
One blusheth lo, as red as fyre,
 anone as pale as claye:
Anone he lookes astonished,
 as one did hym dismaye:
Sometime he mumping mockes and moes,
 sometime he doth repine:
Ymarrie, this is that I would:
 now please me verses mine.

Ep. 8.35 *To a Married Couple, that could not Agree*

Sith that you both are like in life,
 (a naughty man, a wicked wife:)
I muse ye liue not voyd of strife.

Ep. 9.25 *Against Apher*

As oft as I beholde thy wife,*
    when as with thee I dine,
Thou lowryng Apher bendst thy brow,
    as though thou didst repine.
What fault? tell what offence it is
    thy wife for to behold:
The sun, the starres, the thrunbed* thrones
    with siluer perle and gold,
And eak the gods themselues we see:
    what should I turne aside,
And flap my hand on face, as though,
    some Roman grim I spide?
A hoorson fell was Hercules,
    yet Hilas we might see:
With prety Ganimed to play,
    M.* still had licence free.
If thou wilt haue thy guests to wink,
    and not thy wife to see:
Let Phineas blind, and Oedipus,
    thy guests then Apher be.

Ep. 11.92 *Against Zoilus*

He did not terme thee Zoilus right,
    who termde thee vicious elfe:
If he shoulde terme thee truely, he
    should terme thee vice it self.

---

thy wife: in Martial's epigram the object of the guests' attention is a boy-servant, Hyllus
thrunbed: perhaps to be amended to 'hundred'
M.: Mercury

Ep. 12.10 *Of Affricanus*

As riche as Cresus Affric is:
 for more yet hunts the chuffe:
To muche to many, fortune giues,
 and yet to none inuffe.

Xen. 14 *Lettuce*

Sith that our auncients vsde to eate,
 Lettuce when all was doon:
I muse why euery meale of us,
 with Lettuce is begunne.

Xen. 70 *The Peacocke*

Thou wondrest when he spreads abrode,
 his wyngs that glisteryng looke:
And canst thou finde in harte, to giue
 hym to the cruell Cooke?

Xen. 77 *The Swanne*

With warblyng note, he tuneth verse.
 The Swanne doeth sweetely syng
Before his death, tracyng a long
 the streame with fethered wyng.

Apoph. 12 *Chestes made of Iuery*

In coffers these put nothyng els
      saue yellow glisteryng golde:
Chests homely, rude, lesse precious,
      may siluer serue to holde.

Apoph. 19 *Nuttes*

Small dice and nuttes, seme trifling toyes,
      and thinges of slender price:
Yet these haue made boyes buttockes smart
      with rods, not once, nor twice.

Apoph. 67 *A Flye Flap of Peacockes Plumes*

The taile of princely Peacock proud,
      that glisteryng faire doth show,
May serue to flap the filthy flies
      upon thy meate that blow.

Apoph. 73 *The Parret*

I Pratyng Parret am, to speake
      some straunge thing, learne ye me:
This of my selfe I learnd to speake,
      Caesar alhaile to thee.

THOMAS BASTARD (1566–1618)

Poet, satirist and divine. Educated at Winchester and New College, Oxford, graduating BA in 1590 and later MA, he became chaplain to the Earl of Suffolk and through the latter's patronage was made vicar of Beer Regis and rector of Amour (or Hamer). His poetic career began at Oxford, where he contributed to several collections of verse, including one in memory of Sir Philip Sidney. His most famous work was *Chrestoleros: Seuen Bookes of Epigrames* (1598), deeply indebted to Martial, as he acknowledges (see p. xxiv), and which was variously received. Bastard died miserably in a Dorchester prison, to which he had been committed for debt. He did not translate Martial, but his Martialesque epigrams (note the attacks on bodily smells, wealth, personal vanity, hypocrisy and social pretension, and the flattery of the powerful and great) merit some small inclusion here as index of the ancient epigrammatist's influence on Elizabethan poetic practice at the end of the sixteenth century.

From *Chrestoleros: Seuen Bookes of Epigrames* (1598).

Chrest. 2.12 *In Zoilum*

Zoilus now stinkes, cold, wann, and withered,
How shall one know when *Zoilus* is dead.

Chrest. 2.16 *Ad Lectorem*

Reader, there is no biting in my verse;
    No gall, no wormewood, no cause of offence.
And yet there is a biting I confesse
And sharpenesse tempred to a wholsome sense.
    Such are my Epigrams well vnderstood,
    As salt which bites the wound, but doth it good.

Chrest. 2.23

Misus, thy wealth will quickly breath away,
Thine honestie is shorter than thy breath,
Thy flesh will fall, how can it longer stay,
Which is so ripe and mellow after death?
Yet while thou liu'st men make of thee a iest.
Here lies olde *Misus* soule, lockt in his chest.

Chrest. 2.25 *In Habentem Longum Barbam*

Thy beard is long: better it would thee fitt,
To haue a shorter beard, and longer witt.

Chrest. 2.29 *In Papam*

The Pope as king of kings hath power from hye,
To plant, and to roote out successively:
Why fell the king of *France* in wofull case?
Because the Pope did plant him of his grace.
    But our *Elisa* liues, and keepes her crowne,
        Godamercy Pope, for he would pull her downe.

Chrest. 2.30 Ad Reginam Elizabetham

Liue long *Elisa*, that the wolfe of *Spayne*,
In his owne thirst of blood consumde may be.
That forraine princes may enuie thy reigne.
That we may liue and florish vnder thee,
And through the bended force of mighty kings,
With knots of policy confederate,
Ayme at thy royall Scepter, purposing
Confusion to thy country and thy state.
    Heauen fights for thee, & thou shalt haue thy will
    Of all thy foes, for thy Sunne standeth still.

Chrest. 2.32 Ad Comitem Essexiae

Essex, the ends which men so faine would finde,
Riches, for which most are industrious.
Honour, for which most men are vertuous,
Are but beginnings to thy noble minde:
    Which thou as meanes dost frankly spend vpon,
    Thy countries good, by thy true honour wonne.

Chrest. 2.36 Ad Sextum

Sextus in wordes giues me goold wealth and lands
Sextus hath *Crassus* tongue, *Irus* handes.

JOHN MARSTON (1576–1634)

Poet, dramatist and satirist, born in Oxfordshire and educated at Brasenose College, Oxford, and the Middle Temple, where he joined his lawyer father and lodged until 1606. His plays included *Antonio and Mellida* and *Antonio's Revenge* (1599/1600), *The Dutch Courtesan* (before 1603) and *The Malcontent* (1604). He collaborated with Webster, Chapman and Jonson (with whom he quarrelled and made up). After release from prison in 1608 he left the theatre, taking holy orders in 1609 and eventually obtaining the rectorship of Christchurch, Hampshire (1616–31). In 1598 he published *The Metamorphosis of Pigmalions Image and Certaine Satyres* and *The Scourge of Villanie*, both of which were ordered to be burned in 1599. Marston's satires are deeply indebted to both Juvenal and Martial. The latter influenced not only Marston's closed heroic couplets but his epigrammatic mode and much of the material of the satires themselves. Marston's dedication of *The Scourge of Villanie* 'To his most esteemed, and best beloued Selfe' may itself be an imitation of the dedicatory opening of *Ep*. 6.1 (where the 'Martial' addressed, however, is the poet's friend and namesake). The passage quoted below comes from the second of Marston's *Certaine Satyres* (ll. 41–54), and is an expansion of Martial *Ep*. 2.20.

From *The Metamorphosis of Pigmalions Image and Certaine Satyres* (1598).

Ep. 2.20

Who would once dreame that that same Elegie,
That faire fram'd peece of sweetest Poesie,
Which *Muto* put betwixt his Mistris paps,
(When he (quick-witted) call'd her *Cruell chaps*,
And told her, there she might his dolors read
Which she, oh she, vpon his hart had spread)

Was penn'd by *Roscio* the Tragedian.
Yet *Muto*, like a good *Vulcanian*,
An honest Cuckold, calls the bastard sonne,
And brags of that which others for him done.
Satyre thou lyest, for that same Elegie
Is Mutos *owne, his owne deere Poesie:*
Why tis his owne, and deare, for he did pay
Ten crownes for it, as I heard *Roscius* say.

ANONYMOUS
TRANSLATIONS OF THE
SIXTEENTH CENTURY

The Egerton MS 2982 of the British Library contains translations by
various hands of a number of Martial's epigrams, arranged by book
number and more or less in sequence. The following is a selection. As
will be seen the translators do not avoid sexual themes, although they
hold back from writing the 'forbidden words'.

From *Egerton MS* 2982.

Ep. 1.46 *To Hedyla*

When you cry – Now it comes – Stand to me: then
My Courage flags, my Lust abates: But when
You cry – Forbeare: I faster come, restrayn'd.
If you would have mee doe it; ride mee rein'd.

Ep. 5.13 *Of Calistratus*

I am, and alwayes was, poore; I confess:
Yet no obscure, but well knowne, knight, ne'r-less:
Whom the whole world reades; and sayes, this is hee.
Few dead so famous, as I liueing, bee.
But your vast Piles on hundred Columnes rest:
Your massy wealth is in cram'd coffers prest:
Your Granary's from Ægipt stoar'd each yeere:
And Parma's wooll your num'rous flocks doe beare.
Thus wee are each. Yett you can't bee like mee:
What you are, every vulgar man may bee.

Ep. 6.39 *Of Cinna*

Thou father'st for thy wife seav'n births; which I
Can't children call; no: nor yett free-borne. Why?
For thou thy selfe not one of them, nay, not
Thy friend, or honest neighbour, ever gott:
But all, on Matts, conceiu'd, or Couches, they,
Eu'n by their lookes, their Mothers stealths betray.
This that with curled hayre Moore-like doth looke,
Proues himselfe issue of the swarthy Cooke.
Hee, with flat nose and blubber lips, you'ld sweare
The wrastler Pannicus his picture were.
Damas, the third, who (that did him e'r see)
Knows not the bleere-ey'd bakers sonn to bee?
The fowrth, a sweete-fac'd Boy, with wanton Mine,
Was gott by Lygdus, thy Hee-Concubine.
Vse him so too: Thou need'st no Incest feare.
But this, with's taper-head, and his long eare
Which like an Asses moues, who can deny
To bee the Idiot Gyrrha's progeny.

Two daughters, this fox-red, that bacon-browne;
One's Crote's, the piper; t'other Carp's, the Clowne.
Thy Mungrils number had bin now compleate,
Could Dyndymus, and Cores, children gett.

Ep. 6.93 Of Thais

Worse then a Fullers tubb* doth Thais* stinke,
Broak in the streets and leakeing through each chinke;
Or Lyon's belch or Lustfull reakeing Goats
Or skin of dogg that dead o'th' Bank-side floats.
Or halfe-hatch'd chickin from broake rotten eggs,
Or taynted Iarrs of stinking mack'rell-dreggs.
This vile ranke smell, with perfumes to disguise
When e'r shee naked baths shee doth devise:
Shee's with Pomatum smudg'd; or paint good store;
Or oyle of Beane flow'r varnish'd o'r and o'r.
A thousand wayes shee tryes to make all well.
In vaine. For still shee doth of Thais smell.

Ep. 8.32 Of Aretulla's Dove

Through silent ayre the gentle Doue does glide.
And into Aretulla's bosome softly slide.
This seem'd to bee by chance had it not stayd
And, as loath to be gone, a neast there made.
Why shoud shee not from hence take Augury;
It came to say: Cæsar would not deny,
Reversall of her banish'd Brothers Doome;
Did shee now beg it; and would call him home.

Fullers tubb: in Roman times it contained urine for cleaning clothes
Thais: a common 'street-name' for a prostitute

Ep. 9.28 *An Epitaph on Latinus*

The Stage's Fame and pleasing Glory; I,
(Thy pleasure and applause once) here now ly:
That could haue Cato made looke on awhile,
Graue Curio's, and Fabricio's, forc'd to smile.
Yet was my Life vntaynted by my Trade:
My Looser parts myselfe ne'r looser made.
I could not else with Cæsar favour finde.
Hee, God-like, searches to the inward minde.
Apollo's Parasite you may mee call:
Whilst Rome know's mee for her Ioues Menial.

Ep. 11.78 *To Victor*

Female embraces, Victor! now enioy.
Lett P— learne, at length, a new Employ.
The Virgin's ready, now, with Wedding stoale:
Your new Bride, now, your Pages locks will poll.
For once, shee'll giue you leaue to vse your Boy;
Feareing your first encounters to enioy:
After, your Nurse, and Mother, will't deny;
Saying: A wife, now, not a Boy, you'l try.
Alas! What heats must P—, what paines conioynt,
Indure! If then a Stranger to a C—.
Vnto some Subvrbe-whore putt it to Schoole.
A mayde won't teach you play the Man, butt Foole.

FRANCIS DAVISON (?1575–?1619)

Eldest son of William Davison, secretary of state to Elizabeth I. He was admitted to Gray's Inn in 1593, where he participated in the writing of masques, after which he travelled in Europe, substantially in Italy (1595–7). On his return to England he became (for a while) private secretary to Sir Thomas Parry. In 1602 he published with his brother Walter *A Poetical Rapsody Containing Diverse Sonnets, Odes, Elegies, Madrigalls, and other Poesies, both in Rime, and Measured Verse*. It includes poems by several authors, including Ralegh, Sidney, Spenser and (possibly) Donne. He also published *Anagrammata in Nomina Illustrissimorum Heroum* (1603), celebrating in Latin anagrams various prominent figures, including Sir Thomas Egerton and the Earls of Oxford, Southampton and Northumberland.

From *A Poetical Rapsody* (1602).

Ep. 1.19

Foure teeth of late you had, both black and shaking,
Which durst not chew your meate for feare of aking.
But since your Cough, (without a Barbers ayde)
Hath blowne them out, you need not be afrayd.
    On either side to chew hard crusts, for sure
    Now from the Tooth-ache you liue most secure.

Ep. 1.83

I muse not that your Dog turds oft doth eate,
To a tung that licks your lips, a turd's sweete meate.

Ep. 2.15 *A Monsieur Naso, Verolé*

NASO let none drinke in his glasse but he,
Think you tis curious pride? tis curtesie.

Ep. 3.15

CODRVS although but of a meane estate,
Trusts more then any Merchant in the cittie,
For being old and blind, he hath of late,
Married a wife, yong, wanton, faire, and wittie.

Ep. 3.61

What so'ere you coggingly require,
T'is nothing (Cinna) still you cry:
Then Cinna you haue your desire,
If you aske nought, nought I deny.

Ep. 5.47

Philo sweares he ne'er eates at home a nightes:
He meanes, he fasts when no man him inuites.

Ep. 5.75

Thy lawfull wife faire Lælia needs must bee,
For she was forst by lawe to marrie thee.

Ep. 5.81 *To All Poore Schollers*

Faile yee of wealth, of wealth ye still will faile,
None but fat sowes are now greaz'd in the taile.

Ep. 7.43 *To His Frinds*

My iust demands soone graunt or soone deny,
Th' one frendship showes, and th' other curtesie.
But who nor soon doth graunt, nor soone say noe,
Doth not true frendship, nor good manners know.

Ep. 8.35

Why doe your wife and you so ill agree,
Since you in manners so well matched be?
Thou brazen-fac'd, she impudently bould,
Thou still dost brawle, she euermore doth scould.
Thou seldome sober art, she often drunk,
Thou a whore hunting knaue, she a knowne Punck.
Both of you filch, both sweare, and damme, and lie,
And both take pawnes, and *Iewish* vsurie.
     Not manners like make man and wife agree,
     Their manners must both like and vertuous bee.

Ep. 11.67 *To A. S.*

Rich Chremes while he liues will nought bestow,
On his poore Heires, but all at his last day.
If he be halfe as wise as rich I trow,
He thinks that for his life they seldome pray.

Ep. 12.12

You promise mountaines still to mee,
When ouer-night stark-drunk you bee.
But nothing you performe next day,
Hence foorth bee morning drunk, I pray.

SIR JOHN HARINGTON
(*c.*1560–1612)

Courtier and godson of Elizabeth I, educated at Eton, King's College, Cambridge (MA 1581), and Lincoln's Inn. He became known for his translation of Ariosto's *Orlando Furioso* (1591), the self-parodic fantasy of which he captured brilliantly, but which according to tradition was imposed upon him by the queen as a penance for his ribald verse. He angered the queen also with his later satire on water closets, *A New Discourse of a Stale Subject, Called the Metamorphosis of Ajax* (1596). In 1599 he served in Ireland with Essex and was knighted on the field. He was, however, more sympathetic than most to the position of the Irish Catholics, and in 1605 wrote a progressive essay, *A Short History of the State of Ireland*, in the hope of being made chancellor and archbishop there. When James I came to the throne, he was appointed Prince Henry's tutor. He is also remembered as a brilliant epigrammatist, indeed the chief rival of Jonson (who loathed Harington's Ariosto). Although *Epigrams both Pleasant and Serious* appeared after his death (London, 1615), like Martial he circulated his epigrams in manuscript form among friends and at court during his lifetime. Among the reasons for this was undoubtedly personal preference (so too John Donne); but it should be remembered that to be a 'wit' was sometimes dangerous, and in 1599 a book-burning was ordered of the works of several satirists (including John Marston). In 1618 a much larger edition of Harington's epigrams was published, containing some 428 epigrams, at least eighty of which are imitations or translations of Martial. Although

often over-expansive (the two-line epigram 2.20 receives twelve lines
from Harington: cf. Marston's fourteen-line 'version') and at times
rhythmically somewhat stiff, these 'translations' contain some very
faithful renditions, closely imitative of Martial's verbal patterning
(see, e.g., *Ep.* 1.64) and wit, attentive to wordplay (see, e.g., *Ep.* 5.61)
and to the epigrammatist's pointed, conversational style. The selec-
tion below begins with an epigram addressed to Harington's rival
epigrammatist, Thomas Bastard (see pp. 15ff.).

From *The Most Elegant and Witty Epigrams of Sir Iohn Harington,
Knight. . .* (1618).

To Master Bastard, Taxing Him of Flattery

It was a saying vs'd a great while since,
The subiects euer imitate the Prince,
A vertuous Master, makes a good Disciple,
Religious Prelates breede a godly people.
And euermore the Rulers inclination,
Workes in the time the chawnge and alteration.
Then what's the reason, *Bastard*, why thy Rimes
Magnifie Magistrates, yet taunt the times?
  I thinke that he to taunt the time that spares not,
  Would touch the Magistrate, saue that he dares not.

Ep. 1.19 *Of a Toothlesse Shrew*

Old *Ellen* had foure teeth as I remember,
She cought out two of them the last December;
But this shrewd cough in her raign'd so vnruly,
She cought out tother two before twas Iuly.
Now she may cough her heart out, for in sooth,
The said shrewd cough hath left her ne're a tooth.
  But her curst tongue, wanting this common curbe,
  Doth more than erst the houshold all disturbe.

Ep. I.27 *Of Table-talke*

I had this day carroust the thirteene cup,
And was both slipper-tong'd and idle-brain'd,
And said by chance, that you with me should sup.
You thought hereby, a supper cleerely gain'd:
And in your Tables you did quote it vp.
Vnciuill ghest, that hath beene so ill train'd!
    Worthy thou art hence supperlesse to walke,
    That tak'st aduantage of our Table-talke.

Ep. I.38 *To an Ill Reader*

The verses, *Sextus*, thou doost read, are mine;
But with bad reading thou wilt make them thine.

Ep. I.54 *Of Friendship*

New friends are no friends; how can that be true?
The oldest friends that are, were sometimes new.

Ep. I.64 *Of a Faire Shrew*

Faire, rich, and yong? how rare is her perfection,
Were it not mingled with one foule infection?
I meane, so proud a heart, so curst a tongue,
As makes her seeme, nor faire, nor rich, nor yong.

Ep. 1.73 *Of Wittoll*

Cayus, none reckned of thy wife a poynt,
While each man might, without all let or cumber,
But since a watch o're her thou didst appoint,
Of Customers she hath no little number.
     Well, let them laugh hereat that list, and scoffe it,
     But thou do'st find what makes most for thy profit.

Ep. 1.75 *Of Lynus Borrowing*

Lynus came late to me, sixe crownes to borrow,
And sware God damn him, hee'd rapai't to morrow.
I knew his word, as currant as his band,
And straight I gaue to him three crownes in hand;
     This I to giue, this he to take was willing,
     And thus he gaind, and I sau'd fifteene shilling.

Ep. 1.99 *Against Quintus, that Being Poore and Prodigall, Became Rich and Miserable*

Scant was thy Liuing, *Quintus*, ten pound cleare,
When thou didst keepe such fare, so good a table,
That we thy friends praid God thou might'st be able,
To spend, at least, an hundred pounds a yeare.
Behold, our boone God did benignly heare.
Thou gotst so much by Fortune fauourable,
And foure friends deaths to thee both kind and deare:
But suddenly thou grew'st so miserable,
We thy old friends to thee vnwelcome are,
Poore-Iohn, and Apple-pyes are all our fare.

No Salmon, Sturgeon, Oysters, Crab, nor Cunger.
What should we wish thee now for such demerit?
I would thou might'st one thousand pounds inherit,
Then, without question, thou wold'st starue for hunger.

Ep. 2.20 Of Don Pedro and His Poetry

Sir, I shall tell you newes, except you know it,
Our noble friend *Don Pedro*, is a Poet.
His verses all abroad are read and showne,
And he himselfe doth sweare they are his owne.
His owne? tis true, for he for them hath paid
Two crownes a Sonnet, as I heard it said.
So *Ellen* hath faire teeth, that in her purse
She keepes all night, and yet sleepes ne're the worse.
So widdow *Lesbia*, with her painted hide,
Seem'd, for the time, to make a handsome bride.
      If *Pedro* be for this a Poet cald,
      So you may call one hairie that is bald.

*Ep. 2.32 Of One Paulus a Great Man that Expected
to be Followed*

Proud *Paulus* late aduanc't to high degree,
Expects that I should now his follower be.
Glad I would be to follow ones direction,
By whom my honest suits might have protection.
But I sue *Don Fernandos* heyre for land,
Against so great a Peere he dare not stand.
A Bishop sues me for my tithes, that's worse,
He dares not venter on a Bishops curse.
Sergeant Erifilus beares me old grudges,
Yea but, saith *Paulus*, *Sergeants* may be Iudges.

Pure *Cinna* o're my head would begge my Lease,
Who my Lord. – Man, O hold your peace.
Rich widdow *Lesbia* for a slander sues me.
Tush for a womans cause, he must refuse me.
Then farewell frost: *Paulus*, henceforth excuse me,
    For you that are your selfe thrall'd to so many,
    Shall neuer be my good Lord, if I haue any.

Ep. 3.87 *To Galla Going to the Bathe*

When *Galla* for her health goeth to the Bathe,
She carefully doth hide, as is most meete,
With aprons of fine linnen, or a sheete,
Those parts, that modesty concealed hath:
Nor onely those, but eu'n the brest and necke,
That might be seene, or showne, without all checke.
    But yet one foule, and vnbeseeming place,
    She leaues uncouered still: What's that? Her face.

Ep. 4.21 *Against an Atheist*

That heau'ns are voide, & that no gods there are,
Rich *Paulus* saith, and all his proofe is this:
That while such blasphemies pronounce he dare,
He liueth here in ease, and earthly blisse.

Ep. 4.69 *Of Cinna His Gossip Cup*

When I with thee, *Cinna*, doe dine or sup,
Thou still do'st offer me thy Gossips cup:
And though it sauour well, and be well spiced,
Yet I to taste thereof am not enticed.
Now sith you needs will haue me cause alledge,
While I straine curt'sie in that cup to pledge:

One said, thou mad'st that cup so hote of spice,
That it had made thee now a widdower twice.
>   I will not say 'tis so, nor that I thinke it:
>   But good Sir, pardon me, I cannot drinke it.

Ep. 5.61 *In Cornutum*

What curld-pate youth is he that sitteth there
So neere thy wife, and whispers in her eare,
And takes her hand in his, and soft doth wring her,
Sliding her ring still vp and downe her finger?
Sir, tis a Proctor, seene in both the Lawes,
Retain'd by her, in some important cause;
Prompt and discreet both in his speech and action,
And doth her busines with great satisfaction.
And thinkest thou so? a horne-plague on thy head:
Art thou so like a foole, and wittoll led,
>   To thinke he doth the businesse of thy wife?
>   He doth thy businesse, I dare lay my life.

Ep. 5.76 *To One that had Meate Ill Drest*

King Mithridate to poysons so inur'd him,
As deadly poysons, damage none procur'd him.
So you to stale vnsauorie foode and durtie,
Are so inur'd, as famine ne're can hurt yee.

Ep. 6.12 *Of Galla's Goodly Periwigge*

You see the goodly hayre that *Galla* weares,
'Tis certain her own hair, who would have thought it?
She sweares it is her owne: and true she sweares:

For hard by Temple-barre last day she bought it.
> So faire a haire, vpon so foule a forehead,
> Augments disgrace, and showes the grace is borrowed.

Ep. 6.41 *Of an Importunate Prater, out of Martiall*

He that is hoarse, yet still to prate doth please,
Proues he can neither speake, nor hold his peace.

Ep. 9.8 *Of a Bequest without a Legacy*

In hope some Lease or Legacy to gaine,
You gaue old *Titus* yeerely ten pound pension.
Now he is dead, I heare thou dost complaine,
That in his will of thee he made no mention.
Cease this complaint that shewes thy base intention.
> He left thee more, then some he lou'd more deerely,
> For he hath left thee ten pound pension yeerely.

Ep. 12.10 *Of Fortune*

Fortune, men say, doth giue too much to many:
But yet shee neuer gaue enough to any.

Ep. 12.34 *Against Too Much Trust*

If you will shrowde you safe from all mis-haps,
And shunne the cause of many after-claps:
> Put not in any one, too much beliefe;
> Your ioy will be the lesse, so will your griefe.

Ep. 12.90 *Of Cosmus Heyre*

'When all men thought old *Cosmus* was a dying,
And had by Will giu'n thee much goods & lands,
Oh, how the little *Cosmus* fell a crying!
Oh, how he beates his brests & wring his hands!
How feruently for *Cosmus* health he pray'd!
What worthy Almes he vow'd, on that condition:
But when his pangs a little were allayd,
And health seem'd hoped, by the learn'd Physicion,
    Then though his lips, all loue, and kindnesse vanted,
    His heart did pray, his prayer might not be granted.

Ep. 12.93 *Of Lesbias Kissing Craft*

Lesbia with study found a meanes in th'end,
In presence of her Lord to kisse her friend,
Each of them kist by turnes a little Whelpe,
Transporting kisses thus by puppies help.
    And so her good old Lord she did beguile:
    Was not my Lord a puppy all the while?

JOHN DONNE *(c.*1572–1631)

Son of a London ironmonger and recognized as one of the great English poets. Donne's early life, after his education at Hart Hall, Oxford, and Lincoln's Inn, was one of womanizing, military adventure, erotic, intellectually energetic poetry (most of the love poems in *Songs and Sonnets* seem to belong to the 1590s, as do the satires and elegies) and social advancement; it climaxed (socially) in his appointment (1597) as secretary to Sir Thomas Egerton, Lord Keeper of the Great Seal, and election (1601) to a pocket borough seat in Parliament.

In 1602, however, he was dismissed from Egerton's service (having married Egerton's niece, Ann More, in secret the previous year) and lived in varying states of dependency for the next fourteen years, writing both verse and prose, often on religious issues. His wife, to whom he was devoted, bore him twelve children. In 1615 at James I's suggestion he entered the church, later (1621) obtaining through the favour of Buckingham the deanship of St Paul's, where he achieved celebrity as a preacher, especially on the theme of suffering. Although Donne's satires are pervasively epigrammatic, he himself wrote few epigrams and all are datable to his early period (1596–1602). None are translations of Martial, but they show his influence not only in wit, puns and paradox, but in epigrammatic structure, subject-matter and satirical thrust. Fittingly, one of the last epigrams satirizes a recent expurgated edition of Martial himself. Donne's poetry circulated primarily in manuscript form until after his death, when most of it was printed for the first time.

From *Poems, by J. D. with Elegies on the Authors Death* (1633).

Epigrams

Hero and Leander

Both rob'd of aire, we both lye in one ground,
Both whom one fire had burnt, one water drownd.

Pyramus and Thisbe

Two, by themselves, each other, love and feare
Slaine, cruell friends, by parting have joyn'd here.

Niobe

By childrens births, and death, I am become
So dry, that I am now mine owne sad tombe.

A Burnt Ship*

Out of a fired ship, which, by no way
But drowning, could be rescued from the flame,
Some men leap'd forth, and ever as they came
Neere the foes ships, did by their shot decay;
So all were lost, which in the ship were found,
     They in the sea being burnt, they in the burnt ship
          drown'd.

Fall of a Wall

Under an undermin'd, and shot-bruis'd wall
A too-bold Captaine* perish'd by the fall,
Whose brave misfortune, happiest men envi'd,
That had a towne for tombe, his bones to hide.

A Lame Begger

I am unable, yonder begger cries,
To stand, or moue; if he say true, hee *lies*.

A Burnt Ship: The ship is generally thought to have been the Spanish galleon, *San Felipe*, sunk during the storming of Cadiz in 1596 by the English fleet under Essex. Donne took part in the action.
Captaine: Captain Sydenham, who fell at Corunna (1589)

A Selfe Accuser

Your mistris, that you follow whores, still taxeth you:
'Tis strange that she should thus confesse it, though'it be
    true.

A Licentious Person

Thy sinnes and haires may no man equall call,
For, as thy sinnes increase, thy haires doe fall.

Antiquary

If in his Studie he hath so much care
To'hang all old strange things, let his wife beware.

Disinherited

Thy father all from thee, by his last Will
Gave to the poore; Thou has good title still.

Phryne

Thy flattering picture, *Phryne*, is like thee,
Onely in this, that you both painted be.

An Obscure Writer

Philo, with twelve yeares study, hath beene griev'd,
To'be understood, when will hee be beleev'd.

Klockius

Klockius, so deeply hath sworne, ne'r more to come
In bawdie house, that hee dares not goe home.

Raderus*

Why this man gelded *Martiall* I muse,
Except himselfe alone his tricks would use,
As *Katherine*,* for the Courts sake, put downe Stewes.

Mercurius Gallo-Belgicus*

Like *Esops* fellow-slaves, O *Mercury*,
Which could do all things, thy faith is; and I
Like *Esops* selfe, which nothing; I confesse
I should have had more faith, if thou hadst lesse;
Thy credit lost thy credit: 'Tis sinne to doe,
In this case, as thou wouldst be done unto,
To beleeve all: Change thy name: thou art like
Mercury in stealing, but lyest like a *Greeke*.

Ralphius

Compassion in the world againe is bred:
Ralphius is sick, the broker keeps his bed.

Raderus: Matthew Rader, whose bowdlerized edition of Martial appeared in
1602
Katherine: not known, but obviously a queen who wanted to monopolize vice
for the court
Mercurius Gallo-Belgicus: an annual news report

BEN JONSON (1572–1637)

Temperamental actor, poet and prolific dramatist, posthumous child of a clergyman, stepson of a master bricklayer; author of *Sejanus* (1603), *Volpone* (1606), *The Silent Woman* (1609), *The Alchemist* (1610), *Bartholomew Fair* (1614) and other plays. He also wrote verse letters, criticism, numerous lyrics, and a translation of Horace's *Art of Poetry*, and never wavered in his belief in his own talent. He was steeped in Latin literature and drew heavily on Martial for his *Epigrammes*, in which he fuses the Roman's pointed, detached, conversational tone with an irrepressibly dramatic mode of speech. The *Epigrammes* were published in a folio edition of his *Workes* (London, 1616), in the dedication to which he proclaims them 'the ripest of my studies'. Jonson lived a turbulent, combative life (he even slew a fellow actor in a duel), an intellectual controversialist ever (especially in the war of the theatres), but was lucky enough in his patrons and friends, even becoming court poet and writer of masques to James I (with Inigo Jones as his designer). His relationship with the Caroline court, however, was less good. Despite his high estimate of his poetry, he is still best known as a dramatist, primarily as a writer of comedies, although *To Penshurst* (which is much indebted to Martial, cf. especially 48–71 and *Ep.* 3.58.33–44; see also *Ep.* 3.60, 11.39) remains one of the great country-house poems of the language, its vigorous fusion of aristocratic and bourgeois ideals in the image of property, family and home unparalleled. He was educated at Westminster School in London; his funeral was in Westminster Abbey.

From *Epigrammes* (1616) with the exception of *Ep.* 3.58 (from *The Forrest*, 1616), *Ep.* 8.77, 10.47 (from *The Vnder-Wood*, 1640), and *Ep.* 12.61 (uncollected verse).

To the Ghost of Martial

MARTIAL, thou gau'st farre nobler *Epigrammes*
    To thy DOMITIAN, than I can my IAMES:
But in my royall subiect I passe thee,
    Thou flattered'st thine, mine cannot flatter'd be.

Ep. 1.1 *To the Reader*

Pray thee, take care, that tak'st my booke in hand,
    To reade it well: that is, to vnderstand.

Ep. 1.2 *To My Booke*

It will be look'd for, booke, when some but see
    Thy title, *Epigrammes*, and nam'd of mee,
Thou should'st be bold, licentious, full of gall,
    Wormewood, and sulphure, sharpe, and tooth'd withall;
Become a petulant thing, hurle inke, and wit,
    As mad-men stones: not caring whom they hit.
Deceiue their malice, who could wish it so.
    And by thy wiser temper, let men know
Thou art not couetous of least selfe fame,
    Made from the hazard of anothers shame:
Much lesse with lewd, prophane, and beastly phrase,
    To catch the worlds loose laughter, or vaine gaze.
He that departs with his owne honesty
    For vulgar praise, doth it too dearely buy.

Ep. I.3 *To My Booke-Seller*

Thou, that mak'st gaine thy end, and wisely well,
    Call'st a booke good, or bad, as it doth sell,
Vse mine so, too: I giue thee leaue. But craue
    For the lucks sake, it thus much fauour haue.
To lye vpon thy stall, till it be sought;
    Not offer'd, as it made sute to be bought;
Nor haue my title-leafe on posts, or walls,
    Or in cleft-sticks, aduanced to make calls
For termers, or some clarke-like seruing-man,
      Who scarse can spell th'hard names: whose knight lesse
        can.
If, without these vile arts, it will not sell,
    Send it to *Bucklers-bury,** there 'twill, well.

Ep. I.4 *To King Iames*

How, best of Kings, do'st thou a scepter beare!
    How, best of *Poets,** do'st thou laurell weare!
But two things, rare, the FATES had in their store,
    And gaue thee both, to shew they could no more.
For such a *Poet*, while thy dayes were greene,
    Thou wert, as chiefe of them are said t'haue beene.
And such a Prince thou art, wee daily see,
    As chiefe of those still promise they will bee.
Whom should my *Muse* then flie to, but the best
    Of Kings for grace; of *Poets* for my test?

Bucklers-bury: a grocers' area; the book could serve as wrapping paper
best of Poets: the reference is to *His Majesties Poetical Exercises* (1591)

Ep. I.39 *To Beniamin Rudyerd**

If I would wish, for truth, and not for show,
　　The aged SATURNE's age, and rites to know;
If I would striue to bring backe times, and trie
　　The world's pure gold, and wise simplicitie;
If I would vertue set, as shee was yong,
　　And heare her speake with one, and her first tongue;
If holiest friendship, naked to the touch,
　　I would restore, and keepe it euer such;
I need no other arts, but studie thee:
　　Who prou'st, all these were, and againe may bee.

Ep. I.63 *To Provle the Plagiary*

Forbeare to tempt me, PROVLE,* I will not show
　　A line vnto thee, till the world it know;
Or that I'haue by two good sufficient men,
　　To be the wealthy witnesse of my pen:
For all thou hear'st, thou swear'st thy selfe didst doo.
　　Thy wit liues by it, PROVLE, and belly too.
Which, if thou leaue not soone (though I am loth)
　　I must a libell make, and cosen both.

Benjamin Rudyerd: 1572–1658, knighted in 1618; his poems were published
posthumously
PROVLE: 'prowling' means 'stealing'

Ep. 1.98 *On Banck the Vsurer*

BANCK feeles no lamenesse of his knottie gout,
    His monyes trauille for him, in and out:
And though the soundest legs goe euery day,
    He toyles to be at hell, as soone as they.

Ep. 2.12 *To Sir Cod*

Th'expence in odours is a most uaine sinne,
    Except thou could'st, Sir COD, weare them within.

Ep. 3.58 *To Penshurst**

Thou art not, PENSHVRST, built to enuious show,
    Of touch, or marble; nor canst boast a row
Of polish'd pillars, or a roofe of gold:
    Thou hast no lantherne, whereof tales are told;
Or stayre, or courts; but stand'st an ancient pile,
    And these grudg'd at, art reuerenc'd the while.
Thou ioy'st in better markes, of soyle, of ayre,
    Of wood, of water: therein thou art faire.
Thou hast thy walkes for health, as well as sport:
    Thy *Mount*, to which the *Dryads* doe resort,
Where PAN & BACCHVS their high feasts haue made,
    Beneath the broad beech, and the chest-nut shade;
That taller tree, which of a nut was set,
    At his great birth, where all the *Muses* met.
There, in the writhed barke, are cut the names
    Of many a SYLVANE taken with his flames.

Penshurst: the country home of the Sidney family, at the time belonging to Sir
Philip Sidney's brother, Robert; it is situated in Kent

And thence, the ruddy *Satyres* oft prouoke
    The lighter *Faunes*, to reach thy *Ladies oke*.
Thy copp's too, nam'd of GAMAGE, thou hast there,
    That neuer failes to serue the season'd deere,
When thou would'st feast, or exercise thy friends.
    The lower land, that to the riuer bends,
Thy sheepe, thy bullocks, kine, and calues doe feed:
    The middle grounds thy mares, and horses breed.
Each banke doth yeeld thee coneyes; and the topps
    Fertile of wood, ASHORE, and SYDNEY's copp's,
To crowne thy open table, doth prouide
    The purpled pheasant, with the speckled side:
The painted partrich lyes in euery field,
    And, for thy messe, is willing to be kill'd.
And if the high-swolne *Medway* faile thy dish,
    Thou hast thy ponds, that pay thee tribute fish.
Fat, aged carps, that runne into thy net.
    And pikes, now weary their owne kinde to eat,
As loth, the second draught, or cast to stay,
    Officiously, at first, themselues betray.
Bright eeles, that emulate them, and leape on land,
    Before the fisher, or into his hand.
Then hath thy orchard fruit, thy garden flowers,
    Fresh as the ayre, and new as are the houres.
The earely cherry, with the later plum,
    Fig, grape, and quince, each in his time doth come:
The blushing apricot, and wooly peach
    Hang on thy walls, that euery child may reach.
And though thy walls be of the countrey stone,
    They'are rear'd with no mans ruine, no mans grone,
There's none, that dwell about them, wish them downe;
    But all come in, the farmer, and the clowne:
And no one empty-handed, to salute
    Thy lord, and lady, though they haue no sute.
Some bring a capon, some a rurall cake,
    Some nuts, some apples; some that thinke they make

The better cheeses, bring 'hem; or else send
    By their ripe daughters, whom they would commend
This way to husbands; and whose baskets beare
    An embleme of themselues, in plum, or peare.
But what can this (more then expresse their loue)
    Adde to thy free prouisions, farre aboue
The neede of such? whose liberall boord doth flow,
    With all, that hospitalitie doth know!
Where comes no guest, but is allow'd to eate,
    Without his feare, and of thy lords owne meate:
Where the same beere, and bread, and selfe-same wine,
    That is his Lordships, shall be also mine.
And I not faine to sit (as some, this day,
    At great mens tables) and yet dine away.
Here no man tells my cups; nor, standing by,
    A waiter, doth my gluttony enuy:
But giues me what I call, and lets me eate,
    He knowes, below, he shall finde plentie of meate,
Thy tables hoord not vp for the next day,
    Nor, when I take my lodging, need I pray
For fire, or lights, or liuorie: all is there;
    As if thou, then, wert mine, or I raign'd here:
There's nothing I can wish, for which I stay.
    That found King IAMES, when hunting late, this way,
With his braue sonne, the Prince, they say thy fires
    Shine bright on euery harth as the desires
Of thy *Penates* had beene set on flame,
    To entertayne them; of the countrey came,
With all their zeale, to warme their welcome here.
    What (great, I will not say, but) sodayne cheare
Did'st thou, then, make 'hem! and what praise was heap'd
    On thy good lady, then! who, therein, reap'd
The iust reward of her high huswifery;
    To haue her linnen, plate, and all things nigh,
When she was farre: and not a roome, but drest,
    As if it had expected such a guest!

These, PENSHVRST, are thy praise, and yet not all.
    Thy lady's noble, fruitfull, chaste withall.
His children thy great lord may call his owne:
    A fortune, in this age, but rarely knowne.
They are, and haue beene taught religion: Thence
    Their gentler spirits haue suck'd innocence.
Each morne, and euen, they are taught to pray,
    With the whole houshold, and may, euery day,
Reade, in their vertuous parents noble parts,
    The mysteries of manners, armes, and arts.
Now, PENSHVRST, they that will proportion thee
    With other edifices, when they see
Those proud, ambitious heaps, and nothing else,
    May say, their lords haue built, but thy lord dwells.

Ep. 5.34 *On My First Daughter*

Here lyes to each her parents ruth,
MARY, the daughter of their youth:
Yet, all heauens gifts, being heauens due,
It makes the father, lesse, to rue.
At six moneths end, shee parted hence
With safetie of her innocence;
Whose soule heauens Queene, (whose name shee beares)
In comfort of her mothers teares,
Hath plac'd amongst her virgin-traine:
Where, while that seuer'd doth remaine,
This graue partakes the fleshly birth.
Which couer lightly, gentle earth.

Ep. 5.78 *Inuiting a Friend to Supper*

To night, graue sir, both my poore house, and I
    Doe equally desire your companie:
Not that we thinke vs worthy such a ghest,
    But that your worth will dignifie our feast,
With those that come; whose grace may make that seeme
    Something, which, else, could hope for no esteeme.
It is the faire acceptance, Sir, creates
    The entertaynment perfect: not the cates.*
Yet shall you haue, to rectifie your palate,
    An oliue, capers, or some better sallade
Vshring the mutton; with a short-leg'd hen,
    If we can get her, full of egs, and then,
Limons, and wine for sauce: to these, a coney
    Is not to be despair'd of, for our money;
And, though fowle, now, be scarce, yet there are clarkes,
    The skie not falling, thinke we may haue larkes.
Ile tell you of more, and lye, so you will come:
    Of partrich, pheasant, wood-cock, of which some
May yet be there; and godwit, if we can:
    Knat, raile, and ruffe too. How so ere, my man
Shall reade a piece of VIRGIL, TACITVS,
    LIVIE, or of some better booke to vs,
Of which wee'll speake our minds, amidst our meate;
    And Ill professe no verses to repeate:
To this, if ought appeare, which I know not of,
    That will the pastrie, not my paper, show of.
Digestiue cheese, and fruit there sure will bee;
    But that, which most doth take my *Muse*, and mee,

---

cates: food, especially delicacies

Is a pure cup of rich *Canary*-wine,
    Which is the *Mermaids*, now, but shall be mine:
Of which had HORACE, or ANACREON tasted,
    Their liues, as doe their lines, till now had lasted.
Tabacco, *Nectar*, or the *Thespian* spring,
    Are all but LUTHERS beere, to this I sing.
Of this we will sup free, but moderately,
    And we will haue no *Pooly*', or *Parrot** by;
Nor shall our cups make any guiltie men:
    But, at our parting, we will be, as when
We innocently met. No simple word,
    That shall be vtter'd at our mirthfull boord,
Shall make vs sad next morning: or affright
    The libertie, that wee'll enjoy to night.

Ep. 6.29 *On My First Sonne*

Farewell, thou child of my right hand,* and ioy;
    My sinne was too much hope of thee, lou'd boy,
Seuen yeeres tho' wert lent to me, and I thee pay,
    Exacted by thy fate, on the iust day.
O, could I lose all father, now. For why
    Will man lament the state he should enuie?
To haue so soon scap'd worlds, and fleshes rage,
    And, if no other miserie, yet age?
Rest in soft peace, and, ask'd, say here doth lye
    BEN. IONSON his best piece of *poetrie*.
For whose sake, hence-forth, all his vowes be such,
    As what he loues may neuer like too much.

Pooly', *or Parrot*: two spies and informers
child of my right hand: Benjamin in Hebrew means son of the right hand

Ep. 8.35 *On Giles and Ione*

Who sayes that GILES and IONE at discord be?
    Th'obseruing neighbours no such mood can see.
Indeed, poore GILES repents he married euer.
    But that his IONE doth too. And GILES would neuer,
By his free will, be in IONES company.
    No more would IONE he should. GILES riseth early,
And hauing got him out of doores is glad.
    The like is IONE. But turning home, is sad.
And so is IONE. Oft-times, when GILES doth find
    Harsh sights at home, GILES wisheth he were blind.
All this doth IONE. Or that his long yearn'd life
    Were quite out-spun. The like wish hath his wife.
The children, that he keepes, GILES sweares are none
    Of his begetting. And so sweares his IONE.
In all affections shee concurreth still.
    If, now, with man and wife, to will, and nill
The selfe-same things, a note of concord be:
    I know no couple better can agree!

Ep. 8.70 *To Elizabeth Countesse of Rutland*

That *Poets* are far rarer births than kings,
    Your noblest father prou'd: like whom, before,
Or then, or since, about our *Muses* springs,
    Came not that soule exhausted so their store.
Hence was it, that the *destinies* decreed
    (Saue that most masculine issue of his braine)
No male vnto him: who could so exceed
    Nature, they thought, in all, that he would faine.
At which, shee happily displeas'd, made you:
    On whom, if he were liuing now, to looke,
He should those rare, and absolute numbers view,
    As he would burne, or better farre his booke.

Ep. 8.77

Liber, of all thy friends, thou sweetest care,
    Thou worthy in eternall Flower to fare,
If thou be'st wise, with '*Syrian* Oyle let shine
    Thy locks, and rosie garlands crowne thy head;
Darke thy cleare glasse with old *Falernian* Wine;
    And heat, with softest love, thy softer bed.
Hee, that but living halfe his dayes, dies such,
    Makes his life longer then 'twas given him, much.

Ep. 9.35 *To Captayne Hungry*

Doe what you come for, Captayne, with your newes;
    That's, sit, and eate: doe not my eares abuse.
I oft looke on false coyne, to know't from true:
    Not that I loue it, more, then I will you.
Tell the grosse *Dutch* those grosser tales of yours,
    How great you were with their two Emperours;
And yet are with their Princes: Fill them full
    Of your *Morauian* horse, *Venetian* bull.
Tell them, what parts yo'haue tane, whence run away,
    What States yo'haue gull'd, and which yet keepes yo'in
        pay.
Giue them your seruices, and embassies
    In *Ireland*, *Holland*, *Sweden*, pompous lies,
In *Hungary*, and *Poland*, *Turkie* too;
    What at *Ligorne*, *Rome*, *Florence* you did doe:
And, in some yeere, all these together heap'd,
    For which there must more sea, and land be leap'd,
If but to be beleeu'd you haue the hap,
    Then can a flea at twice skip i'the Map.
Giue your yong States-men, (that first make you drunke,
    And then lye with you, closer, then a punque,

For newes) your *Ville-royes*, and *Silleries*,
    Ianin's, your *Nuncio's*, and your *Tuilleries*,
Your *Arch-Dukes* Agents, and your *Beringhams*,
    These are your wordes of credit. Keepe your Names
Of *Hannow*, *Shieter-huissen*, *Popenheim*,
    Hans-spiegle, *Rotteinberg*, and *Boutersheim*,
For your next meale: this you are sure of. Why
    Will you part with them, here, vnthriftely?
Nay, now you puffe, tuske, and draw vp your chin,
    Twirle the poore chaine you run a feasting in.
Come, be not angrie, you are HVNGRY; eate;
    Doe what you come for, Captayne, There's your meate.

Ep. 10.47

The Things that make the happier life, are these,
Most pleasant Martial; Substance got with ease,
Not labour'd for, but left thee by thy Sire;
A Soyle, not barren; a continewall fire;
Never at Law; seldome in office gown'd;
A quiet mind; free powers; and body sound;
A wise simplicity; freindes alike-stated;
Thy table without art, and easy-rated:
Thy night not dronken, but from cares layd wast;
No sowre, or sollen bed–mate, yet a Chast;
Sleepe, that will make the darkest howres swift–pac't;
Will to bee, what thou art; and nothing more:
Nor feare thy latest day, nor wish therfore.

Ep. 12.61 *To a Ffreind an Epigram of Him*

Sr Inigo* doth feare it as I heare
(And labours to seem worthy of y^t feare)
That I should wryte vpon him some sharp verse,
Able to eat into his bones & pierce
The Marrow! Wretch! I quitt thee of thy paine
Thou'rt too ambitious: and dost fear in vaine!
The Lybian Lion hunts noe butter-flyes,
He makes ye Camell & dull Ass his prize.
If thou be soe desyrous to be read,
Seek out some hungry painter, y^t for bread,
Wth rotten chalk, or Cole, vpon a wall
Will well designe thee, to be viewd of all
That sit vpon ye Common Draught: or Strand!*
Thy Forehead is too narrow for my Brand.

Ep. 12.94 *To a Weake Gamster in Poetry*

With thy small stocke, why art thou ventring still,
    At this so subtile sport: and play'st so ill?
Think'st thou it is meere fortune, that can win?
    Or thy ranke setting?* that thou dar'st put in
Thy all, at all: and what so ere I doe,
    Art still at that, and think'st to blow me'vp too?
I cannot for the stage a *Drama* lay,
    Tragick, or *Comick*; but thou writ'st the play.
I leaue thee there, and giuing way, entend
    An *Epick* poeme; thou hast the same end.

Inigo: Inigo Jones, architect, Surveyor of the King's Works, and Jonson's
collaborator in his court masques, about which they quarrelled famously
Draught: or Strand: privy or sewer
ranke setting: excessive betting

I modestly quit that, and thinke to write,
>   Next morne, an *Ode*: Thou mak'st a song ere night.
I passe to *Elegies*; Thou meet'st me there:
>   To *Satyres*; and thou dost pursue me. Where,
Where shall I scape thee? in an *Epigramme*?
>   O, (thou cry'st out) that is thy proper game.
Troth, if it be, I pitty thy ill lucke;
>   That both for wit, and sense, so oft dost plucke,
And neuer art encounter'd, I confesse:
>   Nor scarce dost colour for it, which is lesse.
Pr'y thee, yet saue thy rest; giue ore in time:
>   There's no vexation, that can make thee prime.

THOMAS MAY (1595–1650)

Poet, playwright, translator; graduate of Cambridge University (1612, Sidney Sussex College). He wrote a number of unsuccessful comedies, tragedies and historical narrative poems, but was more successful in his translations of Latin classics. His versions of Lucan's *Pharsalia* (1627 – it was to go through eight editions) and Virgil's *Georgics* (1628) were admired by Jonson. He followed these with translations of Martial, evidencing here as elsewhere his own member-ship of the 'tribe of Ben' (admirers of Jonson). Although he received considerable support at the Stuart court during the body of his literary career, after Jonson's death in 1637 (disappointed, it is said, at not succeeding Jonson as poet laureate) he became a supporter of the Parliament and espoused its cause in the English Civil War. He became secretary to the Long Parliament, and wrote the important *History of the Parliament in England which Began November the Third, 1640 . . .* (1647). May's turncoat politics earned Marvell's unforgiving denunciation of his 'Most servile wit and Mercenary Pen'.

From *Selected Epigramms of Martial Englished* (1629).

Spec. 6 Among Other Spectacles, Ancient Fables were Acted at the Theatre, and among Others, This of the Queen Pasiphaë, Who Unnaturally Lusted after a Bull

Beleeve a bull enioy'd the Cretan Queene;
Th'old fable verifi'd we all have seene.
Let not old times, Cæsar, selfe-praised bee;
Since what fame sings, the stage presents to thee.

Ep. 3.43 *Against Lentinus*

Thou dy'st thy haire to seeme a younger man,
And turn'st a Crow, that lately wert a Swan.
All are not cousen'd; hels queene knows thee grey.
She'll take the vizor from thy head away.

Ep. 3.51 *To Galla*

When ere I praise thy face, hand, leg; far more
(Thou sayst) I'd like thee, if all naked ore;
Yet still thou shun'st the common Baths with me;
Fear'st thou that I should not be lik'd by thee?

Ep. 4.21

That in the Heavens no gods there be
Selius affirmes, and proves, cause he
Still thinking so lives happily.

Ep. 4.32 *Of a Bee Smoother'd in Amber*

Here shines a Bee clos'd in an Amber tombe
As if interr'd in her own honey-combe.
A fit-reward fate to her labours gave;
No other death would she have wish'd to have.

Ep. 4.35

Wee saw faint Deere with furious butts of late
Each other meet, and dye with mutuall fate.
The Dogs beheld their prey, the Hunts-man proud
Admir'd no worke was to his knife allowd.
Whence should faint hearts such furie entertaine?
So fight sterne Buls, so valiant men are slaine.

Ep. 4.49

Thou know'st not, trust me, what are Epigrams,
Flaccus, who thinkst them iests, & wanton games.
He wantons more, who writes what horrid meat
The plagu'd Thyestes, and vex'd Tereus eat,
Or Dædalus fitting his Boy to fly,
Or Polyphemus flocks in Sicily.
My Booke no windy words, nor turgid needes,
Nor swels my Muse with mad Cothurnall weedes.
Yet those things all men praise, admire, adore.
True, they praise those, but read these Poems more.

Ep. 5.72 *Of Bacchus Birth*

Who sayes that Iove was Bacchus mother, he
As well may call his father Semele.

Ep. 8.24 To Cæsar

If my small fearefull Booke do begge of thee,
Grant it, if not too bold my beggings bee;
Or pardon, though thou grant not what I move;
Incense and prayers nere offended Iove.
He makes not gods, who does their figures raise
In gold and marble; but the man that prayes.

Ep. 9.14

Thinkst thou his friendship ever faithful proves,
Whom first thy Table purchas'd? no, he loves
Thy Oysters, Mullets, Bores, Sowes paps, not thee:
If I could feast him so, he would love me.

Ep. 9.56

To Libya goes Spendophorus to warre.
Cupid, thy shafts for this faire Boy prepare,
Those shafts, which youths & tender virgins wound;
Light let thy speare in his soft hand be found.
The breast-plate, helme and shield I leave to thee;
To fight in safety, naked let him bee.
No arrow, sword, nor dart could hurt in warre
Parthenopæus, whilst his face was bare.
He, whom this youth shall wound, will dy of love,
And happy too so sweet a fate to prove.
Whilst yet thy chin is smooth fair boy come home;
Grow not a man in Affricke, but at Rome.

Ep. 10.71 *Upon the Tombe of Rabirius His Parents*

Thou that dost wish thy parents' lives should prove
Both long & blest, this tombs short title love.
Wherein Rabirius dead deare parents rest.
No age with happier fate was ever blest.
Wedlocke of threescore years one night untwines,
And in one funerall flame both bodies ioynes.
But he, as they had dy'd in greener yeares,
Still weepes. What iustice is there in those teares?

Ep. 10.72

In vaine ô wretched Flatterie,
With bare-worne lips thou comst to me,
To call me falsly Lord and God.*
Away; for thee here's no abode;
To Parthia's mitred Monarchs goe;
There falling prostrate, basely low,
The gawdy Kings proud feet adore.
This is no Lord, but Emperour,
Of all the iustest Senatour,*
By whom from Stygian shades, the plaine,
And rustike truth's brought backe againe.
Thou dar'st not, Rome, the Emperour,
To flatter as thou didst before.

Lord and God: form of address demanded by Domitian
Senatour: Trajan, emperor 98–117 CE

Ep. 11.56 *Against Cheræmon*

That thou, Cheræmon, death dost oft desire
Thou wouldst have us thy valiant mind admire.
This high resolve comes from an eareless pot,
A chimney without fire to keepe it hot,
A bedsted eat with wormes, rugs coarse & light,
One short bare gown to weare both day and night.
How brave a man art thou canst want such geere
As straw, coarse bread, and lees of vinegar!
But if a woven purple coverled,
And fine french lawne adorn'd thy downy bed,
Hadst thou a Boy, whose rosie lips would fire,
As wine he fils; the lustfull guests desire:
Then thou to live thrice Nestors years wouldst pray,
And wouldst not lose an houre of any day.
In poore estate tis easie scorning death;
Valiant is he dares draw a wretched breath.

Ep. 11.91

Within this Tombe faire Canace is plac't,
To whom her seventh Winter was her last.
O dire mischance! Reader, why weepst thou there?
Tis not her short life, that requires thy teare.
Deaths manner's worse than death; the dire disease
Beset her face, her tender mouth did seize.
The Monster sicknesse striv'd a kisse to have.
Her faire lips went not wholly to the grave.
If fates so soone had meant to stop her breath,
They should have come some other way. But death
Made haste her tongues sweet Musicke to prevent,
Lest that should make the flintie Fates relent.

ROBERT HERRICK (1591–1674)

Born into a family of goldsmiths and apprenticed to his uncle at the age of sixteen, Herrick went up to Cambridge late, entering St John's College in 1613 and graduating BA from Trinity Hall in 1617 and MA in 1620. He became a friend of Ben Jonson, with whom he associated in London in the early 1620s. In 1623 he was ordained priest and was chaplain to the Duke of Buckingham during the ill-fated expedition to the Île de Rhé in 1627. From 1629 he received a living as Dean Prior in Devon, of which he was deprived as a Royalist in 1647, only to be reinstated in 1662. A prolific writer of verse from the 1620s onward (although a number of poems predate this), he would circulate his poems rather than publish them, and waited until the Parliamentarians ejected him from his living to publish his first major collection, *Hesperides* (1648). The collection features some 1200 poems with both secular and religious themes in a wide variety of literary forms, including hymns and songs, for which he earned from Swinburne the title of 'the greatest song-writer ever born of English race'. Also among the forms used is the epigram (one well suited to Herrick's intricate verbal craftsmanship), and among the epigrams are many direct translations of Martial, with a far greater attention than in Jonson's versions to the satiric or even offensive. Sometimes, as in *The Lilly in a Christal*, the ideas of a Martial epigram (8.68) are transformed into an extraordinary erotic lyric (compare Peter Porter's version on p. 340). The following selection begins with a thoroughly Martialesque epigram with no direct Latin precursor.

From *Hesperides* (1648).

Upon Scobble

> *Scobble* for Whoredome whips his wife; and cryes,
> He'll slit her nose; But blubb'ring, she replyes,
> Good Sir, make no more cuts i'th'outward skin,
> One slit's enough to let Adultry in.

Ep. 1.4 *Poets*

Wantons we are; and though our words be such,
Our Lives do differ from our Lines by much.

Ep. 1.19 *Upon Bridget*

Of foure teeth onely *Bridget* was possest;
Two she spat out, a cough forc't out the rest.

Ep. 1.98 *Upon Urles*

Urles had the Gout so, that he co'd not stand;
Then from his Feet, it shifted to his Hand:
When 'twas in's Feet, his Charity was small;
Now tis in's Hand, he gives no Almes at all.

Ep. 3.2 *To His Booke*

While thou didst keep thy *Candor* undefil'd,
Deerely I lov'd thee; as my first-borne child:
But when I saw thee wantonly to roame
From house to house, and never stay at home;
I brake my bonds of Love, and bad thee goe,
Regardlesse whether well thou sped'st, or no.
On with thy fortunes then, what e're they be;
If good I'le smile, if bad I'le sigh for Thee.

Ep. 4.59 *The Amber Bead*

I saw a Flie within a Beade
Of Amber cleanly buried:
The Urne was little, but the room
More rich then *Cleopatra*'s Tombe.

Ep. 5.10 *Posting to Printing*

Let others to the Printing Presse run fast,
Since after death comes glory, *Ile not haste*.

Ep. 6.39 *Upon Dundridge*

Dundridge his Issue hath; but is not styl'd
For all his Issue, Father of one Child.

Ep. 6.66 *The Custard*

For second course, last night, a Custard came
To th' board, so hot, as none co'd touch the same:
Furze, three or foure times with his cheeks did blow
Upon the Custard, and thus cooled so:
It seem'd by this time to admit the touch;
But none co'd eate it, 'cause it stunk so much.

Ep. 7.25 *On Poet Prat*

Prat He writes Satyres; but herein's the fault,
In no one Satyre there's a mite of salt.

Ep. 7.77 *To the Detracter*

Where others love, and praise my Verses; still
Thy long-black-Thumb-nail marks 'em out for ill:
A fellon take it, or some Whit-flaw come
For to unslate, or to untile that thumb!
But cry thee Mercy: Exercise thy nailes
To scratch or claw, so that thy tongue not railes:
Some numbers prurient are, and some of these
Are wanton with their itch; scratch, and 'twill please.

Ep. 8.35 *Jack and Jill*

Since *Jack* and *Jill* both wicked be;
It seems a wonder unto me,
That they no better do agree.

Ep. 8.55 *To the Patron of Poets, M. End: Porter*

Let there be Patrons; Patrons like to thee,
Brave *Porter*! Poets ne'r will wanting be:
Fabius, and *Cotta*, *Lentulus*, all live
In thee, thou Man of Men! who here do'st give
Not onely subject-matter for our wit,
But likewise Oyle of Maintenance to it:
For which, before thy Threshold, we'll lay downe
Our Thyrse, for Scepter; and our Baies for Crown.
For to say truth, all Garlands are thy due;
The *Laurell*, *Mirtle*, *Oke*, and *Ivie* too.

Ep. 8.68 *The Lilly in a Christal*

You have beheld a smiling *Rose*
    When Virgins hands have drawn
    O'r it a Cobweb-Lawne:
And here, you see, this Lilly shows,
    Tomb'd in a *Christal* stone,
More faire in this transparent case,
    Then when it grew alone;
    And had but single grace.

You see how *Creame* but naked is;
    Nor daunces in the eye
    Without a Strawberrie:
Or some fine tincture, like to this,
    Which draws the sight thereto,
More by that wantoning with it;
    Then when the paler hieu
    No mixture did admit.

You see how *Amber* through the streams
    More gently stroaks the sight,
    With some conceal'd delight;
Then when he darts his radiant beams
    Into the boundlesse aire:
Where either too much light his worth
    Doth all at once impaire,
    Or set it little forth.

Put Purple Grapes, or Cherries in-
    To Glasse, and they will send
    More beauty to commend
Them, from that cleane and subtile skin,

Then if they naked stood,
And had no other pride at all,
But their own flesh and blood,
And tinctures naturall.

Thus Lillie, Rose, Grape, Cherry, Creame,
And Straw-berry do stir
More love, when they transfer
A weak, a soft, a broken beame;
Then if they sho'd discover
At full their proper excellence;
Without some Scean cast over,
To juggle with the sense.

Thus let this *Christal'd Lillie* be
A Rule, how far to teach,
Your nakednesse must reach:
And that, no further, then we see
Those glaring colours laid
By Arts wise hand, but to this end
They sho'd obey a shade;
Lest they too far extend.

So though y'are white as Swan, or Snow,
And have the power to move
A world of men to love:
Yet, when your Lawns and Silks shal flow;
And that white cloud divide
Into a doubtful Twi-light; then,
Then will your hidden Pride
Raise greater fires in men.

Ep. 8.69 *To the Detracter*

I ask't thee oft, what Poets thou hast read,
And lik'st the best? Still thou reply'st, The dead.
I shall, ere long, with green turfs cover'd be;
Then sure thou't like, or thou wilt envie me.

Ep. 10.23 *Vertue*

Each must, in vertue, strive for to excell;
That man lives twice, that lives the first life well.

Ep. 11.16 *On his Booke*

To read my Booke the Virgin shie
May blush, (while *Brutus* standeth by:)
But when He's gone, read through what's writ,
And never staine a cheeke for it.

Ep. 11.104 *What Kind of Mistresse He would Have*

Be the Mistresse of my choice,
Cleane in manners, cleere in voice:
Be she witty, more then wise;
Pure enough, though not Precise:
Be she shewing in her dresse,
Like a civill Wilderness;
That the curious may detect
Order in a sweet neglect;
Be she rowling in her eye,
Tempting all the passers by:

And each Ringlet of her haire,
An Enchantment, or a Snare,
For to catch the Lookers on;
But her self held fast by none.
Let her *Lucrece* all day be,
Thais in the night, to me.
Be she such, as neither will
Famish me, nor over-fill.

SIR RICHARD FANSHAWE
(1608–66)

Educated at Thomas Farnaby's school in London and Jesus College, Cambridge, he was entered at the Inner Temple in 1626 but abandoned the study of law upon the death of his mother in 1631. He was a devoted Royalist and served Charles I in several important offices, including the King's Remembrancer of the Exchequer and Secretary for War to the Prince of Wales. He was captured in 1651. After the Restoration he became ambassador to Portugal, a privy councillor and ambassador to Spain, where he died of a fever in 1666. His translations included Guarini's *Il Pastor Fido* (first edn, 1647), the fourth book of Virgil's *Aeneid* (1648 – in Spenserian stanzas), *Selected Parts of Horace* (1652) and the epic *Lusiads* of the Portuguese poet Camoëns (1655). The following translation is a product of Fanshawe's preoccupation with the theme of rural contentment, itself a reaction to the political and social upheaval of the times.

From *Il Pastor Fido & Divers Other Poems* (1648).

Ep. 10.47 *A Happy Life out of Martiall*

The things that make a life to please
(Sweetest *Martiall*) they are these:
Estate *inherited*, not *got*;
A *thankfull* Field, *Hearth* always hot:
City *seldome*, Law-suits *never*:
Equall Friends agreeing *ever*:
Health of *Body*, *Peace* of *Minde*:
Sleepes that till the Morning binde:
Wise Simplicitie, *Plaine* Fare:
Not *drunken* Nights, yet *loos'd* from *Care*:
A *Sober*, not a *sullen* Spouse:
Cleane strength, not such as *his* that Plowes:
Wish onely what thou *art*, to *bee*;
Death neither *wish*, nor *feare* to *see*.

WILLIAM CARTWRIGHT
(1611–43)

Playwright, poet, scholar, preacher, and member of 'the tribe of Ben'; educated at Westminster School and Christ Church, Oxford, where he received his MA in 1635. His Jonsonian comedies and tragicomedies were admired by the Caroline court. *The Royal Slave* (1636) was performed before Charles I and Queen Henrietta at Christ Church in a production designed by Inigo Jones, and later revived at Hampton Court. His play-writing ceased and his preaching began when he took holy orders in 1638. In 1642 he was nominated one of the Council of War. His collected works, *Comedies, Tragi-Comedies, with Other Poems*, were published in 1651, prefaced by a cornucopia of Royalist tributes.

From *Comedies, Tragi-Comedies, with other Poems* (1651).

Ep. 1.19 *Si Memini Fuerunt*

Thou hadst four Teeth, good *Elia*, heretofore,
But one Cough spit out two, and one two more:
Now thou mayst Cough all day, and safely too;
There's nothing left for the third Cough to do.

Ep. 1.66 *Ad Furem de Libro Suo*

Th'art out, vile Plagiary, that dost think
A Poet may be made at th'rate of Ink,
And cheap-priz'd Paper; none e'er purchas'd yet
Six or ten Penniworth of Fame or Wit:
Get Verse unpublish'd, new-stamp'd Fancies look,
Which th'only Father of the Virgin Book
Knows, and keeps seal'd in his close Desk within,
Not slubber'd yet by any ruffer Chin;
A Book, once known, ne'r quits the Author; If
Any lies yet impolish'd, any stiff,
Wanting it's Bosses, and it's Cover, do
Get that; I've such and can be secret too.
      He that repeats stoln Verse, and for Fame looks,
      Must purchase Silence too as well as Books.

Ep. 5.74 *In Pompeios Juvenes*

Europe and *Asia* doth th'young *Pompeys* hold,
He* lyes, if any where, in *Lybian* Mould:
No wonder if in all the world they dwell;
So great a Ruine ne'r in one place fell.

He: Pompey the Great, killed in Egypt (48BCE); his sons, Gnaeus and Sextus,
died in Europe and Asia

Ep. 7.60 *Ad Iovem Capitolinum*

Thou Swayer of the Capitoll, whom we
Whiles *Cæsar*'s safe, believe a Deity,
Whiles thee with wishes for themselves all tire,
And to be given, what Gods can give, require,
Think me not proud O *Jove*, 'cause 'mongst the rest
I only for my self make no request:
To thee I ought for *Cæsar*'s wants alone
To make my Sute, to *Cæsar* for my own.

Ep. 10.5 *In Maledicum Poetam*

Whoe'r vile slighter of the State, in more
Vile verse, hath libell'd those he should adore,
May be quite banish'd from the Bridge and Hill
Walk through the Streets, and 'mongst hoarse Beggars still
Reserved to the last even then entreat
Those mouldy harder Crusts that Dogs won't eat.
A long and wet December, nay, what's more,
Stewes shut against him, keep him cold and poor.
May he proclame those blest, and wish he were
One of the happy Ones, upon the Beer;
And when his slow houre Comes, whiles yet alive,
May he perceive Dogs for his Carcass strive;
And moving's rags fright eager Birds away:
Nor let his single torments in death stay;
But deep Gash'd now by *Aeacus* whips, anon
Task'd with the restless *Sisyphus* his stone,
Then 'mongst the old blabbers* waters standing dry;
Weary all Fables, tire all Poetry,
And when a Fury bids him on truth hit,
Conscience betraying him, cry out I writ.

---

old blabbers: the reference is to Tantalus

RICHARD CRASHAW (1612/13–49)

A religious poet, son of a Puritan preacher, educated at Charterhouse and Pembroke Hall, Cambridge. From 1635 to 1643 he was a fellow of Peterhouse, Cambridge, his fellowship being officially cancelled in 1644 after the Royalist defeat. He converted to Catholicism in 1645, left England, and, as a consequence of Stuart patronage, obtained some minor ecclesiastical posts in Italy before his early death in Loreto. His *Epigrammatum Sacrorum Liber* was published in Cambridge in 1634 and *Steps to the Temple, with the Delights of the Muses* in London in 1648. The elaborate, baroque conceits which characterize his verse have elicited a varied critical response.

From *The Delights of the Muses* (1648).

Ep. 1.19 *Out of Martiall*

Foure Teeth thou had'st that ranck'd in goodly state
                    Kept thy Mouthes Gate.

The first blast of thy cough left two alone,
                    The second, none.

This last cough Ælia, cought out all thy feare,
Th'hast left the third cough now no businesse here.

SIR EDWARD SHERBURNE
(1616–1702)

Born and educated in London (at Thomas Farnaby's prestigious school), Sherburne succeeded his father by royal patent as Clerk of the Ordnance at the end of 1641, was removed from his position by the Parliamentarians in the following year, in which he joined the Royalist forces at Nottingham and then at Oxford as Commissary General of Artillery. At the fall of Oxford (1646) he was captured, and was reduced to unemployment and poverty. In 1652 he joined the service of Sir George Saville. After the Restoration he regained his post in the Ordnance Office on petition, served diligently in the office, and was knighted for his services in 1682. At the Revolution he retired from public service, since as a Roman Catholic he could not take the oaths. It was after his capture by the Parliamentarians in 1646 that he began his career as a translator, maintaining a principle of close fidelity to the original which was criticized by several, including Johnson, for whom Sherburne was 'a man whose learning was greater than his powers of poetry' (*The Lives of the English Poets*, 1781, vol. ii, 'Dryden', 126). Sherburne's translations included Italian and French poets as well as the ancients, among whom may be cited Seneca (*Medea*, 1648), Colluthus, Theocritus, Martial and Horace (1651), Manilius (1675) and (in ms.) Pindar, Lucretius and Virgil.

From *Poems and Translations* or (alternative title) *Salmacis, Lyrian & Sylvia . . .* (1651).

Ep. 3.26 On Candidus, a Rich Miser

Alone thou dost enjoy a fair Estate,
Alone rare *Myrrhine* Vessels, golded Plate;
Alone rich Wines dost drink; and hast for None
A Heart, nor Wit but for thy self alone.
None shares with thee, it is deny'd by no man:
But *Candidus*, thou hast a Wife that's Common.

Ep. 3.32 *On Martinia, an Old, Old Leacherous* —

VVhat? canst thou not with an old VVoman bed
Thou criest? – yes: but thou art not old but dead.
VVe could with *Hecuba*, or *Niobe*
Make shift, but then (*Martinia!*) it must be
                                Before the one
Into a Bitch be turn'd, t'other to Stone.

Ep. 5.58 *To Postumus, an Ill Liver*

Still, still thou cry'st to morrow I'l live well:
But when will this to morrow come? canst tell?
How far is't hence? or where is't to be found?
Or upon *Parthian*, or *Armenian* Ground?
Priams, or *Nestors* years by this 't has got;
I wonder for how much it might be bought?
Thou'lt live to morrow? – 'tis too late to day:
Hee's wise who yesterday, I liv'd, can say.

Ep. 6.28 *Epitaphium Glauciae*

Here *Meliors* Freed-man, known so well,
Who by all *Rome* lamented, fell,
His dearest Patrons short-liv'd Joy,
Glaucias, beneath this Stone doth lye,
Neer the *Flaminian* Way interr'd:
Chast, modest, whom quick Wit preferr'd
And happy Forme, who to twelve past,
Scarce one year added; that, his last.
If Passenger thou weep'st for such a Loss,
Mayst thou ne'r mourn for any other Cross.

Ep. 8.35 *On an Ill Husband and Wife*

Since both of you so like in Manners be,
Thou the worst Husband, and the worst Wife she,
I wonder, you no better should agree.

Ep. 10.32 *On Marus Anton. Primus: His Picture*

This Picture, which with Violets you see
And Roses dekt, askst thou whose it may be?
Such was *Antonius* in his Prime of Years,
Who here still young, though he grow old, appears.
Ah! could but Art have drawn his Mind in this,
Not all the World could shew a fairer Peece.

Ep. 10.47 *The Happy Life: To Julius Martialis*

Those things which make life truly blest,
Sweetest *Martial* hear exprest:
Wealth left, and not from Labour growing;
A gratefull soyl, a Hearth still glowing;
No Strife, small Business, Peace of Mind,
Quick Wit, a Body well inclin'd,
Wise Innocence, Friends of one Heart,
Cheap Food, a Table without Art;
Nights which nor Cares, nor Surfets know,
No dull, yet a chaste Bedfellow;
Sleeps which the tedious Hours contract;
Be what thou mayst be, nor exact
Ought more; nor thy last Hour of Breath
Fear, nor with wishes hasten Death.

Ep. 10.102 On Philænus

If how *Philænus* may be stil'd
A Father, who ne'r got a Child
Thou'd'st know; *Davus* can tell thee it,
Who is a Poet and ne'r writ.

Ep. 11.100 The Choice of His Mistris

I would not have a VVench with such a VVaste
As might be well with a Thumb-Ring embrac'd;
VVhose bony Hips, which out on both sides stick,
Might serve for Graters, and whose lean Knees prick;
One, which a saw does in her back-Bone bear,
And in her Rump below carries a Spear.
Nor would I her yet of Bulk so grosse
That weigh'd should break the Scales at th'market-cross;
A meer unfathom'd lump of Grease; no, that
Like they that will; 'tis Flesh I love, not Fat.

Ep. 12.17 On Lentinus, being Troubled with an Ague

Lentinus! thou dost nought but fume, and fret,
To think thy Ague will not leave thee yet.
Why? it goes with thee; bathes as thou dost do,
Eats Mushromes, Oysters, Sweet-breads, wild Boar too,
Oft drunk by thee with Falern Wine is made,
Nor *Cæcub* drinks unless with snow allay'd:
Tumbles in Roses dawb'd with unctuous sweets,
Sleeps upon Down between pure Cambrick sheets,
And when thus well it fares with thee, wouldst thou
Have it to go unto poor *Damma** now?

Damma: name of a slave or poor freedman

ROBERT FLETCHER (fl. *c.*1650)

Perhaps the son of Robert Fletcher (fl. 1586), a student of Merton
College, Oxford, who graduated in 1564 and became a Fellow, then
a schoolmaster, preacher and the author of some pious or patriotic
works. If so, the younger Fletcher's translations of selected poems of
Martial in *Ex Otio Negotium. Or Martiall His Epigrams Translated*
(London, 1656) are his only known work. As will be seen from the
following selections, Fletcher did not baulk at translating with evident
relish Martial's more *risqué* epigrams.

From *Ex Otio Negotium. Or Martiall His Epigrams Translated* (1656).

Ep. 2.37 *In Caecilianum*

What's here and there thou dost purloyn,
A pregnant sow's papps, a hoggs chine,
A woodcock, commons for two men,
A whole Jack, half a Barble, then
A Lamprey's side, a Pullet's thigh,
A Stock-dove boyld in pottage by:
When these are hid in greasy clout,
And to thy Boy deliverd out
To be brought to thy home: we sit
An idle crowd without a bit.
    Restore the feast if any shame there bee,
    To morrow I have not invited thee.

Ep. 2.56 *Ad Gallum de Ejus Uxore*

In *Lybia* thy wife they stigmatize
With the foule crime of too much avarice.
But they are lyes they tell: she is not wont
To take, but give for scouring of her ——.

Ep. 4.87 *De Bassa*

Thy *Bassa*'s used to place a childe up by her,
      And calls it her delight her pretty pinck:
Yet loves no childe, which thou mayst more admire,
      What then's the cause? why, *Bassa*'s wont to stinck.

Ep. 6.4 *Adulatorium Cæsarem*

Most Mighty *Cæsar*, King of kings, to whom
Rome owes so many tryumphs yet to come,
So many Temples growing and restored,
So many Spectacles, gods, Cities: Lord
      She yet in debt to thee doth more remain,
      That she by thee is once made chast again.*

Ep. 7.18 *In Gallam*

When th' hast a face of which no woman may
And body without blur, have ought to say,
Why suitors thee so seldom doe repeat
And seek, dost wonder *Galla*? the fault's great,
As oft as thou and I in the worke joynd,
Thy lips were silent, but thou prat'st behinde.
Heavens grant that thou wouldst speak, but bridle that,
I'me angry with thy tatling *Twit com Twat*.
I'de rather hear thee fart: for *Symmachus*
Says that's a means of laughter unto us.
But who can smile to hear the foolish smack
Of thy loose *Toul*? and when it gives a crack

---

made chast again: Domitian issued edicts against sexual immorality (especially child castration and prostitution) and strengthened the laws against adultery

Whose minde and mettle will not fall? at least
Speak something that may usher in a jest
Of thy C—'s noise: but if thou art so mute,
Articulately learn thence to dispute.

Ep. 7.85 Ad Sabellum

Cause thou dost pen *Tetrasticks* clean and sweet
And some few pretty disticks with smooth feet,
    I praise but not admire:
    Tis easie to acquire
Short modest Epigrams that pretty look,
But it is hard and tough to write a book.

Ep. 7.86 In Sextum

Sextus was wont me to his feasts to call,
When I was scarce made known to him at all.
What have I done so late? so sudenly?
That I his old companion am pass'd by?
After so many pledges, many years?
But I perceive the cause: no gift appears
Of beaten silver from me, no light coat,
No cloak, fee, or negotiating groat.
    Sextus invites his gifts, but not his friends:
    Then cryes his servants bones shall make amends.

Ep. 8.12 Ad Priscum

Dost ask why I'de not marry a rich wife?
I'le not be subject in that double strife.
    Let matrons to their heads inferior be
    Else man and wife have no equalitie.

Ep. 9.67 *In Aeschylum*

I enjoyd a buxom lass all night with mee,
Which none could overcome in venerie.
Thousand wayes tyred, I askd that childish thing,*
Which she did grant at the first motioning,
Blushing and laughing I a worse besought,
Which she most loose vouchsafed as quick as thought.
    Yet she was pure, but if she deale with you
    Shee'l not be so, and thou shalt pay dear too.

Ep. 10.47 *Ad Julium Martialem*

Most pleasant *Martial* these are they
That make the happyer life and day,
Means not sweat for, but resign'd,
Fire without end, fields still in kinde,
No strife, no office, inward peace,
Free strength, a body sans disease,
A prudent plainesse, equal friends,
Cheap Cates,* not scraped from the world's ends,
A night not drown'd, but free from care,
Sheets never sad, and yet chast are,
Sleep that makes short the shades of night,
Art such thou would'st be, if there might
A choice be offer'd, nor dost fear
Nor wish thy last dayes exit here.

---

that childish thing: Latin, *illud puerile*, lit. 'that boy's thing', a euphemism for
anal intercourse
Cates: victuals, provisions, often delicacies

Ep. 10.90 *In Ligellam*

Why dost thou reach thy *Merkin* now half dust?
Why dost provoke the ashes of thy lust?
Girles such lasciviousnesse doth best beseem,
For thou art pass'd old woman in esteem.
That trick (*Ligella*) suites not, credit mee,
With *Hecuba*, but young *Andromache*.
Thou err'st, if this a C— thou dar'st to call
To which no Prick doth now belong at all,
    If thou cann'st blush *Ligella*, be afear'd
    To pull a deceas'd Lyon by the beard.

Ep. 11.43 *In Vxorem*

Caught with my *Boyes*, at me my wife the *Froe*
Scolds, and cryes out she hath an ars-hole too.
How oft hath *Juno* thus reprov'd loose *Jove*?
Yet he with *Ganimede* doth act his love.
Hercules bent his Boy,* layd-by his Bow,
Though *Megara* had hanches too we know.
Phoebus was tortured by the flying Wench,*
Yet the *Oebalian* Lad* those flames did quench.
Though much denyed *Briseis* from him lay
Achilles with *Patroclus* yet did play.
Give not male names then to such things as thine,
But think thou hast two Twats o wife of mine.

Boy: Hylas
flying Wench: Daphne
Oebalian Lad: Hyacinthus

Ep. 12.97 *In Bassum*

When thou a wife so youthful hast,
So rich, so noble, wise, and chast,
That the most wicked Goat that is
A better cannot wish for his.
Thou spendst thy strength with Boyes (we see)
Which thy wife's dowry bought for thee,
So to his Mistris thy Prick comes
Tyred, thus redeemed with mighty summs.
Nor will he stand though tempted by
The voyce's or thumbs flattery.
    Blush then, or let the Law unfold it,
      (*Bassus*) this is not thine, th'hast sold it.

THOMAS PECKE (b. 1637, fl. 1664)

Scion of a well-known Norfolk family, who was educated at the free school, Norwich, and entered Gonville and Caius College, Cambridge, in 1655. He did not graduate, but was called to the bar in 1664 on the books of the Inner Temple. His *Parnassi Puerperium* included translations of selected epigrams of John Owen, Sir Thomas More and Martial (from *Liber De Spectaculis*), together with epigrams by himself. Other works by Pecke include *Advice to Balaam's Ass* (1658), *An Elegie upon Mr. John Cleeveland* (1658), and a poem of congratulations to Charles II on his restoration to the throne.

From *Parnassi Puerperium* . . . (1659).

Spec. 1 *Upon the Cæsarean Amphitheater**

No more let Sun-burnt *Cayro* vaunt, that She,
Bequeaths her wonders, to Eternitie.
Let not *Euphrates*, in a superb Style,
Brag her Wall, Girdle, unto sixty Mile.
Who lends *Diana* confidence, to tell;
Her Cedar-Statues, scorn a Parallel?
What if *Apollo*'s horned Altar, stands
Unimitable, by *Lysippus* Hands?
Let *Carian* Impudence, presume so far;
As to make *Mausoleum*, kiss a Star.
Dame *Tellus*! and thy Prodigies confer;
They must kneel to the *Amphitheater*.
This Miracle, Grac'd by *Vespasian*'s Name:
Hath the Monopoly, of checquer'd Fame.

Spec. 4 *To the Emperour Titus, upon His Banishing Sycophants*

Those Caterpillers of the Commonwealth,
The Poor Mans Wolfe, whose livelihood was Stealth;
Growing too Numerous, are ship'd away;
To Feast the Lions, of *Getulia*:
And those Informers, who have many sent
Into Exile; now suffer Banishment.

---

the Cæsarean Amphitheater: The Flavian Amphitheatre or Colosseum in Rome, dedicated in 80 CE by the emperor Titus. The poem catalogues wonders of the ancient world now inferior to the Colosseum: 1–2, Egyptian pyramids; 3–4, walls of Babylon; 5–6, Diana's temple at Ephesus; 7–8, Apollo's altar at Delos; 9–10, tomb of Mausolus.

Spec. 6 *Upon Pasiphae**

That *Minos* lustful Wife, Trepan'd a Bull;
Now we have seen it, is not wonderfull:
Let not Antiquity, her Fictions boast:
We fancy most, they should the Stage accost.

Spec. 7 / 8 *The Conflict of a Woman, with a Lion: As it was Performed in the Amphitheater*

Caesar's Munificence, 'twill not suffice;
That virile Hands, should grasp the crimson Price.
Delicate body, can't Fair *Cypria* shield:
As well as *Mars*, She conquers, or is Kil'd.
Alcides kil'd a Lion, and it is
Blown through the world by Fame, with Emphasis.
Be silent Authors! For *Cæsar*'s command;
Made this Achievement, of a Female hand.

Spec. 9 *The Punishment of Laureolus*

Prometheus to cold *Caucasus* is chain'd;
Whilst by his Entrails, Vultures are sustain'd:
Wretched *Laureolus*, a Northern Bear;
Very sincerely, did asunder tear.
Every Vein, to weep Bloud was inclin'd:
Strict search in's Carkass, could no Body finde.

Upon Pasiphae: This epigram describes a re-enactment 'for real' of Pasiphaë's mating with the Cretan bull. Similarly *Spec.* 9 and 24 below describe bloody re-enactments of the crucifixion and dismemberment of Laureolus and of the dismemberment of Orpheus. Criminals were used for these roles and were torn apart in the arena.

Thus one that stab'd his Master, must have dy'd;
Or Actors of infernal Parricide.
This Torment is his due, who dares *Rome* Fire;
Or who deflowres, the Gods most sacred Quire.
Obsolete Mischiefs, resalute the Stage:
Fables prove True; in this our conscious Age.

Spec. 24 *Upon Orpheus*

Whatever *Hæmus* polisht Vales comprise;
The Theatre vouchsafes to *Cæsar*'s Eyes.
The Rocks creep from their place; Woods give the start:
Splendid as *Ægles*, in the Western Part.
The Wolf, and Lamb, the Hound, and Hare desist
From enmity; to hear this Lutanist.
Rare *Philomel*, and the Cock-Linnet, fly
Hither to learn, *Orphean* Harmony:
Yet he was rent, by an unthankful Bear:
Let *Thrace* choose Fictions; at *Rome*, Truths these are.

Spec. 28/29 *Upon Leander*

Leander wonder not, curl'd Waves thee spare;
These inoffensive Surges, *Cæsars* are.
When *Tethys* stopt, Love-sick *Leander*'s Breath;
And some few drops, would hurry him to Death,
The poor Wretch begg'd: O waft Me safe to ground:
When I have seen my Dear; let me be Drown'd.

Spec. 34 *Upon a Sea-fight*

The Palm of Glory, to *Augustus* yeeld;
For framing Sea, into a pitched Field.
How then may *Cæsar* Triumph? Such Beasts are,
Guests to the Waves, as Sea-green *Thetis* scare.
Swift Chariots track the Main; at whose approach,
Triton cri'd out; Here coms King *Neptune*'s Coach.
Whilst *Nereus* for the Skirmishes provides;
And a Whale's Back, victoriously Bestrides.
What *Cæsar*'s pleasure, shall the Circk command;
The Flouds React; as Mimicks to the Land.
On *Claudius*; *Nero*'s Lake;* let Scorn reflect:
Domitian's shows, merit entire Respect.

Claudius, *Nero*: had staged spectacular sea-fights previously

II. THE RESTORATION TO THE AUGUSTANS: 1660–*c*.1700

INTRODUCTION

Martial's technique of surprise, commonly called wit, became ever more prevalent in the satire of the latter half of the seventeenth century, and with the removal of the Puritans and the restoration of the monarchy there was much to be witty about. Released from Puritan fetters, the verbal and sexual licence of the Elizabethans was restored, although the excesses of a Rochester had to be hidden under the publishing label of 'Antwerp', society's acceptance reserved for Sedley's more refined manner. This was a period of extensive translation practice and varied translation intent, the close fidelity of Thomas Creech's Lucretius (1682) operating alongside the expansive 'imitations' of Cowley (1668) and the creative reformulations of Rochester. Indeed Dryden's famous tripartition (Preface to *Ovid's Epistles*, 1680) of *Metaphrase* (literal translation), *Paraphrase* (in which the author's 'words are not so strictly followed as his sense') and *Imitation* (creative adaptation) signalled both the nature of contemporary practice and its literary and social importance. Dryden's *Miscellanies* and his own transformation from satirist to translator indexed the tenor of the times. The ancients were not so much admired as venerated, oftentimes viewed as keepers of a lost wisdom and truth, the applicability of which to late-seventeenth-century England was self-evident. The notion of cultural difference, let alone that of 'historical translation' (translation which sought to represent for contemporary readers the historically conditioned form and meaning of an ancient text), was scarcely entertained. There were substantial, 'close' translations of Martial in this period (see especially Killigrew), as of other classical authors, and excellent paraphrases in Dryden's sense (see Brown and Sedley); but in both modes the ancient epigrammatist is turned into a Restoration wit, often complete with knowledge of seventeenth-century life. As for poetic honours, these may be thought to go to the more creative versions of Cowley and the innovations and developments of Rochester and Dryden. Although (apart from a few epitaphs) Dryden wrote no epigrams, his verse's sustained epigrammatic brilliance joins Rochester's graphic sexual satire and Cowley's imaginative re-creations as perhaps the Restoration's most worthy inheritance of the poet from Bilbilis.

TRANSLATIONS AND IMITATIONS

JAMES WRIGHT (1643–1713)

Born at Yarnton, Oxfordshire, and educated by neither university, Wright yet entered the Middle Temple in 1669 and was called to the bar in 1672. He was also an antiquary and had one of the finest collections of old manuscripts, especially of plays, in the country. His chief loves were perhaps the theatre and country life. Among the interesting works ascribed to him are *A Poem . . . on the Present Ruins in St. Paul's Cathedral* (1668), *The History and Antiquities of the County of Rutland* (1684), *A Compendious View of the Late Tumults and Troubles in this Kingdom* (1685), *Country Conversations* (1694) and the now neglected account of the English stage before the Restoration, *Historia Histrionica: An Historical Account of the English Stage* (1699), which frequently prefaced Colley Cibber's *Apology* from its third edition (1750) onwards. He was also a translator of Martial, author of *Sales*

Epigrammaton, Being the Choicest Disticks of Martials Fourteen Books of Epigrams . . . Made English (London, 1663). By 'choicest' Wright meant (among other things) 'not obscene', since the more *risqué* and sexually explicit distichs are omitted. Contemporaries remark that he died a papist.

From *Sales Epigrammaton . . .* (1663).

Ep. 1.28 *Of Acerra*

Who says with last nights Wine *Acerra* stinks,
Is much deceived; till day *Acerra* drinks.

Ep. 1.32 *To Sabidius*

I love thee not, *Sabidius*; Ask you why?
I do not love thee, let that satisfie!

Ep. 1.47 *Of Diaulus the Physician*

Diaul the Dectour is a *Sexton* made;
Though he is changed, he changeth not his Trade.

Ep. 1.110 *To Velox*

You say my Epigrams, *Velox*, too long are:
You nothing write; sure yours are shorter far.

Ep. 2.20 Of Paulus

Bought Verses, for his own, Paul doth recite;
For what you buy, you may call yours by right.

Ep. 2.88 Upon Mamercus

You'd Poet seem, yet nothing you rehearse;
Be what you will, so we nere hear your verse.

Ep. 3.28 Upon Nestor

Wonder you *Nestor*, Marius ear smells strong?
Your breaths the Cause, you whisper there so long.

Ep. 4.65 Of Philænis

With but one eye *Philænis* weeps; how done
If you enquire, know she hath got but one.

Ep. 4.85 Upon Ponticus

We drink in glass, but you in stone, and why?
Least clear glass should your better Wine descry.

Ep. 5.43 Of Thais and Lecania

Lecania's teeth why white, *Thais* black are?
Lecania bought, *Thais* her own doth wear.

Ep. 5.47 *Of Philo*

That he ne're sups at home, *Philo* makes Oath;
He never sups, but when invited forth.

Ep. 5.57 *To Cinna*

When *Sir* I call thee, be not pleas'd; for know
Cinna, I often call my servant so.

Ep. 7.3 *To Pontilianus*

Why send I not to thee these Books of mine?
'Cause I, *Pontilian*, would be free from thine.

Ep. 7.9 *Of Cassellius*

Cassellius now to threescore years doth rise;
He witty is, when will he grow to wise?

Ep. 7.94 *To Papilus*

Sweet oyntment once was in that Onyx stone;
You smelt, and see 'tis putrefaction grown.

Ep. 9.15 *On Chloe*

On her seven Husbands tombs she doth impress,
This Chloë did; what can she more confess?

Xen. 4 *Frankincense*

Send perfum'd prayers to *Jove*, that *Cæsar* may
Long rule on earth, e're he heaven's scepter sway.

Xen. 53 *A Turtle-dove*

Lettuce farewell; fat Turtles give to me;
And poynant hunger the best sawce will be.

Xen. 127 *A Coronet of Roses to Cæsar*

Winter a Rose presents unto thy Throne;
Once 'twas the Springs, but now 'tis *Cæsars* grown.

Apoph. 34 *A Sithe Made of a Sword*

Me to a better Trade calme Peace doth change,
I, in the Camp did serve, do in the Scange.

Apoph. 44 *A Wooden Candlestick*

Unless you mind, and mend the light, you'l see
The Candlestick it self will Candle be.

Apoph. 75 *A Nightingale*

Wrong'd *Philomel*, while woman, mute was she;
But since a bird, sings her own Eligy.

Apoph. 76 *A Pie**

Did you not see, (such a true voyce I fain)
Thinking me man, you would Salute again.

Apoph. 177 *Corinthian Hercules**

See how the Child doth the two Serpents tear,
And squeeze out life; *Hydra* even now may fear.

Apoph. 181 *Leander in Marble*

Thus bold *Leander* spake to the swel'd wave;
Spare me till I return, be then my grave.

Apoph. 190 *Livy in Parchment*

In a small Parchment see great *Livy* roll'd;
Whom all my Study is too small to hold.

Apoph. 194 *Lucan*

There some be say I do not poetize;
But he who sells me finds it otherwise.

Pie: magpie
Hercules: The infant Hercules strangled two snakes in his cradle; the killing of
the Hydra was one of the Twelve Labours.

ABRAHAM COWLEY (1618–67)

Renowned in his own day as the greatest living poet, this son of a London stationer was educated at Westminster School and at Trinity College, Cambridge, where he was both scholar and fellow. It was at Cambridge that Cowley wrote his biblical epic, *Davideis*. He moved to France in 1644 after the Royalist defeat, accompanying Queen Henrietta as her secretary. He returned to England in 1654 and was arrested as a Royalist agent, but released, after which he studied medicine at Oxford. He was in fact suspected by both sides in the Civil War. Following the Restoration he got (with some difficulty) the pension he thought he deserved, and retired to Barnes and Chertsey, where he died. His works include *Essays*, *The Mistress* (1647) and *Poems* (1656), which contained *Miscellanies, Pindaric Odes* and *Davideis* together with a critical preface. In Samuel Johnson's *Lives of the English Poets* (1781), vol. i, 'Cowley', 27ff., he furnishes the opportunity for Johnson's reflections on 'metaphysical poetry' generally. Cowley's poetic activity covers the whole period of the English Civil War and its aftermath. Since *Several Discourses by Way of Essays in Verse and Prose*, which contains all but one of the ensuing versions, was published posthumously in 1668, it seemed appropriate to include him in this section. Several of Cowley's 'imitations' promote an ideology of withdrawal from public life appropriate to the poet's final years. Their celebration of retirement and their at times intimate, even polite tone of personal address look forward to the Augustans, who held Cowley in high esteem. His creative renditions of Martial helped to establish the *Imitation* as a literary form in itself.

From *Several Discourses by Way of Essays in Verse and Prose* (1668), except *Ep.* 5.20, which is from *Miscellanies* (1656).

Ep. 1.55

Well then, Sir, you shall know how far extend
The Prayers and Hopes of your Poetick Friend.
He does not Palaces nor Manors crave,
Would be no Lord, but less a Lord would have
The ground he holds, if he his own, can call,
He quarrels not with Heaven because 'tis small:
Let gay and toilsome Greatness others please,
He loves of homely Littleness the Ease.
Can any Man in guilded rooms attend,
And his dear houres in humble visits spend;
When in the fresh and beauteous Field he may
With various healthful pleasures fill the day?
If there be Man (ye Gods) I ought to Hate
Dependance and Attendance be his Fate.
Still let him Busie be, and in a crowd,
And very much a Slave, and very Proud:
Thus he perhaps Pow'rful and Rich may grow;
No matter, O ye Gods! that I'le allow.
But let him Peace and Freedome never see;
Let him not love this Life, who loves not Me.

Ep. 2.53

Would you be Free? 'Tis your chief wish, you say,
Come on; I'le shew thee, Friend, the certain way,
If to no Feasts abroad thou lov'st to go,
Whilst bounteous God does Bread at home bestow,
If thou the goodness of thy Cloaths dost prize
By thine own Use, and not by others Eyes.
(If onely safe from Weathers) thou can'st dwell,
In a small House, but a convenient Shell,

If thou without a Sigh, or Golden wish,
Canst look upon thy Beechen Bowl, and Dish;
If in thy Mind such power and greatness be,
The *Persian* King's a Slave compar'd with Thee.

Ep. 2.68

That I do with humble Bowes no more,
And danger of my naked Head adore.
That I who Lord and Master cry'd erewhile,
Salute you in a new and different Stile;
By your own Name, a scandal to you now,
Think not that I forget my self or you:
By loss of all things by all others sought
This Freedome, and the Freemans Hat is bought.
A Lord and Master no man wants but He
Who o're Himself has no Autoritie.
Who does for Honours and for Riches strive,
And Follies, without which Lords cannot Live.
If thou from Fortune dost no Servant crave,
Believe it, thou no Master need'st to have.

Ep. 2.90

Wonder not, Sir (you who instruct the Town
In the true Wisdom of the Sacred Gown)
That I make haste to live, and cannot hold
Patiently out, till I grow Rich and Old.
Life for Delays and Doubts no time does give,
None ever yet, made Haste enough to Live.
Let him defer it, whose preposterous care
Omits himself, and reaches to his Heir.
Who does his Fathers bounded stores despise,
And whom his own too never can suffice:

My humble thoughts no glittering roofs require,
Or Rooms that shine with ought but constant Fire.
I well content the Avarice of my sight
With the fair guildings of reflected Light:
Pleasures abroad, the sport of Nature yields
Her living Fountains, and her smiling Fields:
And then at home, what pleasure is't to see
A little cleanly chearful Familie?
Which if a chast Wife crown, no less in Her
Than Fortune, I the Golden Mean prefer.
Too noble, nor too wise, she should not be,
No, not too Rich, too Fair, too fond of me.
Thus let my life slide silently away,
With Sleep all Night, and Quiet all the Day.

Ep. 4.5

Honest and Poor, faithful in word and thought;
What has thee, *Fabian*, to the City brought?
Thou neither the Buffoon, nor Bawd canst play,
Nor with false whispers th'Innocent betray:
Nor corrupt Wives, nor from rich Beldams get
A living by thy industry and sweat;
Nor with vain promises and projects cheat,
Nor Bribe or Flatter any of the Great.
But you'r a Man of Learning, prudent, just;
A Man of Courage, firm, and fit for trust.
Why you may stay, and live unenvyed here;
But (faith) go back, and keep you where you were.

Ep. 5.20

If, dearest *Friend*, it my good Fate might be
T' enjoy at once a *quiet Life* and *Thee*;
If we for *Happiness* could *leisure* find,
And *wandring Time* into a *Method* bind,
We should not sure the *Great Mens* favour need,
Nor on long *Hopes*, the *Courts thin Diet*, feed.
We should not *Patience* find daily to hear,
The *Calumnies*, and *Flatteries* spoken there.
We should not the *Lords Tables* humbly use,
Or talk in *Ladies* Chambers *Love* and *News*;
But *Books* and wise *Discourse*, *Gardens* and *Fields*,
And all the joys that *unmixt Nature* yields.
Thick *Summer* shades where *Winter* still does ly,
Bright *Winter* Fires that *Summers* part supply.
Sleep not controll'd by *Cares*, confin'd to *Night*,
Or bound in any rule but *Appetite*.
Free, but not savage or ungracious *Mirth*,
Rich *Wines* to give it quick and easie birth.
A few *Companions*, which our selves should chuse,
A *Gentle Mistress*, and a *Gentler Muse*.
Such, dearest Friend, such without doubt should be
Our *Place*, our *Business*, and our *Companie*.
Now to *Himself*, alas, does neither *Live*,
But sees good *Suns*, of which we are to give
A strict *account*, set and march thick away;
Knows a man how to Live, and does he stay?

Ep. 5.58

To morrow you will Live, you always cry;
In what far Country does this morrow lye,
That 'tis so mighty long 'ere it arrive?
Beyond the *Indies* does this Morrow live?
'Tis so far fetcht this Morrow, that I fear
'T will be both very Old and very Dear.
To morrow I will live, the Fool does say;
To Day it self's too Late, the wise liv'd Yesterday.

Ep. 10.47

Since, dearest Friend, 'tis your desire to see
A true Receipt of Happiness from Me;
These are the chief Ingredients, if not all;
Take an Estate neither too great nor small,
Which *Quantum Sufficit* the Doctors call;
Let this Estate from Parents Care descend;
The getting it too much of Life does spend.
Take such a Ground, whose gratitude may be
A fair Encouragement for Industry.
Let constant Fires the Winters fury tame,
And let thy Kitchens be a Vestal Flame.
Thee to the Town let never Suit at Law;
And rarely, very rarely Business draw.
Thy active mind in equal Temper keep,
In undisturbed Peace, yet not in sleep.
Let exercise a vigorous health maintain,
Without which all the Composition's vain.
In the same weight Prudence and Innocence take,
*Ana** of each does the just mixture make.

Ana: an equal quantity

But a few Friendships wear, and let them be
By Nature and by Fortune fit for thee.
In stead of Art and Luxury in food,
Let Mirth and Freedome make thy Table good.
If any Cares into thy Day-time creep,
At Night, without Wines Opium, let them sleep.
Let rest, which Nature does to Darkness wed,
And not Lust, recommend to thee thy Bed,
Be satisfi'd, and pleas'd with what thou art;
Act cheerfully and well th'allotted part,
Enjoy the present Hour, be thankful for the Past,
And neither fear, nor wish th'approaches of the last.

Ep. 10.96

Me who have liv'd so long among the great,
You wonder to hear talk of a Retreat:
And a retreat so distant, as may show
No thoughts of a return when once I go.
Give me a Country, how remote so e're,
Where Happiness a mod'rate rate does bear,
Where poverty it self in plenty flowes,
And all the solid use of Riches knowes.
The ground about the house maintains it there,
The House maintains the ground about it here.
Here even Hunger's dear, and a full board,
Devours the vital substance of the Lord.
The Land it self does there the feast bestow,
The Land it self must here to Market go.
Three or four suits one Winter here does wast,
One suit does there three or four winters last.
Here every frugal Man must oft be cold,
And little Luke-warm fires are to you sold.
There Fire's an Element as cheap and free.
Almost as any of the other Three.

Stay you then here, and live among the Great,
Attend their sports, and at their tables eat.
When all the bounties here of Men you score:
The Places bounty there, shall give me more.

SIR JOHN DENHAM (1615–69)

Irish-born poet, educated at Trinity College, Oxford, and Lincoln's
Inn. He supported the Royalists in the Civil War and was governor
of Farnham Castle when it surrendered to the Parliamentarians in
1642. A principal participant during the 1650s in the negotiations for
the king's return, he was rewarded after the Restoration with appoint-
ment as Surveyor of the Royal Works (with Christopher Wren as
his deputy) and a knighthood. His later years, however, were marred
by a period of madness and domestic unhappiness. He was the author
of a verse tragedy, *Sophy*, performed in 1641, a translation of Virgil,
and the long topographical, political and satirical poem, *Cooper's Hill*
(1642), praised by Johnson and Dryden. His use of the heroic couplet
was influential in the transition from the Metaphysical poets to the
Augustans. Most of his poetry was written before the Restoration
(primarily in the period 1636–41), but the first edition of his collected
works was in 1668.

From *Poems and Translations, with the Sophy* (1668).

Ep. 11.104 *Out of an Epigram of Martial*

Prithee die and set me free,
     Or else be
Kind and brisk, and gay like me;
I pretend not to the wise ones,
     To the grave, to the grave,
Or the precise ones.

Tis not Cheeks, nor Lips nor Eyes,
  That I prize,
Quick Conceits, or sharp Replies,
If wise thou wilt appear, and knowing,
  Repartie, Repartie
To what I'm doing.

Prithee why the Room so dark?
  Not a Spark
Left to light me to the mark;
I love day-light and a candle,
  And to see, and to see,
As well as handle.

Why so many Bolts and Locks,
  Coats and Smocks,
And those Drawers with a Pox?
I could wish, could Nature make it,
  Nakedness, Nakedness
Itself were naked.

But if a Mistress I must have,
  Wise and grave,
Let her so her self behave
All the day long *Susan* Civil,
  Pap by night, pap by night
Or such a Divel.

JOHN WILMOT, SECOND EARL OF ROCHESTER (1647–80)

Notorious for his dissolute courtier's life and scandalous verse, paradigmatically famous for his deathbed abjuration of his intellectual scepticism and hitherto fleshly life, Rochester has provoked a number of strong responses from his readers over the centuries. Educated at Wadham College, Oxford, he served bravely in the second Dutch War (1665) and became close to the restored monarch, Charles II, but had to be banished from court because of his behaviour. He divided his time between living with his wife in the country and a libertine existence in London with several friends and mistresses, including the actress Elizabeth Barry. Himself a poet, he was also the patron of poets. Rochester's *Poems on Several Occasions* was published in London shortly after his early death, despite his dying request that his writings be burned. To elude prosecution the place of publication was stated to be Antwerp, and this practice was followed by the several other editions of these poems which quickly followed. Rochester translated no poems of Martial but he was deeply influenced by him, as by other Roman satirists, especially Horace. The first two great poems below can instructively be regarded as a creative adaptation of the Martial satiric inheritance, and not only in satiric pungency and wit. Rochester's sexual ideology differs considerably from Martial's, but the sexual detail and graphic obscenity, the rasping, cutting, trenchant couplets, the obsession with semen and with female body parts and odours, the scathing treatment of male hypocrisy, social pretension and, above all, female promiscuity, the animal imagery, the fusion of fiery indignation and black laughter, the self-deprecating humour are in the spirit of the Latin epigrammatist. Even the variation in verse form is typical of Martial, though the length of the poems is more reminiscent of Jonson. Martial's longest epigram was a mere fifty lines. The Rochester selection concludes with a handful of epigrams attributed to him by various sources.

From *Poems on Several Occasions* (1680) and *The Complete Poems of John Wilmot, Earl of Rochester* (1968).

A Ramble in St. James's Park

Much Wine had past with grave discourse,
Of who Fucks whom and who does worse;
Such as you usually do hear,
From them that dyet at the *Bear*;
When I, who still take care to see,
Drunkenness reliev'd by *Lechery*;
Went out into *St. James's Park*,
To cool my Head, and fire my heart:
But though *St. James* has the honor on't,
'Tis consecrate to *Prick* and *Cunt*.
There by a most incestuous *Birth*;
Strange *Woods*, Spring from the teeming Earth
For they relate how heretofore,
When Ancient *Pict*, began to Whore.
Deluded of his Assignation,
(Jilting it seems was then in fashion.)
Poor pensive *Lover*, in this place,
Would Frigg upon his *Mothers* Face:
Whence Rowes of *Mandrakes* tall did rise,
Whose lewd Tops Fuck'd the very Skies.
Each imitative Branch does twine,
In some lov'd fold of *Aretine*.
And Nightly now beneath their shade,
Are *Bugg'ries*, *Rapes*, and *Incests* made.
Unto this All-sin-sheltring *Grove*,
Whores of the *Bulk*, and the *Alcove*.
Great *Ladies Chamber-Maids, Drudges*;
The *Rag-picker*, and *Heiresse* trudges:
Carr-men, Divines, great *Lords*, and *Taylors*,
Prentices, Pimps, Poets and *Gaolers*;

Foot-Men, fine *Fops*, do here arrive,
And here promiscuously they swive.
     Along these hallow'd Walks it was,
That I beheld *Corinna* pass;
Who ever had been by to see,
The proud disdain she cast on me.
Through charming Eyes, he wou'd have swore,
She dropt from *Heav'n* that very hour;
Forsaking the Divine abode,
In scorn of some despairing *God*.
But mark what Creatures *Women* are,
So infinitely vile, and fair.
     Three *Knights*, o'th'Elbow, and the flurr,
With wrigling Tails, made up to her.
     The First was of your *Whitehall Blades*
Near Kin to th'*Mother* of the *Maids*,
Grac'd by whose favour he was able,
To bring a *Friend* to th'*Waiters Table*.
Where he had heard Sir *Edward S——*
Say how the *K——* lov'd *Bansted Mutton*.
Since when he'd ne'er be brought to eat,
By's good will any other Meat.
In this, as well as all the rest,
He ventures to do like the best.
But wanting common Sence, th'ingredient,
In choosing well, not least expedient.
Converts Abortive imitation,
To Universal affectation;
So he not only eats, and talks,
But feels, and smells, sits down and walks.
Nay looks, and lives and loves by Rote,
In an old tawdrey *Birth-Day-Coat*.
     The Second was a *Grays Inn Wit*,
A great Inhabiter of the *Pit*;
Where *Critick-like*, he sits and squints,
Steals Pocket-Handkerchiefs, and hints,

From's *Neighbor*, and the *Comedy*,
To Court, and Pay his *Landlady*.
    The Third a *Ladies Eldest Son*,
Within few years of Twenty One;
Who hopes from his propitious Fate,
Against he comes to his Estate.
By these Two *Worthies* to be made
A most accomplisht tearing *Blade*.
One in a strain 'twixt Tune and *Nonsense*,
Cries, *Madam, I have lov'd you long since*,
Permit me your fair hand to kiss.
When at her *Mouth* her C— says yes.
    In short, without much more ado,
Joyful, and pleas'd, away she flew;
And with these Three confounded *Asses*,
From *Park* to *Hackney-Coach*, she passes.
So a proud *Bitch* does lead about,
Of humble *Currs*, the Amorous rout;
Who most obsequiously do hunt,
The sav'ry scent of Salt-swolne *Cunt*.
Some Pow'r more patient now relate;
The sense of this surprizing Fate.
Gads! that a thing admir'd by me,
Shou'd taste so much of Infamy.
Had she pickt out to rub her Arse on,
Some stiff-Prick'd *Clown*, or well hung *Parson*.
Each job of whose Spermatick Sluce,
Had fill'd her *Cunt* with wholsome Juice.
I the proceeding shou'd have prais'd,
In hope she had quencht a Fire I rais'd:
Such nat'rall freedoms are but just,
There's something gen'rous in meer Lust.
But to turn damn'd abandon'd *Jade*,
When neither *Head* nor *Tail* perswade;
To be a *Whore*, in understanding,
A Passive *Pot* for *Fools* to spend in.

The *Devil* plaid booty, sure with thee,
To bring a blot of infamy.
But why was I of all *Mankind*,
To so severe a fate design'd?
Ungrateful! why this Treachery
To humble fond, believing me?
Who gave you priviledges above,
The nice allowances of Love?
Did ever I refuse to bear,
The meanest part your Lust cou'd spare?
When your lew'd *Cunt*, came spewing home,
Drencht with the Seed of half the *Town*.
My Dram of Sperme, was supt up after,
For the digestive Surfeit Water.
Full gorged at another time,
With a vast *Meal* of Nasty Slime;
Which your devouring *Cunt* had drawn
From *Porters Backs*, and *Foot-mens Brawn*.
I was content to serve you up,
My *Ballock* full, for your *Grace Cup*;
Nor ever thought it an abuse,
While you had pleasure for excuse.
You that cou'd make my Heart away,
For Noise and Colours, and betray,
The Secrets of my tender hours,
To such *Knight Errant Paramours*;
When leaning on your Faithless Breast,
Wrapt in security, and rest.
Soft kindness all my pow'rs did move,
And Reason lay dissolv'd in Love.
May stinking *Vapour* choak your *Womb*,
Such as the *Men* you doat upon;
May your deprav'd Appetite,
That cou'd in whiffling *Fools* delight,
Beget such *Frenzies* in your *Mind*,
You may go mad for the *North-Wind*.

And fixing all your hopes upon't,
To have him Bluster in your *Cunt*.
Turn up your longing Arse to th'Air,
And perish in a wild despair.
But *Cowards* shall forget to Rant,
School-Boys to Frigg, Old *Whores* to Paint:
The *Jesuits Fraternity*,
Shall leave the use of *Buggery*.
Crab-Lowse, inspir'd with Grace Divine,
From Earthy *Cod*, to *Heav'n* shall climb;
Physicians, shall believe in *Jesus*,
And disobedience cease to please us.
E're I desist with all my Pow'r,
To plague this *Woman* and undo her.
But my revenge will best be tim'd,
When she is *Marry'd* that is lym'd;
In that most lamentable State,
I'll make her feel my scorn, and hate;
Pelt her with Scandals, Truth or Lies,
And her poor *Curr* with jealousies.
Till I have torn him from her *Breech*,
While she whines like a *Dog-drawn Bitch*.
Loath'd, and depriv'd, kickt out of *Town*,
Into some dirty hole alone,
To Chew the *Cud* of Misery,
And know she owes it all to me.
And may no Woman *better thrive,*
Who dares prophane the Cunt *I Swive.*

The Imperfect Enjoyment

Naked she lay, claspt in my longing Arms,
I fill'd with Love, and she all over charms,
Both equally inspir'd with eager fire,
Melting through kindness, flaming in desire;

With *Arms*, *Legs*, *Lips*, close clinging to embrace,
She clips me to her *Breast*, and fucks me to her *Face*.
The nimble *Tongue* (*Love's* lesser Lightning) plaid
Within my *Mouth,* and to my thoughts conveyd.
Swift Orders, that I shou'd prepare to throw,
The *All-dissolving Thunderbolt* below.
My flutt'ring *Soul*, sprung with the pointed kiss,
Hangs hov'ring o're her *Balmy Limbs* of Bliss.
But whilst her busie hand, wou'd guide that part,
Which shou'd convey my *Soul* up to her *Heart*.
In liquid *Raptures*, I dissolve all o'er,
Melt into Sperme, and spend at ev'ry Pore:
A touch from any part of her had don't,
Her Hand, her Foot, her very look's a *Cunt*.
Smiling, she chides in a kind murm'ring *Noise*.
And from her *Body* wipes the clammy joys;
When with a Thousand Kisses, wand'ring o'er,
My panting *Breast*, and is there then no more?
She cries. All this to Love, and *Rapture's* due,
Must we not pay a debt to pleasure too?
But I the most forlorn, lost *Man* alive,
To shew my wisht Obedience vainly strive,
I sigh alas! and Kiss, but cannot Swive.
Eager desires, confound my first intent,
Succeeding shame, does more success prevent,
And *Rage*, at last, confirms me impotent.
Ev'n her fair Hand, which might bid heat return
To frozen *Age*, and make cold *Hermits* burn,
Apply'd to my dead *Cinder*, warms no more,
Than Fire to *Ashes*, cou'd past Flames restore.
Trembling, confus'd, despairing, limber, dry,
A wishing, weak, unmoving lump I ly.
This *Dart* of love, whose piercing point oft try'd,
With *Virgin blood, Ten thousand Maids* has dy'd.
Which *Nature* still directed with such *Art*,
That it through ev'ry *C—t*, reacht ev'ry *Heart*.

Stiffly resolv'd, twou'd carelesly invade,
Woman or *Boy*, nor ought its fury staid,
Where e're it pierc'd, a *Cunt* it found or made.
Now languid lies, in this unhappy hour,
Shrunk up, and Sapless, like a wither'd *Flow'r*.
Thou treacherous, base, deserter of my flame,
False to my passion, fatal to my *Fame*;
By what mistaken *Magick* dost thou prove,
So true to lewdness, so untrue to Love?
What *Oyster*, *Cinder*, *Beggar*, common *Whore*,
Didst thou e're fail in all thy Life before?
When *Vice*, *Disease* and *Scandal* lead the way,
With what officious hast does thou obey?
Like a Rude roaring *Hector*, in the *Streets*,
That Scuffles, Cuffs, and Ruffles all he meets;
But if his *King*, or *Country*, claim his Aid,
The *Rascal Villain*, shrinks, and hides his head:
Ev'n so thy *Brutal Valor*, is displaid,
Breaks ev'ry *Stews*, does each small *Whore invade*,
But if great *Love*, the onset does command,
Base Recreant, to thy *Prince*, thou darst not stand.
Worst part of me, and henceforth hated most,
Through all the *Town*, the common *Fucking Post*;
On whom each *Whore*, relieves her tingling *Cunt*,
As *Hogs*, on *Goats*, do rub themselves and grunt.
May'st thou to rav'nous *Shankers*, be a *Prey*,
Or in consuming *Weepings* waste away.
May *Stranguries*, and *Stone*, thy *Days* attend,
May'st thou Piss, who didst refuse to spend,
When all my joys, did on false thee depend.
And may *Ten thousand* abler *Pricks* agree,
To do the wrong'd *Corinna*, right for thee.

Miscellaneous Epigrams

Spoken Extempore to a Country Clerk, after Hearing Him Sing Psalms

Sternhold and *Hopkins* had great Qualms,
When they Translated *David's* Psalms,
    To make the Heart full glad;
But had it been poor *David's* Fate,
To hear thee Sing, and them Translate,
    By God! 'twould have made him Mad.

On Charles II

God bless our Good and Gracious *King*,
    Whose *Promise* none relies on;
Who never said a Foolish Thing,
    Nor ever did a Wise One.

On the English Court

Here's *Monmouth* the witty,
And *Lauderdale* the pretty,
And *Frazier*, that learned Physician;
But above all the rest,
Here's the *Duke* for a jest,
And the *King* for a grand Politician.

*On Cary Frazier**

Her *Father* gave her *Dildoes* six;
    Her *Mother* made 'em up a score;
But she loves nought but living *Pricks*,
    And swears by God she'll Frigg no more.

*On Mrs Willis**

Against the Charmes our *Ballocks* have
    How weak all humane skill is?
Since they can make a *Man* a *Slave*,
    To such a *Bitch* as *Phillis*.

Whom that I may describe throughout,
    Assist me *Bawdy Pow'rs*,
I'll write upon a double *Clout*,
    And dip my *Pen* in *Flow'rs*.*

Her look's demurely impudent,
    Ungainly *Beautiful*,
Her *Modesty* is insolent,
    Her Mirth is pert and dull.

A *Prostitute*, to all the *Town*,
    And yet with no *Man Friends*,
She rails, and scolds, when she lyes down,
    And curses when she spends.

Cary Frazier: a celebrated beauty at the Restoration court, daughter of Charles
II's physician, Sir Alexander Frazier
On Mrs Willis: The title in Vieth's edition, where *Willis* in line 4 is read for
Phillis. The text is the 'Antwerp' 1680 collection (Huntington ed.). Sue Willis
was a well-known prostitute with access to court circles.
Flow'rs: menstrual blood

Bawdy in thoughts, precise in words,
    Ill natur'd, and a *Whore*,
Her *Belly*, is a *Bag* of *T—ds*,
    And her *C—t*, a common shore.*

A Rodomontade on His Cruel Mistress

Trust not that thing call'd *Woman*: she is worse
Than all ingredients cram'd into a *Curse*,
Were she but ugly, peevish, proud, a *Whore*,
Poxt, painted, perjurd so she were no more,
I could forgive her, and connive at this,
Alledging still she but a *Woman* is.
But she is worse: in time she will forestall
The *Devil*, and be the *Damning* of us all.

Epigram on Samuel Pordage

Poet, whoe'er thou art, *God* damn thee;
Go hang thyself, and burn thy *Mariamne*.*

JOHN DRYDEN (1631–1700)

Dramatist, satirist and the major poet and leading figure in English
letters in the last quarter of the seventeenth century. He is also the
major translator of Latin poetry in the English language. Educated at
Westminster School and Trinity College, Cambridge, he began liter-
ary life primarily as a dramatist, turning from 1681 onwards to satire

---

shore: sewer
Mariamne: Pordage's tragedy *Herod and Mariamne*

and other controversial writing, acting as the prime literary advocate of Royalists and Tories. Falling from royal favour after the revolution of 1688, he returned to drama but devoted most of his creative activity to translation, and in this later period produced versions of Juvenal, Persius and (most especially) Virgil's *Eclogues*, *Georgics* and *Aeneid*, which are regarded in themselves as English classics. He did not, however, translate Martial, but the Latin epigrammatist informed his whole compositional style, whether Dryden derived it directly, through his study of Juvenal, or from the evolving English epigrammatic tradition. There is a sense in which *Absalom and Achitophel* (1681), *The Medal* (1682), *Mac Flecknoe* (1682), etc., are constructs of epigrams. One such epigrammatic section follows: the description of Zimri (= Duke of Buckingham) in the list of Israelite 'malcontents' in *Absalom and Achitophel*. It is followed by Dryden's variation on Martial, *Ep.* 8.18, in his *Discourse on Satire* (1693), and three epitaphs.

From *Absalom and Achitophel* (1681), *Discourse on Satire* (1693) and Epitaphs of various dates.

Absalom and Achitophel, 543–68

Some of their Cheifs were Princes of the Land:
In the first Rank of these did *Zimri* stand,
A man so various, that he seem'd to be
Not one, but all Mankinds Epitome.
Stiff in Opinions, always in the wrong;
Was every thing by starts, and nothing long:
But, in the course of one revolving Moon,
Was Chymist, Fiddler, Stats-Man, and Buffoon:
Then all for Women, Painting, Rhiming, Drinking;
Besides ten thousand freaks that dy'd in thinking.
Blest Madman, who could every hour employ,
With something New to wish, or to enjoy!
Rayling and praising were his usual Theams.
And both (to shew his Judgment) in Extreams:

So over Violent, or over Civil,
That every man, with him, was God or Devil.
In squandring Wealth was his peculiar Art:
Nothing went unrewarded, but Desert.
Begger'd by Fools, whom still he found too late,
He had his Jest, and they had his Estate.
He laught himself from Court, then sought Releif
By forming Parties, but could ne'er be Chief;
For spight of him, the weight of Business fell
On *Absalom* and wise *Achitophel*:
Thus, wicked but in will, of means bereft,
He left not Faction, but of that was left.

After *Ep.* 8.18 *Discourse concerning Satire*

For I may say it, with all the severity of Truth, that every Line of
yours is precious. Your Lordship's* only fault is, that you have not
written more: Unless I cou'd add another, and that yet greater, but I
fear for the Publick, the Accusation wou'd not be true, that you have
written, and out of a vicious Modesty will not Publish. *Virgil* has
confin'd his Works within the compass of Eighteen Thousand Lines,
and has not treated many Subjects; yet he ever had, and ever will
have the Reputation of the best Poet. *Martial* says of him, that he
cou'd have excell'd *Varius* in Tragedy, and *Horace* in Lyrick Poetry,
but out of deference to his Friends, he attempted neither. The same
prevalence of Genius is in your Lordship, but the World cannot
pardon your concealing it on the same consideration; because we
have neither a Living *Varius*, nor a *Horace*, in whose Excellencies,
both of *Poems*, *Odes* and *Satires*, you had equall'd them, if our Lan-
guage had not yielded to the *Roman* Majesty, and length of time had
not added a Reverence to the Works of *Horace*.

Your Lordship: Charles, Earl of Dorset and Middlesex, to whom the *Discourse* is
dedicated

Epitaphs

Lines on Milton

Three *Poets*,* in three distant *Ages* born,
Greece, *Italy*, and *England* did adorn.
The *First* in loftiness of thought Surpass'd;
The *Next* in Majesty; in both the *Last*.
The force of *Nature* cou'd no farther goe:
To make a *Third* she joynd the former two.

Upon Young Mr. Rogers of GLOCESTERSHIRE

Of gentle Blood, his Parents only Treasure,
Their lasting Sorrow, and their vanish'd Pleasure,
Adorn'd with Features, Virtues, Wit and Grace,
A large Provision for so short a Race;
More mod'rate Gifts might have prolong'd his Date,
Too early fitted for a better State;
But, knowing Heav'n his Home, to shun Delay,
He leap'd o'er Age, and took the shortest Way.

Epitaph on Mrs. Margater Paston Of Barningham in Norfolk

So fair, so young, so innocent, so sweet;
So ripe in Judgment, and so rare a Wit,
Require at least an Age, in One to meet.
In her they met; but long they cou'd not stay,
'Twas Gold too fine to fix without Allay:

Three Poets: Homer, Virgil, Milton

Heav'ns Image was in her so well exprest,
Her very Sight upbraided all the rest.
Too justly ravish'd from an Age like this;
Now *she* is gone, the World is of a Piece.

JOHN OLDHAM (1653–83)

Poet, satirist and schoolteacher, educated at Tetbury Grammar School
and St Edmund Hall, Oxford. He was best known for his Juvenalian
and Horatian imitations, his *Satyr against Vertue* (1676) and the anti-
Catholic virulence of *Satyrs upon the Jesuits* (1681), a reaction to the
'Popish Terror' of the period subsequent to the discovery of the plot
of Titus Oates. His admirers included Rochester, Sedley and Dryden,
who composed a poem on his early death from smallpox. His *Poems
and Translations*, first published in London in 1683, enjoyed a wide
readership in the years following his death.

From *Poems and Translations* (1683).

Ep. 1.117 *An Allusion to Martial*

As oft, Sir *Tradewel*, as we meet,
You're sure to ask me in the street,
When you shall send your Boy to me,
To fetch my Book of Poetry,
And promise you'l but read it o're,
And faithfully the Loan restore:
But let me tell ye as a Friend,
You need not take the pains to send:
'Tis a long way to where I dwell,
At farther end of *Clarkenwel*:

There in a Garret near the Sky,
Above five pair of Stairs I lie.
But, if you'd have, what you pretend,
You may procure it nearer hand:
In *Cornhil*, where you often go,
Hard by th' *Exchange*, there is, you know,
A Shop of Rhime, where you may see
The Posts all clad in Poetry:
There *H*—* lives of high renown,
The noted'st TORY in the Town:
Where, if you please, enquire for me,
And he, or's Prentice, presently,
From the next Shelf will reach you down
The Piece well bound for half a Crown:
The Price is much too dear, you cry,
To give for both the Book, and me:
Yes doubtless, for such vanities,
We know, Sir, you are too too wise.

CHARLES COTTON (1630–87)

Restoration translator, poet and literary figure, friend of Lovelace
and Izaak Walton, and staunch Royalist. He is best remembered for
his contribution to the fifth edition of Walton's *The Compleat Angler,
or the Contemplative Man's Recreation* (1676) and his translation of
Montaigne's *Essais* (1685–6), which substantially replaced the 1603
version of Florio. His landscape poetry, including *The Wonders of the
Peake* (1681) and *Poems on Several Occasions* (1689), influenced both
Wordsworth and Coleridge, and his burlesque of Virgil's *Aeneid*,
Scarronides, the first book of which was published in 1664, went

---

H—: Hindmarsh, Oldham's publisher from 1680 on and bookseller to the
Duke of York, against whose enemies he published several tracts

through several editions right to the nineteenth century. It was fol-
lowed by a burlesque of Lucian, *The Scoffer Scoft*, in 1675. The
following, which are sometimes versions of a line or two from the
relevant epigram, come from his translation of Montaigne, himself
less than a fervent admirer of Martial: 'Yet there is no good Judge . . .
that does not incomparably more admire the equal Smoothness, and
that perpetual Sweetness and Beauty which flourishes in the Epigrams
of *Catullus*, than all the Stings with which *Martial* has armed the
Tails of his' (*Essays* II,x, 'Of Books').

From *The Essays of Michael Seigneur de Montaigne* . . . (1685–6).

Ep. 1.13

When the chaste *Arria* gave the reeking Sword,
That had new gor'd her Heart, to her dear Lord;
Pætus, the Wound I've made hurts not, quoth she;
The Wound which thou wilt make, 'tis that hurts me.

Ep. 2.80

Can there be greater Madness, pray reply,
Than that one should, for Fear of dying, die?

Ep. 4.38

Galla deny, be not too eas'ly gain'd,
For Love will glut with Joys too soon obtain'd.

Ep. 6.53

Andragoras bath'd, supp'd, and merry went to Bed
Last Night, but in the Morning was found dead;
Would'st know, *Faustinus*, what was his Disease?
He dreaming saw the Quack, *Hermocrates*.

Ep. 6.55

Because thou *Coracinus* still dost go
With Musk and Ambergrease perfumed so,
We under thy Contempt, forsooth, must fall;
I'd rather than smell sweet, not smell at all.

Ep. 7.10

Ollus, what matters it to thee,
What with their Skin does he or she?

Ep. 8.15

No greater Virtue can a Prince enjoy
Than well to know the Men he wou'd employ.

Ep. 10.23

He liveth twice, who can the Gift retain
Of Mem'ry, to enjoy past Life again.

Ep. 11.20

'Cause *Anthony* is fir'd with *Glaphire*'s Charms,
Fain would his *Fulvia* tempt me to her Arms:
If *Anthony* be false, what then? Must I
Be Slave to *Fulvia*'s lustful Tyranny?
Then would a thousand wanton, waspish Wives
Swarm to my Bed like Bees into their Hives.
Declare for LOVE or WAR, she said, and frown'd;
No Love I'll grant: To Arms bid Trumpets sound.

Ep. 11.56

The Wretched well may wish for Death, but he
Is brave, who dares to live in Misery.

Ep. 12.63

But the Truth is, and all the Critics shew it,
None's more conceited than a sorry Poet.

Xen. 2

Be nos'd, be all Nose, till thy Nose appear
So great, that *Atlas* it refuse to bear;
Though ev'n against *Latinus* thou inveigh,
Against my Trifles thou no more canst say
Than I have said myself: Then to what End
Should we to render Tooth for Tooth contend?
You must have Flesh, if you'll be full, my Friend,
Lose not thy Labour; but on those that do
Admire themselves thy utmost Venom throw;
That these Things nothing are, full well we know.

THOMAS HEYRICK (1651–94)

Grand-nephew of Robert Herrick and scholar of Peterhouse, Cambridge, where he graduated BA in 1670 and MA in 1675. In 1671 he contributed to a collection of verses on the death of the Duchess of York. He was ordained deacon at Peterborough in 1672 and priest in 1681. In his last years he was a schoolmaster in Market Harborough, Leicestershire, where he had grown up and where he died in 1694. Apart from some published sermons, he was the author of *The New Atlantis: A Poem . . . with Some Reflections on the Hind and the Panther* (1687) and *Miscellany Poems* (1691), from which the following four versions are taken.

From *Miscellany Poems* (1691).

Ep. 4.40 *On a Covetous Man*

When Heaven to You a small Estate did lend,
You kept your Coach and Footmen did attend:
But when blind *Fortune* had your Store increas'd,
And ten times doubled what You had at least:
Your Narrow Soul, contracted with the Store,
Lost all the Pleasure, it did tast before.
A Curse into your Treasures Heaven did put;
You groan'd beneath their weight, and went afoot.
For all your Merits what doth then remain;
But that we pray, Heaven send your Coach again?

Ep. 9.14

Dost think, He whom thy liberal Table drew,
Can ever be to *Love* or *Friendship* true? . . .
He loves thy Mullets, Oysters, and not *Thee*:
Could I so entertain him, hee'd love Me.

Ep. 10.47 *Martial's Happy Life*

What things our Life do happy make
From me, my sweetest *Martial*, take.
A left *Estate*, not got with pain;
A fruitfull *Field*, that swells with grain;
A *Kitching*, that is ever warm;
Life free from Quarrels and from Harm.
Rarely to be concern'd with State,
Never to have *Law-sutes*, or debate;
But on the Mind *Content* to wait.
The *Strength* intire and *Body found*,
And *Innocence* with *Prudence* crown'd:
An Equal and a Faithfull *Friend*,
Discourse, that may in *Pleasure* end,
Nor *Feasts*, that may to *Riot* tend.
No *drunken* Nights, yet *such*, as may
Wash off the sully of the Day.
No lonely *Bed*, yet One, that's *chast*;
And *Sleep*, that tedious Nights may wast.
With what we have to be *Content*,
Nor, what we have not, to resent:
Not fear our last approaching Day,
And yet not rashly fling our Life away.

Ep. 12.25

When Mony I on my bare Bond do crave,
Youv' none: I'le Mortgage, Sir, – oh! now you have.
Thus, *Thelesine*, you will not trust a Friend,
But on the Credit of his Field You'l lend.
You'r cast at Law; tell not me, tell my Land –
You want a Friend – not I, my Field shall stand.

HENRY KILLIGREW (1613–1700)

Educated by Thomas Farnaby, the English editor of Martial, Killi-
grew entered Christ Church, Oxford, in 1628, graduating in 1632.
Younger brother of the playwright and theatre manager, Thomas
Killigrew, he himself was the author of a play, *The Conspiracy* (1638).
During the Civil War he was chaplain to the king's army and was
created a DD at Oxford. He served the Duke of York after the
Restoration and held a number of public posts and benefices, includ-
ing Master of the Savoy. Many held him responsible (through incom-
petence or greed) for the Savoy Hospital's collapse and eventual
dissolution in 1702. Given his training by Farnaby and his abilities in
Latin and English verse, the attribution to him of *Select Epigrams of
Martial Englished*, published in 1689 and reprinted with additions in
1695, is perfectly plausible.

From *Epigrams of Martial Englished* (1695).

Spec. 1 *On Cæsar's Amphitheatre*

Egypt, forbear thy Pyramids to praise,
A barb'rous Work up to a Wonder raise;
Let *Babylon* cease th' incessant Toyl to prize,
Which made her Walls to such immensness rise;
Nor let th' *Ephesians* boast the curious Art,
Which Wonder to their Temple does impart.
Delos dissemble too the high Renown,
Which did thy Horn-fram'd Altar lately crown;
Caria to vaunt thy Mausoleum spare,
Sumptous for Cost, and yet for Art more rare,
As not borne up, but pendulous i'th' Air:
All Works to *Cæsar*'s Theatre give place,
This Wonder *Fame* above the rest does grace.

Spec. 2 *On the Publick Works*

Where the Etherial *Coloss* does appear,
The towring Machin to the Stars draw near,
The hated Court, which so much blood did spill,
Late stood; one House* the City seem'd to fill!
    Where the stupendious Theatre's vast Pile
Is rear'd, there *Nero*'s Fish-ponds were e'er-while.
    Here, where the Baths,* a great, yet speedy, Gift,
All Men admire, (the People left to shift
For Dwellings) late was a proud ample Space,
Reserv'd to boast an insolent State and Grace.
    Where now a goodly Tarras does extend,
The City both with Shade and Walks befriend,
Was but the Courts Fagg and expiring End.
    Rome's to it self restor'd; in *Cæsar*'s Reign,
The Prince's Pleasures now the People gain.

Spec. 20 *On an Elephant's Kneeling to Cæsar*

That thee an Elephant suppliant did adore,
Who stroke with Terror a fierce Bull before,
To 's Keeper's Art, cannot imputed be;
We must ascribe it to thy Deity.

---

one House: the Golden House of Nero, built after the great fire of Rome in
64 CE in a private parkland which occupied most of the centre of Rome. The
artificial lake in this park (*Nero's Fish-ponds*, 6) was drained and filled with
concrete to form the foundations of the Colosseum
Baths: of Titus, also constructed on land belonging to Nero's Golden House

Spec. 28/29* *On Leander*

Leander, cease t'admire the Seas did spare
Thy last-nights Passage, *Cæsar*'s Seas they were.
While to enjoy Loves Sweets thou didst address,
And boist'rous Waves thee threaten'd to oppress,
Thus, Wretch, the raging Seas thou didst implore,
Drown me returning, waft me safely o'er.

Ep. 1 *Pref. To Cato*

When thou the Wanton Rites of *Flora*'s Feast
Didst know, the Peoples License then exprest,
Why cam'st thou in, sour *Cato*, 'mong the Rout?
Did'st enter only, that thou might'st go out?*

Ep. 1.4 *To Cæsar*

If my Book, *Cæsar*, comes into thy Hand,
Lay by those Looks, which do the World command.
When thou in Triumph rid'st, thou dost submit,
To be the Subject of the Soldier's Wit.
My Verses read with so serene a Face,
As *Thymele* and *Latine* thou dost Grace.
The *Censor* does with harmless Pastime bear,
My Leaves are wanton, but my Life's severe.

28–29: originally numbered 25 and printed as a single epigram in earlier editions

go out: the story is preserved of Cato leaving the theatre during the Floralia of 55 BCE, when he observed that his presence repressed the actors' usual licence

Ep. 1.10 *On Gemellus and Maronilla*

Gemellus, Maronilla fain would wed,
Aspires by Pray'rs, by Gifts, unto her Bed,
By Friends, by Tears: *So wond'rous fair is she?*
Nothing that lives can more deformed be.
What is't that pleases then, and takes his Eye?
She's rich, and coughs, and gives good hopes she'll dye.

Ep. 1.13 *On Arria and Petus*

When *Arria* to her *Petus* gave the Sword,
With which her chast and faithful Breast sh'ad gor'd,
Trust me, said she, that I my self have slain,
I do not grieve, 'tis thy Death gives me Pain.

Ep. 1.62 *On Levina*

Levina chast as *Sabins* were of old,
Than her strict Husband yet more strict and cold:
While in the common Baths she did descend,
And in those Freedoms many Hours did spend,
She fell in Love; in the cold Streams took Fire;
And burning with a Youth in loose Desire,
She left her Husband, and her vertuous Name;
Helen went thence, *Penelope* that came.

Ep. 1.83 *On Manneja*

That thy Dog loves to lick thy Lips, th'art pleas'd;
He'll lick that too, of which thy Belly's eas'd;
And not to flatter, and the Truth to smother,
I do believe, he knows not one from t'other.

Ep. 1.88 *An Epitaph on Alcimus*

Alcime, who didst in Years yet blooming die,
And, by a light Turf cover'd, here dost lie.
I rear no towring Tombs of massie Stone,
A vain Expence, that Fame confers on None:
But plant frail Box and Palms, whose verdant shade,
Drench'd by my Tears, shall be immortal made.
Receive thou then the Monument I give,
A Verse that will unto all Ages live:
And when my Life is spun, and Days expire,
No nobler Monument I my self Desire.

Ep. 1.107 *To Lucius Julius*

Oft, Noble *Lucius*, thou dost this repeat,
Th'art Idle, Martial, *something write that's Great.*
Then give me Ease, such as *Mecenas* gave,
When the like Work from *Virgil* he would have;
I'll frame a Verse with such Immortal Flame,
As to all Ages shall preserve my Name.
The Yoke does pinch that's born in Barren Soyl,
The Rich Ground tires, but Sweeter is the Toyl.

Ep. 2.50 *On Lesbia*

Lesbia talks Baudy, and does Water drink,
Thou dost well, *Lesbia*, so to wash the Sink.

Ep. 3.14 *On Tuccius*

Starved *Tuccius* from remotest *Spain* did come,
Full of great Hopes, Plenty to find in *Rome*:
But at the very Port being told the hard
Duty of Clients, and their lean Reward,
He turned straight his Horses Head again,
With Switch and Spur posted him back to *Spain*.

Ep. 3.20 *On Canius*

Tell me my Muse, how *Canius* spends his Time
In lasting Leaves, and in immortal Rhime,
Does he the Facts of *Nero* rightly state,
From Malice and from Flatt'ry free, relate?
Light Elegies, or grave Heroicks write?
I'th'Comick, or the Tragick Strain delight?
Or in the Poets School does *Canius* sit,
Regaling all with his choice *Attick* Wit?
Or else, being free from Study, does he talk
I'th'Temples, and the Shady Porches walk?
Bathes he? Or from the City Toyl retir'd,
Are Fields and Rivers more by him admir'd,
Baias or *Lucrins* Sweet Recess desir'd?
How Canius *spends his Time, wouldst have me show?*
He laughs at all which most Men, serious, do.

Ep. 3.32 *To Matrinia*

Dost ask, if an old Woman I could wed?
An Old I could, *Matrinia*, not a Dead,
As thou art. Even *Niobe* I could take,
And Mother *Hecuba* a Mistress make:
But then before they were transform'd so fur.
One to a Stone, the other to a Cur.

Ep. 3.69 *To Cosconius*

That all thy Epigrams thou dost indite
In cleanest Terms, not one broad Word dost write,
I praise, admire; how Chast alone thou art;
Such Crimes my Pages shew in ev'ry Part,
The which, the waggish Youth and Maids approve,
The Older, too, who feel the Sting of Love.
But yet, I must confess, thy Holy Verse
Deserves much more with Children to converse.

Ep. 4.53 *On a Counterfeit Cynick*

He who i'th'Temples, you so often meet,
In publick Porches, *Cosmus*, and the street,
With Bag and Staff, nasty, and antique dress'd,
His Hair an End, Beard hanging down his Breast;
Who, for a Cloke, a Coverlet does use;
Barkes for his Meat, the Givers of t'abuse;
A Cynick to be thought, does make this Stir:
But he no Cynick is. What then? A Cur.

Ep. 4.59 *On a Viper Inclosed in Amber*

As 'mong the Poplar Boughs a Viper crawls,
The Liquid Gum upon him struggling falls:
With Drops alone, while wond'ring, to be held,
He straight within the Amber was congeal'd.
Then of thy Tomb, proud Queen* think not too high.
A Worm far nobler here entomb'd doth lie.

Ep. 6.1. *To Julius Martialis*

This my sixth Book, *Julius, to thee* I send,
Dear 'mong the first, and my judicious Friend:
If it shall pass approv'd thy learned Ear,
When 'tis in *Cæsar*'s Hand, I less shall fear.

Ep. 6.4 *To Domitian*

Censor of Manners is thy Glory more,
Than Prince of Princes which thou had'st before.
Tho' for so many Triumphs *Rome* does owe,
Which, thy Heroick Valour did bestow,
So many Temples new, so many old,
So many Shows, and Gods by thee enroll'd,
So many Cities won, or else laid Waste;
Yet more she owes, that thou hast made her Chast.*

Queen: Cleopatra
Chast: See note p. 76

Ep. 6.7 On Thelesina

Since the Law 'gainst Adultery took place,
And all are forced Chastity t'embrace:
In less than thirty Days, thou has been wed
Ten times, ten Men admitted to thy Bed.
Who weds so oft, not weds, but plays the Whore:
And than Adultery offendeth more.

Ep. 7.19 On a Fragment of the Ship Argus

This piece thou see'st of rotten, useless Wood,
Was the first Ship that ever plow'd the Flood:
Which not the Billows of *Cyanean* Seas
Of old could wreck, or *Scythian* worse than these.
Age conquer'd it; but in Time's Gulf thus drown'd,
One Plank's more Sacred, than the Vessel sound.

Ep. 8.3 To His Muses

Five had suffic'd, six Books or seven do cloy,
Why dost as yet delight, *my Muse*, to toy?
Give o're for shame: Fame has not more to grace
My Verse, the Business made in ev'ry place.
And when proud Tombs, in which for Fame men trust,
O'rethrown and broken lye reduc'd to Dust,
I shall be read, Strangers will make 't their care,
Unto their sev'ral Soils my Works to bear.
       She of the *Sacred Nine*, (when I had spoke)
Whose Locks with Odors drop, thus Silence broke.
       And wilt thou then thy pleasant Verse forsake?
What better Choice, Ungrateful, canst thou make?

Exchange thy Mirthful for a Tragick Vein?
Thunder harsh Wars in an Heroick Strain;
Which strutting Pedants, till they're hoarse, may rant,
While the Ripe Youth detest to hear the Cant:
Let the o're-sowre and dull that way delight,
Whose Lamps at Midnight see the Wretches write.
But season thou thy Lines with sharpest Wit,
That all may read their Vices smartly hit.
Altho' thou seem'st to play but on a Reed,
Thy slender Pipe the Trumpet does exceed.

Ep. 9 Pref. To Avitus

Tho' thy learn'd Breast, Great Poet, 's known to me,
And that thy Verse will raise me 'bove mine own;
Yet this short Title on my Statue place,
Which 'mong no common Authors thou dost grace.
    I'm He, in Sportive Verse, none is above,
    Who none astonish, yet all Readers love;
    In vaster Works vast uncouth things are said,
    My glory is, that I am often read.

Ep. 9.12 On Earinus*

Thy Name the sweetest Season in does bring,
(Joy of the plund'ring Bees) the flow'ry Spring;
Which to decypher *Venus* may delight,
Or *Cupid*, with a Plume from 's own Wing, write;
Which those, that Amber chase, shou'd only note,
Or be upon, or with a Jewel wrote;

Earinus: Domitian's castrated catamite, whose name = 'vernal'

A Name the Cranes do figure as they fly,
And boast to *Jove*, as they approach the Sky:
A Name that does with no place else comport,
But where 'tis fix'd, only in *Cæsar*'s Court.

Ep. 11.3 *To His Book*

Not only those at Ease my Verses love,
And the more Civiliz'd my Muse approve:
But the rough Soldier does my Leaves o'erlook,
'Mongst Snows and Martial Ensigns reads my Book.
The *Britains* too are said, my Verse to sing.
What does this unto my Coffers bring?
What living Numbers from my Quill would flow!
What Blasts would my *Pierian* Trumpet blow!
If an *Augustus* now again does reign.
I also a *Mecenas* could obtain.

Ep. 11.27 *To Flaccus*

Thou'rt iron, *Flaccus*, if to such a Dame,
Who begs vile Gifts, thou can'st keep up a Flame;
Cow-heels does ask, Tripes, Sprats, and Scraps of Fish,
And a whole Pompion, holds too much, to wish:
To whom her Maid, joyful t'have got, does pour
Cheap Pulse, which greedily she does devour:
And when she's bold, and will all shame depose,
Begs Yarn enough to knit a pair of Hose.
　　My Wench Perfumes exacts, both Rich and Rare,
Rubies and Pearls, and those must also Pair;
Choice Naples Silk, with her, will only pass,
An hundred Crowns in Gold, she begs, like Brass.
Give I such Gifts, dost say, a Miss to please?
No: But I'd have her Merit such as these.

Ep. 11.71 *On Leda*

To her old Husband *Leda* made her moan,
That her Hysterick Fits were helpless grown:
And that her Life, no hope there was, to save,
Unless her Honour, for her Life, she gave.
But Sighing then, and drown'd in Tears, she said,
Than that way cur'd, 'twere better to be dead.
  The old Man begg'd, that she her Life would spare,
And of her youthful Years have tender Care:
Said, He'd give leave that others might supply,
What Age in him did to her help deny.
Straight young and able Doctors *Leda* knew,
Were sent for; and the Women all withdrew.
They laid her gently on the Bed, for cure.
Ah Cruel Help, says she, *that I endure.*

THOMAS BROWN (1663–1704)

Author of miscellaneous works in prose and verse, although now best known to every schoolboy for his irreverent translation of *Ep.* 1.32. Brown was educated at Newport school in Shropshire and Christ Church, Oxford, which he entered in 1678. He left Oxford without a degree, becoming a schoolmaster – even a headmaster – for a time, when he found it impossible to earn his living as a writer. He gave up schoolteaching for satirical writing and political pamphleteering. He was also an occasional translator of ancient (Petronius, Martial, Lucian) and modern (French and Spanish) authors. *A Collection of Miscellany Poems, Letters, &c.* was published in 1699, *Amusements Serious and Comical* in 1700 and his collected *Works* in three volumes in 1707–8.

From *A Collection of Miscellany Poems, Letters, &c.* (1699), and *The Fourth and Last Volume of the Works of Mr. Thomas Brown . . .* (7th edition, 1730).

Ep. 1.18 *Advice to a Vintner*

What Planet distracts thee, what damnable Star,
To dash honest *Bourdeaux* with vile *Bar a Bar*?
Why shou'd innocent Claret be murder'd by Port,
Thou'lt surely be sentenc'd in *Bacchus*'s Court?
As for us Drunken Rakes, if we hang, or we drown,
Or are decently poyson'd, what loss has the Town?
But to kill harmless Claret, that does so much good,
Is downright effusion of Christian Blood:
Ne'r think what I tell you is matter of laughter,
Thou'lt be curst for't in this world, and damn'd for't
    hereafter.

Ep. 1.19

When Gammar *Gurton* first I knew
    Four Teeth in all she reckon'd:
Come's a damn'd Cough, and whips out two,
    And t'other two a second.

Courage, old Dame, and never fear,
    The third when e're it comes;
Give me but t'other Jugg of Beer,
    And I'll ensure your Gums.

Ep. 1.32

I do not love thee, Doctor *Fell*;*
The reason why I cannot tell.
But this I'm sure I know full well,
I do not love thee, Doctor *Fell*.

Ep. 2.3 *Mr. Brown's Extempore Version of Two Verses out of Martial, Occasion'd by a Clamorous Dun, Who Vow'd She wou'd not Leave Him 'till She had Her Money.*

Sextus thou nothing ow'st, nothing I say;
He something owes that something has to pay.

Ep. 2.5

In some vile Hamlet let me live forgot,
Small Beer my portion, and no Wine my lot:
To some worse Fiend in Church-Indentures bound
Than ancient *Job*, or modern *Sh-l-ck** found.
And with more aches plagu'd, and pains, and ills,
Than fill our *Salmon*'s Works, or *Tilburgh*'s Bills;
If 'tis not still the burden of my prayer
The night with you, with you the day to share.
But Sir (and the complaint you know is true),
Two damn'd long miles there lie 'twixt me & you,
And these two miles, by help of calculation,
Make four, by that I've reach'd my habitation.

Fell: Dr John Fell, Bishop of Oxford, classical scholar and Dean of Christ Church, Brown's college; he died in 1686
Sh-l-ck: William Sherlock (1641–1707), master of the Temple and Dean of St Paul's; his son Thomas succeeded him in the former position in 1704

You're near Sage *Wills*, the land of Mirth and Claret,
I live stow'd up in a *White-chappel* Garret.
Oft when I've walk'd so far, your hands to kiss,
Flatter'd with thoughts of the succeeding bliss,
I'm told you're gone to the vexatious *Hall*,
Where with eternal Lungs the Lawyers bawl;
Or else stole out, some Female friend to see;
Or, what's as bad, you're not at home for me.
Two miles I've at your service, and that's civil,
But to trudge four, and miss you, is the Devil.

Ep. 3.43

Thou that not many months ago
Wast white as Swan, or driven Snow,
Now blacker far than *Æsop*'s Crow,
Thanks to thy Wig, set'st up for Beau.
    Faith *Harry*, thou'rt i'the wrong box,
Old Age these vain endeavours mocks,
And time that knows thou'st hoary locks,
Will pluck thy Mask off with a pox.

Ep. 3.44

That Cousins, Friends, and Strangers fly thee,
Nay, thy own Sister can't sit nigh thee;
That all men thy acquaintance shun,
And into holes and corners run,
Like *Irish* Beau from *English* Dun:
The reason's plain, and if thoud'st know it,
Thou'rt a most damn'd repeating Poet.
Not Bayliff sowr, with horrid Beard,
Is more in poor *Alsatia* fear'd,

Since the stern Parliament of late
Has stript of ancient rights their State:
Not Tygers, when their Whelps are missing;
Not Serpents in the Sun-shine hissing;
Not Snake in tail that carries rattle;
Not Fire, nor Plague, nor Blood, nor Battle,
Is half so dreaded by the throng,
As thy vile persecuting Tongue.
If e're the restless Clack that's in it
Gives thy Head leave to think a minute,
Think what a pennance we must bear
Thy damn'd impertinence to hear.
Whether I stand, or run, or sit,
Thou still art i'th'repeating fit:
Weary'd I seek a nap to take,
But thy curst Muse keeps me awake.
At Church too, when the Organ's blowing,
Thy louder pipe is still a going.
Nor Park, nor Bagnio's from thee free,
All places are alike to thee.
Learn Wisdom once, at a Friend's instance,
From the two Fellows at St. *Dunstan*'s,
Make not each Man thou meet'st a Martyr;
But strike like them but once a quarter.

Ep. 3.63

Oh *Jemmy* you're a Beau, not I alone
Say this, but 'tis the talk of all the Town.
Prithee be free, and to thy friend impart
What is a Beau – Ay Sir, with all my heart.
He's one, who nicely curls and combs his hair,
And visits *Sedgwick* monthly all the year:
Sings bawdy Songs, and humms them as along
Flanting he walks thro the admiring throng;

All the day long sits with the charming fair,
And whispers pretty stories in their ear.
Writes *Billets-doux*, shuns all men as he goes,
Lest their unhallow'd touch shou'd daub his cloaths.
He knows your Mistress. Nay, at every Feast
He'll tell the Pedigree of every Guest.
Is this a Beau? Faith *Jemmy* I'll be plain,
A Beau's a Bawble, destitute of Brain.

Ep. 5.56

When e're I meet you, still you cry,
What shall I do with *Bob*, my Boy?
Since this Affair you'd have me treat on,
Ne'r send the Lad to *Paul*'s or *Eaton*.
The Muses let him not confide in,
But leave those Jilts to *Tate* or *Dryden*.
If, with damn'd Rimes he racks his wits,
Send him to *Mevis* or *St. Kit*'s.
Wou'd you with wealth his Pockets store well,
Teach him to pimp, or hold a door well.
If he has a head not worth a Stiver,
Make him a Curate, or Hog Driver.

Ep. 11.60

Nothing than *Chloe* e're I knew
    By Nature more befriended:
Cælia's less Beautiful, 'tis true,
    But by more hearts attended.

No Nymph alive with so much art
    Receives her Shepherd's firing,
Or does such cordial drops impart
    To love when just expiring.

Cold niggard Age, that does elsewhere
    At one poor offering falter,
To her whole Hecatombs wou'd spare,
    And pay them on her Altar.

But *Chloe*, to Love's great disgrace,
    In Bed nor falls, nor rises,
And too much trusting to her face,
    All other Arts despises.

No half form'd words, nor murmuring sighs,
    Engage to fresh performing
Her breathless Lover; when he lies,
    Disabled after storming.

Dull as a Prelate when he prays,
    Or Cowards after listing,
The fair insensible betrays
    Love's rites by not assisting.

Why thus, ye powers that cause our smart,
    Do ye Love's gifts dissever;
Or why those happy Talents part,
    That shou'd be joyn'd for ever.

For once perform an Act of Grace,
    Implor'd with such devotion,
And grant my *Cælia Chloe*'s face,
    Or *Chloe Cælia's* motion.

Ep. 11.104

Sweet Spouse, you must presently troop and be gone,
    Or fairly submit to your betters,
Unless for the faults that are past, you atone,
    I must knock off my Conjugal-Fetters.

When at night I am paying the tribute of Love,
    You know well enough what's my meaning,
You scorn to assist my devotion, or move,
    As if all the while you were dreaming.

At Cribbage and Put and All Fours I have seen
    A Porter more passion expressing,
Than thou, wicked *Kate*, in the rapturous scene,
    And the height of the amorous blessing.

Then say I to myself, is my Wife made of Stone,
    Or does the old Serpent possess her;
Better motion and vigor by far might be shown
    By dull Spouse of a *German* Professor?

So *Kate* take advice and reform in good time,
    And while I'm performing my duty,
Come in for your Club, and repent of the crime
    Of paying all scores with your Beauty.

All day thou mayst cant, and look grave as a Nun,
    And run after *Burgess* the surly;
Or see that the Family business be done,
    And chide all thy Servants demurely.

But when you're in Bed with your Master & King,
    That tales out of School ne'r does trumpet,
Move, riggle, heave, pant, clip round like a Ring,
    In short, be as lewd as a Strumpet.

Ep. 12.65

To Charming *Cælia*'s arms I flew,
    And there all night I feasted;
No God such transports ever knew,
    Nor mortal ever tasted.

Lost in the sweet tumultuous joy,
    And pleas'd beyond expressing:
How can your Slave, my Fair, said I,
    Reward so great a Blessing?

The whole Creation's wealth survey,
    Thro both the *Indies* wander:
Ask what brib'd Senates give away,
    And fighting Monarchs squander.

The richest spoils of earth and air;
    The rifled Ocean's treasure;
'Tis all too poor a bribe by far
    To purchase so much pleasure.

She blushing cry'd – My Life, my Dear,
    Since *Cælia* thus you fancy.
Give her, but 'tis too much, I fear,
    A Rundlet of right *Nantcy*.

SIR CHARLES SEDLEY (1639–1701)

A notoriously dissolute courtier of Charles II, Restoration wit, and friend of Rochester, Dryden and Thomas Shadwell, a product like Rochester of Wadham College, Oxford, which he left without a degree. He entered parliament after the Restoration and at the time of the Revolution supported William III. Although prominent as a dramatist (*The Mulberry Garden*, 1668, *Antony and Cleopatra*, 1677, *Bellamira, or the Mistress*, based on Terence's *Eunuch*, 1687 – he appears as Lisideius in Dryden's *Essay of Dramatic Poesy*, 1668), he is best remembered for his songs and satiric *vers de société*, which, pointed and unemotional, included his witty imitations of Martial, entitled *Epigrams: Or, Court Characters*. Other Martial translations occur in *Poems and Translations*, both collections being found in Captain Ayloffe's 1702 edition of Sedley's works. In neither will the reader encounter the graphic obscenities of a Rochester, but rather a refined sexual–textual play, reflective of court proprieties, combined with a brilliant and sustained sense of the contemporary applicability of Martial's satire.

From *The Miscellaneous Works of the Honourable Sir Charles Sedley* . . . (1702).

Ep. 1.13 *On Arria and Poetus*

When *Arria* to her *Poetus* gave the Steel,
    Which from her bleeding Side did newly part;
From my own Wound, she said, no Pain I feel:
    And yet thy Wound will stab me to the Heart.

Ep. 1.58 *The Maidenhead*

Cloris, the prettyest Girl about the Town,
        Askt fifty Guineas, for her Maidenhead;
I laught, but *Cascus* paid the Money down,
        And the young Wench did to his Chamber lead.
This Thrift my eager *Catso* did upbraid,
        And wisht that he had grown 'twixt *Cascus* Thighs;
Get me but half what his got him, I said,
        And to content thee, I'll ne'er stick at Price.

Ep. 1.90 *To Bassa*

That I ne'er saw thee in a Coach with Man,
        Nor thy chast Name in wanton Satyr met;
That from thy Sex thy liking never ran,
        So as to suffer a Male-servant yet.
I thought thee the *Lucretia* of our time:
        But, *Bassa*, thou the while a *Tribas** wert,
And clashing —, with a prodigious Crime,
        Didst act of Man th'inimitable part.
What *Odipus* this Riddle can untye?
Without a Male, there was Adultery.

Tribas: lesbian. Martial's word is actually *fututor*, 'fucker'.

Ep. 2.12 *To Posthumus*

That thou dost *Cashoo** breath, and Foreign *Gums*,
Enough to put thy Mistress into Fits;
Tho' *Rome* thy Hair, and *Spain* thy Gloves perfumes,
Few like, but all suspect, those borrow'd Sweets:
The Gifts of various Nature come and go,
He that smells always, well does never so.

Ep. 2.41 *To Maximina*

Ovid, who bid the Ladies laugh,
    Spoke only to the Young and Fair;
For Thee his Council were not safe,
    Who of sound Teeth hast scarce a Pair;
If thou thy Glass, or Me believe,
    Shun Mirth, as Foplings do the Wind;
At *Durfey*'s Farce affect to grieve;
    And let thy Eyes alone be kind.
Speak not, tho't were to give Consent;
    For he that sees those rotten Bones,
Will dread their monumental Scent,
    And fly thy Sigh's like dying Groans.
If thou art wise, see dismal Plays,
    And to sad Stories lend thy Ear;
With the afflicted, spend thy Days,
    And laugh not above once a Year.

Cashoo: a sweetmeat

Ep. 2.43 *To Candidus*

All Things are common amongst Friends, thou say'st;
    This is thy Morning and thy Ev'ning-song,
Thou in rich Point, and Indian-Silk art dress'd
    Six foreign Steeds to thy Calash belong,
Whilst by my Cloaths the Ragman scarce wou'd gain;
    And an uneasie Hackny jolts my Sides;
A Cloak embroider'd interrupts thy Rain,
    A worsted Camblet my torn Breeches hides;
Turbots and Mullets thy large Dishes hold,
    In mine a solitary Whiting lies;
Thy Train might Fire the impotent and old,
    Whil'st my poor Hand a *Ganimede* supplies:
For an old wanting Friend thou'lt nothing do,
Yet all is common among Friends we know:
Nothing so common, as to use 'em so.

Ep. 2.44 *On Sextus*

When I had purchast a fresh Whore or Coat,
    For which I knew not how to pay,
Sextus, that wretched covetous old Sot,
    My ancient Friend, as he will say;
Lest I shou'd borrow of him, took great care,
    And mutter'd to himself aloud,
So as he knew I cou'd not chuse but hear
    How much he to *Secundas* ow'd,
And twice as much he paid for Interest,
Nor had one Farthing in his trusty Chest:
If I had ask'd, I knew he wou'd not lend;
'Tis new, before-hand, to deny a Friend.

Ep. 2.53 *To Maximus*

Wou'd'st thou be free, I fear thou art in jest;
But if thou wou'd'st, this is the only Way,
Be no Man's Tavern, nor Domestick Guest;
Drink wholsom Wine, which thy own Servants draw;
Of knavish *Curio*, scorn the ill–got Plate,
    The numerous Servants, and the cringing Throng:
With a few Friends on fewer Dishes eat,
    And let thy Cloaths, like mine, be plain and strong;
Such Friendships make, as thou may'st keep with ease,
Great Men expect, what good Men hate to pay;
    Be never thou thy self in pain to please,
But leave to Fools, and Knaves, th'uncertain Prey.
    Let thy Expence with thy Estate keep pace;
Meddle with no Man's Business, scarce thy own;
    Contented pay for a Plebeian Face,
And leave vain Fops the Beauties of the Town.
If to this Pitch of Vertue thou can'st bring
Thy Mind, th'art freer than the *Persian* King.

Ep. 2.55 *To Sextus*

I Offer Love, but thou Respect wilt have;
Take, *Sextus*, all thy Pride and Folly crave;
But know, I can be no Man's Friend and Slave.

Ep. 2.64 *To Milo*

One Month a Lawyer, thou the next wilt be
    A grave Physician, and the third a Priest;
Chuse quickly one Profession of the three;
    Marry'd to her, thou yet may'st court the rest.

Whil'st thou stand'st doubting, *Bradbury** has got
  Five Thousand Pound, and *Conquest** as much more;
W—* is made B—, from a drunken Sot:
  Leap in, and stand not shiv'ring on the Shore;
On any one amiss thou can'st not fall,
Thou'lt end in nothing, if thou grasp'st at all.

Ep. 2.69 *To Classicus*

When thou art ask'd to Sup abroad,
  Thou swear'st thou hast but newly din'd;
That eating late does overload
  The Stomach, and oppress the Mind;
But if *Appicius* makes a Treat,
  The slend'rest Summons thou obey'st,
No Child is greedier of the Teat,
  Than thou art of the bounteous Feast.
Then wilt thou drink till every Star
  Be swallow'd by the rising Sun:
Such Charms hath Wine we pay not for,
  And Mirth, at others Charge begun.
Who shuns his Club, yet flies to ev'ry Treat
  Does not a Supper, but a Reck'ning hate.

Bradbury: George Bradbury, a well-known contemporary barrister and (from 1689) a Baron of the Exchequer
Conquest: a Popish physician
W—: probably Thomas Watson, made Bishop of St David's in 1687

Ep. 2.77 *On Coscus*

Coscus, thou say'st my Epigrams are long;
    I'd take thy Judgment on a Pot of Ale:
So thou may'st say the Elephant's too strong,
    A Dwarf too short, the Pyramid too tall;
Things are not long, where we can nothing spare;
But, *Coscus*, even thy Disticks tedious are.

Ep. 2.89 *To Gaurus*

That thou dost shorten thy long Nights with Wine,
    We all forgive thee, for so *Cato* did;
That thou writ'st Poems without one good Line,
    Tully's Example may that Weakness hide;
Thou art a Cuckold, so great *Cæsar* was;
    Eat'st till thou spew'st, *Antonius* did the same;
That thou lov'st Whores, *Jove* loves a bucksom Lass;
    But that th'art whipt,* is thy peculiar Shame.

Ep. 3.42 *To Cloe*

Leave off thy Paint, Perfumes, and youthful Dress,
And Nature's failing Honesty confess;
Double we see those Faults which Art wou'd mend,
Plain downright Ugliness wou'd less offend.

. . . *whipt*: noteworthy substitution for the Latin, *quod fellas*, 'that you suck (pricks)'

Ep. 8.77 *To Liber*

Liber, thou Joy of all thy Friends,
    Worthy to live in endless Pleasure:
While Knaves and Fools pursue their Ends,
    Let Mirth and Freedom be thy Treasure.
Be still well dress'd, as now thou art,
    Gay, and on charming Objects thinking;
Let easie Beauty warm thy Heart,
    And fill thy Bed when thou leav'st drinking.

Delay no pressing Appetite,
    And sometimes stir up lazy Nature;
Of Age the envious Censure slight;
    What Pleasure's made of, 'tis no matter:
He that lives so but to his Prime,
Wisely doubles his short Time.

Ep. 9.70 *To Coscus*

O Times! O Manners!* *Cicero* cry'd out,
    But 'twas when enrag'd *Catilin* conspir'd
To burn the City, and to cut the Throat
    Of half the Senate, had his Ruffians hir'd:

When Son and Father did the World divide,
    And *Rome* for Tyrants, not for Empire fought;
When slaughter'd Citizens on either side
    Cover'd that Earth, her early Valour bought.

O Times! O Manners!: a famous quotation from Cicero's first speech *Against Catiline* (1.2)

Of Times and Men, why dost thou now complain?
    What is it, *Coscus*, that offends thee, say?
Our Laws the License of the Sword restrain;
    And our Prince wills that his arm'd Troops obey:
His Reign, Success, Freedom and Plenty crown,
Blame not our Manners then, but mend thy own.

ANONYMOUS TRANSLATIONS OF THE SEVENTEENTH CENTURY

The following is a selection from the seventeenth-century British Library MS Add. 27343, which like the Egerton MS 2982 contains translations of a substantial number of Martial's epigrams by various hands. The translators do not avoid sexual themes, although once again the 'forbidden words' are not actually written.

From *MS Add. 27343*.

Ep. 5.10 To Regulus. Of the Fame of Poetts

Whence is't, so few doe liueing men approue,
And Readers seldome their owne times doe loue?
From envyous mindes, whose customes ever were
Things Antique before moderne to preferr.
So wee, ingrate, Pompeys old Buildings prayse,
And worser Temples built in Catulus dayes.
Ennius is read now, Virgill layd aside:
And his owne Age ev'n Homer did deride.

Few Stages brought Menander crowned forth;
Only Corinna knew her Ovids worth.
Yet you (my Bookes!) hast not too much, I pray:
If fame come not till after death, I'll stay.

Ep. 5.37 *Of the Virgin Erotion*

Then aged swanns more beautyfull,
And softer then Galesian wooll,
Then Lucrine shells more delicate,
Whose whiteness Pearles did emulate,
Or Ivory new polished,
Lillys untoucht, or snow new-shedd;
Whose hayre more golden lustre hurld
Then Betick Fleece, or German curld;
Whose breath was sweet as Roses bloome,
Or purest honey from the Combe,
Or in your hand when Gumms you rowle:
To whom compar'd the Peacock's fowle,
No Squerrell's louely, Phœnix rare;
Erotions bones yett smoakeing are
On fun'rall Pile, whom cruell Fate
Snatcht from mee ere her sixth yeeres date,
My Loue, my Joy, my deare Content:
Yett Pete forbids mee to lament.
Hee beates his breast, his hayre doth teere
And says: For shame weepe nott for her,
Your vassall. I've just lost a wife, which
You know was gallant, noble, rich,
Yett I doe liue, and all this beare.
O Mighty valour! past compare!
Her death does thousands to him giue,
Yett hee does beare her loss, and liue.

Ep. 5.64 *To His Servants*

You, Boy, two measures of briske wine lett flow,
And, You, powre on it summer cooleing snow:
Lett my moyst hayre with rich perfumes abound,
With loades of Rosy wreaths my temples crown'd.
Liue now: our neighb'ring stately Tombes doe cry;
Since kings you see (your petty Gods) can dy.

Ep. 6.12 *Of Fabulla*

Shee sweares tis her owne hayre. Who would haue thought
        it?
Shee's nott forsworne though: I know where shee bought it.

Ep. 6.31 *To Charidemus*

Knowing't, thou lettst the Doctour — thy wife.
Thou'lt dye without a feaver, on my life.

Ep. 6.34 *To Diadumenus*

Come kiss mee, Sweet. How often? wouldst thou know?
Thou bidst mee number the salt waues that flow;
Or shells spread on th' Ægean shoares to count;
Or swarming Bees on the Cecropian Mount;
Or tell the Hemms and Clapps oth' crowded Rout,
When to the Theater Cæsar first comes out.

Not all those kisses, Lesbia frankly gaue
To sharpe Catullus, are what I would haue:
Those are too few which any numbers hold.
Give mee the kisses* that can ne'r bee told.

Ep. 10.47 *To Julius Martiall*

To make my life of all mens happyest,
Sweet Martiall, I w'ld bee with these things blest:
A good Estate, nott gott with mine owne toyle,
But by Descent: plac'd in a fruitfull soyle:
Well woodded, that may constant fyres mayntayne:
No private Suites: few publicke Cares: A Brayne
Untroubled: Body healthfull; actiue, strong;
Harmeless, butt prudent, in converse; among
Few friends of my owne rank: No curious Fare,
Butt wholesome: Nights, nott drunke, butt free from Care:
A Wife though chast yett frolick in my Bedd:
Sound sleepe all Night to seize my drowsy head;
Wish to bee what thou art, and wish no higher:
And thy last End nor feare, nor yett desire.

Ep 11.8 *Of His Boyes Kisses*

Like Balsams chaf'd by some Exotick fayre:
Or from a saffron feild fresh gliding ayre:
In winter chests like Apples ripening:
Or grounds o'r spread with budding trees in spring:
Like silken roabes in royall presses: and
Gumms suppled by a virgin's soft white hand;
As broaken jarrs of Falerne wines doe smell,
Farr off: or flowry Gardens where Bees dwell:

. . . *kisses*: the reference is to Catullus, *Poems* 5 and 7, in which the poet demands
from Lesbia an infinite multiplicity of kisses

Perfumers potts: Burnt Incence lost ith' ayre;
Chapletts new fall'n from rich perfumed hayre:
What more? All's not enough: mixed all express
My deare Boys morning kisses sweetnesses.
You'ld know his Name. I'll nought butt's kisses tell.
I doubt, I sweare, you'ld know him faine too well.

Ep 11.104 *To His Wife*

Wife, out of doores:* or else conforme to mee.
No Curius, Numa, Tatius, I'll bee.
I loue with iolly cupps to spend the night.
You dully to drinke water doe delight.
You loue the darke: but by a candle I,
Or by daylight, had rather —.
You boddyes weare, coats, gownes, and such like stuff:
I never woman thought naked enough.
To mee the Doue-like kiss is sweate:
You kiss as if your Gran-dame you did meete:
Helpe not with motion, voyce, or hand; and rise
As graue as if you went to sacrifise.
The servants — themselues behind the doore,
When Hectors wife did ride him, like a whore.
And when Ulisses snoar'd, and nought did stand,
Ev'n chast Penelope there layd her hand.
You deny t'other thinge. Cornelia
Did giue't, so did chast Julia, Portia.
Before Joue had his Ganymede, to fill
His Cupps: Juno supply'd his function still.
If you must needs bee graue; then Lucrece bee
All day: but Lais-like, at night bee free.

---

out of doores: the Latin, *uade foras*, is a Roman formula for divorce

III. THE EIGHTEENTH CENTURY: AUGUSTANS AND NEOCLASSICISTS

INTRODUCTION

When Dryden died in 1700 the English Augustan age was substantially under way. At this time, perhaps more than at any other, a poet-translator could rely upon his readers' wide knowledge of classical, especially Latin, literature, for the purposes of exploitation in his own adaptations. Pope's *Imitations of Horace* (1738) are a paradigm case, product of a self-consciously mature literary culture – but one which yet tended unreflectively to appropriate its past. Although a historical purpose is sometimes articulated, translation in the main energetically assimilates the world of Augustan Rome, even of Homeric Greece, to that of eighteenth-century England. Pope's *Iliad* is itself a contemporary poem – definitely, as Dr Bentley observed, not Homer. Confidence in the reader's familiarity with the original left the translator free to create between the source text and his version a witty and editorial counterpoint, which became the basis of much of the translation's value. Horace was the chief figure here, supplying the eighteenth century with its principal model of order, decorum, harmony; but Martial's influence too was substantial, attested by the popularity of his work as a quotable source of wisdom in *The Rambler* and *The Spectator*, and by the frequency of imitations and even parodies in *The Gentleman's Magazine* and other journals. His acceptability to the great reading public was evident. Notable essayists who found a place for him in their lucubrations were Joseph Addison, Sir Richard Steele and Aaron Hill. What emerges from these quotations and translations of Martial is the image of him as a man of the world, a person of taste and discernment, experienced and hard to outrage. Dr Johnson's partiality to him somewhat shocked some of his contemporaries, to judge from the reaction recorded by Boswell of the father of one of his female acquaintances, but the evidence is undeniable. At the other end of the spectrum, the rakish Matthew Prior would be no surprise in the ranks of his admirers. And although the two main luminaries of the Augustan period, Pope and Swift, contributed but a few versions to the store of English translations of Martial, their debt to Martial in satiric language, theme and wit and, especially where Pope is concerned, in the heroic couplet itself, is considerable.

The first serious extensive selection of the epigrams in verse translation during this century was that of William Hay in 1755, whose versions are conspicuous for the assurance with which they transpose Martial into the contemporary London world at the very time that the archaeological rediscovery of Herculaneum and Pompeii was changing Europe's perception of antiquity. Included in Hay's collection are a number of imitations by Cowley and some versions by other hands. The extraordinary and absurd translation of the schoolmaster James Elphinston followed in 1782. Elphinston completely rearranged the epigrams by subject-matter into twelve books to accord with eighteenth-century taste, omitting the obscene poems, and elevating the historically informative, moralizing and imperial poems to positions of importance. Short satirical epigrams and misogynistic attacks were confined without title to the last of Elphinston's twelve books. The strategy enabled Martial to be presented to the late-eighteenth-century reader as a frank, moral and informative writer of genius and wisdom. This dismemberment of Martial's literary *corpus* had an enormous impact on the general perception of the Latin poet despite the vilification which the translation received at the hands of Johnson and Burns (see p. xxxii above). A more creative and fitting response to Martial was that of the intriguing Nathaniel Brassey Halhed, who, as the century drew to a close (1793–4), gave fresh impetus to Martial's possibilities for contemporary political and social satire.

TRANSLATIONS AND IMITATIONS

MATTHEW PRIOR (1664–1721)

Poet, essayist, satirist and important diplomatic figure during the reign of Queen Anne. Educated at Westminster School and St John's College, Cambridge (of which he was elected a fellow in 1688), he combined prolific writing with an active diplomatic and political life, and was employed in the negotiations of the treaties of Ryswick (1697) and, as minister plenipotentiary, the treaty of Utrecht (1713), which was popularly known as 'Matt's Peace'. He suffered imprisonment for over a year on returning to England in the year following the death of Queen Anne. On release in 1716 he retired to private life. His poetic works were many and varied, ranging from lyrics, epistles, burlesques and other occasional poetry, to such large-scale works as *Solomon on the Vanity of the World*, published in three books (1718). His first publication (written with Charles Montague) was *The Country Mouse and the City Mouse* (1687), a rewriting of Horace *Satires* 2.6 as a satire on Dryden's *The Hind and the Panther*. Horace remained his favourite Roman poet, but Prior's knowledge of both the classics and French literature was extensive and his epigrams were influenced not only by Martial but by such French poets as De Cailly, Lebrun, De Brébeuf and Gombauld. Translation as such is rare ('Scarcely any one of our poets has written so much and translated so little,' Johnson, *Lives of the Poets*). But all his epigrams, even those where the French influence is most apparent, evidence unmistakable Martialesque qualities in their misogyny, their attacks on physical deficiencies, old age, hypocrisy, medical practitioners, and parasites – and in their wit. Prior's light elegance sometimes surpasses that of Martial himself (see his version of *Ep*. 5.52). He is buried in Westminster Abbey.

From _Poems on Several Occasions_ (1707, 1718, 1727), _Miscellaneous Works_ (1740) and (in the case of the last epigram) from a Prior ms.

_Ep._ 1.13 _Arria and Petus out of Martial: Paraphrase_

With Roman constancy and decent pride
The dying Matron from her wounded side
    Drawing forth the guilty blade
To her lov'd Lord the fatal gift convey'd.
But then in streams of blood and sorrow drown'd,
Pardon, she crys, an unbecoming Tear
    (The Womans weakness will appear)
Yet think not tis that I repent the Deed
    Or that my firm resolves give ground.
Witness just Heav'n 'tis nothing that I bleed
But that You must, there Petus, there's the Wound.

_Ep._ 5.52*

To JOHN I ow'd great Obligation;
    But JOHN, unhappily, thought fit
To publish it to all the Nation:
    Sure JOHN and I are more than Quit.

_Ep._ 6.12 _Pontius and Pontia_

PONTIUS, (who loves you know a joke,
    Much better than he loves his life)
Chanc'd t'other morning to provoke
    The patience of a well-bred wife.

_Ep. 5.52_: Probably modelled on the version of the French epigrammatist Gombauld (1657).

Talking of you, said he, my dear,
    Two of the greatest wits in town,
One ask'd, If that high fuzz of hair
    Was, *bona fide*, all your Own.

Her own, most certain, t'other said,
    For NAN, who knows the thing, will tell ye,
The hair was bought, the money paid,
    And the receipt was sign'd DUCAILLY.

PONTIA, (that civil prudent She,
    Who values wit much less than sense,
And never darts a repartee,
    But purely in Her own defense)

Reply'd, These friends of your's, my dear,
    Are given extremely much to satire,
But pr'ythee husband, let one hear,
    Sometimes less wit, and more good-nature.

Now I have one unlucky thought,
    That wou'd have spoil'd your friend's conceit;
Some hair I have, I'm sure, unbought,
    Pray bring your brother-wits to see't.

Miscellaneous Epigrams

The Remedy, Worse than the Disease

I sent for RADCLIFFE,* was so ill,
    That other Doctors gave me over,
He felt my Pulse, prescribed his *Pill*
    And I was likely to recover.

Radcliffe: Prior's physician until 1711 and a regular butt of social humour

But when the *Wit* began to wheeze,
    And Wine had warmed the *Politician*,
Cur'd yesterday of my Disease,
    I died last night of my *Physician*.

Epigram

Ten months after FLORIMEL happen'd to wed,
And was brought in a laudable Manner to Bed;
She warbl'd Her Groans with so charming a Voice,
That one half of the Parish was stun'd with the Noise.
But when FLORIMEL deign'd to lie privately in,
Ten Months before She and her Spouse were a-kin;
She chose with such Prudence her Pangs to conceal,
That her Nurse, nay her Midwife, scarce heard her once
    squeal.
Learn, Husbands, from hence, for the Peace of your Lives,
That Maids make not half such a Tumult, as Wives.

A Reasonable Affliction

On His Death-Bed poor LUBIN lies:
    His Spouse is in Despair:
With frequent Sobs, and mutual Cries,
    They Both express their Care.

A diff'rent Cause, says Parson SLY,
    The same Effect may give:
Poor LUBIN fears, that He shall Die;
    His Wife, that He may Live.

Phyllis' Age

How old may PHYLLIS be, You ask,
    Whose Beauty thus all Hearts engages?
To Answer is no easie Task;
    For She has really two Ages.

Stiff in Brocard, and pinch'd in Stays,
    Her Patches, Paint, and Jewels on;
All Day let Envy view her Face;
    And PHYLLIS is but Twenty-one.

Paint, Patches, Jewels laid aside,
    At Night Astronomers agree,
The Evening has the Day bely'd;
    And PHYLLIS is some Forty-three.

Forma Bonum Fragile

What a frail Thing is Beauty, says Baron LE CRAS,
Perceiving his Mistress had one Eye of Glass:
    And scarcely had He spoke it;
When She more confus'd, as more angry She grew,
By a negligent Rage prov'd the Maxim too true:
    She dropt the Eye, and broke it.

A Critical Moment

How capricious were Nature and Art to poor NELL?
She was painting her Cheeks at the time her Nose fell.

Epigram

Her time with equal prudence Celia shares,
First writes her billet doux then says her prayrs
Her Mass and Toylet, Vespres and the Play;
Thus God and Astorath divide the day:
Constant she keeps her Ember week and Lent
At Easter calls all Israel to her tent:
Loose without bound, and pious without zeal
She still repeats the Sins she would conceal;
Envy her Self from Celias life must grant
An artfull Woman makes a modern Saint.

Epigram

LUKE Preach–ill admires what we Laymen can mean
    That thus by our Profit and pleasure are Sway'd.
He has but Three Livings, and wou'd be a Dean,
    His Wife dy'd this Year, He has Marri'd his Maid.

To suppress all his Carnal desires in their Birth
    At all Hours a lusty young Hussy is near;
And to take off his thought from the things of this Earth
    He can be Content with Two Thousand a Year.

Epigram

At Noble Mens table NED every day Eats
And rails against all but the Bubble that treats.
To what real Use does He manage his Sence
Who ne'r opens his mouth but at others Expence?

JOSEPH ADDISON (1672–1719)

Essayist, poet, dramatist and classical scholar. Educated at Charter-house and at Magdalen College, Oxford, of which he was made a fellow, he became a prominent Whig, held various political posts, including Chief Secretary for Ireland (1715), and was a Member of Parliament from 1708 until his death. In his later years he was a figure of considerable literary standing and a patron of other writers. His earliest poetical works were in Latin and he published translations of several Latin poets, including Virgil and Ovid, from his early twenties onwards. Several of his translations feature in Dryden's *Miscellanies*, vols. 4 (1694), 5 (1704) and 6 (1706). His plays include the verse tragedy, *Cato* (1713), and the prose comedy, *The Drummer* (1715). He was until the last years of his life a friend of Sir Richard Steele, who founded the English magazine *The Tatler*, to which Addison contributed, and together with Steele founded another famous English magazine, *The Spectator*, in 1711. Along with Swift, Steele, Congreve and others, he was a member of the famous Whig Kit-cat Club. In his last years he founded two political newspapers, *The Freeholder* and *The Old Whig*. As a prose writer he was lauded by Johnson as 'the model of the middle style' and his advocacy and practice of refined taste and judgement drove him to reject what he saw as the literary coarseness of the Restoration period. It is noticeable that the poems of Martial which he translated are selected to accord with his literary ideology. He is buried in Westminster Abbey.

The following come from *The Spectator* (1711–12: nos. 68, 86, 446), *Remarks on Several Parts of Italy, &c.* (1705) and *Dialogues upon the Usefulness of Ancient Medals* (1721).

Ep. 1 *Pref.*

Why dost thou come, great Censor* of thy Age,
To see the loose Diversions of the Stage?
With awful Countenance and Brow severe,
What in the Name of Goodness dost thou here?
See the mixt Crowd! how Giddy, Lewd, and Vain!
Didst thou come in but to go out again?

Ep. 2.68

By thy plain name though now addrest,
Though once my King and Lord confest,
Frown not: with all my goods I buy
The precious Cap of Liberty.

Ep. 3.43

Why should'st thou try to hide thy self in youth?
Impartial *Proserpine* beholds the truth,
And laughing at so fond and vain a task,
Will strip thy hoary noddle of its mask.

Ep. 3.56

Lodg'd at *Ravenna*, (water sells so dear)
A cistern to a vineyard I prefer.

Censor: Cato the Younger; see note on p. 126

Ep. 3.57

By a *Ravenna* vintner once betray'd,
So much for wine and water mix'd I paid;
But when I thought the purchas'd liquor mine,
The rascal fobb'd me off with only wine.

Ep. 4.44

Vesuvio, cover'd with the fruitful vine,
Here flourish'd once, and ran with floods of wine,
Here *Bacchus* oft to the cool shades retir'd,
And his own native *Nisa* less admir'd;
Oft to the mountain's airy tops advanc'd,
The frisking Satyrs on the summets danc'd;
Alcides here, here *Venus* grac'd the shore,
Nor lov'd her fav'rite *Lacedæmon* more:
Now piles of ashes, spreading all around,
In undistinguish'd heaps deform the ground,
The Gods themselves the ruin'd seats bemoan,
And blame the mischiefs that themselves have done.

Ep. 4.57

While near the *Lucrine* lake consum'd to death
I draw the sultry air, and gasp for breath,
Where streams of Sulphur raise a stifling heat,
And through the pores of the warm pumice sweat;
You taste the cooling breeze, where, nearer home
The twentieth pillar marks the mile from *Rome*:

And now the Sun to the bright Lion turns,
And *Baja* with redoubled fury burns;
Then briny seas and tasteful springs farewel,
Where fountain-nymphs confus'd with *Nereids* dwell,
In winter you may all the world despise,
But now 'tis *Tivoli* that bears the prize.

Ep. 4.64

All shun the raging Dog-star's sultry heat,
And from the half-unpeopled town retreat:
Some hid in *Nemi*'s gloomy forests lye,
To *Palestrina* some for shelter fly;
Others to catch the breeze of breathing air,
To *Tusculum* or *Algido* repair;
Or in moist *Tivoli*'s retirements find
A cooling shade, and a refreshing wind.

Ep. 7.93

Preserve my better part, and spare my friend;
So, *Narni*, may thy bridge for ever stand.

Ep. 10.51

Ye warbling fountains, and ye shady trees,
Where *Anxur* feels the cool refreshing breeze
Blown off the sea, and all the dewy strand
Lyes cover'd with a smooth unsinking sand!

Ep. 10.58

On the cool shore, near *Baja*'s gentle seats,
I lay retir'd in *Anxur*'s soft retreats.
Where silver lakes, with verdant shadows crown'd,
Disperse a grateful chilness all around;
The Grasshopper avoids th'untainted air,
Nor in the midst of summer ventures there.

Ep. 10.72

In vain, mean flatteries, ye trie
To gnaw the lip, and fall the eye;
No man a God or Lord I name:
From *Romans* far be such a shame!
Go teach the supple *Parthian* how
To veil the Bonnet on his brow:
Or on the ground all prostrate fling
Some *Pict*, before his barbarous King.

Ep. 12.46

In all thy Humours, whether grave or mellow,
Thou'rt such a touchy, testy, pleasant Fellow;
Hast so much Wit, and Mirth, and Spleen about thee,
There is no living with thee, nor without thee.

Ep. 12.54

Thy Beard and Head are of a diff'rent Die;
Short of one Foot, distorted in an Eye;
With all these Tokens of a Knave compleat,
Should'st thou be honest, thou'rt a dev'lish Cheat.

Ep. 12.98

Fair *Bætis*! Olives wreath thy azure locks;
In fleecy gold thou cloath'st the neighb'ring flocks:
Thy fruitful banks with rival-bounty smile,
While *Bacchus* wine bestows, and *Pallas* oil.

SIR RICHARD STEELE (1672–1729)

Influential literary figure and Whig politician of the Augustan period. Educated at Charterhouse and Merton College, Oxford, he held various administrative positions before being elected the Member of Parliament for Stockbridge in 1713. In 1715 he was knighted and was appointed patentee of the Drury Lane Theatre. He wrote a moral treatise on virtue, *The Christian Hero* (1701), and a number of moralizing, sentimental comedies (including *The Funeral*, 1701, *The Conscious Lovers*, 1722), but his main impact was through the magazines *The Tatler*, *The Spectator*, *The Guardian* and *The Englishman*, which he started between 1709 and 1714. He also engaged in political pamphleteering: *The Crisis* (1714), on the Hanoverian succession, brought about a charge of seditious libel. He was a member of the famous Whig Kit-cat Club and, until 1718, a close friend of Joseph Addison, who founded *The Spectator* with him (1711) and contributed to others of Steele's magazines.

The following appeared in *The Tatler*, no. 72 (1709), *The Spectator*, nos. 113 (1711), 490 (1712) and 52 (1711), respectively. The last poem, *De Vetula* ('On an Old Woman'), is a translation of a Latin distich written in imitation of Martial.

Ep. 1.13

When Arria pull'd the Dagger from her Side,
Thus to her Consort spoke th'illustrious Bride:
The Wound I gave my self I do not grieve,
I die by that which Paetus must receive.

Ep. 1.68

Let *Rufus* weep, rejoice, stand, sit or walk,
Still he can nothing but of *Nævia* talk:
Let him eat, drink, ask Questions, or dispute,
Still he must speak of *Nævia* or be mute.
He writ to his Father, ending with this Line,
I am, my lovely *Nævia*, ever thine.

Ep. 4.22

When my bright Consort, now nor Wife nor Maid,
Asham'd and wanton, of Embrace afraid,
Fled to the Streams, the Streams my Fair betray'd.
To my fond Eyes she all transparent stood,
She blush'd, I smil'd at the slight covering Flood.
Thus through the Glass the lovely Lilly glows,
Thus through the ambient Gem shines forth the Rose.
I saw new Charms, and plung'd to seize my Store,
Kisses I snatch'd, the Waves prevented more.

De Vetula

Whilst in the Dark on thy soft Hand I hung,
And heard the tempting *Syren* in thy Tongue,
What Flames, what Darts, what Anguish I endur'd?
But when the Candle enter'd I was cur'd.

AARON HILL (1685–1750)

London poet, playwright, theatre-manager, librettist (for Handel's
Rinaldo) and historian, pilloried by Pope in his *Dunciad*. He was
educated at Barnstaple Grammar School and Westminster. Author
of *A Full Account of the Ottoman Empire* (1709), several unsuccessful
plays and the unfinished epic poem *Gideon* (1749). He participated in
the turbulent periodical life of the capital, founding (1724) *The Plain
Dealer* and editing (with William Popple) the theatrical bi-weekly,
The Prompter (1734–6). His literary coterie included John Dyer,
Charles Churchill and James Thomson. Two versions of Martial are
here followed by an epitaph for Newton, with which the version of
Pope (p. 179) should be compared.

From *The Works of the Late Aaron Hill* . . . (1753).

Ep. 1.13 *Arria and Pætus, from Martial*

When, from her breast, chaste *Arria* dragg'd the sword,
And, faintly, reach'd it her expecting lord;
My wound, said she, but wastes unvalu'd breath,
'Tis thine, dear *Paetus*, gives the *sting* to death.

Ep. 7.60 *Ad Jovem Capitolinum*

Great *Capitolian Jove*! thou God, to whom
Our *Cæsar* owes that bliss, he sheds on *Rome*,
While prostrate crowds thy daily bounty tire,
And all thy blessings, for themselves, desire:
Accuse me not of pride, that I, alone,
Put up no pray'r, that may be call'd *my own*:
For *Cæsar*'s wants, O *Jove*! I sue to thee,
Cæsar himself can grant what's fit for me.

On Sir Isaac Newton

O'er *nature*'s laws, GOD cast the veil of *night*,
Out-blaz'd a NEWTON's *soul* – and *all* was *light*.

ALEXANDER POPE (1688–1744)

English Augustan poet and satirist. Essentially self-educated, he achieved financial independence through the proceeds of his translation into heroic couplets of Homer's *Iliad* (1715–20) and (with Fenton and Broome) *Odyssey* (1725–6). His major works include *An Essay on Criticism* (1711), *The Rape of the Lock* (1712–14), *The Dunciad*, a satire on dullness (1728–43), and *An Essay on Man* (1733–4). Throughout his life Pope suffered from ill health and a weak body, and his Roman Catholicism was always a problem in post-1688 London. He left the anti-Catholic Whig circle of Addison to align himself more with the Tories, and became a member of the famous collection of early-eighteenth-century Tory intellectuals and literati known as the Scriblerus Club (1714), which included Swift, Arbuthnot, Gay, Parnell, Robert Harley and others. Pope was the Augustan poet *par excellence*, influenced greatly by the Roman Augustan poet Horace, whom he openly acknowledges in a series of creative translations, *Imitations of Horace* (1733–8). His debt to Martial is less overt, but perhaps more profound. Although his translations/imitations of Martial are few, his epigrammatic couplets are the direct descendants of Martial's elegiac distichs, as the selections from Pope's poems and epitaphs following the two Martial poems show.

The following are taken from the 1751 nine-volume London edition of Pope's *Works* or the 1776 *Additions*.

Ep. 10.23

At length my Friend (while Time with still career
Wafts on his gentle wing this eightieth year)
Sees his past days safe out of Fortune's pow'r,
Nor dreads approaching Fate's uncertain hour;
Reviews his life, and in the strict survey
Finds not one moment he could wish away,
Pleas'd with the series of each happy day.
Such, such a man extends his life's short space,
And from the goal again renews the race:
For he lives twice, who can at once employ
The present well, and ev'n the past enjoy.

Ep. 12.50 *Upon the Duke of Marlborough's House at Woodstock*

See, Sir, here's the grand approach,
This way is for his Grace's coach;
There lies the bridge, and here's the clock,
Observe the lion and the cock,
The spacious court, the colonnade,
And mark how wide the hall is made!
The chimneys are so well design'd,
They never smoke in any wind.

This gallery's contriv'd for walking,
The window's to retire and talk in;
The council-chamber for debate,
And all the rest are rooms of state.
    Thanks, Sir, cry'd I, 'tis very fine,
But where d'ye sleep, or where d'ye dine?
I find by all you have been telling,
That 'tis a house, but not a dwelling.

The Rape of the Lock,* Canto 1.121–48 *Belinda's Toilet*

And now unveil'd, the Toilet stands display'd,
Each silver Vase in mystic order laid.
First, rob'd in white, the Nymph intent adores,
With head uncover'd, the Cosmetic pow'rs.
A heav'nly Image in the glass appears,
To that she bends, to that her eyes she rears;
Th'inferior Priestess, at her altar's side,
Trembling begins the sacred rites of Pride.
Unnumber'd treasures ope at once, and here
The various off'rings of the world appear;
From each she nicely culls with curious toil,
And decks the Goddess with the glitt'ring spoil.
This casket India's glowing gems unlocks,
And all Arabia breathes from yonder box.
The Tortoise here and Elephant unite,
Transform'd to combs, the speckled, and the white.
Here files of pins extend their shining rows,
Puffs, Powders, Patches, Bibles, Billet-doux.
Now awful beauty puts on all its arms;
The fair each moment rises in her charms,

The Rape of the Lock: For the epigraph Pope chose Martial *Ep.* 12.84.1–2,
substituting *Belinda* for *Polytime*: 'Nolueram, Belinda, tuos violare capillos; sed
juvat hoc precibus me tribuisse tuis. MART.'

Repairs her smiles, awakens ev'ry grace,
And calls forth all the wonders of her face;
Sees by degrees a purer blush arise,
And keener lightnings quicken in her eyes.
The busy Sylphs surround their darling care,
These set the head, and those divide the hair,
Some fold the sleeve, whilst others plait the gown;
And Betty's prais'd for labours not her own.

Epitaphs (1723-)

On Sir Godfrey Kneller
In Westminster Abbey, 1723

Kneller, by Heav'n and not a Master taught,
Whose Art was Nature, and whose Pictures thought;
Now for two Ages having snatch'd from fate
Whate'er was beauteous, or whate'er was great,
Lies crown'd with Princes honours, Poets lays,
Due to his Merit, and brave Thirst of praise.
    Living, great Nature fear'd he might outvie
Her works; and, dying, fears herself may die.

On Mr. Elijah Fenton
At Easthamsted in Berks, 1730

This modest Stone, what few vain Marbles can,
May truly say, Here lies an honest Man:
A Poet, blest beyond the Poet's fate,
Whom Heav'n kept sacred from the Proud and Great:
Foe to loud Praise, and Friend to learned Ease,
Content with Science in the Vale of Peace.

Calmly he look'd on either Life, and here
Saw nothing to regret, or there to fear;
From Nature's temp'rate feast rose satisfy'd,
Thank'd Heav'n that he had liv'd, and that he dy'd.

Intended for Sir Isaac Newton
In Westminster Abbey

Nature and Nature's Laws lay hid in Night:
GOD said, *Let Newton be!* and all was Light.

Epigrams from the Letters

On Damning a Poet

Damnation follows death in other men,
But your damn'd Poet lives and writes agen.

To a Lady

You know where you did despise
(T'other day) my little eyes,
Little legs, and little thighs,
And some things of little size,
            You know where.

You, 'tis true, have fine black eyes,
Taper legs, and tempting thighs,
Yet what more than all we prize
Is a thing of little size,
            You know where.

On Fame

What's Fame with Men, by custom of the Nation,
Is call'd in Women only Reputation:
About them both why keep we such a potter?
Part you with one, and I'll renounce the other.

On Wit

Jove was alike to *Latian* and to *Phrygian*,
For you well know, that Wit's of no Religion.

*On his Birthday**

With added days if life give nothing new,
But, like a Sieve, let ev'ry Pleasure thro';
Some Joy still lost, as each vain Year runs o'er,
And all we gain, some sad Reflection more!
Is this a Birth-day? – 'Tis, alas! too clear,
'Tis but the Fun'ral of another Year.

On Two Lovers Struck by Lightning

When Eastern lovers feed the fun'ral fire,
On the same pile the faithful pair expire:
Here pitying Heav'n that virtue mutual found,
And blasted both, that it might neither wound.
Hearts so sincere th' Almighty saw well pleas'd,
Sent his own lightning, and the victims seiz'd.

On his Birthday: Extracted by Pope from his poem 'To Mrs. M. B. on her Birthday'.

On the Same

Here lye two poor Lovers, who had the mishap
Tho very chaste people, to die of a Clap.

JONATHAN SWIFT (1667–1745)

One of the pre-eminent literary figures of the period: satirist, poet,
political and religious pamphleteer, author of *The Battle of the Books*
(1697), *Tale of a Tub* (1704) and *Gulliver's Travels* (1726). Born in
Dublin, where he attended Trinity College, he came to England in
1689, and became secretary to Sir William Temple, on whose support
he depended until Temple's death in 1699. He was ordained in 1694.
Much of his early life was spent in London, where he mingled with
Addison, Steele, Congreve and other Whigs, and contributed to *The
Tatler*, but he later moved over to Toryism and launched a series of
attacks upon Whig ministers. He became a close associate of the
Tory statesman Robert Harley and a prominent member of the
Scriblerus Club (see Pope). After the death of Queen Anne (1714)
and the formation of a Whig administration, Swift returned to Ire-
land, where he had been made Dean of St Patrick's in Dublin, and
apart from two visits to England he remained in Ireland until his
death. Swift translated little (if any, see below) Martial, though of
course conscious of the fashion:

> Translate me now some Lines, if you can,
> From *Virgil, Martial, Ovid, Lucan*;
> They could all Pow'r in Heav'n divide,
> And do now Wrong to either Side:
> They teach you how to split a Hair,
> Give —* and *Jove* an equal Share. (*On Poetry, A Rapsody*)

Give —: George (King George II)

The few Martial versions attributed to Swift by some scholars (Graves, Bohn, Sullivan and Whigham) are here followed by two satirical poems, Martialesque in language, theme and wit, and notable for their focus on physical ugliness and disgusting female smells. The first, *Dick, A Maggot*, is from *Miscellanies* 10 (1745), the second, *The Lady's Dressing Room*, was published in 1732.

Ep. 1.86

My Neighbour *Hunk*'s House and mine
Are built so near they almost join;
The Windows too project so much,
That through the Casements we may touch.
Nay, I'm so happy, most Men think,
To live so near a Man of Chink,
That they are apt to envy me,
For keeping such good Company:
But he's as far from me, I vow,
As London is from good Lord Howe;
For when old *Hunks* I chance to meet,
Or one or both must quit the Street.
Thus he who would not see old *Roger*,
Must be his Neighbour – or his Lodger.

Ep. 2.88

Arthur, they say, has Wit. 'For what?
For Writing?' No – for Writing not.

Xenia 18 *Green Leeks*

For it is every Cook's Opinion;
No savoury Dish without an Onion.
And, lest your Kissing should be spoil'd,
Your Onions must be thoroughly boil'd:
        Or else you may spare
        Your Mistress a Share,
The Secret will never be known;
        She cannot discover
        The Breath of a Lover,
But think it as sweet as her own.

Dick, A Maggot

As when from rooting in a Bin,
All powder'd o'er from Tail to Chin;
A lively Maggot sallies out,
You know him by his hazel Snout:
So, when the Grandson of his Grandsire,
Forth issues wriggling *Dick Drawcensir*,
With powder'd Rump, and Back and Side,
You cannot blanch his tawny Hide;
For 'tis beyond the Pow'r of Meal,
The Gypsey Visage to conceal:
For, as he shakes his Wainscot Chops,
Down ev'ry mealy Atom drops
And leaves the Tartar Phiz, in show
Like a fresh T—d just dropt on Snow.

The Lady's Dressing Room

Five Hours, (and who can do it less in?)
By haughty *Celia* spent in Dressing;
The Goddess from her Chamber issues,
Array'd in Lace, Brocade and Tissues.
    Strephon, who found the Room was void,
And *Betty* otherwise employ'd;
Stole in, and took a strict Survey,
Of all the Litter as it lay;
Whereof, to make the Matter clear,
An Inventory follows here.
    And first, a dirty Smock appear'd,
Beneath the Arm-pits well besmear'd;
Strephon, the Rogue, display'd it wide,
And turn'd it round on ev'ry Side.
On such a Point few Words are best,
And *Strephon* bids us guess the rest;
But swears how damnably the Men lie,
In calling *Celia* sweet and cleanly.
Now listen while he next produces,
The various Combs for various Uses,
Fill'd up with Dirt so closely fixt,
No Brush could force a Way betwixt.
A Paste of Composition rare,
Sweat, Dandriff, Powder, Lead and Hair;
A Forehead Cloth with Oyl upon't
To smooth the Wrinkles on her Front;
Here Allum Flower to stop the Steams,
Exhal'd from sour unsavoury Streams,
There Night-gloves made of *Tripsy*'s Hide,
Bequeath'd by *Tripsy* when she dy'd,
With Puppy Water, Beauty's Help
Distill'd from *Tripsy*'s darling Whelp;

Here Gallypots and Vials plac'd,
Some fill'd with Washes, some with Paste,
Some with Pomatum, Paints and Slops,
And Ointments good for scabby Chops.
Hard by a filthy Bason stands,
Fowl'd with the Scouring of her Hands;
The Bason takes whatever comes
The Scrapings of her Teeth and Gums,
A nasty Compound of all Hues,
For here she spits, and here she spues.
But oh! it turn'd poor *Strephon*'s Bowels,
When he beheld and smelt the Towels,
Begumm'd, bematter'd, and beslim'd
With Dirt, and Sweat, and Ear-wax grim'd.
No Object *Strephon*'s Eye escapes,
Here Pettycoats in frowzy Heaps;
Nor be the Handkerchiefs forgot
All varnish'd o'er with Snuff and Snot.
The Stockings, why shou'd I expose,
Stain'd with the Marks of stinking Toes;
Or greasy Coifs and Pinners reeking,
Which *Celia* slept at least a Week in?
A Pair of Tweezers next he found
To pluck her Brows in Arches round,
Or Hairs that sink the Forehead low,
Or on her Chin like Bristles grow.
     The Virtues we must not let pass
Of *Celia*'s magnifying Glass.
When frighted *Strephon* cast his Eye on't
It shew'd the Visage of a Gyant.
A Glass that can to Sight disclose,
The smallest Worm in *Celia*'s Nose,
And faithfully direct her Nail
To squeeze it out from Head to Tail;
For catch it nicely by the Head,
It must come out alive or dead.

Why *Strephon* will you tell the rest?
And must you needs describe the Chest?
That careless Wench! no Creature warn her
To move it out from yonder Corner;
But leave it standing full in Sight
For you to exercise your Spight.
In vain, the Workman shew'd his Wit
With Rings and Hinges counterfeit
To make it seem in this Disguise,
A Cabinet to vulgar Eyes;
Which *Strephon* ventur'd to look in,
Resolv'd to go thro' thick and thin;
He lifts the Lid, there needs no more,
He smelt it all the Time before.
As from within *Pandora*'s Box,
When *Epimetheus* op'd the Locks,
A sudden universal Crew
Of human Evils upwards flew;
He still was comforted to find
That *Hope* at last remain'd behind;
So *Strephon* lifting up the Lid,
To view what in the Chest was hid.
The Vapours flew from out the Vent,
But *Strephon* cautious never meant
The Bottom of the Pan to grope,
And fowl his Hands in Search of *Hope*.
O never may such vile Machine
Be once in *Celia*'s Chamber seen!
O may she better learn to keep
'Those Secrets of the hoary Deep'!

     As Mutton Cutlets, Prime of Meat,
Which tho' with Art you salt and beat,
As Laws of Cookery require,
And toast them at the clearest Fire;
If from adown the hopeful Chops
The Fat upon a Cinder drops,

To stinking Smoak it turns the Flame
Pois'ning the Flesh from whence it came;
And up exhales a greasy Stench,
For which you curse the careless Wench;
So Things, which must not be exprest,
When plumpt into the reeking Chest;
Send up an excremental Smell
To taint the Parts from whence they fell.
The Pettycoats and Gown perfume,
And waft a Stink round every Room.

    Thus finishing his grand Survey,
Disgusted *Strephon* stole away
Repeating in his amorous Fits,
Oh! *Celia, Celia, Celia*, shits!

    But Vengeance, Goddess never sleeping
Soon punish'd *Strephon* for his Peeping;
His foul Imagination links
Each Dame he sees with all her Stinks:
And, if unsav'ry Odours fly,
Conceives a Lady standing by;
All Women his Description fits,
And both Ideas jump like Wits:
By vicious Fancy coupled fast,
And still appearing in Contrast.
I pity wretched *Strephon* blind
To all the Charms of Female Kind;
Should I the Queen of Love refuse,
Because she rose from stinking Ooze?
To him that looks behind the Scene,
Satira's but some pocky Quean.
When *Celia* in her Glory shows,
If *Strephon* would but stop his Nose;
(Who now so impiously blasphemes
Her Ointments, Daubs, and Paints and Creams,
Her Washes, Slops, and every Clout,
With which he makes so foul a Rout;)

He soon would learn to think like me,
And bless his ravisht Sight to see
Such Order from Confusion sprung,
Such gaudy Tulips rais'd from Dung.

WILLIAM HAY (1695–1755)

Educated at Lewes Grammar School and Christ Church, Oxford, he
entered the Middle Temple in 1715, being called to the bar in 1723.
Although he suffered from being a hunchbacked dwarf, he had an
active career in legal and civil administration and in politics. As
Whig Member of Parliament for Seaford (1734–55), Hay was a
supporter of Sir Robert Walpole, but himself campaigned repeatedly
(and unsuccessfully) for the passing of legislation to improve the
condition of the English poor. He later held the offices of commis-
sioner for victualling the navy, and keeper of records in the Tower of
London. He was the author of various poems and of several essays on
government and philosophy. He describes his version of Martial as
follows: 'It is a translation or imitation of Martial; or both. Not of all
his epigrams; that would be unpardonable. Many are full of obscen-
ity, beneath a man: others of adulation, unbecoming a Roman: and
great numbers concerning his own writings are omitted, for fear of
cloying the reader ... What I have selected are generally moral or
instructive; in which a great variety of characters is introduced; and
the follies and foibles of many are justly ridiculed. These follies and
foibles are the same in all ages; and among all people, resembling
each other in opulence. What was practised at Rome, near seventeen
hundred years since, is now going on at London.'

From *Select Epigrams of Martial* (1755).

Ep. 1.25

Your book, Sir George, now give to public use;
From your rich fund the polish'd piece produce:
Which will defy the Louvre's nicer laws;
And from our critics here command applause.
Fame at your portal waits; the door why barr'd?
Why loth to take your labour's just reward?
Let works live with you, which will long survive;
For honours after death too late arrive.

Ep. 1.73

Your wife's the plainest piece a man can see:
No soul would touch her, whilst you left her free:
But since to guard her you employ all arts,
The rakes besiege her. – You're a man of parts!

Ep. 1.89

Your powder'd nose you thrust in every ear;
And whisper that, which all the world may hear:
In whispers smile, or wear a dismal face:
In whispers state, or else lament, the case:
Now hum a tune, judicious now appear,
Now hold your tongue, now hollow, in the ear.
Is this a secret too? Your accent raise:
We love the king, whom you in whispers praise.

Ep. 2.11

See you the cloud on yonder mortal's face?
Walking the Mall, the last who quits the place:
In tragic silence, and in dumps profound,
His nose almost draws furrows on the ground:
His wig he twitches, and he canes the air.
Is he for friend or brother in despair?
'Tis no such thing. Two sons with him do dwell:
They both are promising, they both are well:
So his good wife, for whom we all do pray:
Safe are his bags; nor servants run away:
Duly accounts his steward for his rent;
And by his bailiff's care his crops augment.
Say, from what cause can such affliction come!
Is there not cause? ye gods! he sups at home.

Ep. 2.37

You sweep my table: sausages, and chine,
A capon on which two at least may dine,
Smelts, salmon, sturgeon, birds of every feather,
Dripping with sauce, you wrap up all together;
And give it to your servant home to bear;
Leaving us nothing, but to sit and stare.
For shame restore the dinner; ease our sorrow:
I did not ask you, sir, to dine to-morrow.

Ep. 2.65

Why seem you dead to all the joys of life?
Have I not cause? you say: – I've lost my wife.
Oh! cursed fate! and oh! misfortune dire!
That one so wealthy should so soon expire!
Who left you twice five hundred annual rent!
– I'm sorry you have had this accident.

Ep. 2.71

Nothing I see your candour can exceed,
My distichs whensoe'er you please to read:
From Dryden or from Pope you cite a line,
To show how much they both fall short of mine,
Such foils, no doubt, make mine appear more taking.
Yet I should chuse some verses of your making.

Ep. 4.54

You, whom your country's honours high do raise,
And crown with merited, but early praise;
If you are wise, make use of every hour;
And never think another in your power.
No man could ever soften cruel fate;
But what, that once decrees, must be our date.
Were you polite as Sidney, or as great,
Had Cato's soul, or Marlborough's estate;
Still is life's line by the three sisters sped:
Not one prolongs, but one still cuts, the thread.

Ep. 4.78

Thrice twenty years you've seen your grass made hay:
Your eyebrows too proclaim your hair is grey:
Yet through all quarters of the town you run;
At every ball, and levee, you make one.
No great man stirs, but you are at his heels;
And never fail both them, who have the seals.
You never miss St. James's; ever chat
Of lord or bishop this, or general that.
To youth leave trifles: have you not been told,
That of all fools no fool is like the old?

Ep. 6.8

Welsh judges two, four military men,
Seven noisy lawyers, Oxford scholars ten,
Were of an old man's daughter in pursuit.
Soon the curmudgeon ended the dispute,
By giving her unto a thriving grocer.
What think you? did he play the fool, or no, Sir?

Ep. 6.39

'Tis a strange thing, but 'tis a thing well known,
You seven children have, and yet have none:
No genuine offspring, but a mongrel rabble,
Sprung from the garret, hovel, barn, and stable.
They every one proclaim their mother's shame:
Look in their face, you read their father's name.
This swarthy, flat-nos'd, Shock is Africk's boast;
His grandsire dwells upon the golden coast.

The second is the squinting butler's lad;
And the third lump dropp'd from the gardener's spade.
As like the carter this, as he can stare:
That has the footman's pert and forward air.
Two girls with raven and with carrot pate;
This the postillion's is, the coachman's that.
The steward and the groom old hurts disable,
Or else two branches more had graced your table.

Ep. 8.6

In leathern jack* to drink much less I hate,
Than in Sir William's antique set of plate.
He tells the gasconading pedigree,
Till the wine turns insipid too as he.
This tumbler, in the world the oldest toy,
Says he, was brought by Brute himself from Troy.
That handled cup, and which is larger far,
A present to my father from the Czar:
See how 'tis bruis'd, and the work broken off;
'Twas when he flung it at prince Menzicoff.
The other with the cover, which is less,
Was once the property of good queen Bess:
In it she pledg'd duke d'Alençon, then gave it
To Drake, my wife's great uncle: so we have it.
The bowl, the tankard, flagon, and the beaker,
Were my great-grandfather's, when he was speaker.
What pity 'tis, that plate so old and fine,
Should correspond no better with the wine.

---

jack: jug

Ep. 8.18

In epigram so happy is your strain,
You might be read, and I might write in vain:
But your regard to friendship's so sincere,
Your own applause, than mine, you hold less dear.
So Maro left to Flaccus Pindar's flight,
Able himself to soar a nobler height:
And warm'd with a superior tragic rage,
To Varius gave the honour of the stage.
Friends oft to friends in other points submit;
Few yield the glory of the field in wit.

Ep. 8.44

'Tis late: begin to live, old gentleman:
It would be late, if you at school began.
You a long race of misery have run;
But have not yet the race of life begun.
Your every morning is in labour spent,
This man to dun, or that to compliment.
With dirty stockings you to Hall resort,
A well-known party now in every court.
Through every quarter of the town you range,
Guild-hall, the Bank, the Custom-House, the Change.
Heap, scrape, oppress, use every fraudful art;
Oh! dismal thought! your wealth and you must part!
Of cash and mortgages though huge your store,
Your graceless son will wonder 'tis no more.
And when the plumes shall o'er your coffin wave,
And sable's venal train attend your grave,
Chief mourner he, and heir to your embrace,
Shall with your whore that night supply your place.

Ep. 8.54

So very fair! and yet so very common!
Would you were plainer! or a better woman!

Ep. 9.35

By these stale arts a dinner you pursue;
You trump up any tale, and tell as true.
Know, how the councils at the Hague incline:
What troops in Italy and on the Rhine.
A letter from the general produce,
Before the offices could have the news.
Know to an inch the rising of the Nile:
What ships are coming from each sugar isle:
What we expect from this year's preparation:
Who shall command the forces of the nation.
Leave off these tricks; and with me if you chuse
To dine to-day, do so; but then, no news.

Ep. 10.2

The verses in this book too soon took air:
My want of care at first renew'd my care.
Some, that are old, you here retouch'd will find:
The greater part are new: to both be kind.
When Fate to me a constant reader gave;
Receive, she said, the greatest boon I have.
By this beyond oblivion's stream arrive;
And in your better part by this survive.
Statues may moulder; and the clown unbred
Scoff at young Ammon's horse without his head.
But finish'd writings theft and time defy;
The only monuments, which cannot die.

Ep. 10.3

The porter's joke, the chairman's low conceit,
The dirty style of angry billingsgate,
Such as a strolling tinker would not use,
Nor hawker of old cloaths, or dreadful news,
A certain poet privately disperses,
And fain would fob them off for Martial's verses.
Will then the parrot steal the raven's note?
At country wakes Italians strain their throat?
Far from my writings be th'envenom'd lye:
My name on purer wings shall mount the sky.
Rather than strive an evil fame to own,
Cannot I hold my tongue, and die unknown?

Ep. 10.63

By this small stone as great remains are hid,
As sleep in an Egyptian pyramid,
Here lies a matron, for her years rever'd;
Who through them all with spotless honour steer'd.
Five sons, as many daughters, nature gave,
Who drop'd their pious tears into her grave.
Nor her least glory, though too rarely known;
One man she held most dear, and one alone.

Ep. 12.26

She ravish'd was by highwaymen, she cries:
Flatly the fact each highwayman denies.

SAMUEL JOHNSON (1709–84)

Essayist, poet, translator, biographer, editor, lexicographer, political pamphleteer, brilliant conversationalist (as his biographer Boswell and others amply testify) and one of the most eminent literary figures of the eighteenth century. Educated at Lichfield Grammar School and Pembroke College, Oxford, he contributed regularly to *The Gentleman's Magazine* (founded in 1731), founded *The Rambler* (1750), most of which he wrote, and published his acclaimed *Dictionary of the English Language* in 1755. The literary and artistic association known as The Club, based at the Turk's Head in London, was founded by him and Joshua Reynolds in 1764, and included the Whig politicians, Burke and Fox, the actor David Garrick, James Boswell and Oliver Goldsmith. The main achievements of Johnson's later years were his edition of Shakespeare (1765) and *The Lives of the English Poets* (1779–81). Apart from the above, he is perhaps best known for his didactic romance, *Rasselas, Prince of Abyssinia* (1759) and his creative imitations of Juvenal in *London* (1738) and *The Vanity of Human Wishes* (1749). Boswell's *Life of Samuel Johnson LL.D* (1791) gave almost mythic status to a life of intellectual achievement. Johnson is buried in Westminster Abbey.

The following (except for *Ep*. 6.11) come from *The Rambler* (1750–52), *The Adventurer* (1753) and Boswell's *Life* (1791). *Ep*. 6.11 is attributed to Johnson by Sullivan and Whigham (1987).

Ep. 1.8

Not him I prize who poorly gains
From death the palm which blood disdains;
But him who wins with nobler strife
An unpolluted wreath from life.

Ep. 2.55

The more I honour thee, the less I love.

Ep. 2.86

How foolish is the toil of trifling cares.

Ep. 2.89

Gaurus, pretends to *Cato*'s fame;
    And proves, by *Cato*'s vice,* his claim.

Ep. 5.81

Once poor, my friend, still poor you must remain,
    The rich alone have all the means of gain.

Ep. 6.11

You wonder now that no man sees
    Such friends as those of ancient Greece.
Here lies the point – Orestes' meat
    Was just the same his friend did eat;
Nor can it yet be found his wine
    Was better, Pylades! than thine.
In home-spun russet I am drest,
    Your cloth is always of the best.

Cato's vice: excessive drinking of wine

But, honest Marcus, if you please
    To choose me for your Pylades,
Remember, words alone are vain;
    Love – if you would be lov'd again.

Ep. 7.98

Who buys without discretion, buys to sell.

Ep. 10.4

We strive to paint the manners and the mind.

Epigram on Colley Cibber

Augustus still survives in Maro's strain,
And Spencer's verse prolongs Eliza's reign;
Great George's acts let tuneful Cibber sing;
For Nature form'd the Poet for the King.

REVD MR SCOTT (*c.*1725–*c.*1800)

The author, 'late of Trinity College, Cambridge', of a translation of a small selection of Martial's epigrams, together with 'mottoes from Horace, &c.', aimed at the 'amusement and improvement' of the Nobility, Clergy and Gentry (to which they are addressed) 'both in their *serious* and *laughing* hours, from the *Press* as well as from the *Pulpit*'. He has been identified as the Revd William Scott, born in King's Lynn and admitted as a sizar to Trinity College in January 1743, having previously attended Lynn school and Eton. Scott was ordained deacon in 1747 and priest in 1750, when he also received his

MA. He was at one time assistant morning preacher at St Sepulchre's, Snow Hill, London. In addition to his Martial, Scott translated some works of John Chrysostom and was responsible for several ecclesiastical publications. In his translation Scott adopts a self-consciously free mode, asking to be forgiven 'for not sticking so much altogether to the *Letter*, since he has endeavoured to keep up the *Spirit* of his [Martial's] EPIGRAMS and MOTTOS throughout'.

From *Epigrams of Martial, &c.* (1773).

Ep. I.13 *To the memory of the late LORD and LADY SUTHERLAND, who died but a few years ago, very soon after each other.*

When the chaste *Arria* gave the reeking sword,
Drawn from her bowels, to her honour'd *Lord*:
Pætus! she cry'd, for *this* 'I do *not* grieve,'
But for the *Wound* that *Pætus* must receive.

Ep. I.39 *To the Honourable Sir STEPHEN THEODORE JANSSEN, Bart, Chamberlain of the City of London. – A Man of Integrity.*

If there's one shall arise amongst all his rare friends,
Whose fam'd honour and virtue knows no private ends:
If One, whose great skill leaves us much at a strife,
If in arts he excels, or most simple in life:
If One, who's the guardian of Honesty's cause,
And in *secret* asks nothing against divine laws:
If there's One, who on greatness of mind builds his plan,
May I die, if the CHAMBERLAIN won't be that man!

201] EP. 8.43 · REVD MR SCOTT

Ep. 4.10 *To Mr. GARRICK, COLMAN, and FOOTE. To whom (the Translator) sends his Work lately finished.*

While my Book is quite new, and yet lying in sheets,
And while the moist Page does not fear whom it meets:
Go Boy! and bear this little Gift to my Friends,
Who well deserve such *Bagatelles* he intends.
Run, but pray now beware! that your *Sponge* does hang to't:
As *that* all such Gifts will be found best to suit.
O my *Friends*! many Blots cannot mend every jest:
But *one general Blot* may be all for the best!

Ep. 7.83 *To — TURVILLE, Esq. of the Temple, on his Barber who is very slow.*

While good Master *Temple* but *drawls* o'er your Face,
Another Beard rises, and steps in it's Place.

Ep. 8.43 *To the Honourable THOMAS WEBB, Esq. and LADY DOROTHY, his Wife, near Portman-Square, one of whom has buried only FIVE Wives, and the other as many Husbands.*

While TOM and DOLLY *many* Mates
    Does *carry off*, ('tis said)
Each shakes by turns (so will the Fates!)
    The *Fun'ral* Torch in bed;

O fye, Ma'am *Venus*! end this rout,
    Commit Them to the *Fleet*:
And grant They may be *carry'd out*
    Both cover'd with *one Sheet*!

Ep. 8.51 *To the Honourable EDWARD MORRIS, Esq. near Hanover-Square; in love with a Young Lady whom he never saw.*

The girl was handsome it is plain,
    But *Ned* himself was blind:
For, to be short, Love turn'd his brain,
    And left his *sight* behind.

Ep. 10.39 *To the Honourable Mrs. LAWES, near Hyde-Park, very old, but affects to be thought much younger.*

Why do you swear that you was born
    In good *Queen Anna*'s reign?
You're out – for by your face forlorn,
    In *James*'s, it is plain;

Nay *here* you're out, – for as your age
    Does shew, (as one may say)
That you was form'd, and in a rage,
    Of the *Promethean Clay*!

Ep. 12.92 *To WILLIAM PARS, Esq. Portrait-Painter, in Piercy-Street, Tottenham-Court-Road. About a Man's future Behaviour was he Great.*

You've often been used, *my good friend*, for to ask
    What sort of a man I might prove
Was I *rich* or soon *great*? but 'tis no easy talk,
    For 'faith I can't tell you, by Jove!
For who do You think, of the men that are here
    Can his manners divine, that You see?
And was you at *Jonathan's bull* or a *bear*,
    Pray what sort of *beast* would you be?

JAMES ELPHINSTON (1721–1809)

A Scots schoolmaster, educated at Edinburgh University and one-time tutor to Lord Blantyre, who established a school in London in 1753. He wrote several educational textbooks, including translations of Racine, and in 1778 devised an eccentric plan to publish a verse translation of Martial by subscription, submitting a specimen of them to the public. The translations, published in 1782, exerted a great influence on the general reading public's perception of Martial and figure largely in the 1860 Bohn Classical Library translation of the complete *Epigrams*. Bohn comments: '[Elphinston] has always stood to the public as the accepted versifier of Martial, and his pompous quarto, dignified by a long array of subscribers' names, still occupies a prominent place in many libraries.' In the opinion of Bohn Elphinston's translations were 'very indifferent'. Other critics were not so kind (see p. xxxii). Elphinston's rearrangement of the epigrams by subject-matter into twelve books of his own making and his removal of obscenity completely transformed the Bilbilis poet. Few would agree with the translator's claim that the epigrams were thus 'illuminated by arrangement'. His view of the epigram is more to the matter: 'Epigram, animated as free, owns to but one limit; is more or less requisite to every human labor; essential to this, brevity. Quick as thought it begins without form, procedes without interruption, tho' not without order, and flies to its *point*, which enters head and heart; with unavoidable, as often, unexpected power.' One incidental virtue of Elphinston's translations was that he did not avoid the Domitianic poems, unfavoured by modern translators; indeed, he gave them especial prominence, gathering them together to form his first book. A few of them are included here. The reader may also wish to observe the strategies, primarily omission and obfuscation, used by Elphinston to avoid translating the 'obscenities' of the *risqué* epigram, 3.82. After *Martial* Elphinston spent the rest of his life developing a fantastic system of quasi-phonetic spelling.

From *The Epigrams of M. Val. Martial, in Twelve Books . . .* (1782).

Ep. 1.21 *On MUCIUS SCAEVOLA and PORSENA*

The hand that, for the king, his captain slew;
Into the hallow'd flame, with ardor flew.
The desp'rate deed astounds the gen'rous foe:
Snatcht from the fire, he bids the heroe go.
The limb, that in combustion still seem'd cold;
The feeling PORSENA could not behold.
The hapless hand, by error, sav'd her fame:
She less had hit, had she not mist her aim.

Ep. 1.32 *To SABIDIUS*

SABBY, I love thee not, nor can say why.
One thing I can say, SAB: thee love not I.

Ep. 3.50 *To LIGURINUS*

The single cause why you invite,
Is that your works you may recite.
I hardly had my slippers dropt,
Nor dremt the entertainment stopt;
When, mid the lettuces and sallad,
Is usher'd in a bloody ballad.
Then lo! another bunch of lays,
While yet the primal service stays.
Another, ere the second course!
A third, and fourth, and fifth you force.
The boar, beroasted now to rags,
Appears in vain: the stomach flags.
The labors, that destroy each dish,
Were usefull coats for frying fish.
Affirm, my BARD, this dire decree:
Else you shall sup alone for me.

Ep. 3.82 On ZOILUS

Whoe'er with a ZOILUS' treat can put up,
As well at a prostitute's table may sup:
And e'en, while yet sober, were far better off
From Leda's lame porringer* humbly to quaff.

Behold him betrickt on the couch he has seiz'd,
On either side elb'wing that he may be eased;
Supported on purple, and pillows of silk:
The catamite standing, that nothing may bilk.

To ZOILUS squeamish his minister lends
The ruddy provokers,* and lentisk extends:
And now in a swim while he's stewing, poor man!
A lolloping concubine flaps the green fan.

As thus she restores him to regions of light,
A minion with myrtle puts insects to flight.
Meantime the bold stroker his person must skim,
And ply her arch palm o'er his each lazy limb.

The fingers, now snapt, give the eunuch the sign,
My lord has a mind to alembic his wine.
The latter unwearied persisting the filler,*
The dextrous emasculate guides the distiller.*

---

porringer: shallow bowl; 'Leda' is the name of a prostitute
provokers: feathers
filler: euphemism for 'urine'
distiller: euphemism for 'penis'

The treater converts, the repast to complete,
His thoughts and his eyes on the crew at his feet.
He duly reflects what to servants he ows:
And so to the dogs the goose-gibblets he throws.

The kernels, and other nice bits of the boar,
He portions to those who have toil'd on his floor:
And, sleek to plump up his most favourite widgeon,
He deals the plump thighs of his best potted pidgeon.

To us while the rocks of Liguria present,
Or fumes of Massilia, their must and their tent;
The nectar Opimian he gives to refine,
In crystals and myrrhines, for zanies the wine!

Himself made essential, from Cosmus' first flasks,
His guests to accept a few droplings he asks.
From out his gold shell scarce sufficing to shed
The unguent upon an adulteress' head.

O'erpower'd with deep goblets, sweet ZOIL besnores:
And, though we recline, none the music deplores.
We smile, or we swet, or we swill, now by nods;
Nor can we revenge – such a feast of the gods!

Ep. 4.38 *To GALLA*

GALLA, deny; and render passion strong:
But, prudent GALLA, not deny too long.

Ep. 5.5 *To SEXTUS*

SEXTUS, whose winning Muse presumes t'explore
The Palatine Minerva's* matchless lore,
'Tis thine t'approach her friend, the earthly god;*
T'imbibe his graces, and attend his nod.
'Tis thine to scan and sooth each springing care;
To mark the hue his inmost secrets wear.
Oh! to thy friend some little nook assign,
Where Pedo, Marsus, and Catullus shine:
But place the heavenly Capitolian strains,*
Fast by the buskin'd Maro's grand remains.

Ep. 6.2 *To CESAR*

They sported erst, with wedloc's holy flame;
And, innocence t' unman, they held no shame.
Both, CESAR, thou forbidst* with gen'rous scorn;
And sayst: O coming age, be guiltless born.
No castrate or suborner shall there be:
Erewhile the castrate was the debauchee.

Palatine Minerva: the libraries associated with the temple of Apollo on the
Palatine, of which the addressee seems to have been the curator
earthly god: Domitian, addressed as 'master and god' (*dominus et deus*, Suetonius,
Domitian, 13.2)
Capitolian strains: Domitian's youthful poem on the fighting round the Capitol
in the civil war of 69 CE
forbidst: the reference is to Domitian's ban on castration and his revival of the
punitive Augustan laws on adultery

Ep. 6.3 *To the SON of DOMITIAN*

Come, promis'd name; Iulus' race* adorn.
True offspring of the gods! blest babe, be born:
To whom thy sire, when many an age has roll'd;
May give th' eternal reins with him to hold.
The golden threds, shall Julia's* fingers draw;
And Phryxus' fleece the willing world shall aw.

Ep. 7.22 *On the Birth of LUCAN*

APOLLO's bard exalts to day:
Glad Aon's choir, attune the lay.
When bounteous Betis* LUCAN gave,
He blended with Castalia's wave.

Ep. 7.61 *To DOMITIAN*

When the bold hucster bore the town away,
And within bounds no boundary would stay;
Thou bad'st obstruction* sound a quick retreat;
And what was now a lane, became a street.
Concatenated pots no post surround:
No pretor waddling in mid-mud is found.
No rasor, drawn in darkness, now we feel:
Whole streets of tipplers dance no more their reel.

Iulus' race: ambivalent; ostensibly 'Roman race', but literally the Julian family, of which Domitian's niece was a member
Julia: Domitian's niece, recently dead and deified
Betis: Lucan was born at Corduba (Cordova) on the Baetis (Guadalquivir)
bad'st obstruction . . .: Domitian's urban regulations prohibited stalls spreading into the street

The tonsor, taverner, the butcher, cook;
Who, each forsaking, curst the bounds forsook;
All their respective mounds submiss explore:
And she is ROME, that was a stall before.

Ep. 8.22 To GALLICUS

You bid to a boar, and you treat with a hog.
You make us both mongrels, if thus you're a dog.

Ep. 9.5 To CESAR

O thou, who couldst the Rhine restore,
    Dread guardian of mankind;
Meek modesty, with blushing lore,
    Was to thy care* consign'd.

To thee their everlasting praise,
    Let town and country pay;
Who fairly may their offspring raise,
    To people and obey.

By avarice no more beguil'd,
    Virility shall mourn:
Nor shall the prostituted child
    Be from the mother tor'n.

Shame, tho', before thy blest decree,
    The bridal bed's disdain;
Now sanctifi'd again by thee,
    Must in a brothel reign.

---

to thy care: Domitian's edicts against castration and child prostitution and his revival of the Augustan adultery laws are alluded to here and in the following lines; cf. *Ep.* 6.2 above

Ep. 9.93 *To CALATHISSUS*

Crown the deathless Falernian, my boy;
    Draw the quincunx from out the old cask.
Of the gods who shall highten the joy?
    It is for CESAR five swellers I ask.

Let the garland ten times bind the hair,
    To the heroe that planted the fane:
Twice five goblets replete will declare
    The kind god from th' Odrysian domain.

Ep. 10.53 *On SCORPUS*

Erewhile I set the Circus in a roar;
O ROME, thy fav'rite and delight no more.
When envious Lachesis my triumphs told,
Rapt in the cube of three, she thought me old.

NATHANIEL BRASSEY HALHED (1751–1830)

Youthful collaborator of Richard Sheridan, distinguished orientalist and linguistic scholar, civil servant, politician, polemical satirist, pamphleteer and one of the most controversial and perplexing figures of the late eighteenth century. Educated at Harrow and Christ Church, Oxford, he spent his early manhood in Bengal, having obtained a writership with the East India Company, for whom he worked while Warren Hastings was governor-general of India. During this early period he helped lay the foundations of the study of Sanskrit in the West and pioneered the study of classical Indian culture and of comparative linguistics. His translation (at Hastings's suggestion) from Persian of *A Code of Gentoo Laws, or, Ordinations of the Pundits* (1776), followed by a *Grammar of the Bengal Language* (1778), made him famous – not only in learned circles. He became a Member of Parliament in 1791, but his political and social reputation were fatally damaged by his involvement in popular millenarianism and fervent support for the self-styled prophet, Richard Brothers, who was eventually committed to an asylum. In 1793–4 he published anonymously in four separate fascicles some tart versions and imitations of Martial, rewriting the originals to eulogize Hastings and Pitt, to attack political enemies and even to poke fun at friends such as Sheridan and Samuel Parr. The versions are much less obscene than their Latin originals, but the translator happened also to print the Latin text opposite the English 'imitations' to show their ingenuity, thereby also drawing the reader's attention to the less savoury aspects of Martial's genius. Both Martial and his translator were castigated in the response which followed. Nevertheless some of the versions are very sprightly, indeed keen verbally, and powerful. They are curiously unlike Halhed's other writings on religion, linguistics and Warren Hastings.

From *Imitations of Some of the Epigrams of Martial* (1793).

Ep. I.106

Dear Tom,* while with cordial of raisin
    Our spirits and energies rise,
Your gruel, how little in season!
    The water-decanter supplies:
And press'd by your neighbour more nimble

Tom: Tom Paine, later viciously attacked (in a translation of 10.5 below) as a traitor against the king for his pamphlet on the Rights of Man

The life-giving bottle to pass,
You sip what might go in a thimble,
　　Diluted three-fourths, from your glass.
To revisit your once-lov'd French beauty
　　Perhaps may to-night be your plan:
If so, to be sober's your duty,
　　For urging *the Rights*, Tom, *of Man*.
But your sighs and your silence deny it;
　　Then tipple – no matter how deep:
If forc'd to be chaste and lie quiet,
　　Let Claret at least give you sleep.

Ep. 2.58

In velvet clad, and lace so fine,
You scorn this thread-bare suit of mine.
– Thread-bare I grant ye, Mr. Beau,
– But then – 'twas paid for long ago.

Ep. 3.70

For years neglected and turn'd off at last,
D–dw–ll's* fair wife upon the town was cast. –
Now D–dw–ll's coach is ever at her door:
He likes the danger of a common whore.

D-dw-ll's: Dodwell's

Ep. 3.90

You will and you won't – half no and half yes,
I'm quite at a loss for your meaning, dear Miss.
Long enough in all conscience you've shuffled and shamm'd:
– Say yes and be kissed – or say no, and be —.

Ep. 6.70

Two lustres now their period bring,
That Pitt has ably serv'd the King;
Foster'd the nation, and its purse,
Without one glimpse of a reverse;
And rais'd our happiness the more,
From contrast with the ills before.
He shakes his head (and well he may)
At Fox, and Sheridan, and Grey,
Whose desp'rate aims for his disgrace,
Just help to rivet him in place.
      But should comparison draw forth
The long-spun ministry of North,
And sum up all the time he spent
In blunders, and mismanagement;
Compute the provinces he lost,
The mighty sums his systems cost,
The vast expence of blood and tea
Profusely shed by land and sea,
Then set, as far as they would go,
The days of weal 'gainst those of woe,
His whole official term, comprest,
Would make one hour of Pitt's, at best.
'Tis fallacy, by years to count
A ministerial life's amount:
The wise Politician's creed,
Is, *not to last*, but to *succeed*.

Ep. 9.2

Howe'er depress'd and fall'n thy state
From all that's splendid, France, and great,
Triumphant o'er thy King enchain'd,
Marat at least in blood has reign'd.
Howe'er thy harass'd subjects pine,
As famine spreads, and arts decline;
Though wealth be lost, and commerce dead,
There's store of *ammunition-bread*:
Thy armies, too, no void regret,
– There's food enough for powder yet.
Custine, in democratic tents
Consum'd the precious wines of Mentz:
But what, in jail, thy Monarch's fare!
His potion what, but fell despair? –

Ep. 9.29

Art thou so soon to Stygian comforts fled,
        Decrepit ghost, who once wert Charlotte Hayes?
Ill could'st thou brook to number with the dead,
        Dame Shipton's junior, by a dozen days!
Hush'd is the thunder of thy pow'rful tongue,
        Whose din a thousand forges far outvied:
Clos'd are thy labours for the fair and young,
        The daily widow, and the nightly bride.
Ah! who shall now the virgin's mind bewitch,
        Stifle her fears, and bargain for her fall:
What vent'rous bawd shall pander for the rich,
        When thou'rt a skeleton in Surgeon's Hall?

Ep. 9.80

Feignlove, half-starv'd, a rich old hag has wed: —
Poor Feignlove, doom'd to earn his board in bed.

Ep. 10.5

O may the scoundrel Pamphleteer,*
Disseminating libel here,
Who would with trait'rous pen write down
Our King, his dignity, and crown,
Be kick'd and cuff'd, and bang'd and hurl'd,
From post to pillar, through the world,
(Shunn'd, as an universal pest)
Like Cain, without a place of rest!
Outcast of beggars, be his meals
Nought but the bones from curs he steals!
One long december, drear and chill,
His whole extended twelvemonth fill,
With not a hovel's nook, to warm
His limbs, all shiv'ring in the storm;
That ev'n the very dead excite
His envy, at their happier plight!
Dismal and dreadful be the woes
That haunt his life's last ling'ring close:
Then let him rue, with tenfold smart,
The throbbings of a guilty heart,
Anticipate a hell alive,
Suffer its pangs, and still survive!
Dogs, let him think, and vultures greedy,
Devour his mangled flesh already;

Pamphleteer: Tom Paine, addressed in *Ep.* 1.106 above

Think his yet panting carcase cramm'd
Amongst the lowest of the damn'd:
There fiends and devils let him feel,
With whips of flame, and fangs of steel! –
– Gnaw him, ye worms, that ne'er expire!
Burn him, thou everlasting fire! –
Thus while he draws his tainted breath,
In agonies far worse than death,
Let conscience (in the act to die)
Wring from his struggling soul, "Twas I,
'(Curs'd be the hour I form'd the plan)
"Twas I compos'd the Rights of Man.'

Ep. 10.8

I laugh at Poll's perpetual pother
    To make me her's for life.
She's old enough to be my mother –
    But not to be my wife.

Ep. 10.75

When Charlotte first increas'd the Cyprian corps,
She ask'd a hundred pounds – I gave her more.
Next year, to fifty sunk the course of trade:
I thought it now extravagant, but paid.
Six months elapsed: 'twas twenty guineas then;
In vain I pray'd, and press'd, and proferr'd ten.
Another quarter barely slipp'd away,
She begg'd four guineas of me at the play:
I boggled – her demand still humbler grew,
'Twas 'thank you kindly, Sir,' for two–pounds–two.

Next, in the street her favours I might win,
For a few shillings and a glass of gin: –
– And now, (though sad and wonderful it sounds)
I would not touch her for a hundred pounds.

Ep. 10.81

One morn, at Susan's levee, in King's-place,
Two elders quarell'd for her first embrace:
She, *knowing both*, the fierce dispute to close,
Gave one her smock to air, and one her hose.

Ep. 11.60

Sophy and Jane the Bond-Street beaus divide:
Their merits all can judge – for all have tried.
Sophy's the belle – but Jane's eternal spunk
Would tempt a Bramin, and exhaust a monk.
Jane into love-worn Wilkes new life would pour,
And bid old Queensb-r- be old no more.
Jane's am'rous flame all wish their nymphs to catch:
The *Brighton Taylor** is not half her match.
– No fires in Sophy's marble bosom glow,
Tame as St. Austin's bed-fellow of snow. –
Ah! might we ask the gods one precious boon,
Too great, perhaps, for aught below the moon:
'Tis, that they'd Sophy's charms on Jane confer,
And breathe Jane's ardent feelings into her.

Brighton Taylor: a well-known whore

IV. THE ROMANTICS TO POUND: 1800–c.1950

INTRODUCTION

It is commonplace to suggest that the Romantic movement ought to have generated a spirit hostile to Martial; and certainly large-scale imitation of Martial disappears. But there was much too for the Romantic movement to admire and Martial's influence can be felt in the epigrams of Coleridge and the satiric verve of Byron, even if it was now thought that epigram was a truly minor form. Byron's self-consciously ironic description of 'all those nauseous epigrams of Martial' nevertheless contained within it what was to be the prevailing nineteenth-century rejection of Martial on the grounds of obscenity and his 'perfectly nauseating' flattery of Domitian. Noticeably, Macaulay's eulogy of Martial's imagery was qualified by disgust at 'his indecency . . . servility and . . . mendacancy' (see p. xxxiii). Moreover the 'Grecian taste' of the nineteenth century ensured that translation activity focused on Hellenic literature, sometimes, as in the case of Browning's radical version of Aeschylus' *Agamemnon* (1877), with an intention to reproduce its strangeness or difference. Matthew Arnold's quintessentially Victorian vision of Greek 'nobility', articulated in his lectures 'On Translating Homer' (1861–2), reflected and sustained the Hellenic prejudice. Not surprisingly, epigrammatists of the period, such as Landor and Kipling, owe as much to the *Greek Anthology* as to Martial. In Kipling's case Hellenic indebtedness is especially marked. The few self-professed admirers of the Roman epigrammatist either, like Robert Louis Stevenson and Goldwin Smith, created an image of him as an English gentleman acceptable to the Victorian public, or, like George Augustus Sala and his friends, swam against the tide by concentrating on those poems most offensive to the ostensible ethos of nineteenth-century Britain. The paucity and immense selectivity of scholarly editions of Martial produced during this period underscore the epigrammatist's fragmentation and neglect.

It was the bowdlerized Martial that the early twentieth century inherited and even so he held little interest for anyone except schoolmasters and their pupils, as the reader will see from the selections which close this section. There is one exception to this, and a most seminal one: Ezra Pound, whose creative innovations in translation practice and deep respect for and affinity with Martial (though he translated only one epigram) were to bear fruit in the second half of the twentieth century.

TRANSLATIONS AND IMITATIONS

SAMUEL TAYLOR COLERIDGE (1772–1834)

Poet, critic, philosopher and one of the major figures of English Romanticism; author of *Frost at Midnight* (1798), *The Rime of the Ancient Mariner* (1798), *Kubla Khan* (1816), and *Christabel* (1816). He was educated at Christ's Hospital and Jesus College, Cambridge, and won early respect on the basis of his political and religious lectures and sermons. During this period he produced a Christian weekly, *The Watchman* (1796), and contributed regularly to *The Morning Post*. His friendship and creative collaboration with Wordsworth resulted in *Lyrical Ballads* of 1798, which revolutionized English

poetry and literary sensibility. Although his famed addiction to
opium and an unhappy marriage debilitated his creative energies in
middle life, he lectured widely and with distinction (especially on
Shakespeare), produced a new paper *The Friend* (1809–10), a play
Remorse (1813), many political articles and the *Biographia Literaria*
(1817), a philosophical autobiography. *Christabel and other Poems* was
published in 1816. Although Coleridge made no direct translations
of Martial or any acknowledged imitations, his own epigrammatic
production displays unmistakably Martialesque qualities, derived in
part from his occasional choice of Lessing (1729–81), epigrammatist,
literary theorist and advocate of Martial, as a model for imitation.
Few of Coleridge's epigrams found their way into his own final
collection of his works in 1834, but were scattered throughout news-
papers, periodicals and other publications. Some received publication
only after his death. The following epigrams have been selected to
illustrate their Martialesque wit, range of subject-matter and rhetori-
cal strategies.

The first three epigrams are from *Poetical Works* (3rd edn, 1834). *On
Donne's Poetry* was first published in *Literary Remains* (1836); the
remainder, printed in chronological order of their first publication,
were published in *The Watchman*, 1796, *Morning Post*, 1799–1802,
Annual Anthology, 1800, *The Friend*, 1809, and the *Biographia Literaria*,
1817.

On an Insignificant

No doleful faces here, no sighing –
Here rots a thing that *won* by dying.*
'Tis Cypher lies beneath this crust –
Whom Death *created* into dust.

Lines 1 and 2 were not included in the 1834 edition.

On a Volunteer Singer

Swans sing before they die – 'twere no bad thing
Should certain persons die before they sing.

Epitaph on an Infant

Ere Sin could blight or Sorrow fade,
    Death came with friendly care:
The opening Bud to Heaven convey'd,
    And bade it blossom *there*.

On Donne's Poetry

With Donne, whose muse on dromedary trots,
Wreathe iron pokers into true-love knots;
Rhyme's sturdy cripple, fancy's maze and clue,
Wit's forge and fire-blast, meaning's press and screw.

On an Amorous Doctor

From Rufa's eye sly Cupid shot his dart
And left it sticking in Sangrado's heart.
No quiet from that moment has he known,
And peaceful sleep has from his eyelids flown.
And opium's force, and what is more, alack!
His own orations cannot bring it back.
In short, unless she pities his afflictions,
Despair will make him take his *own prescriptions*.

Hippona

Hippona lets no silly flush
Disturb her cheek, nought makes her blush.
Whate'er obscenities you say,
She nods and titters frank and gay.
Oh Shame, awake one honest flush
For this, – that nothing makes her blush.

On a Reader of His Own Verses

Hoarse Mævius reads his hobbling verse
      To all and at all times,
And deems them both divinely smooth,
      His voice as well as rhymes.

But folks say, Mævius is no ass!
      But Mævius makes it clear
That he's a monster of an ass,
      An ass without an ear.

The Prodigal

Jack drinks fine wines, wears modish clothing,
But prithee where lies Jack's estate?
In Algebra for there I found of late
A quantity call'd less than nothing.

To a Lying Youth

If the guilt of all lying consists in deceit,
    Lie on – 'tis your duty, sweet youth!
For believe me, then only we find you a cheat
    When you cunningly tell us the truth.

Rufa*

Thy lap-dog, Rufa, is a dainty beast,
It doesn't surprise me in the least
To see thee lick so dainty clean a beast.
But that so dainty clean a beast licks thee,
Yes – that surprises me.

To a Certain Modern Narcissus

Do call, dear Jess, whene'er my way you come;
My looking-glass will always be at home.

On Epigram

What is an Epigram? a dwarfish whole,
Its body brevity, and wit its soul.

Cf. Martial, *Ep.* 1.83.

To Aurelia

From me, Aurelia! you desired
　　Your proper praise to know;
Well! you're the FAIR by all admired –
　　Some twenty years ago.

For a House-Dog's Collar

When thieves come, I bark: when gallants, I am still –
So perform both my Master's and Mistress's will.

On Kepler

No mortal spirit yet had clomb so high
As Kepler – yet his Country saw him die
For very want! the *Minds* alone he fed,
And so the *Bodies* left him without bread.

Modern Critics

No private grudge they need, no personal spite,
The *viva sectio* is its own delight!
All enmity, all envy, they disclaim,
Disinterested thieves of our good name –
Cool, sober murderers of their neighbours' fame!

WALTER SAVAGE LANDOR
(1775–1864)

Poet and major epigrammatist of nineteenth-century Britain, al-
though in many ways himself an eighteenth-century man, a
neo-classicist in the age of Romantics and Victorians. Educated (in-
completely) at Rugby and Trinity College, Oxford, he spent much
of his life abroad, primarily in Italy (1814–35). A prolific writer,
famous for his many-volumed prose work, *Imaginary Conversations*,
and steeped in the classics, he not only translated poets such as Virgil,
Horace and Catullus, but composed poetic works on Greek themes
(e.g. *Simonidea*, 1806, *Pericles and Aspasia*, 1836, *Hellenics*, 1847), influ-
enced by the rediscovery of Greece and the taste for Hellenic culture
which began to define Victorian England. He translated no epigrams
of Martial. The range and quality of his own epigrammatic produc-
tion, however, is impressive, and owes more than he would have
admitted to Martial (and Martial's influence on the English epigram-
matic tradition). It did little, however, to affect the genre's ambigu-
ous, indeed lowly status, in the nineteenth century, reflected in the
comment Landor himself placed in the mouth of his 'imaginary'
Richard Porson (see p. xxxii above). Some of his own verses (see
From 'Interlude' below) pay at least lip-service to this devaluation. The
following selection includes some poems, not classified as 'epigrams'
in the various collections, but according fully with the epigrammatic
tradition as represented by Martial and Ben Jonson. Landor was the
'model' for Lawrence Boythorn in Dickens's *Bleak House*.

From various sources including *The Poems of Walter Savage Landor*
(1795), *Miscellaneous Poems* (1846), *The Last Fruit of an Old Tree*
(1853), *Additional Poems* (1863).

On a Quaker's Tankard

Ye lie, friend Pindar! and friend Thales! –
Nothing so good as water? Ale is.

On a Certain Print

That cockt-up nose there, shining like the knob
    Of greasy plow-boy's hazle switch,
Is a vile woman's. – tho' upon this globe
    Few are so high, and none so rich,
A tinker of tin-shavings she would rob,
    Or ointment from Scotch pedlar's breech.
Who that comes filching farthings from one's fob
    Need ever feel a fouler itch?

Dirce

Stand close around, ye Stygian set,
    With Dirce in one boat conveyed!
Or Charon, seeing, may forget
    That he is old and she a shade.

On Reade's Cain

The reign of justice is return'd again:
    Cain murders Abel, and Reade* murders Cain.

Reade: John Edmund Reade, author of the dramatic poem, *Cain the Wanderer*
(1830)

Ternissa

Ternissa! you are fled!
I say not to the dead,
But to the happy ones who rest below:
For, surely, surely, where
Your voice and graces are,
Nothing of death can any feel or know.
Girls who delight to dwell
Where grows most asphodel,
Gather to their calm breasts each word you speak:
The mild Persephone
Places you on her knee,
And your cool palm smoothes down stern Pluto's cheek.

Untitled

Various the roads of life; in one
All terminate, one lonely way.
We go; and 'Is he gone?'
Is all our best friends say.

Untitled

One tooth has Mummius; but in sooth
No man has such another tooth:
Such a prodigious tooth would do
To moor the bark of Charon to,
Or, better than the Sinai stone,
To grave the Ten Commandments on.

From 'Interlude'

Idle and light are many things you see
In these my closing pages: blame not me.
However rich and plenteous the repast,
Nuts, almonds, biscuits, wafers come at last.

To One Who Quotes and Detracts

Rob me and maim me! Why, man, take such pains
On your bare heath to hand yourself in chains?

Untitled

Joy is the blossom, sorrow is the fruit,
Of human life; and worms are at its root.

Untitled

Alas! 'tis very sad to hear,
Your and your Muse's end draws near:
I only wish, if this be true,
To lie a little way from you.
The grave is cold enough for me
Without you and your poetry.

Untitled

In the odor of sanctity Miriam abounds,
Her husband's is nearer the odor of hounds,
With a dash of the cess-pool, a dash of the sty,
And the water of cabbages running hard-by.

Untitled

Stop, stop, friend Cogan!* would you throw
That tooth away? You little know
Its future: that which now you see
A sinner's, an old saint's may be,
And popes may bless it in a ring
To charm the conscience of some king.

A Quarrelsome Bishop

To hide her ordure, claws the cat;
You claw, but not to cover that.
Be decenter, and learn at least
One lesson from the cleanlier beast.

Cogan: dentist of Bath

The Georges

George the First was always reckoned
Vile, but viler George the Second;
And what mortal ever heard
Any good of George the Third?
When from earth the Fourth descended
(God be praised!) the Georges ended.

To a Poet

I never call'd thy Muse splay-footed,
Who sometimes wheez'd, and sometimes hooted,
As owls do on a lonely tower,
Awaiting that propitious hour
When singing birds retire to rest,
And owls may pounce upon the nest.
I only wish she would forbear
From sticking pins into my chair,
And let alone the friends who come
To neutralize thy laudanum.

On Man

In his own image the Creator made,
     His own pure sunbeam quicken'd thee, O man!
Thou breathing dial! since thy day began
     The present hour was ever markt with shade!

GEORGE LAMB (1784–1834)

Literary journalist, theatrical entrepreneur, translator and political figure, product of Eton and Cambridge (Trinity College). Called to the bar at Lincoln's Inn, Lamb quickly abandoned law for theatre and literature, and was one of the early writers for the *Edinburgh Review*. His circle included Douglas Kinnaird and Byron, with whom he ran the Drury Lane Theatre in London. He was a member of the British Parliament from 1819 to 1820, and again from 1826 to 1834, becoming in 1830 under-secretary of state in the Home Office to his brother, Lord Melbourne. His most famous translation was of the poems of Catullus (1821), which was widely criticized, but which received sufficient commendation to be republished in Bohn's Classical Library (1854). It is in the notes and preface to his Catullus translation that Lamb's Martial versions are to be found.

From *The Poems of Caius Valerius Catullus* (1821).

Ep. 1.7 *Upon Stella's Poem – Addressed to Maximus*

The lines my Stella wrote to praise
    The Dove, so long to him most dear,
Are, Maximus, far sweeter lays
    (I speak, though all Verona hear)

Than those in which Catullus tells
    Of that fond Sparrow,* once his Love's;
And Stella him as much excels
    As sparrows are surpass'd by doves.

Sparrow: Lesbia's pet sparrow in Catullus poems 2 and 3; also the title of a book of poems by Catullus

Ep. 1.42

When the sad tale, how Brutus fell,* was brought,
And slaves refused the weapon Portia sought;
'Know ye not yet,' she said, with towering pride,
'Death is a boon that cannot be denied?
I thought my father* amply had imprest
This simple truth upon each Roman breast.'
Dauntless she gulp'd the embers as they flamed,
And, while the heat within her raged, exclaim'd;
'Now, troublous guardians of a life abhorr'd,
Still urge your caution, and refuse the sword.'

Ep. 1.61 *To Licinius*

Verona loves her learned poet's* strains;
    His Mantua Maro's lofty numbers bless.
From Livy's birth its rank Aponus gains;
    From Stella scarce, nor epic Flaccus less.

Apollodorus sound the waves of Nile;
    Loud the Peligni ring with Ovid's fame.
Corduba tells in high but simple style
    Two Senecas, and Lucan's unmatch'd name.

With Canius gladdens Cadiz, prone to glee;
    Emerita doth Decianus own,
Kind Decianus, ever dear to me;

Brutus fell: he committed suicide at Philippi in 42 BCE, defeated by Mark Antony and Octavian
father: Cato, the Stoic, who committed suicide after his own defeat at the hands of Julius Caesar in 46 BCE
learned poet: Catullus

And ever, Bilbilis, our native town
    Shall thee, Licinius, proudly boast;
    Nor let my name be wholly lost.

Ep. 1.88

Dear boy, whom, torn in early youth away,
The light turf covers in Labicum's way,
Receive no tomb hewn from the Parian cave
By useless toil to moulder o'er the grave;
But box and shady palms shall flourish here,
And softest herbage green with many a tear.

Dear boy, these records of my grief receive,
These simple honours that will bloom and live;
And be, when Fate has spun my latest line,
My ashes honour'd, as I honour thine!

Ep. 2.80

Brave Fannius slew himself from foes to fly.
What madness this, for fear of death to die!

Ep. 3.12

Faith! your essence was excelling;
    But you gave us nought to eat:
Nothing tasting, sweetly smelling
    Is, Fabullus, scarce a treat.

Let me see a fowl unjointed,
    When your table next is spread:
Who not feeds, but is anointed,
    Lives like nothing but the dead.

Ep. 4.14 *To Silius Italicus, the Poet*

> Oh thou, whose strains in loftiest style
> (Oh, Silius, glory of the Nine!)*
>> Tell barbarous warfare's varied wile,
> Hannibal's ever new design;
>>> And paint the Scipios in the field,
>>> Where Carthage false was forced to yield,
>
>> Awhile your grandeur put away.
> December now, with rattling dice
>> Cast from the doubtful box, is gay;
> And Popa plied his false device.
>>> 'Tis now an easy festive time
>>> That well befits my careless rhyme.
>
>> Then smooth your frowns: with placid brow
> Read, pr'ythee, these my trifling lays,
>> My lays where wanton jests o'erflow;
> For thus, perchance, his sparrow's praise
>>> Catullus, whom sweet strains attend,
>>> To mighty Maro dared to send.

Ep. 5.73 *To Theodorus*

> I give thee, friend, no works of mine,
> For fear you should return me thine.

Nine: the Muses

Ep. 6.34

Come kiss me, love, with rapture's fiercest fire.
Ask me how many kisses I desire?
You bid me sum the waves of Ocean's roar,
The shells dispersed upon th' Egean shore,
The bees that wander on Cecropia's hill,*
The rapturous shouts with which the people fill
The crowded theatre, and rend the air,
When they unwarn'd behold their Cæsar there.

'Twould not content me from your lips to gain
The kisses* claim'd by sweet Catullus' strain,
That Lesbia yielding gave, his lyre's fond due:
He who can tell the number wants but few.

Ep. 8.40 *To Priapus*

Priapus, thou the placed defence
     Of no fair garden or rich vine;
But of this thin plantation, whence
     Thou'rt sprung, and may'st prolong thy line.

I warn thee from all theft protect
     And save this strong and growing brood
To serve my hearth. Should'st thou neglect,
     I'll make thee know thyself art wood.

Cecropia's hill: Hymettus, a mountain in Attica south-east of Athens, famous
for its bees and honey
kisses: see note on p. 155

Ep. 8.73 *To Instantius*

Instantius, dearest friend, than whose no heart
    Can truth's or honour's voice more warmly move,
If thou wouldst fire to my cold muse impart,
    And wish immortal verses – give me love.

Cynthia, Propertius, lit thy tuneful flame;
    Thy genius, Gallus, was Lycoris' praise;
Fair Nemesis gave flowing Albius fame,
    And Lesbia, learn'd Catullus, taught thy lays.

Not the Peligni, graced by Ovid's flow,
    Nor Mantua's self my strains shall dare despise;
If some Corinna will her love bestow,
    Some Galatea my caresses prize.

Xen. 77 *Swans*

And how to swans, their truth's reward, belong
A joyful death, and sweet expiring song.

Apoph. 77 *Address to an Ivory Bird-Cage*

E'en such a bird, so fond and gay,
    As Lesbia loved so well,
As mourn'd in sweet Catullus' lay,*
    In thee might happy dwell.

Catullus' lay: poem 3 in modern editions of Catullus

Apoph. 195 *On Catullus*

Much as great Mantua to her Virgil's flow,
Doth small Verona to her Catullus owe.

GEORGE GORDON, LORD BYRON (1788–1824)

One of the major poetic figures and prime satirist of the English Romantic movement. Educated at Aberdeen Grammar School, Harrow, and Trinity College, Cambridge, English peer, indefatigable traveller, sexual libertarian, champion of liberal causes, especially the freedom of Greece, he was one of the most widely read as well as prolific poets of his day. His works include *English Bards and Scotch Reviewers* (1809), *The Bride of Abydos* (1813), *The Corsair* (1814), *Manfred* (1817) and *The Vision of Judgment* (1822). His *Childe Harold's Pilgrimage* (1812–18) and *Don Juan* (1819–24), although attacked by some contemporary critics, were immensely popular and remain classics of English Romanticism. After separation from his wife he left England in 1816 never to return. His death (of fever) in Greece, assisting armed insurrection against the Turks with his own 'Byron Brigade', was mourned throughout that country, but his body was refused interment at both Westminster and St Paul's. Most of his translations of classical poets belong to his early period, his most extensive imitation being *Hints from Horace* (1811), based on the *Ars Poetica*. Although Byron 'translated' less than a dozen epigrams (most unpublished in his lifetime), he seems to have been deeply influenced by Martial in the formation of his own satiric stanzas, most particularly in *Don Juan*, which contains a brilliantly Martialesque description of Juan's classical education (including his protection from Martial's 'grosser parts') and a witty variation on *Ep.*

10.46. The *Don Juan*, Canto 1, stanzas signal both the prevalent contemporary attitude to Martial and Byron's contemptuous rejection of it.

From 'Poetical Works 1812' and 'Poetical Works 1822', *Lord Byron: The Complete Poetical Works* (1980–93); and *Don Juan* (1819–24).

Ep. 1.1

He unto whom thou art so partial,
Oh, reader! is the well-known Martial,
The Epigrammatist: while living,
Give him the fame thou wouldst be giving;
So shall he hear, and feel, and know it:
Post-obits rarely reach a poet.

Ep. 2.55

To love you well you bid me know you better,
And for that wish I rest your humble debtor;
But, if the simple truth I may express,
To love you better, I must know you less.

Ep. 2.88

You don't recite, but would be deemed a poet;
You shall be Homer – so you do not show it.

Ep. 3.26

Dear friend, thou hast a deal of cash,
And wherewithal to cut a dash –
Of every kind in food and raiment,
Cooks, taylors praise thy punctual payment –
Thy wealth, thy wine, thy house thine own,
With none partaken, thine alone. –
Thy very heart and soul and wit
No partnership with man admit. –
All – all is thine – and were for life,
But that the Public share thy wife.

Ep. 6.34

Give me thy kisses – ask me not to count
The sweet but never to be summed amount;
Or rather bid me number unto thee
Shells on the shore, or billows on the sea,
Or bees that wander with the busy wing
And hum in gladness through their wealthy spring;
Or every voice or clapping hand that hails
The face of every sovereign – but of Wales.
Even then the reckoning would be scarce begun –
But he who counts his kisses, merits none.

Ep. 6.53

Jack supped – and drank – and went to bed,
Morn breaks – and finds the sleeper dead.
What caused this healthy man's perdition?
Alas! he *dreamt* of his *Physician*.

Ep. 6.60

I print sometimes – to judge of praise or blame –
Sam's face is my thermometer of fame. –
If he looks gay, the critic's was most fearful;
If sad, my publisher is wondrous cheerful.

After Ep. 10.46 Don Juan, Canto 15.21

'Omnia vult *belle* Matho dicere – dic aliquando
    Et *bene*, dic *neutrum*, dic aliquando *male*.'*
The first is rather more than mortal can do;
    The second may be sadly done or gaily;
The third is still more difficult to stand to;
    The fourth we hear, and see, and say too, daily:
The whole together is what I could wish
To serve in this conundrum of a dish.

Ep. 11.92

Who calls thee vicious, Jack, is rather nice;
Thou art no vicious mortal – but a Vice.

Ep. 11.93

Fitzgerald's house hath been on fire – the Nine
All smiling saw that pleasant bonfire shine.
Yet – cruel Gods! Oh! ill-contrived disaster!
The house is burnt – the house – without the Master!

'*Omnia . . . male*': these two lines comprise Martial, *Ep.* 10.46

Ep. 12.12

You drink all night, and promise fairly;
But getting sober somewhat early,
Your promise is not worth a d——n:
For God's sake take a Morning dram!

Don Juan, Canto 1.39—45

But that which Donna Inez most desired,
  And saw into herself each day before all
The learned tutors whom for him she hired,
  Was, that his breeding should be strictly moral;
Much into all his studies she inquired,
  And so they were submitted first to her, all,
Arts, sciences, no branch was made a mystery
To Juan's eyes, excepting natural history.

The languages, especially the dead,
  The sciences, and most of all the abstruse,
The arts, at least all such as could be said
  To be the most remote from common use,
In all these he was much and deeply read;
  But not a page of anything that's loose,
Or hints continuation of the species,
Was ever suffer'd, lest he should grow vicious.

His classic studies made a little puzzle,
  Because of filthy loves of gods and goddesses,
Who in the earlier ages made a bustle,
  But never put on pantaloons or boddices;

His reverend tutors had at times a tussle,
    And for their Aeneids, Iliads, and Odysseys,
Were forced to make an odd sort of apology,
For Donna Inez dreaded the mythology.

Ovid's a rake, as half his verses show him,
    Anacreon's morals are a still worse sample,
Catullus scarcely has a decent poem,
    I don't think Sappho's Ode a good example,
Although Longinus tells us there is no hymn
    Where the sublime soars forth on wings more ample;
But Virgil's songs are pure, except that horrid one*
Beginning with 'Formosum Pastor Corydon.'

Lucretius' irreligion is too strong
    For early stomachs, to prove wholesome food;
I can't help thinking Juvenal was wrong,
    Although no doubt his real intent was good,
For speaking out so plainly in his song,
    So much indeed as to be downright rude;
And then what proper person can be partial
To all those nauseous epigrams of Martial?

Juan was taught from out the best edition,*
    Expurgated by learned men, who place,
Judiciously, from out the schoolboy's vision,
    The grosser parts; but fearful to deface
Too much their modest bard by this omission,
    And pitying sore his mutilated case,
They only add them all in an appendix,
Which saves, in fact, the trouble of an index;

---

horrid one: Eclogue 2
best edition: Vincent Collesso's Delphin edition (1680), which segregated the
obscene poems into an Appendix

For there we have them all at one fell swoop,
      Instead of being scatter'd through the pages;
They stand forth marshall'd in a handsome troop,
      To meet the ingenuous youth of future ages,
Till some less rigid editor shall stoop
      To call them back into their separate cages,
Instead of standing staring all together,
Like garden gods – and not so decent either.

LEIGH HUNT (1784–1859)

Poet, essayist, dramatist, literary editor and journalist. Born of poor parents, he was educated as a charity boy at Christ's Hospital and became one of the most influential literary catalysts of the nineteenth century. Between 1808 and 1834 he founded and/or edited such literary journals as *The Examiner, Reflector, Indicator, Liberal, Companion, Tatler* and *London Journal*, through which he introduced to the world the poetry of Keats, Shelley and Byron's *The Vision of Judgment*. *The Examiner*, which he founded with his brother and edited from 1808 to 1821, was renowned for its liberal views, and in 1811 Hunt himself was imprisoned together with his brother for publishing an anti-royalist piece. His friends and protégés comprised the main literary and intellectual luminaries of the Romantic and early Victorian periods, including Charles Lamb, Thomas Moore, Bentham, Mill, Hazlitt, Carlyle and Tennyson. His most famous poems, 'Abou Ben Adhem' and 'Jenny Kissed Me', have been frequently anthologized; he was the model for the early Skimpole of Dickens's *Bleak House*. The following was included in the final collection of his poems (1860), revised by himself.

From *The Poetical Works of Leigh Hunt* . . . (1860).

Ep. 10.61 *Epitaph on Erotion*

Underneath this greedy stone
Lies little sweet Erotion;
Whom the Fates, with hearts as cold,
Nipp'd away at six years old.
Thou, whoever thou may'st be,
That hast this small field after me,
Let the yearly rites be paid
To her little slender shade;
So shall no disease or jar
Hurt thy house, or chill thy Lar;
But this tomb here be alone,
The only melancholy stone.

GEORGE AUGUSTUS SALA
(1828–96)

Victorian journalist, illustrator, novelist, travel-writer and wit. He
was an editor of *Chat* and contributed in the 1850s to *Household
Words*, a weekly literary periodical begun by Dickens. His books
included *A Journey Due North* (1858), on Russia, and *A Diary in the
Midst of War* (1865), a construct of his work as a newspaper corres-
pondent during the American Civil War. He and some Oxford
friends, such as Captain Edward Sellon (d. 1886), were responsible
for the anonymous *Index Expurgatorius of Martial, Literally Translated,
Comprising All the Epigrams hitherto Omitted by English Translators*,
printed privately in 150 copies (London, 1868). Prose translations
with abundant, often fanciful, notes explaining sexual matters, were
accompanied by original metrical versions in a bouncy Swinburn-
esque style. An address to the reader defends the translation on the

grounds that 'the abnormal vices of a highly civilized though extra-ordinarily demoralized society form an essential and important study for the historian, moralist or legislator . . . and facilitates our compre-hension of the last act of the drama of imperial despotism'. Despite this self-professedly pious claim (undermined by the wit and verbal pleasure evidenced by the translators), the book was a bold riposte to the censorious ideology of the times. Even in 1994 it remained under lock and key in the Oxford Bodleian library, bearing the restricted Phi classification and available for perusal only with difficulty, as one of the present book's editors discovered.

From *The Index Expurgatorius of Martial* (1868).

Ep. 1.92 *To Mamurianus*

Cestos, with tearful eyes, while with me lingering,
Often complains of your indecent fingering;
              Mamurianus!

You need not only use your finger, really
Appropriate the youth you love so dearly,
If your abode is wanting Cestos merely;
              Mamurianus!

But if your chilly hearth's forgot to glow;
If your vile bedstead ne'er a leg can show;
If you can boast a vessel no more pure
Than some poxed harlot's cracked and cast-off ewer;
If a worn greasy cloak entraps your heels;
If a starved jacket half your arse reveals;
– You drink with curs foul water on your knees;
– The distant kitchen's smell your guts appease;
My finger up your arsehole I'd not pass.
An arse that wants no paper's not an arse;
              Mamurianus!

Call me not harsh or envious; but your eye
's The only hole my finger cares to try.
I'd gouge the orb from out its socket's snuggery;
First fill your belly, then you go to buggery;
                  Mamurianus!

Ep. 2.45 To Glyptus

What, Glyptus! cut your cock off! Where's the good?
     Save 'twas too short to hand, it never stood.
Without the knife, you'd be a sexless Priest;
     You never could have woman, man, or beast.

Ep. 2.70 To Cotilus

Friend Cotilus, why can't you wash in
The hip bath that your comrades splash in?
Is 't 'cause you'll not your lather mix
With creamy streaks from fetid pricks?
If so, next time you take your tub,
Your lower parts you first must scrub.
To give your face the first ablution
Would taint the water with far worse pollution.

Ep. 4.48 To Papilus

What! want to be buggered, and cry when it's done!
     Here clear contradictions seem blended!
Do you grieve that the sodding was ever begun,
     Or lament that the pleasure is ended?

Ep. 7.67 *To Philaenis, a Tribade*

Abhorrent of all natural joys,
Philaenis sodomises boys,
And like a spouse whose wife's away
She drains of spend twelve cunts a day.
With dress tucked up above her knees
She hurls the heavy ball with ease,
And, smeared all o'er with oil and sand,
She wields a dumb bell in each hand,
And when she quits the dirty floor,
Still rank with grease, the jaded whore
Submits to the schoolmaster's whip
For each small fault, each trifling slip:
Nor will she sit her down to dine
Till she has spewed two quarts of wine:
And when she's eaten pounds of steak
A gallon more her thirst will slake.
After all this, when fired by lust,
For pricks alone she feels disgust,
These cannot e'en her lips entice,
Forsooth it is a woman's vice!
But girls she'll gamahuche for hours,
Their juicy quims she quite devours.
Oh, you that think your sex to cloak
By kissing what you cannot poke,
May God grant that you, Philaenis,
Will yet learn to suck a penis.

Ep. 7.75 *To a Deformed Old Woman*

Tho' deformed, old, and ugly as sin,
     For gratuitous fucking you tout,
'Tis absurd, you request a put-in,
     And refuse in return to fork out.

Ep. 9.27 To Chrestus

Chrestus, though not two hairs your scrotum deck,
Though your prick's softer than the vulture's neck,
Though your mild face, effeminate smooth and plump,
Rivals the Pathic's prostituted rump,
And girlish in your hairless thighs and hips,
Art hides all trace of manhood on your lips;
You talk of deeds the great, and good, and bold
Have done, with stern pomposity, and hold
Forth on the vices that corrupt the age;
But while this virtuous war on vice you wage,
If some bright lad, who's just outgrown his school,
While thoughts of freedom swell his youthful tool,
Come up, you lead aside the sprightly boy,
And when replete of what you most enjoy,
Your Cato's tongue would never dare confess t' us,
How very much you had behaved like Chrestus.

Ep. 9.41 To Ponticus

While you never indulge in a woman's embrace,
     But rely on your whorish left hand,
And call yourself chaste, yourself you debase
     By a crime men can scarce understand.
Horatius once fucked the delight of his home,
     And three noble offspring she bore;
And Mars lay but once with the mother of Rome,
     And made one and one into four.
But if either of their fingers in lust had imbrued,
     Nor with these good ladies had lain,
Those happy results would have never accrued;
     So listen while now I explain,

What your fingers are recklessly throwing away
    Without stint or the least hesitation,
Is God's divine image, repeated in clay,
    Is Man, our Lord's noblest creation!

Ep. 9.67 To Aeschylus

Last night the soft charms of an exquisite whore
    Fulfilled every whim of my mind,
Till, with fucking grown weary, I begged something more,
    One bliss that still lingered behind.
My prayer was accepted; the rose in the rear
    Was opened to me in a minute;
One rose still remained, which I asked of my dear, –
    'Twas her mouth and the tongue that lay in it.
She promised at once, what I asked her to do;
    Yet her lips were unsullied by me,
They'll not, my old friend, remain virgins for you,
    Whose penchant exceeds e'en her fee.

Ep. 9.69 To Polycharmus

When you lie with a woman, at least so girls say,
    You shit the same moment you come.
But what do you do, Polycharmus, I pray,
    When a lover's stiff prick stops your bum?

Ep. 11.21 To Lydia

The roomy Lydia's private parts surpass
The lusty dray horse's elephantine arse;
Wide as the school boy's ringing iron hoop;
Vast as the ring the agile riders stoop

And leap through neatly, touching not the side,
As round and round the dusty course they ride;
Capacious as some old and well worn shoe,
That's trudged the muddy streets since first 'twas new;
Stretched like the net the crafty fowler holds;
And drapery as a curtain's heavy folds;
Loose as the bracelet, gemmed with green and scarlet,
That mocks the arm of some consumptive harlot;
Slack as a feather bed without the feathers;
And baggy as some ostler's well used leathers;
Relaxed and hanging like the skinny coat
That shields the vulture's foul and flabby throat.
'Tis said, while bathing once we trod love's path,
I know not, but I seemed to fuck the bath.

Ep. 11.25 *To Linus*

Linus' prick of rare renown,
Well known to every girl in town,
Cannot be waxed to raise its head,
So Tongue beware you're not employed instead.

Ep. 11.43 *To His Wife*

My better half, why turn a peevish scold,
When round some tender boy my arms I fold,
And point me out that nature has designed
In you as well a little hole behind?
Has Juno ne'er said this to lustful Jove?
Yet graceful Ganymede absorbs his love.
The stout Tirynthian left his bow the while, as
The lusty hero drove his shaft in Hylas:
Yet think you Megara had not her bulls-eye?
And startled Daphne turning round to fly,

Her bottom lit a lust for virile joys
Phoebus needs quench in the Oebalian boy's:*
However much Briseis towards Achilles
Turned her white buttocks, fairer than twin lilies,
He found below the smooth Patroclus' waist
Enjoyment more congenial to his taste.
Then gibe no manly names to back or front,
A woman every where is only cunt.

Ep. 11.61 *On Manneius*

Oh husband that ne'er became father,
    Oh lover whose sweetheart's a maid,
Who would delve love's soft acreage rather
    With ought save its natural spade,
More foul than the cheeks of a harlot
    With the slime of stale kisses o'erhung,
Oh potent, yet impotent varlet,
    That's man but in tongue.
At whose coming the vilest whores hasten
    To shut and to bar up their den,
From lips that care only to fasten
    On what's shameful of women and men:
E'en the o'erburdened womb's gaping threshold
    By him is lasciviously sipped,
And he'll guess, as he sucks the soft flesh fold,
    If a boy or a girl's to be slipped.
Oh tongue that was meant for a penis,
    Oh head that was meant for a tail,
No more shall ye riot, and Venus
    No more at your riots grow pale,

Oebalian boy: Hyacinthus

> To thighs ye shall be no more mated,
>   No more shall soft cunnies be rung
> With agonies not to be sated
>   By merely a tongue!
> For while this most lustful of mortals
>   His slavering member had glued
> To a vivified womb's hanging portals,
>   This terrible vengeance ensued:
> The gods the closed fountain releasing
>   Of the woman, there rolled down a flood,
> Ropy and clotted, unceasing,
>   Of menstrual blood,
> And he rose amid gasping and choking,
>   And from his mouth hung
> No longer a potent and poking
>   But paralysed tongue.

ROBERT LOUIS
STEVENSON (1850–94)

Eminent Scottish literary figure of the Victorian era. He studied law at the University of Edinburgh (being admitted advocate in 1875) before becoming an extremely popular novelist of adventure and a widely read travel-writer, essayist and poet. His works include *An Inland Voyage* (1878), *Treasure Island* (1883), *The Strange Case of Dr Jekyll and Mr Hyde* (1886), *Kidnapped* (1886), *The Wrong Box* (1889), and the poetry collections *A Child's Garden of Verses* (1885) and *Underwoods* (1887). He was a regular contributor to such journals as *The Cornhill Magazine* and *Longman's Magazine*. He spent his last years in Samoa because of his health. His ventures into translating Martial needed some help from French translations and were careful to avoid some of the more shocking aspects of the epigrams, but his published appreciation of the poet (in *The British Weekly*, 1887 – see above, pp. xxxivf.) was remarkable, given the period and the contempt in which the Roman poet was then held. The following translations cannot be dated with certainty, but may have been written at Hyères in 1883–4. They were first published in *BBS* II (1916) or *BBS* III (1921).

From *Boston Bibliophile Society* II (1916) and III (1921).

Ep. 2.53 *In Maximum*

Wouldst thou be free? I think it not, indeed
But if thou wouldst, attend this simple rede:
When quite contented thou canst dine at home
And drink a small wine of the march of Rome;
When thou canst see unmoved thy neighbour's plate,
And wear my threadbare toga in the gate;
When thou hast learned to love a small abode,
And not to choose a mistress *à la mode*;
When thus contained and bridled thou shalt be,
Then, Maximus, then first shalt thou be free.

Ep. 2.59 *De Cænatione Micæ*

Look round: You see a little supper room;
But from my window, lo! great Cæsar's tomb!
And the great dead themselves, with jovial breath,
Bid you be merry and remember death.

Ep. 2.68 *Ad Olum*

Call me not rebel, though in what I sing
If I no longer hail thee Lord and King,
I have redeemed myself with all I had,
And now possess my fortunes poor but glad.

With all I had I have redeemed myself,
And escaped at once from slavery and pelf.
The unruly wishes must a ruler take,
Our high desires do our low fortunes make:
Those only who desire palatial things
Do bear the fetters and the frowns of Kings;
Set free thy slave; thou settest free thyself.

Ep. 2.90 *Ad Quintilianum*

O chief director of the growing race,
Of Rome the glory and of Rome the grace,
Me, O Quintilian, may you not forgive
Though, far from labour, I make haste to live?
Some burn to gather wealth, lay hands on rule,
Or with white statues fill the atrium full.
The talking hearth, the rafters swart with smoke,
Live fountains and rough grass, my love invokes:
A sturdy slave: a not too learned wife:
Nights filled with slumber, and a quiet life.

Ep. 4.30 *Ad Piscatorem*

For these are sacred fishes all
Who know that lord who is lord of all;
Come to the brim and nose the friendly hand
That sways and can beshadow all the land.
Nor only so, but have their names, and come
When they are summoned by the Lord of Rome.
Here once his line an impious Libyan threw;
And as with tremulous reed his prey he drew,
Straight, the light failed him.
He groped, nor found the prey that he had ta'en.

Now as a warning to the fisher clan
Beside the lake he sits, a beggarman.
Thou, then, while still thine innocence is pure,
Flee swiftly, nor presume to set thy lure;
Respect these fishes, for their friends are great
And in the waters empty all thy bait.

Ep. 4.64 De Hortis Julii Martialis

My Martial owns a garden, famed to please,
Beyond the glades of the Hesperides;
Along Janiculum lies the chosen block
Where the cool grottos trench the hanging rock.
The moderate summit, something plain and bare,
Tastes overhead of a serener air;
And while the clouds besiege the vales below,
Keeps the clear heaven and doth with sunshine glow.
To the June stars that circle in the skies
The dainty roofs of that tall villa rise.
Hence do the seven imperial hills appear;
And you may view the whole of Rome from here:
Beyond, the Alban and the Tuscan hills;
And the cool groves and the cool falling rills.
Rubre Fidenæ, and with virgin blood
Anointed once Perenna's orchard wood.
Thence the Flaminian, the Salarian way,
Stretch far abroad below the dome of day;
And lo! the traveller toiling toward his home;
And all unheard, the chariot speeds to Rome!
For here no whisper of the wheels; and tho'
The Mulvian Bridge, above the Tiber's flow,
Hangs all in sight, and down the sacred stream
The sliding barges vanish like a dream,
The seaman's shrilling pipe not enters here,
Nor the rude cries of porters on the pier.

And if so rare the house, how rarer far
The welcome and the weal that therein are!
So free the access, the doors so widely thrown
You half imagine all to be your own.

Ep. 5.20 *Ad Martialem*

God knows, my Martial, if we two could be
To enjoy our days set wholly free;
To the true life together bend our mind,
And take a furlough from the falser kind,
No rich saloon, nor palace of the great,
Nor suit at law should trouble our estate;
On no vainglorious statues should we look,
But of a walk, a talk, a little book,
Baths, wells, and meads and the verandah shade,
Let all our travels and our toils be made.
Now neither lives unto himself, alas!
And the good suns we see, that flash and pass
And perish; and the bell that knells them cries,
'Another gone: O when will ye arise?'

Ep. 5.34 *Epitaphium Erotii*

Mother and sire, to you do I commend
Tiny Erotion, who must now descend,
A child, among the shadows, and appear
Before hell's bandog and hell's gondolier.
Of six hoar winters she had felt the cold,
But lacked six days of being six years old.
Now she must come, all playful, to that place
Where the great ancients sit with reverend face;
Now lisping, as she used, of whence she came,
Perchance she names and stumbles at my name.

O'er these so fragile bones, let there be laid
A plaything for a turf; and for that maid
That swam light-footed as the thistle-burr
On thee. O Mother earth, be light on her.

Ep. 5.37 *De Erotio Puella*

This girl was sweeter than the song of swans,
And daintier than the lamb upon the lawns
Or Lucrine oyster. She, the flower of girls,
Outshone the light of Erythræan pearls;
The teeth of India that with polish glow,
The untouched lilies or the morning snow.
Her tresses did gold-dust outshine
And fair hair of women of the Rhine.
Compared to her the peacock seemed not fair,
The squirrel lively, or the phoenix rare;
Her on whose pyre the smoke still hovering waits,
Her whom the greedy and unequal fates
On the sixth dawning of her natal day
My child-love and my playmate – snatcht away.

Ep. 6.16 *An Imitation, Pudoris Causa*

Lo, in thy green enclosure here,
Let not the ugly or the old appear,
Divine Priapus; but with leaping tread
The schoolboy, and the golden head
Of the slim filly twelve years old –
Let these to enter and to steal be bold!

Ep. 6.27 *Ad Nepotem*

O Nepos, twice my neighbour (since at home
We're door by door by Flora's temple dome,
And in the country, still conjoined by fate,
Behold our villas, standing gate by gate!)
Thou hast a daughter, dearer far than life,
Thy image and the image of thy wife;
But why for her neglect the flowing can
And lose the prime of thy Falernian?
Hoard casks of money, if to hoard be thine;
But let the daughter drink a younger wine!
Let her go rich and wise, in silk and fur;
Lay down a bin that shall grow old with her;
But thou, meantime, the while the batch is sound,
With pleased companions pass the bowl around:
Nor let the childless only taste delights,
For Fathers also may enjoy their nights.

Ep. IO.23 *De M. Antonio*

Now Antonius, in a smiling age,
Courts of his life the fifteenth finished stage.
The rounded days and the safe years he sees
Nor fears death's water mounting round his knees,
To him remembering not one day is sad,
Not one but that its memory makes him glad.
So good men lengthen life; and to recall
The past, is to have twice enjoyed it all.

Ep. 10.61 *Epitaphium Erotii*

Here lies Erotion, whom at six years old
Fate pilfered. Stranger (when I too am cold
Who shall succeed me in my rural field),
To this small spirit annual honours yield.
Bright be thy hearth, hale be thy babes, I crave,
And this, in thy green farm, the only grave.

Ep. 11.18 *In Lupum*

Beyond the gates, you gave a farm to till:
I have a larger on my window-sill!
A farm, d'ye say? Is this a farm to you? —
Where for all woods I spy one tuft of rue,
And that so rusty, and so small a thing,
One shrill cicada hides it with a wing;
Where one cucumber covers all the plain;
And where one serpent rings himself in vain
To enter wholly; and a single snail
Eats all, and exit fasting — to the jail.
Here shall I wait in vain till figs be set,
Or till the spring disclose the violet.
Through all my wilds a tameless mouse careers,
And in that narrow boundary appears,
Huge as the stalking lion of Algiers,
Huge as the fabled boar of Calydon.
And all my hay is at one swoop impresst
By one low-flying swallow for her nest.
Strip god Priapus of each attribute
Here finds he scarce a pedestal to foot.
The gathered harvest scarcely brims a spoon;
And all my vintage drips in a cocoon.
Generous are you, but I more generous still:
Take back your farm and hand me half a gill!

Ep. 11.39 *In Charidemum*

You, Charidemus, who my cradle swung
And watched me all the days that I was young –
You, at whose steps the laziest slaves awake
And both the bailiff and the butler quake –
The barber's suds now blacken with my beard
And my rough kisses make the maids afeard:
Still, in your eyes, before your judgement seat,
I am the baby that you used to beat.
You must do all things, unreproved; but I
If once to play or to my love I fly,
Big with reproach, I see your eyebrows twitch,
And for the accustomed cane your fingers itch.
If something daintily attired I go,
Straight you exclaim: 'Your father did not so!'
And, frowning, count the bottles on the board,
As though my cellar were your private hoard.
Enough, at last! I have borne all I can,
And your own mistress hails me for a man.

Ep. 12.61 *De Ligurra*

You fear, Ligurra – above all, you long –
That I should smite you with a singing song,
This dreadful honour you both fear and hope:
Both quite in vain: you fall below my scope.
The Libyan lion tears the roaring bull,
He does not harm the midge along the pool.
But if so close this stands in your regard,
From some blind tap fish forth a drunken bard,
Who shall, with charcoal, on the privy wall,
Immortalize your name for one and all.

GOLDWIN SMITH (1823–1910)

Historian and influential literary and political figure, educated at Eton and Christ Church, Oxford, where he was Regius Professor of Modern History, 1858–66. He left Oxford for the USA where he became the first professor of English and constitutional history at Cornell University in New York State, from where he moved to Toronto, Canada, in 1871. He was a prominent religious sceptic and liberal activist, opposed to British imperialism, a supporter of the North in the American Civil War and an advocate of Canadian independence. His works include *The Empire* (1863), political histories of the United States (1893) and the United Kingdom (1899), books on Cowper (1880) and Jane Austen (1892), and his translations, *Bay of Leaves: Translations from the Latin Poets* (1893), which contains versions of Lucretius, Catullus, Tibullus, Propertius, Ovid, Horace, Seneca, Lucan and Claudian, as well as of twenty-one epigrams of Martial. His approach to the Bilbilis poet is adequately articulated in his description of Martial as 'the mirror of the social habits of Imperial Rome, amidst whose heaps of rubbish and ordure are some better things and some pleasant pictures of Roman character and life' (*Bay of Leaves*, p. vii). These 'better things' and 'pleasant pictures' include nothing sexual, political or harshly satirical, but poems on death, friendship, marriage, country life, art and the like, sentimentalized to accord with Smith's late-nineteenth-century taste. What merits comment too is that, despite the increasing historicization of the classical world, especially the ancient Greek world, Smith can still write (p. v): 'The translator of Latin poetry has the comfort of knowing that he is separated from his authors by no chasm of thought and sentiment . . . The men are intellectually almost his contemporaries.' With Smith's assimilation of *Ep.* 3.58 compare that of Jonson above ('To Penshurst', pp. 43ff.).

From *Bay of Leaves* (1893).

Ep. 1.13 *On the Death of Arria and Pætus*

The poniard, with her life-blood dyed,
    When Arria to her Pætus gave,
''Twere painless, my beloved,' she cried,
    'If but my death thy life could save.'

Ep. 1.93 *On Two Old Roman Officers Buried Side by Side*

Aquinus here by his Fabricius lies,
Glad that he first was summoned to the skies:
The equal honours of each martial chief
Their tombs set forth. This record is more brief –
Comrades they were in virtue to the end,
And each, rare glory! earned the name of friend.

Ep. 3.21

When, scarred with cruel brand, the slave
    Snatched from the murderer's hand
His proscript lord, not life he gave
    His tyrant, but the brand.

Ep. 3.35 *On a Work of Art*

These fishes Phidias wrought: with life by him
They are endowed; add water and they swim.

Ep. 3.40 *On Another Work of Art*

That lizard on the goblet makes thee start.
Fear not; it lives only by Mentor's art.

Ep. 3.58

Faustinus is a man of taste;
Yet is his Baian seat no waste
Of useless myrtle, barren plane,
Clipped box, like many a grand domain
That covers miles with empty state:
But country unsophisticate.
In every corner grain is crammed,
Casks fragrant of old wine are jammed.
Here, at the turning of the year,
Vinedressers house the vintage sere.
Grim bulls in grassy valleys low
And the calf butts with hornless brow.
Poultry of every clime and sort
Ramble in dirt about the court,
The screaming geese, flamingoes red,
Peacocks with jewelled tail outspread,
Pied partridges, pheasants that come
From Colchian strand, dark magic's home,
And Afric's birds of many spots.
The cock amidst his harem struts
While on the tower aloft doves coo
And pigeons flap and turtles woo.
Pigs to the good wife's apron scurry,
Lambs to their milky mothers hurry.
The fire, well-heaped, burns bright and high,
Around it crowds the nursery.

No butler here from lack of toil
Grows sick, no trainer wastes his oil,
Lounging at ease; but forth they fare
The fish with quivering line to snare,
The crafty springe for birds to set,
Or catch the deer with circling net.
Pleased with the garden's easy work
The city hands take spade and fork;
The curly-headed striplings ask
The bailiff for a merry task
Without their pedagogue's command;
E'en the sleek eunuch bears a hand.
Then country callers, many a one,
Troop in, and empty-handed none;
This brings a honeycomb, that a pail
Of milk from green Sassinum's dale;
Capons or dormice plump another,
Or kid, reft from his shaggy mother.
Basket on arm, stout lasses come
With gifts from many a thrifty home.
Work over, each, a willing guest,
Is bidden to no niggard feast,
Where all may revel at their will,
And servants eat, like guests, their fill.
But thou, friend Bassus, close to town,
On trim starvation lookest down,
Seest laurels, laurels everywhere;
No need the thief from fruit to scare.
Town bread thy vinedresser must eat;
The town sends greens, eggs, cheese, and meat.
Such country is – my friend must own –
Not country, but town out of town.

Ep. 4.8 *The Occupation of a Roman Day*

Visits consume the first, the second hour;
When comes the third, hoarse pleaders show their power;
At four to business Rome herself betakes;
At six she goes to sleep, by seven she wakes;
By nine well breathed from exercise we rest,
And in the banquet hall the couch is pressed.
Now, when thy skill, greatest of cooks, has spread
The ambrosial feast, let Martial's rhymes be read,
With mighty hand while Cæsar holds the bowl,
When draughts of nectar have relaxed his soul.
Now trifles pass. My giddy Muse would fear
Jove to approach in morning mood severe.

Ep. 4.13 *On a Friend's Wedding*

My Pudens shall his Claudia wed this day.
Shed, torch of Hymen, shed thy brightest ray!
So costly nard and cinnamon combine,
So blends sweet honey with the luscious wine.
So clasps the tender vine her elm, so love
The lotus leaves the stream, myrtles the cove.
Fair Concord, dwell for ever by that bed;
Let Venus bless the pair so meetly wed;
May the wife love with love that grows not cold,
And never to her husband's eye seem old.

Ep. 10.47 *A Roman Gentleman's Idea of Happiness*

What makes a happy life, dear friend,
If thou would'st briefly learn, attend.
An income left, not earned by toil;
Some acres of a kindly soil;

The pot unfailing on the fire;
No lawsuits; seldom town attire;
Health; strength with grace; a peaceful mind;
Shrewdness with honesty combined;
Plain living; equal friends and free;
Evenings of temperate gaiety;
A wife discreet, yet blithe and bright;
Sound slumber that lends wings to night.
With all thy heart embrace thy lot,
Wish not for death and fear it not.

ANONYMOUS TRANSLATIONS OF THE NINETEENTH CENTURY

From the *Westminster Review, English Journal of Education* and the *Gentleman's Magazine*, collected in *The Epigrams of Martial*, ed. H. Bohn (London, 1860).

Ep. 1.10

Strephon most fierce besieges Cloe,
A nymph not over young nor showy.
What then can Strephon's love provoke? –
A charming paralytic stroke.

Ep. 1.109

Issa's more full of sport and wanton play
    Than that pet sparrow by Catullus sung;
Issa's more pure and cleanly in her way
    Than kisses from the amorous turtle's tongue.

Issa more winsome is than any girl
    That ever yet entranced a lover's sight;
Issa's more precious than the Indian pearl;
    Issa's my Publius' favourite and delight.
Her plaintive voice falls sad as one that weeps;
    Her master's cares and woes alike she shares;
Softly reclined upon his neck she sleeps,
    And scarce to sigh or draw her breath she dares.
When nature calls, she modestly obeys,
    Nor on the counterpane one drop will shed;
But warns her lord with gentle foot, and prays
    That he will raise and lift her from the bed.
So chaste is she, of contact so afraid,
    She knows not Venus' rites, nor do we find
A husband worthy of such dainty maid
    'Mong all the clamorous suitors of her kind.
Her, lest the day of fate should nothing leave,
    In pictured form my Publius hath portray'd;
Where you so lifelike Issa might perceive,
    That not herself a better likeness made.
Issa together with her portrait lay,
Both real or both depicted you would say.

Ep. 2.66

One single curl beyond its bounds had stray'd;
The wandering hair-pin one false loop had made.
This fault to Lalage her mirror shows;
Plecusa's head receives its stunning blows.
Cease, Lalage, to deck thy brows; forbear;
Cease, maidens, cease to dress that fury's hair.
Let scissors clip, or asps among it sit;
Then, then her face that mirror shall befit.

Ep. 4.21

That there's no God, John gravely swears,
And quotes, in proof, his own affairs;
For how should such an atheist thrive,
If there was any God alive?

Ep. 8.10

Gay Bassus for ten thousand bought
    A Tyrian robe of rich array,
And was a gainer. How? Be taught:
    The prudent Bassus did not pay.

Ep. 9.102

My bond for four hundred you proudly present;
One hundred, kind Phœbus, I'd rather you lent.
In the eyes of another such bounty may shine;
Whate'er I can't pay you, dear Phœbus, is mine.

Ep. 12.65

With me fair Phyllis pass'd the night
And strove to please with new delight:
As at the dawn I musing lay
How all her favours to repay,
In china ware, or tea, or snuff,
Or in some gaudy piece of stuff;
She clasp'd my neck and chuck'd my chin,
And softly begg'd a quart of gin.

AN ETON MASTER (fl. 1900)

Fifty Epigrams from the First Book of Martial was published anonymously (by 'an Eton Master') in London in 1900 in 'the belief that they may prove useful to teachers'. The primary purpose behind the volume was historical instruction: 'Martial is an excellent vehicle for information concerning Roman manners and customs under the Emperors of the first two centuries AD.'

From *Fifty Epigrams from the First Book of Martial* (1900).

Ep. 1.5

When I show you each night a great naval sham fight
    Will you plague me with epigrams, Mark?
What a fine sight you'd look, Messrs. Author and Book,
    If I chucked you both in for a lark.

Ep. 1.17

My friend Q.C. would have me be
    An active special pleader.
He thinks 'twould pay. Well, so it may
    To be a great horse breeder!

Ep. 1.30

Both as surgeon and sexton it must be confessed,
Old Sawyer's helped many a man to his rest.

Ep. 1.41

Old Boreham thinks himself a wit,
But there's a claim we can't admit.
What then? Some too familiar butler,
A sharp-tongued, Shoreditch, travelling cutler,
Who trades in knives and old umbrellas
With impecunious Cinderellas;
The kind of man who sells cheap sweets
To crowds of idlers in the streets;
Snake-charmer at suburban *fête*,
Or fishwife fresh from Billingsgate;
Itinerant pieman hoarse with crying
The tripe and onions no one's buying;
A third-rate ginshop poetaster,
Or foreign travelling circus master.
Cease then to fancy, Mr. B.,
What no one but yourself can see;
Namely, that you surpass Corelli,
And could improve upon 'Cleg Kelly'.
Some have no nose for wit's real spice;
But he who jokes at any price,
Whose tongue *will* wag, unless you lock it,
May be a crock – but not a Crockett.

Ep. 1.59

Since I have to live at Brighton to obtain my two bob daily,
I spend twice the sum you give me on my bed and breakfast
    gaily.
If you mean to let me starve in luxury, why need I tarry?
Give me back the gloomy baths frequented by Tom, Dick,
    and Harry.
Baths are scarcely worth the fancy price that suits a millionaire,
If I subsequently find myself compelled to sup on air.

Ep. 1.70

Go, book, and call on Proculus for me,
His house is rich: he bids you go and see.
You ask the way?* Keep Castor on your right,
Past Vesta's temple and unfading light,
Till from the Vestal's house on sacred ground
You skirt the Palatine. Here all around
Stand statues of our Master.* Here the rays
That crown a loftier head* than Rhodians praise
Will light you on your road, until you gain
By winding street the tipsy Wine-God's fane;
Near which the great Earth Mother's* painted dome
Displays her Phrygian Corybants to Rome.
Then to your left a lordly house will rise.
Approach – but not with timorous, downcast eyes.
Here you need fear no churlishness or pride:
These doors to all are open. Step inside.
Did Art and Intellect a palace build,
Scarce could that palace be more wisely filled.
And should one ask: 'Why is your lord not come?'
Give him this reason why he stays at home.
'E'en my poor verses could have ne'er been writ
Had duty-visits dulled my writer's wit.'

---

the way: Martial describes the journey of his book from his house on the
Quirinal across to that of his friend and patron Julius Proculus on the Palatine,
pointing out the various buildings en route; e.g. the temples of Castor and
Vesta in the Forum, the imperial palace and the temple of Cybele on the
Palatine
our Master: Domitian
loftier head: of Nero's Colossus
Earth Mother: Cybele

Ep. 1.78*

His cheeks all wasted by the cankering pest,
    His features tainted by the creeping ill,
Dry-eyed himself, soothing his friends' unrest,
    He spoke of death ordained by his own will.
No secret poison tainted his pure breath,
    No need for him to feel starvation's throes:
A Roman he, that faced a Roman's death,
    And brought life thus to a more fitting close;
Bolder than Cato thus to make an end:
    For Cato had not Caesar* for his friend.

Ep. 1.80

On your death-bed you sent in your bill, Moses Moss,
And you died of the fear of increasing a loss.

Ep. 1.100

'Papa! Mamma!' Miss Afra cries – what stupid affectation!
She's old enough to be the grandmamma of half the nation.

Ep. 1.78: An epigram on the death of Festus, a friend of Domitian.
Caesar: Julius Caesar was Cato's enemy; the present 'Caesar' is Festus' friend

A. E. STREET (1855–1938)

King's scholar of Eton, who later went on to Magdalen College, Oxford. After graduating, he became apprenticed to his architect-father, G. E. Street (of whom he was to write a memoir), and became an architect himself. In 1907 he published a translation of selected epigrams, designed to represent Martial as the 'kind, wise, and self-respecting gentleman' of Robert Louis Stevenson, and not as 'the unseemly jester'. He arranged his translations thematically: 'Epitaphs', 'On His Writings', 'On Country Life', 'On General Subjects'. Like much translation of the period, Street's versions are marred by a penchant for romantic diction and (by now) archaic 'poetic' conventions. Some of his attempts at the relatively down-to-earth epigrams are a little more successful.

From *Martial* (1907).

Ep. 1.116

To his dear dead hath Fænius sanctified
This grove, these acres fair of laboured plain.
Antulla filched by death this tomb doth hide,
Here shall her parents join their child again.
Then covet not this land for ever tied
In service to its lords, 'twould be in vain.

Ep. 4.24

All Vivien's lady-friends get tired of life;
Would I could introduce her to my wife.

Ep. 5.53

Medea and Thyestes dire
Ever and aye thy Muse inspire;
Why, Bassus? What are they to thee,
What Niobe and Andromache?

Floods that o'erwhelm, consuming fires,
Make aptest matter for thy quires;
Be wise, and try thy mettle on
Phaëthon or Deucalion.

Ep. 6.52

Pantagathus, a boy too young for death,
Snatched from his sorrowing master lies beneath.
Cunning he was with blade as light as air
To nip stray locks, and rob the chin of hair,
The earth for very shame must lightly lie
On him whose fingers fell so daintily.

Ep. 7.89

Go, happy rose, and softly garlanded
Wreathe our Apollinaris' curling head;
And when his curls are white – far be the hour! –
Still wreathe them, and be Love's e'er cherished flower.

Ep. 8.20

Varus writes facile verse and keeps it mum,
He's weakly garrulous, and wisely dumb.

Ep. 9.52 To Quintus Ovidius

Ovid, as your deserts are high,
Know that our natal mornings I
Keep with a like fidelity;
How blest the light
Of those twin days we mark with white!
Mine gave me life, but yours a friend,
And that's the gift I more commend.

Ep. 10.1

If brevity's the soul of wit,
And my tailpiece too far a cry,
You've got a certain remedy;
Read, or read not, as you think fit,
Full many a little piece I've writ;
If short you make me, short am I.

Ep. 10.47 To Julius Martialis

Martial, my best of friends, believe
Upon these terms 'tis good to live.
Wealth handed down, not bought by toil,
A genial hearth, a kindly soil;
Scant ceremonial, lawsuits none,
A mind at peace, a healthy tone
Of body, native strength withal,
Wise frankness, friends congenial,
Good company, a simple fare,
Of wine enough to banish care,

A bedfellow who's fondly shy,
Sound sleep to make the night go by,
Divine contentment with your lot,
Death, not desired, but dreaded not.

Ep. 10.50 *On Scorpus, a Celebrated Charioteer*

Break, Victory, your Idumæan palms for woe,
Strike, Favour, with fierce hand your bosom bare,
Honour, put on your weeds, and drooping Glory, throw
To the cruel flames the crown that twined your hair!
Woe, Scorpus, basely robbed of your first youth you die,
And, all too early, yoke black steed to steed!
Why were your wheels so quick to win the goal, and why
Life's goal attained with such untimely speed?

Ep. 10.59

You have no patience for the page-long skit,
Your taste is ruled by brevity, not wit.
Ransack the mart, make you a banquet rare,
You'll pick the titbit from the bill of fare;
I have no use for such a dainty guest;
Who ekes his dinner out with bread is best.

Ep. 11.1

Whither, my book, with heart so light,
All in your festal purple dight,
To see Parthenius? Even so;
Return unread then as you go!

Memorials are his only lore,
His very Muse he knows no more;
Will you accept it as your due
If meaner readers handsel you?

Seek then Quirinus' portico;*
Not Pompey's, nor Europa's, no,
Nor that of Jason,* fickle swain,
Doth a more idle crowd contain.

A few there may be who'll surprise
The bookworms in my drolleries,
When bets are done and every tale
Of steed and charioteer grown stale.

Ep. 12.51

What if Fabullinus gulp lies on lies?
Why, Aulus, goodness ne'er grows worldly-wise.

PAUL NIXON (1882–1956)

American classical scholar, educated at Wesleyan College and
Oxford, where he was the first Rhodes Scholar from Connecticut.
He taught at Bowdoin College, Maine, where he became Dean, and
was known widely for his translations of Plautus and Martial. He
also published an influential study, *Martial and the Modern Epigram*
(London, 1927). His selection of some two hundred of Martial's

---

Quirinus' portico: the temple of Quirinus was near Martial's house
Jason: the portico of the Argonauts, built by Agrippa in 26/25 BCE, was
decorated with Jason's exploits

epigrams in *A Roman Wit* focuses on those on which 'Martial's reputation as a wit' depends, avoiding those which are 'rankly offensive to the modern ear'.

From *A Roman Wit* (Boston and New York, 1911).

Ep. 2.21 *The Salutation of Postumus*

'My lips or hand? Kiss which you choose.
    It does n't matter.'
It does n't. Either way I lose.
    I'll try the latter.

Ep. 2.38 *To Linus*

You ask what I grow on my Sabine estate.
    A reliable answer is due.
        I grow on that soil –
        Far from urban turmoil –
    Very happy at not seeing you.

Ep. 4.24 *What Might Have Been*

I hear that Lycoris has buried
    Every friend that she's had in her life.
I sincerely regret, Fabianus,
    She's not introduced to my wife.

Ep. 5.43 *Darkness Visible*

The teeth of Thais look like jet;
    Læcania's are white.
The cause, you ask? The pallid set
    Go out at night.

Ep. 5.47 *In Society*

Philo swears he was never known
    To dine alone:
        He was n't.
Dine at all, when it comes about
    He's not asked out,
        He does n't.

Ep. 5.66 *To Pontilianus*

I always greet you but you never greet me
    When we meet at a house or a store.
        Since I get no reply
        Let me wish you good-bye
Till we meet – on that beautiful shore.

Ep. 6.30 *To Paetus*

If you'd actually made me that fifty pound loan
    At the time that you told me you'd make it,
I'd pay you back twice for the kindness you'd shown
    As a BENE.MERENTI.M.FECIT.

Ep. 8.60 *Divinely Tall*

With Nero's Colossus you'd easily compete,
Fair Claudia, – if shorter by barely two feet.

Ep. 12.12 *To Pollio*

When drunk at night you promise gifts
    Which don't appear next day.
        Instead of evening exhibitions,
            Give a matinée.

Ep. 12.70 *The Root of Evil*

When a bow-legged slave took his towels to the baths
    And a hag with one eye watched his clothes,
        And a ruptured slave rubbed
        Him with grease when he'd tubbed,
    Aper hated *bon ton* as mere pose.
As for liquor he thought it all beastly and vile,
    And exclaimed that if he had his way,
        He'd smash every stein,
        Spill Falernian wine –
    'Only foppish knights use it,' he'd say.
Since his uncle, however, has left him his heir,
    From the baths he's come drunk each P.M.
        Cups of gold richly chased
        And fair slaves change our taste.
    Aper poor never thirsted – *pro tem.*

W. J. COURTHOPE (1842–1917)

Son of a Sussex rector, educated at Harrow, and Corpus Christi and New College, Oxford, after which he served in the Education Department and Civil Service Commission. Author of the allegorical burlesque on women's rights, *Ludibria Lunae* (1869), *Paradise of Birds* (1870), a *History of English Literature* (1895–1910) and *The Country Town and other Poems* (1920). He also collaborated in editing Pope (1881–9) and was one of the founding editors (1893) of the conservative journal, *National Review*. He held the Poetry Professorship at Oxford from 1896 to 1901.

From *Selections from . . . Martialis* (London, 1914).

Ep. I.2 *To the Public*

If books you'd order without fail
As company for boat or rail,
Buy this, whose small octavo page
Reflects the spirit of our age.
More weighty volumes desks demand,
But this you'll manage, sit or stand,
To hold with ease in either hand.
Where you may buy it I'll next tell.
Mount from the Club-land of Pall Mall
To where St. James by roadway hilly
Conducts your feet to Piccadilly.
If with the publisher you'd parle,
Cross the street of Albemarle;
There (in an ancient house, whose fame
Is sung by bards of mighty name)
You'll find him at his work each day
In 50 or in 50A.

Ep. 4.64 *RVS IN VRBE: Julius Martialis at Home*

My Julius' bounded pleasances,
More rich in their abundant ease
Than gardens of th' Hesperides,
Rise o'er Janiculum's long hill
In deep recesses, wide and still:
With gentle slope the hill-top fair
Enjoys an always milder air,
And when the mists the valleys hide
Spreads its own sunshine far and wide.
The lofty roofs I fondly love
See only the clear stars above;
Hence one may look from Julius' home
On all Seven Hills, and value Rome,
Tusculum's height and Alba's glow,
And the cool spots that lie below,
Fidenae old and Rubrae small,
The apple-orchards that recall
Anna Perenna, and the wood
That revelled once in virgin's blood.
Who watches from that high abode
The Salt or the Flaminian Road,
With distant chariots, need not feel
The jarring of a noisy wheel,
Nor spoil his slumbers with the rout
Of bargemen or the boatswain's shout,
Though near the Milvian Bridge be spied,
And all that fares on Tiber's tide.
This Seat (or House, if so best known)
Its lord makes free; 'twill seem your own;
So open, frank, ungrudging, he,
In courteous hospitality,
You'd fancy Fate did here restore
Alcinoüs' house-gods, or the door

Of good Molorchus, poor no more.
You millionaires! who, having all,
Consider what you have too small,
Go! with a hundred mattocks till
Praeneste's plain or Tibur's hill;
Or swallow all the hanging charm
Of Setia in one monstrous farm!
How much do I prefer to these
My Julius' bounded pleasances!

Ep. 10.47

Julius, the things that make for ease
And happiness in life are these:
Lands left me, not acquired with toil;
Unfailing fuel; kindly soil;
No suits; light work; mind void of whims;
Good constitution; healthy limbs;
Frank thoughts; plain board; congenial friends;
Meals that, with Plenty, Mirth attends;
Nights with good cheer, not drinking, sped;
A glad, but not immodest bed;
Sound sleep that makes the darkness fly;
Content with life, if I be I,
Without the fear, or wish, to die.

Ep. 12.57

Why am I brought so oft, and by what charm,
To dry Nomentum and this humble farm?
For poor men, Sparsus, who would find a space
For sleep and thinking, Rome affords no place.
You claim to live; but all deny your right,
By morn schoolmasters, bakers' men by night;

Armies of copper-smiths, a thousand strong,
Go hammer, hammer, hammer all day long.
Your money-changers here, a lazy horde,
Rattle gold coins upon their dirty board;
There ponderous mallets, pounding Spanish rock
For lumps of gold, the midnight chamber shock.
Add to the noise Bellona's drunken crew,
The shipwrecked mariner, the begging Jew,
Ay, and blind beggars, selling matches, too!
He, who can tell how many clamours keep
The weary Roman from his noonday sleep,
Can count the brazen instruments as soon
Of those who beat their gongs to help the moon.
You, Sparsus, of these plagues can nothing tell,
Who, far-removed, in dainty villa dwell,
And on the slumbering hills look down at home,
To see your farm and vineyard both in Rome.
Your grapes are large as what Falernum stores;
Your house so spacious you may drive indoors;
No noise breaks in upon your sleep at night;
By day nought wakes you but admitted light.
For me the laughter of the passing crowd,
All Rome beneath my bedroom, shrill and loud,
Disgust me ever with some fresh alarm:
Hence, when I wish to sleep, I seek this farm.

J. A. POTT (d. 1920) and
F. A. WRIGHT (fl. 1924)

Classical scholars, who published in 1924 a translation of all the epigrams in the twelve books, omitting *De Spectaculis, Xenia* and *Apophoreta*, motivated by a belief in Martial's historical importance and contemporary relevance: 'The chief value of Martial's Epigrams . . . lies in the picture they give us of Roman society towards the end of the first century AD, that period in the world's history which, beyond all others, bears the closest resemblance to our own' (p. viii). The translation is interesting as indicating a movement towards a re-acceptance of Martial, although sexual explicitness is avoided through euphemism or verbal evasion (not always clever: cf. the version of 1.77 below with Martial's actual epigram on 'cunt-licking Charinus'), and the most 'obscene' poems are left in the original to be enjoyed presumably by incorruptible Latinists. The epigrams marked # are translated by Wright.

Ep. 1.16 *Olla Podrida*

Good work you'll find, some poor, and much that's worse,
It takes all sorts to make a book of verse.

Ep. 1.67 *To Cerylus*

You often say my work is coarse. 'Tis true
But then it must be so – it deals with you.

Ep. 1.77 *On Charinus*

His health is good yet he is always pale;*
He drinks but little, 'tis of no avail,
So wan his face no sun can darken it,
And good digestion aids him not a whit,
Not even rouge that pallid cheek can flush –
And e'en his vices do not make him blush!

Ep. 2.49# *Attraction*

'I won't marry Betty: she's too fond of men.'
'Well, boys find her charming.' 'I'll marry her then.'

Ep. 3.8 *In the Country of the Blind*

'Tis one-eyed Thais sets his love aglow;
She is half-blind – *and he entirely so.*

Ep. 4.4# *To Bassa*

Stench from the pools of marshes newly drained,
Vapours from springs that bubble sulphur-stained,
Reek of a fish-pond old and salt and black,
Of he-goat straining on his partner's back,
Of soldiers' boots, when they have been long worn,
Of Jews who take no food on Sabbath morn,
Of fleeces dipped too much in purple dye,
Of criminals as loud they sob and sigh;

---

pale: pallor is often represented in Martial as a side-effect of cunnilingus

Leda's foul lamp whose fumes the ceiling soil,
Ointment that's made from lees of Sabine oil,
A fox in flight, a viper in her lair,
All these compared with you are perfumes rare.

Ep. 4.12# *The Universal Provider*

At night no man do you refuse,
    And what is worse, dear Nancy,
There's nothing you refuse to do,
    Whatever be his fancy.

Ep. 5.21 *Pelmanism*

No name of old could he recall,
    But always mixed them thus,
A Mr. Gross was Mr. Small,
    And Quintus Decimus;

But now his greetings are correct,
    Each name he rightly quotes;
How much can care and toil effect,
    He learned them from his notes!

Ep. 5.24# *The Pride of the Ring*

Hermes the Martial darling of our day,
Hermes well-skilled in every kind of fray,
Hermes a fighter-teacher, both in one,
Hermes whom Helius fears and fears alone,
Hermes before whom Advolans falls mute,
Hermes himself his only substitute,

Hermes to whom his frightened pupils bow,
Hermes who wins nor needs to strike a blow,
Hermes from whom the theatre wealth derives,
Hermes the bane of gladiators' wives,
Hermes the joy of lady-connoisseurs,
Hermes whose spear the victory ensures,
Hermes terrific with his drooping crest,
Hermes whose trident lays the foe to rest,
Hermes who does each kind of fighting grace,
Hermes in all unique, the triple ace.

Ep. 7.23# *On the Anniversary of Lucan's Birth*

Come, Phoebus, come; as when thou didst inspire
The second singer of our Roman quire
To thunderous strains of war. What shall I pray
From heaven that may befit this glorious day?
Only that Polla still her love may show
To his great shade, and he her love may know.

Ep. 9.11# *To Domitian's Cupbearer Earinos ('Springboy')*

A name that's born with the primrose,
Wherefrom the year its best part knows,
Which draws from Attic flowers their scent
And phoenix perfumes subtly blent,
Sweeter than nectar's juice divine,
Which, Atys, thou wouldst wish were thine,
And he who holds* for Jove his cup;
A name which in our court brings up

---

he who holds: Ganymede

Venus and Cupid to the call,
Soft, delicate, and famed withal;
This in deft verse I fain would tell,
But, stubborn syllable, you rebel.
'Eiarinos' the poets write;
But they are Greeks who may indite
Whate'er they please and in their song
Have Ares short and Ares long.
We cannot such glib license use,
For Romans court a sterner Muse.

Ep. 10.47# *The Happy Life*

The things that make a happy life,
  My genial friend, are these:
A quiet dwelling free from strife,
  Health, strength, a mind at ease;
Money bequeathed, not hardly won,
A blazing fire when work is done.

Ingenuous prudence, equal friends,
  Bright talk and simple fare,
A farm that crops ungrudging lends,
  Soberness free from care,
A wife who's chaste yet fond of sport,
And sleep that makes the night seem short.

With what you are be satisfied,
  Nor let ambition range;
Contented still whate'er betide
  And caring naught for change.
Pray not for death, nor yet feel fear
When the last hour of life draws near.

Ep. 10.84 *The Bedfellow*

He sits up late, you think it odd demeanour?
Think of his wife! Good heavens, have you seen her?

A. L. FRANCIS (1848–1925) and
H. F. TATUM (1853–1925)

Two English schoolmasters who produced a set of translations and imitations of Martial in the same year as Pott and Wright: 1924. The selection is extensive and covers almost half of the epigrams. The whole enterprise is informed by a belief in Martial as private, simple and sincere. 'Martial stands alone in his age as the poet of friendship, private life and simple emotions. Modest, simple and affectionate, he is as much at home in idyll or elegy as in epigram; the latter in a sarcastic sense is rare with him. For his flattery of patrons we may blame his want of spirit but shall not question his sincerity. He saw no doubt the best side of their characters.' Their 'imitation' of 2.13 below may be read as an index of the times.

From *Martial's Epigrams: Translations and Imitations* (Cambridge, 1924).

Ep. 1.15

Julius,* of all my friends the most unfailing,
If faith and hoary trust are aught availing,
Nigh sixty winters do besiege your brow
Yet few the days that you have lived till now;
Delay's the danger; think of time and tide;
'Tis ill postponing what may be denied.
Cares dog the path and sorrow drags her chain,
And but a moment truant joys remain.
Tighten your grasp, and cling with all your might,
Even so they fleet and vanish into night.
'I'll live to-morrow,' no wise man will say;
To-morrow is too late. Then live to-day.

Ep. 2.13

If you don't pay old Shylock at once when you may,
You'll have counsel, judge, jury, Jew, devil to pay.

Ep. 5.19

If truth be told, great Caesar, then your age
Outrivals all the best on history's page.
When were our shores graced with such well-earned bays?
When did the Palatine win louder praise?

Julius: Martial's namesake, Julius Martialis, a lawyer and the poet's closest
friend during the thirty-four years he lived in Rome; this is the first of the
many epigrams in which he appears

When was our Rome so fair and great to see?
What other time basked in such liberty?
But we lay one great blemish at its door;
Never were friends less generous to the poor.
Who showers his gifts upon a trusty friend?
When does a knight only for love attend?
To send a half-pound spoon as Christmas fee
Or half-crown coat is prodigality.
Our purse-proud patrons praise this bounty mean;
Who prate of gold are 'few and far between'.
Since all men fail, Caesar, to you I turn;
No greater laurels could a sovereign earn.
I see you smile with an indulgent wink;
This counsel's for myself, not you, I think.

Ep. 5.74

The East and West* yield Pompey's children graves:
His home is Libya or the salt sea waves:
Three continents must fence such ruins round.
This wreck could not be gathered in one mound.

Ep. 7.4

Poor Oppius, to account for his complexion,
For writing verse conceived a predilection.

East and West: see n. on p.68

Ep. 7.19 *A Relic*

This piece of useless lumber you disdain,
'Twas the first keel that sailed the uncharted main,
Which through the Clappers' havoc landed free
And the fell anger of the Scythian sea.
Time's had his way; but through an age-worn wreck
This plank is holier than the stoutest deck.

Ep. 9.6

When, Afer, you returned from Libya home,
Five times I sought to welcome you to Rome.
'He's busy, he sleeps,' five times I heard and fled:
You want no welcome: well, good-bye instead.

Ep. 9.58 *A Dedication*

Queen of the sacred pool, sweet Nymph divine,
To whom Sabinus gives a grateful shrine,
A joy for ever, so may Umbria love you
Nor Sassina rate the Baian waves above you,
Accept my anxious verse with kindly smile;
You'll be my Hippocrene spring the while.
'Who to the Nymphs their verses dedicate
Give a shrewd forecast of their destined fate.'

Ep. 9.81

Reader and hearer, Aulus, love my stuff;
A certain poet says it's rather rough.
Well, I don't care. For dinners or for books
The guest's opinion matters, not the cook's.

Ep. 9.101*

Immortal Appius, upon whose road*
Our sovereign Hercules* new fame bestowed,
Would you his predecessor's worth compute,
He felled Antaeus, won the golden fruit,
The warrior maiden's girdle bore away,
The boar and lion flayed, foul birds from day
Cut off, from woods the brazen-footed deer,
And dragged the monster from the Stygian mere,
The Hydra's issue dried, that grew with slaughter,
And bathed his western herd in Tiber's water.
Thus far the less; now of the greater learn,
Whose altar-lamps by the sixth milestone burn.
The oppressor from the seat of power he threw
And sovereign Jove his young defender knew.
Sole lord, Iulus' mantle he laid down,
Third ruler in a world late all his own.
Three times he crushed the treacherous Danube's pride
And bathed his charger in its snow-fed tide.
Thrifty of triumphs, yet he won a name,
And from the northern world a conqueror came.
Shrines to the gods he gave and rest from wars,
To his folk virtue, fame to his own, new stars*
To heaven; for Hercules a rôle too great,
That rather might beseem the Thunderer's state.

Ep. 9.101: The Labours of Hercules are described in lines 4–10; Domitian's partici-
pation in the defeat of the Vitellian forces at the Capitol in 69 CE, his subsequent
deputizing for Vespasian and his military 'victories' in the north-east in lines
13–20.
road: *Via Appia* or Appian Way
our sovereign Hercules: Domitian, who dedicated a temple to Hercules on the
Appian Way with a statue sculpted in his own likeness
new stars: Domitian deified several members of his family, most especially his
father and brother

Ep. 10.9 *To Himself*

Martial, renowned throughout the world's domain,
The moral jester in Catullus' vein,
There is small ground for envy at thy star;
The horse Andraemon is more famed by far.

Ep. 10.10 *The Struggle for Patronage*

When you, whose brows the laurel wreaths adorn,
Beset a thousand thresholds every morn,
What shall I do? Paulus, what's left to me,
A man of common, vulgar quality?
I call my patron lord and master too;
The same, how much more daintily, do you.
I wait on chair or litter, you take hire
Yourself and fight for passage through the mire.
I rise when he recites; amazed you stand
And blow him favouring kisses with each hand.
God help the would-be client if he's poor!
Your purple robes have shown our gowns the door.

Ep. 11.108 *A Postscript*

Contented reader – I had thought to say;
But something's wanting? Then perhaps you'll pay.
My bailiff's broke, my lads for victuals cry;
What? Silent? Can't afford it? Then good-bye.

EZRA POUND (1885–1972)

American poet and prominent intellectual figure of the twentieth century. Born in Idaho and educated at the University of Pennsylvania and Hamilton College, New York, he lived most of his life in Europe, where he participated in founding such intellectual movements as Imagism and Vorticism, promoted the talents of writers such as James Joyce, Robert Frost and T. S. Eliot, and himself wrote some of the century's most enduring poems: *Homage to Sextus Propertius* (1917), *Hugh Selwyn Mauberley* (1920) and his epic work, *The Cantos* (1917–70), the first of which 'translates' a Renaissance Latin version of Homer's *Nekuia* (*Odyssey* 11). In the 1930s he became a supporter of Italian fascism and even broadcast on behalf of the Axis from Rome during the Second World War. He was declared insane by the Americans in 1945 and confined to a hospital until 1958. Important volumes of criticism include *Pavannes and Divisions* (1918), *How to Read* (1931), *The ABC of Reading* (1934) and *A Guide to Kulchur* (1938). From the beginning Pound was committed to creative translation, adapting poems in French, Provençal, early Italian, Chinese, as well as Latin. Martial was held in high regard by Pound (see p. xxxvi), who seems to have been substantially influenced by him, as is especially evident in the scattered sequence *Xenia* and in the epigrams in *Lustra* (1913–15), reprinted in *Personae* (1926) and praised by Eliot (despite the latter's aversion to the genre). Pound's plain diction, terse syntax, sexual themes and ironic twist, held together by taut verse form and sharp intellect, owe much to the Roman poet. Pound, however, translated only one two-line epigram of Martial.

The translation of *Ep.* 5.43 is from *Imagi* 5.2 (1950); the Miscellaneous Epigrams are from *Personae: The Collected Poems of Ezra Pound* (1926).

Ep. 5.43

Thais has black teeth, Laecania's are white because
  she bought 'em last night.

Miscellaneous Epigrams

Epitaph

Leucis, who intended a Grand Passion,
Ends with a willingness-to-oblige.

Arides

The bashful Arides
Has married an ugly wife,
He was bored with his manner of life,
Indifferent and discouraged he thought he might as
Well do this as anything else.

Saying within his heart, 'I am no use to myself,
Let her, if she wants me, take me.'

He went to his doom.

The Temperaments

Nine adulteries, 12 liaisons, 64 fornications and something
        approaching a rape
Rest nightly upon the soul of our delicate friend Florialis,
And yet the man is so quiet and reserved in demeanour
That he passes for both bloodless and sexless.
Bastidides, on the contrary, who both talks and writes of
        nothing save copulation,
Has become the father of twins,
But he accomplished this feat at some cost;
He had to be four times cuckold.

Phyllidula

Phyllidula is scrawny but amorous,
Thus have the gods awarded her,
That in pleasure she receives more than she can give;
If she does not count this blessed
Let her change her religion.

The Patterns

Erinna is a model parent,
Her children have never discovered her adulteries.
Lalage is also a model parent,
Her offspring are fat and happy.

Society

The family position was waning,
And on this account the little Aurelia,
Who had laughed on eighteen summers,
Now bears the palsied contact of Phidippus.

V. THE MODERN WORLD: THE LATE TWENTIETH CENTURY

INTRODUCTION

Martial now comes out of the closet. Perhaps no period since the early seventeenth century has taken to him with such gusto and passion. Translators abound: they range from 'faithful' to 'free', all excited by the verbal dexterity of the Roman poet, his wit, humour, unsentimental treatment of sex and satiric punch. In the Sullivan–Whigham collection (1987) post-1950 translators number almost forty. What we also see emerging at long last are female writers willing to translate this misogynistic poet. With an irony which Martial may not have appreciated (despite his praise of the poetess Sulpicia), this anthology ends with the epigrammatist from Bilbilis englished by a woman (Fiona Pitt-Kethley).

There are, however, losses. Some of the attraction of Martial to recent translators seems to lie in their perception of his straightforwardness and simplicity, manifested not only in his coarse language and unsubtle barbs, but in his tirades against Alexandrianism and its learned preciosity. In the multitudinous rush to liberate Martial from the shackles of sexual repression, some translators misread the Roman poet as an ally of their own anti-modernism, distorting the range, focus, intricacy and shifting tonality of the Martial corpus. The so-called 'obscene' poems, to which attention will be seen to be drawn, often possess a more allusive refinement and urbane sexuality, as well as a richer linguistic context, than several versions seem to indicate. A comparison of Harrison's brutal rendition of *Ep.* 3.32 (p. 363) with the linguistically more sensitive translations of Sir Edward Sherburne (p. 72) or Henry Killigrew (p. 130) is instructive (see also H. A. Mason, *Cambridge Quarterly*, 1988). More attuned to the complexities and dynamics of a Martial epigram are the handful of translations by J. V. Cunningham, one of America's finest epigrammatists, whose terse phrases, verbal ambiguities and spare, cynical wit create an interplay with Martial's own text, which makes of the translations themselves allusive, resonant re-creations.

Even more successful perhaps (and far more extensive) are the versions of the Australian-British poet, Peter Porter. Though apparently attracted to Martial in part because of his perceived anti-modernism (see below his translation of *Ep*. 2.86, placed programmatically at the head of the collection in *After Martial*), Porter produces tough, self-conscious, intellectually fertile, satiric verse, which generates from its deceptively simple surface a complex intellectual and emotional effect analogous to that of the original epigrams. Unlike many anti-modernists, Porter does not deintellectualize Martial's verse, but, like Cunningham, produces a rewriting of the Latin text which derives much of its meaning from its *historical* relation to Martial's original (and sometimes to the translations intervening between the latter and Porter's own version). As Hooley has shown (*The Classics in Paraphrase*, London and Toronto, 1988), such historicizing, palimpsestic translation derives ironically from the arch-modernist Pound, whose *Homage to Sextus Propertius* (1917), though pilloried by traditional classicists, not only led the way in diction, versification and imagistic precision, but (perhaps more importantly) provided the model of a creative, interactive translation which is itself a critical approach to, rewriting and repositioning of, the original poems. This repositioning of Martial involves a positioning and historicizing of the translator and his text, a form of historical self-consciousness at work in the process of the interpretative re-creation of the ancient texts. It signals a very different kind of translation from the assimilating *imitations* of a Jonson, Cowley, Pope or Stevenson. It is a quintessentially twentieth-century mode. Acknowledged or not, it shapes the versions which follow.

TRANSLATIONS AND IMITATIONS

ROLFE HUMPHRIES (1894–1969)

American poet, schoolteacher, professor and classical and English scholar. Author of eight volumes of original verse and one of the most widely known translators of Latin verse in the middle of this century. Born in Philadelphia, he was educated at Stanford University and Amherst College, and taught at the Woodmere Academy, and at Hunter and Amherst Colleges. His versions of Virgil's *Aeneid*, Ovid's *Metamorphoses* and *Art of Love*, Martial's *Epigrams*, Juvenal's *Satires*, and Lucretius' *De Rerum Natura*, retitled as *The Way Things Are*, have been widely used in university and college literature courses in the UK, USA and Australia. He also translated García Lorca's *Gypsy Ballads* and *Poet in New York*. Dudley Fitts called him 'one of the most gifted of modern translators', praising his 'directness, unpretentiousness and integrity' and his 'swift, lucid English'.

From *Selected Epigrams of Martial* (1963)

Ep. 1.64

You're beautiful, oh yes, and young, and rich;
But since you tell us so, you're just a bitch.

Ep. I.107

Often, my dearly beloved Lucius Julius, you nag me:
    'Write something grand for a change; oh, what a loafer
        you are!'
Give me a life of ease, the kind that Vergil and Horace
    Once on a time enjoyed, the gift of Maecenas their lord.
Then I would try to provide works that would live through
        the ages,
    Works that would render my name safe from the funeral
        flame.
Oxen won't carry the yoke into fields that are salted and
        barren –
    In a luxurious soil, how delightful the toil!

Ep. 2.9

I wrote. No answer. Nothing doing. Still,
Naevia read my letter. So – she will.

Ep. 3.18

You say, to start with, you have laryngitis;
Stop right there, Maximus, and you'll delight us.

Ep. 3.25

Sabinus, our distinguished rhetorician,
Has such a subantarctic disposition
That when he jumps into the hot baths of Nero
The temperature goes promptly down to zero.

Ep. 9.18

I have, and by your grace I hope to keep,
Caesar, my dwellings in and out of town,
But the curved pole, bucket, and swinging sweep
Hardly suffice to wet my garden down.
My house complains that it is worse than dry
Though the great Marcian flume* is rushing near:
Grant water to my household gods, and I
Will think Jove's golden rain descended here.

Ep. 9.19

In some three hundred lines of verse you praise
The baths of Ponticus. (His feasts are good.)
Don't think, Sabellus, I mistake your ways:
It's not a bath you really want, but food.

Ep. 9.33

If you're passing the baths and you hear,
From within, an uproarious cheer,
        You may safely conclude
        Maro's there, in the nude,
With that tool which has nowhere a peer.

Marcian flume: the great aqueduct, Aqua Marcia, from which Martial wants to
have a supply of water connected to his house; the request seems to have been
turned down

Ep. 9.46

Gellius has an edifice complex.
He's always building, cellars or sundecks,
Purchasing bolts and bars, and fitting keys,
Altering window frames, now those, now these,
Building forever, building without end.
His 'Building!' fixes every borrowing friend.

Ep. 9.62

Philaenis, night and day,
Wears garments drenched in dye,
Not that she's so soignée,
But Tyrian dyes, they say,
Outrank Philaenis' smell:
This serves Philaenis well.

Ep. 10.40

My Polla, people often said,
Was cheating on me with a sodomite.
I caught the pair of them in bed –
The story simply wasn't right!

Ep. 10.47

Here are the things, dear friend, which make
Life not impossible to take:
Riches bequeathed, not won by toil;
Fire on the hearth; responsive soil;

No law suits; seldom formal dress;
A frank but wise disarmingness;
A healthy body, and a mind
Alert, but peaceably inclined;
Congenial guests; a table set
Without excessive etiquette;
Nights free from exigence and worry,
But not too bleary or too blurry;
In bed, a wife not frigid nor
Too reminiscent of a whore;
Slumber, to make the shadows swift;
Contentment with your native gift;
And, without longing or dismay,
The prospect of your final day.

DUDLEY FITTS (1903–68)

American poet and critic. Born in Boston and educated at Harvard, he taught English at the Choate School, Wallingford, Connecticut, and at Phillips Academy. He contributed verse and criticism to such magazines as *Atlantic Monthly, The Criterion* and *New Directions*, with which he was associated. His translation with Robert Fitzgerald of Euripides' *Alcestis* was performed by the BBC in 1937 and both he and Fitzgerald became leaders in the attempt to revitalize the classics through translation. His translations of the Greek comic playwright, Aristophanes, were especially successful in reviving interest in Attic drama. Important for Fitts's concern with epigram are his *One Hundred Poems from the Palatine Anthology* (1938) and *More Poems from the Palatine Anthology* (1941). He began to translate Martial in the mid-fifties and published a collection of these translations in 1967.

From *Sixty Poems of Martial* (1967).

Ep. 1.35 *To a Censorious Critic*

So my verse offends you.
'No taste,' you say, 'no dig-
nity,' as though the class-
room were my proper sphere.
My lines, Cornelius,
like husbands, have licence
to hone the pleasure point.
No stag-party ballad
goes to a psalm tune, your
Mardi-Gras whore would look
absurd frocked by Dior.
No; what I want in verse
is: scratch where you itch.
Then screw solemnity:
carnival's today. You'd
not castrate my poems,
I hope? Gelded Priá-
pus? There's obscenity!

Ep. 2.87 *Valentine*

You claim that all the pretties are panting for you:
for you, Fitts,
face of a drowned clown floating under water.

Ep. 3.53 *To Chloë*

Take oh take that face away,
that neck away, those arms away,
hips and bottom, legs and breast –
Dear, must I catalogue the rest?
Take, Chloë, take yourself away.

Ep. 3.96 *To a Bragging Rival*

You don't lay her, you lick her, you sick fraud,
and you tell the whole damn town you're her lover.

Gargilius, I swear to God,
if I catch you at it you'll be tongue-tied for ever.

Ep. 5.60 *To a Detractor*

Yap-yap at me, you yap,
huff your stinking breath: you'll get
no fame from me, the look
of your name in my book, for all to see.

You exist, yap, you exist; but why
should the world know? Die,
cypher. Go down as you've lived, without recognition.
It's a big city,
and there may be a man, or two men, or even three,
with a taste for dead dog-flesh;
                              as for me,
I'll keep my fingernails clean of your infection.

Ep. 6.57 *Every Man His Own Absalom*

With fictive locks and scented glue
You hide your dome: who's fooling who?

A haircut? That's a simple matter.
No clippers, please; just soap and water.

Ep. 7.73 '. . . *Are Many Mansions'*

That's a fine place you have on Beacon Hill, Max,
and that unlisted duplex out Huntington Avenue,
and the old homestead in Tewksbury.
                                    From one you can see
the big gilt dome; the second
gives you an uninterrupted ecstatic view
of the Mother Church; the third
commands the County Poorhouse.
                                    And you
invite me to dinner?
                    There?
                          There?
                                Or there?
Max, a man who lives everywhere
                                lives nowhere.

Ep. 8.69 *To His Critics*

You puff the poets of other days,
        the living you deplore.
Spare me the accolade: your praise
        is not worth dying for.

Ep. 10.68 *Local Products Preferred*

Abigail, you don't hail from La Ville
Lumière, or Martinique, or even Québec, P.
Q., but from plain old Essex County;
Cape Ann, believe me, for ten
generations.
                        Accordingly, when
you gallicize your transports, such as they are,
and invoke me as *mon joujou!, petit
trésor!, vit de ma vie!*, I grow
restive.
            It's only bed-talk, I know,
but not the kind of bed-talk you
were designed for, darling.
                        Let's you and me
go native. Damn your Berlitz. Please,
woman, you're an Abigail,
                        not a *pièce exquise*.

Ep. 11.85 *On Zoilus, a Linguist*

Paralysis engaged the tongue
        of Zoilus, I grieve to say,
as he was testing beauty's bung.
        Now he must try the triter way.

Ep. 11.104 *A Marital Declaration*

There's only one thing for it: put up
with my 'degenerate ways', as you call them, or
go home to Mama.

                    Admittedly, I'm not one
of those stern & rockbound types, homespun
whiskers, bores
bugling from pulpit and podium. When I drink
it's a long wet night for me; you go to bed
with a bumper of water at sunset. When I make love
I want every light on full blast; you insist
upon darkness,

                    a nightgown,

                              a wrapper,

                                        & blankets –

     (For me, who've never found
          a naked girl naked enough!)

                                        – Kissing? I like it,
but I like it as doves kiss, beaks ajar; you kiss
as though you were greeting your grandmother at breakfast.
A loving technic?
What a technic! Paralyzed, wordless, never so much
as a curious hand:

                    your hand's reserved, I take it,
for Ladies' Day at the altar.

                    Ah the old days
when his wife rode Hector, that bucking gay horse,
and the Phrygian slaves
played with themselves outside the bedroom door!
Those halcyon days
when Ulysses snorted asleep, yet wise Penelope
employed her instructed fingers!

                              Those blessed days
when good Cornelia gave (what you deny)
herself reversed to her Gracchus!

                              and Julia to Pompey!

                                                  and

Portia, Brutus, to you!

                    when Juno herself
was Ganymede enough for Lord Jupiter!

All right.

This is my point: I can bear Lucretia by daylight,
but at night
I want a Laïs in my bed who knows her business.

Apoph. 175 *On a Painting of Danaë in the Golden Rain*

Why put out cash for Danaë, Chairman of Heaven,
        when you could have Leda for nothing?

PHILIP MURRAY (1924–)

American poet and translator. Born in Philadelphia and trained in Latin by nuns, Christian brothers and Jesuits, he graduated from St Joseph's College, Overbrook, Pennsylvania, received an MA from Columbia University, New York, and taught English at CUNY and Hofstra University, 1955–61. Since then he has devoted himself to poetry, giving especial attention to the translation of Latin verse. He describes his *Poems after Martial* as 'a book of creative translations that aspires to demonstrate without fustian footnotes and humourless explanations that Marcus Valerius Martialis . . . is still the funniest poet alive'.

From *Poems after Martial* (1967).

Ep. 1.103 *Advice to Scaevola*

'Ye gods,' you cried, 'if I had the money,
How lavishly I should live.'
The gods, who enjoy being funny,
Granted your wish. You're rich.

Yet your clothes are coarse; your manners, worse.
Your shoes are patched; your socks don't match;
You need a comb, you constantly scratch;
You live in rooms abandoned by rats.
A stingy dinner for six serves eleven;
Out of ten large olives, you hoard seven.
That tepid brine you call pea soup
Costs as little as your penny love-whoops.
You drink nothing but the worst red wine,
Neatest when returned to the jar as urine.
As a wealthy man you're a foolish fraud,
The butt of bored and playful gods.
If you're only going to live like a beggar,
Give me the money. I'll show them better.

Ep. 2.83 *The Point*

The cuckold finally caught the culprit,
Boxed his ears and broke his jaw.
But hasn't he missed the point?

Ep. 3.93 *The Old Gal*

This old gal has three hairs, four teeth,
Cucumber nose, eyes like dried peas,
Complexion of a crab, crocodile jaws,
A hum like a gnat, a frog's voice,
A breath that kills flowers,
She sits at stool for hours
Windy in the morning, gaseous at night.
She has the vision of an owl in the light,
Spider-web dugs, a belly like a sack,
The legs of an ant, a stiff bent back,

She smells like a she-goat, has a duck's ass,
Skinny as a starving hermit at death.
Two hundred husbands she's put under the earth
And now she's rutting to start on her third.
My great-granddaddy called her 'grandma';
Who'll want to call this old crone, a spouse?
There isn't a marriage torch under the moon
That could tickle a blaze in this charred ruin.

Ep. 7.53 *Thanks*

Thanks for the holiday presents.
Thanks for the six three-leaved tablets;
Thanks for the seven toothpicks;
Thanks for the sponge, the napkin and cup;
Thanks for the small figs and the dried prunes;
All the junk you didn't want
Carried to me in full procession
By your bevy of Syrian slaves.
One small boy might have brought
Five pounds of silver plate.

Ep. 9.37 *Portrait of an Old Pro*

Even when you are at home in your cheap flat,
You lie around in an Egyptian wig like Cleopatra,
Flashing false teeth and winking phony eyelashes,
Rummaging through silk dresses in a hundred drawers.
With an artificial face unfit to launch a sinking barge
You expose your manhandled baubles and hoary targe,
Heirlooms borrowed from your great-grandmother.
Still you give out generously to all comers,
And though my battered sceptre is deaf and half-blind,
Your battle-scarred target is easy to find.

Ep. 9.63 Coq au Vin

Lewd dinner hosts keep asking you back.
Are you the entrée, or the midnight snack?

Ep. 9.97 'For Envy is a kind of praise' — John Gay

I know a guy who's ready to bust
Because I am so widely published,
Because I don't work,
Or clerk, or soda-jerk,
Because I don't teach or preach,
Because I spend my winters at the beach,
Because I keep my summers out of reach
In Barcelona or Ibiza,
Because I sleep with the Queen of Sheba,
Because I live on Riverside Drive,
Because I'm the luckiest man alive,
Because I won't get a Ph.D.,
Or catch TB or even VD,
This green-groined bastard hates my guts.
My advice to you is — buster, bust.

Ep. 11.56 To a Stoic

Nobody praises death
Like you, poor stoic,
In your short rough toga,
With your cold hearth,
Your threadbare rug,
Lumpy bed full of bugs,
Broken jugs, black bread,
And just the dregs of wine.

321] EP. 12.82 · PHILIP MURRAY

I don't admire a mind
So easily resigned.

If you had a cozy couch
With plush pillows,
And a handsome lad
Who turned all heads
To toss your salad,
Then you'd be glad
To hold fast;
Nestor, he died young!

But strong men last,
Even when they're wretched.

Ep. 12.23 *A Sad Case*

A wig, you can buy.
Teeth, you can buy.
But Laelia, an eye?

Ep. 12.56 *To a Sick Friend*

Ten times a year or more, you take to your bed.
All those get-well gifts, all that fuss . . .
It doesn't hurt you, it hurts us.
Do your friends a favor. Drop dead.

Ep. 12.82 *Someone You Know*

I defy you to escape him at the baths.
He'll help you arrange your towels;
While you're combing your hair, scanty as it may be,
He'll remark how much you resemble Achilles;

He'll pour your wine and accept the dregs;
He'll admire your build and spindly legs;
He'll wipe the perspiration from your face,
Until you finally say, 'Okay, let's go to my place.'

J. V. CUNNINGHAM (1911–85)

American poet, born in Maryland and educated at Stanford. He taught English at the Universities of Hawaii, Chicago and Virginia, and at Brandeis University. Described by Richard Wilbur as 'our best epigrammatic poet', he was the author of some nine volumes of poetry, including *The Helmsman* (1942), *The Judge is Fury* (1947), *Doctor Drink* (1950), *Trivial, Vulgar and Exalted: Epigrams* (1957), *The Exclusions of Rhyme: Poems and Epigrams* (1960), *To What Strangers What Welcome* (1964). He also published critical work on Shakespeare and poetic structure. His *Collected Poems and Epigrams* (London, 1971) features eight versions of Martial, which are reprinted below. Cunningham's own poetry is remarkably Martialesque in tone, range, wit, metrical precision, verbal economy, clarity and punch. Like Martial, Cunningham exploited traditional forms for new, satiric effect.

From *Collected Poems and Epigrams* (1971).

Ep. 1.32

Sabinus, I don't like you. You know why?
Sabinus, I don't like you. That is why.

Ep. 1.33

In private she mourns not the late-lamented;
If someone's by her tears leap forth on call.
Sorrow, my dear, is not so easily rented.
They are true tears that without witness fall.

Ep. 2.4

Bert is beguiling with his mother,
She is beguiling with Bert.
They call each other *Sister, Brother,*
And others call them something other.
Is it no fun to be yourselves?
Or is this fun? I'd say it's not.
A mother who would be a sister
Would be no mother and no sister.

Ep. 2.5

Believe me, sir, I'd like to spend whole days,
Yes, and whole evenings in your company,
But the two miles between your house and mine
Are four miles when I go there to come back.
You're seldom home, and when you are deny it,
Engrossed with business or with yourself.
Now, I don't mind the two-mile trip to see you;
What I do mind is going four not to.

Ep. 2.55

You would be courted, dear, and I would love you.
But be it as you will, and I will court you.
But if I court you, dear, I will not love you.

Ep. 2.68

That I now call you by your name
Who used to call you sir and master,
You needn't think it impudence.
I bought myself with all I had.
He ought to sir a sir and master
Who's not himself, and wants to have
Whatever sirs and masters want.
Who can get by without a slave
Can get by, too, without a master.

Ep. 4.33

You write, you tell me, for posterity.
May you be read, my friend, immediately.

Ep. 4.69

You serve the best wines always, my dear sir,
And yet they say your wines are not so good.
They say you are four times a widower.
They say . . . A drink? I don't believe I would.

Miscellaneous Epigrams

Lip was a man who used his head.
He used it when he went to bed
With his friend's wife, and with his friend,
With either sex at either end.

Here lies my wife. Eternal peace
Be to us both with her decease.

She has a husband, he a wife.
What a way to spend a life!
So whenever they are free
They synchronize adultery,
And neither one would dare to stop
Without a simultaneous plop.

Cocktails at six, suburban revelry;
He in one corner with the Chest Convex,
She in another with Virility.
So they went home, had dinner, and had sex.

Some twenty years of marital agreement
Ended without crisis in disagreement.
What was the problem? Nothing of importance,
Nothing but money, sex, and self-importance.

Prue loved her man: to clean, to mend,
To have a child for his sake, fuss
Over him, and on demand
Sleep with him with averted face.

Leisure and summer vistas and life green
Within the limits of the sky. What more
Could one want if he also had a clean,
Accommodating, inexpensive whore?

Reader, goodbye. While my associates
Redeem the world in moral vanity
Or live the casuistry of an affair
I shall go home: bourbon and beer at five,
Some money, some prestige, some love, some sex,
My input and my output satisfactory.

DONALD C. GOERTZ

Classical scholar and translator of Brecht, Rilke, Goethe and Greek
lyric poetry, as well as of Martial. Graduate of the University of
Texas, he has taught at Randolph-Macon and Hollins Colleges and
at Wayne State University, Michigan.

From *Select Epigrams of Martial* (1971).

Ep. 3.79

Sertorius only begins
          but never ends.
When he fucks, in fact,
      I don't believe he spends.

327] EP. 7.59 · DONALD C. GOERTZ

Ep. 4.43

Coracinus,
I never said you were nasty
to women,
I never said you bad-mouthed
the fair sex
or carried on unnaturally
with females.

All I said was
now and then
you like to get
a few licks in.

Ep. 4.50

Why do you call me old,
my Thais?
No one's old who fucks
like I do.

Ep. 7.59

Caecilianus always serves steak,
    but only when dining alone.

Ep. 7.90

Matho's mad,
upset,
says my book
is unfair.

That's good,
I'm glad:
fair books
are dull books.

Ep. 8.54

Catulla's a great broad:
    she's glamorous
        and quite amorous
trouble is
    she's also
        promiscuous!
I like Catulla lots
but
I wish that
she were either
        colder
perhaps even
        uglier
or
at least a little
        choosier.

Ep. 8.74

Once as gladiator
    you used to specialize
        as eye remover.
Now as eye doctor
    you've a new profession,
        the same specialty.

Ep. 9.10

Paula's wise and wants to marry Priscus
    because he is very wise;
But Priscus doesn't want to marry Paula
    because he is very wise.

Ep. 9.33

It's easy to tell
by the roar of applause
in which of the baths
Maron is bathing.

Ep. 11.17

Not all my poems are meant
for cocktail parties –
a few are fit for morning tea.

Ep. 11.19

I can't marry you, Galla,
because in high society
my penis has problems
behaving with propriety.

Ep. 12.20

Brother never
    had a wife:
he had sister
    all his life.

Ep. 12.33

Labienus sold an orchard
to buy some slave boys:
he traded fruit trees
for real live fruits.

Ep. 12.40

You tell out-
    rageous lies, and
        I believe you.
You read your
    awful poetry, and
        I applaud you.

You loudly
    sing off key,
        I sing with you.
You drink en-
    tirely too much, and
        I get plastered.
You fart tre-
    mendous blasts,
        I take the blame.
You play your
    boring games,
        I lose to you.
You run a-
    round on your wife,
        I close my eyes.
You give me
    not a thing,
        I humbly accept.
You promise to
    will me plenty,
        I only want
You to die.

PETER PORTER (1929–)

Australian poet, born in Brisbane, who emigrated to England in 1951. Author of some twenty books of poetry, ranging from satirical indictment of the London world of the 1960s (*Once Bitten, Twice Bitten*, 1961, *Poems Ancient and Modern*, 1964) through cultural conservatism (*Preaching to the Converted*, 1972, *Living in a Calm Country*, 1975) to more allusive, contemplative lyric (*The Cost of Seriousness*, 1978, *English Subtitles*, 1981). His *Collected Poems* were published by Oxford in 1983. He has received honorary doctorates from the

Universities of Melbourne (1985) and Loughborough (1987), and was awarded the Gold Medal of the Australian Literature Society in 1990. His *After Martial* is a self-conscious rewriting of the Roman poet, employing a wide range of devices 'from comedians' jokes to sonorous Keatsian cadences' to reproduce the effect of the *Epigrams*, without any attempt to catch the 'perfection of form which Martial, though he encompasses the most amazing degree of reality and grotesquerie, never fails to achieve'. Despite these disclaimers, in the view of the present editors Porter's versions are the most successful versions of Martial in this century, their complex allusiveness and energetic counterpoint with the original epigrams (and – frequently – with intervening translations) serving both to historicize and to expand the Latin poems and Porter's text. A generous selection follows, in which it will be clear that Porter, who regards Martial as 'the best bawdy poet who ever lived', neither avoids the ribald epigrams nor focuses disproportionately on them. The thematic range, shifting tonality and intellectual intricacy of Martial's poetry become apparent in Porter's versions perhaps for the first time since the seventeenth century.

From *After Martial* (1972).

Ep. 1.43

What a host you are, Mancinus;
there we were, all sixty of us,
last night, decently invited guests
and this was the order of the dishes
you pampered us with:
>   NO late-gathered grapes
>   NO apples sweet as honeycomb
>   NO ponderous ripe pears lashed to the branch
>   NO pomegranates the colour of blowing roses
>   NO baskets of best Sassina cheese
>   NO Picenian jars of olives

Only a miserable boar so small
a dwarf could have throttled it
one-handed. And nothing to follow,
no dessert, no sweet, no pudding, nothing . . .

> We were the spectres, this was the feast,
> a boar fit for the arena, duly
> masticated by us –

> I don't want to see you struggle
> in your turn for a share of the crackling –
> no, imitate instead
> that poor devil Charidemus
> who was shredded in the ring –
> rather than miser eats boar
> lets have boar eats miser:
> *bon appétit*, my host of nothings,
> I can almost feel the tushes in your throat.

Ep. 2.17

At the entrance to the dark Subura
    where you catch a glimpse of
the executioners' masterpieces,
    blood-stained bodies hanging
in their beaten racks; where many a cobbler
    knocks out the rhythms of the Potters'
Field – there, Ammianus, sits a famous
    female barber. I said a female barber
but she shears no heads – not for her
    the basin cut, the pudding crop.
What does she do, this female barber,
    if she doesn't clip into a dish?
And why do men flock to her? She won't
    carve or slice you but she'll plate you.

Ep. 2.52

Dasius, chucker-out
at the Turkish Baths,
is a shrewd assessor;
when he saw big-titted
Spatale coming, he decided
to charge her entry for three
persons. What did she do?
Paid with pride of course.

Ep. 2.86

Because I don't attempt those modern poems
like lost papyri or Black Mountain lyrics
stuffed with Court House Records, *non sequiturs*,
and advice on fishing; and since my lines
don't pun with mild obscenities in
the *Sunday Times*; nor yet ape Ezra's men
in spavined epics of the Scythian Marsh,
The Florentine Banking Scene, or hip-baths
in Northumberland; nor am I well-fledged
in the East European Translation Market,
whose bloody fables tickle liberal tongues;
despite this I make my claim to be a poet.
I'm even serious – you don't ask a runner
to try the high-jump, and if my trade is words
I'd be a misfit in the People Show.
From Liverpool to San Francisco, poets
are turning to the Underground, a pop-
ulous place where laurels pale. My pleasure
is to please myself and if the Muses listen
I may find an ear or two to echo in.

Ep. 3.22

Twice thirty million sesterces spent
In the service of his famous stomach
Apicius followed where his money went
under a wide and grassy hummock.

He'd counted his wealth and found there were
Ten million left. Mere hunger and thirst!
Soon life would be more than he could bear
So he drank a beaker of poison first.

Romans are noble in everything – yes,
Even Apicius, the notorious glutton.
He died for his principles – to eat the best
And deny the very existence of mutton.

Ep. 3.35

Instant fish
by Phidias!
Add water
and they swim.

Ep. 4.18

Near the Vipsanian columns where the aqueduct
        drips down the side of its dark arch,
the stone is a green and pulsing velvet
        and the air is powdered with sweat
from the invisible faucet: there winter
        shaped a dagger of ice, waiting till

a boy looked up at the quondam stalactites,
    threw it like a gimlet through his throat
and as in a murder in a paperback the clever
    weapon melted away in its own hole. Where
have blood and water flowed before from one wound?
    The story is trivial and the instance holy –
what portion of power has violent fortune
    ever surrendered, what degraded circumstance
will she refuse? Death is everywhere
    if water, the life-giving element,
will descend to cutting throats.

Ep. 4.21

    'The skies are empty
    and the gods are dead',
says Segius, the proof of which
is that he sees himself made rich.

Ep. 4.44

Hear the testament of death:
yesterday beneath Vesuvius' side
the grape ripened in green shade,
the dripping vats with their viny tide
squatted on hill turf: Bacchus
loved this land more than fertile Nysa:
here the satyrs ran, this was Venus' home,*
sweeter to her than Lacedaemon
or the rocks of foam-framed Cyprus.

Venus' home: Pompeii, of which Venus was the patron deity

One city* now in ashes the great name
of Hercules once blessed, one other
to the salty sea was manacled.
All is cold silver, all fused in death
murdered by the fire of Heaven. Even
the Gods repent this faculty,
that power of death which may not be recalled.

Ep. 5.34

To you, the shades of my begetters, Fronto
and Flacilla, where you lie in sweet
decay, I commend with love the body
of my darling child Erotion.
                              A home-
bred slave yet tender as a golden dormouse,
rarer than the Phoenix, whiter than
an unsmudged lily –
                        guide her spirit home
so she may look for lights in Tartarus
and miss the snapping jaws of hell-hound
Cerberus. She'd have lived six shivering winters
if she hadn't died that many days before
the anniversary.
                    Now let her play
light-heartedly in the ever-darkened house
beside such sure protectors.
                              May my name
be burbling on her tongue, the childish gift
of sorrow spent on age.

One city: Herculaneum, sacred to Hercules

                    And monumental earth,
draw back eternal weight from her
small bones;
                    don't be severe and tread
on her with gravity: she never did on you.

Ep. 6.26

Sotades' head is in the noose.
How come? Who would accuse
so upright and so straight a man?
He's under a different sort of ban –
a pity a chap who's so well-hung
has to rely upon his tongue.

Ep. 6.47

In sickness the world has double purity;
with death so close a cold transparency
descends upon the skin of life; the stream
that snakes as quickly as a dream
beneath the house of Stella and concurs
with jewelled halls and chalcedony doors,
this is no local freshet, for it springs
from Aricia, sipping place of kings;
solemn Egeria set it flowing, Numa
was often there when troubled by a tumour,
Diana of the Crossways' Water-Course,
sacred to the Ninth Italian Muse.
So, pale-boned nymph, your Marcus here complies
with his sickness-vow to offer sacrifice –
a sucking pig that sniffs your garden borders –
I drank your water against doctor's orders

and I'm much better: pardon me my fault,
may dam or upland never give you halt,
instead your crystal waters always slake
my living thirst. The world is warm, opaque,
but death sees through, so one transparent slave
begs of his nymph her light and curing wave –
I watch the crust of earth returning to
its salutary self and drink to you!

Ep. 6.49

I am not made of fragile elm
and though I wear a fluted helm
I always stand with rigid shaft
however deep or fierce the draught!
My sappy life is given dress
in carvings of long-lived cypress –
a thousand days within my sight
are one tired moon and one bright night,
and like the rose that roots in clay
I live to shoot another day.
Then all who come here out of bounds,
be warned that these are sacred grounds,
just lay a hand on plant or house
and I who guard as well as rouse
will punish the offender where
my kingdom stops by half a hair.
Take note, I am Priapus who
engenders love and virtue too;
my punishments in clusters come,
I plant ripe figs inside your bum
and every thief who jail avoids
shall bear my crop of haemorrhoids.

Ep. 8.68

You are king of gentleman-farmers, Entellus,
      Alcinous's orchards pale by yours;
you have destroyed the very Seasons. Your grapes
      sway through brutal Winter in
corybantic clusters: you hold Bacchus himself
      under glass as an ant in amber –
a woman's limbs are outlined thus in silk,
      so shines a sunken pebble in a stream –
you have bent Nature itself to your mind,
      my Lord of Greenhouses, yet I fear
that, when it comes to factory-farming, death
      has the best of ever-bearing crops.

Ep. 10.47

Friend and namesake, genial Martial, life's
happier when you know what happiness is:
money inherited, with no need to work,
property run by experts (yours or your wife's),
Town House properly kitchened and no bus-
iness worries, family watchdogs, legal quirks.
Hardly ever required to wear a suit,
mind relaxed and body exercised
(nothing done that's just seen to be done),
candour matched by tact; friends by repute
won and all guests good-natured – wise
leavers and warm stayers like the sun;
food that isn't smart or finicky,
not too often drunk or shaking off
dolorous dreams; your appetite for sex
moderate but inventive, nights like sea-
scapes under moonlight, never rough;

don't scare yourself with formulae, like x
equals nought, the schizophrenic quest!
What else is there? Well, two points at least –
wishing change wastes both time and breath,
life's unfair and nothing's for the best,
but having started finish off the feast –
neither dread your last day, nor long for death.

Ep. II.47

Why does Lattara keep away from the Baths
where all the pretty women congregate?

So he won't be tempted to fuck them!

Why won't he go where all the high class tarts are –
outside Pompey's Porch or the Temple of Isis?

So he won't be tempted to fuck them!

Why does he cover himself with yellow linament
like an athlete and take cold baths apart from the girls?

So he won't be tempted to fuck them!

Why, when he appears to avoid the whole generation
of women like the plague, is he a known licker of cunts?

So he won't be tempted to fuck them!

Ep. 11.99

Yours is a classic dilemma, Lesbia;
whenever you get up from your chair
your clothes treat you most indecently.
Tugging and talking, with right hand and left
you try to free the yards of cloth swept
up your fundament. Tears and groans
are raised to Heaven as the imperilled
threads are pulled to safety from
those deadly straits: the huge Symplegades
of your buttocks grip all that pass.
What should you do to avoid such
terrible embarrassment? Ask Uncle Val –
don't get up girl, and don't sit down!

Ep. 11.104

You're my wife and you must fit my ways
Or leave the house: I don't keep fastdays,
Nor do I care how Tatius, Curius, Numa
Acted – founding fathers and consumer
Research heroes don't make me repent –
Sex is sex whichever way it's bent!
I prefer it served up elegantly:
A bladder full of wine's no enemy
To what we want to do (if it lies longer
At the point it makes the pleasure stronger),
But keep to water as you always choose,
Not caring to make love on top of booze,
And see what happens – half-way through your stint
You feel the urge, you disengage and sprint
To the loo, sad-eyed water-spiller, and then
You're back berating the appetites of men.

Another thing, I set no limit to
Love's duration: if before I'm through
Daylight's screaming in the floral pane
I say it's night-time still, so once again!
What's night to you? No night is dark enough
To get a head of steam up, no rough stuff
Keeps away the dragomans of sleep
Nor touch upon your haunches gets love's bleep!
It's bad enough, god knows, that you're inclined
To go to bed at half-past bloody nine
In opaque winceyette and cummerbund –
I like a girl that's naked, with her sun
Blazing its circuit for my solar lips
Or playing lost in space to fingertips;
For kissing I make doves my paradigm,
Beak to beak to dribble out the time;
Your sort of kissing is a woolly smother
Offered at breakfast to your old grandmother
And nothing will persuade you, neither words
Nor noises like those Kama Sutra birds,
To use a hand upon my other altar
Or try that *reservatus* style from Malta.
Consider the tradition of the service:
Andromache rode Hector like a war horse
While posted at the bedroom door the Phrygian
Slaves were masturbating (that's religion
For you), and in legendary days,
When heroes lived on earth and not in plays,
On Ithaca the while the Master slept
Penelope's well-instructed fingers kept
Their own appointment. You say that your arsehole
Is not for use, though good Cornelia, soul
Of Rome and glory of our past, reversed
Herself to Gracchus, Julia reimbursed
Her Pompey at the northern postern, and
Brutus's Portia served him contraband,

While long before the gods had Ganymede
To mix their drinks, proud Juno had agreed
To play the pretty boy to Jupiter –
Then why can't I with you, if Him with Her?
The gods and heroes gave all sex its due
But only abstinence will do for you:
I tolerate Lucretia by daylight
But I want Lais in my bed at night.

Ep. 12.31

This phalanx of pines, these demi-fountains,
this subtle pleaching, this irrigation system
ductile as a vein (water meadows under mountains),
and my twice-blooming roses richer than Paestum's,
the rare herb-garden – even in January, green –
my tame eel that snakes about its pond,
white dovecote outshone by its birds – I've been
a long time coming home and you, my fond
benefactress, dear Marcella, gave all this
to me. A miniature kingdom to do
with as I please. If Nausicaa with a kiss
should offer me her Father's gardens,* you
need not worry: to everything that's grown
I give one answer, *I prefer my own.*

Father's gardens: the gardens of Alcinous, lavishly described in Homer's
Odyssey

BRIAN HILL (1896–1978)

British writer, poet, and translator, son of a physiologist and grandson of G. Birkbeck Hill, editor of Boswell's Johnson. Hill was educated at Merchant Taylor's and served in the Durham Light Infantry during the First World War, publishing his first book of poems while on active service. He was the author of several books of poetry, detective stories (the latter under the pseudonym of Marcus Magill) and of translations of Rimbaud, Verlaine, Nerval, Gautier and Heredia – as well as of Martial. His Martial versions appeared in two small books published in the early 1970s: *Ganymede in Rome* (1971) and *An Eye for Ganymede* (1972). Hill's poetry has featured in such British journals as the *Listener*, *New Statesman*, *Poetry Review* and *Country Life*.

From *An Eye for Ganymede* (1972).

Ep. 1.24 *Appearances Deceive*

You see that fellow with his roundhead crop,
    His godly talk and manner dignified?
Do not be duped. Why, only yesterday
    He acted as a 'bride'.

Ep. 1.88 *The Grave of Alcimus*

Snatched from me in your Springtime years! I vow
Only the lightest turves shall shroud you now;
I shall not raise a weighty Parian stone
(Such pomp pays tribute to vain toil alone),
But plant a box-tree and a shady vine
And green grass washed by these sad tears of mine;
These transient tokens of my grief I give,
But in my verse, loved boy, your fame shall live.

And, when the Fates decree *my* time has come,
May I be honoured thus, find such a tomb!

Ep. 3.71 *Evidence*

Your lad is sore in front
    And you itch at the rear;
I'm no clairvoyant, but
    I see things crystal-clear!

Ep. 3.88 *Like or Unlike?*

Down to a different crotch goes each twin brother:
Are they then more alike or less alike each other?

Ep. 5.18 *True Liberality*

Since in December
When gifts fly
Me you'll remember
Only by
These little verses,
You may think:
The stingy fellow
Wasting ink!
But those obsequious
Folk I hate
Who use their presents
As a bait;
A poor man's truly
Liberal when
He baits no hooks
For richer men.

Ep. 6.79 *The Ingrate*

Lucky yet sad? My friend, should Fortune find
You lacking gratitude, she'll change her mind.

Ep. 7.89 *Go, Happy Rose*

Go, happy rose, and wreathe my dear friend's brow;
Not only now,
But when his shining locks have turned to grey,
(Though distant be that day!)
So, from this hour,
Be love's own flower!

Ep. 9.57 *Worse for Wear*

What is rubbed smoother than Hedylus' cloak?
Not vase's rim, nor captive's iron-chafed shin;
Not mule's galled neck, nor sea-turned pebble shore;
Deep rutted road, nor hoe worked paper-thin,
Dead pauper's toga, nor the dragged cart's wheel,
Boar's tusk, nor cage-scraped ribs. Oh, but I swear
There is one thing – and this he won't deny –
More rubbed than all, his bum, and worse for wear.

Ep. 9.63 *He Who Touches Pitch*

You dine with queers, so it appears,
Each day;
I'm very sure you don't keep pure
That way.

Ep. 10.42 *To Dindymus*

Your face reveals a down so light
    A breeze might steal it, or a breath;
    Soft as a quince's bloom that might
    Find in a finger's touch its death.
Five kisses – and your face is cleared
While mine has grown another beard.

Ep. 12.71 *A Change of Heart*

To everything I ask you now say 'no',
Who always answered 'yes' a year ago.

Ep. 12.75 *Martial's Favourites*

Polytimus? Chases girls to find a mate;
Hypnus? He thinks his boyhood infra-dig;
Secundus? Buttocks like a peach-fed pig;
Dindymus? Hates to seem effeminate;
Amphion? Could have been a girl from birth.
The charms, the pride, the petulant display
Of these five boys to my mind far outweigh
The golden dowry that a bride is worth.

Ep. 12.86 *To a Blasé Individual*

Thirty boys and thirty girls you have at your command,
But cannot get a stand.
If you can't screw,
What *do* you do?

Apoph. 171 *On a Statuette of a Boy*

Small as is this statuette
  Its glory shines out clearly;
This is he whom Brutus loved
  So dearly.

JAMES MICHIE (1927–)

British poet and scholar who was educated at Marlborough College in England and read Classics at Trinity College, Oxford. His publications include *Possible Laughter* and translations of *The Odes of Horace* (London, 1964; Penguin Books, Harmondsworth, 1967) and *The Poems of Catullus* (London, 1969). His translation of selections from *The Epigrams of Martial* (London, 1973) was published in Penguin Books in 1978. From the latter the following selection has been taken.

From *Martial: The Epigrams* (Penguin, 1978).

Ep. 2.27

When Selius spreads his nets for an invitation
To dinner, if you're due to plead a cause
In court or give a poetry recitation,
Take him along, he'll furnish your applause:
'Well said!' 'Hear, hear!' 'Bravo!' 'Shrewd point!' 'That's
  good!',
Till you say, 'Shut up now, you've earned your food.'

Ep. 2.36

I wouldn't like you with tight curls
Nor yet too tousled. Both a girl's
Complexion and a gipsy's tan
Are unattractive in a man.
Beards, whether Phrygianly short
Or wild like those defendants sport,
Put me off, Pannychus, for I hate
The 'butch' and the effeminate
Equally. As it is, your trouble
Is that despite the virile stubble
That mats your chest and furs your leg
Your mind's as hairless as an egg.

Ep. 3.5

Since, little book, you're bent on leaving home
Without me, do you want, when you reach Rome,
Lots of introductions, or will one suffice?
One will be quite enough, take my advice –
And I don't mean some stranger, but the same
Julius whom you've often heard me name.
Go to the Arcade entrance – right beside it
You'll find his house (Daphnis last occupied it).
He has a wife, who even if you land
Dust-splattered at the door will offer hand
And heart in hospitable welcome. Whether
You see her first, or him, or both together,
All you need say is, 'Marcus Valerius sends
His love.' A formal letter recommends
Strangers to strangers; there's no need with friends.

Ep. 3.43

You've dyed your hair to mimic youth,
Laetinus. Not so long ago
You were a swan; now you're a crow.
You can't fool everyone. One day
Prosperina, who knows the truth,
Will rip that actor's wig away.

Ep. 3.90

She's half-and-half inclined
To sleep with me. No? Yes?
What's in that tiny mind?
Impossible to guess.

Ep. 5.9

I was unwell. You hurried round, surrounded
By ninety students, Doctor. Ninety chill,
North-wind-chapped hands then pawed and probed and
      pounded.
I was unwell: now I'm extremely ill.

Ep. 6.17

'Address me,' you insist, 'as Long,'
Longbottom. The contraction's wrong.
Surely you wouldn't make the same
Mistake if Cockburn were your name?

Ep. 7.61

The thrusting shopkeepers had long been poaching
Our city space, front premises encroaching
Everywhere. Then, Domitian, you commanded
That the cramped alleyways should be expanded,
And what were footpaths became real roads.
One doesn't see inn-posts, now, festooned with loads
Of chainéd flagons; the praetor walks the street
Without the indignity of muddy feet;
Razors aren't wildly waved in people's faces;
Bar-owners, butchers, barbers know their places,
And grimy restaurants can't spill out too far.
Now Rome is Rome, not just a huge bazaar.

Ep. 8.27

If you were wise as well as rich and sickly,
You'd see that every gift means, 'Please die quickly.'

Ep. 8.69

Rigidly classical, you save
Your praise for poets in the grave.
Forgive me, it's not worth my while
Dying to earn your critical smile.

Ep. 9.9

Although you're glad to be asked out,
Whenever you go, you bitch and shout
And bluster. You must stop being rude:
You can't enjoy free speech *and* food.

Ep. 10.55

Marulla's hobby is to measure
Erections. These she weighs at leisure
By hand and afterwards announces
Her estimate in pounds and ounces.
Once it's performed its exercise
And done its job and your cock lies
Rag-limp, again she'll calculate,
Manually, the loss in weight.
Hand? It's a grocer's balance-plate!

Ep. 10.90

Why poke the ash of a dead fire?
Why pluck the hairs from your grey fanny?
That's a chic touch which men admire
In girls, not in a flagrant granny;
Something, believe me, which might suit
Andromache, but looks far from cute
In Hecuba. Ligeia, you err
If you think sex could rear its head
To burrow in your mangy fur.
Remember what the wise man said:
'Don't pluck the lion's beard when he's dead.'

Ep. 11.62

Lesbia claims she's never laid
Without good money being paid.
That's true enough: when she's on fire
She'll always pay the hose's hire.

Ep. 11.77

For hours, for a whole day, he'll sit
On every public lavatory seat.
It's not because he needs a shit:
He wants to be asked out to eat.

Ep. 11.99

Whenever you rise from a chair, Lesbia, your wretched
    clothes jump,
Like buggers, right up your rump –
I've often observed the sight.
You try twitching them to the left or the right
And finally wrench them free with a tearful shriek,
So deep is the creek they've sailed up, so fierce the squeeze
Of those huge twin Symplegades.
Would you like to cure this unattractive defect? Do you want
    my advice? This is it:
Don't get up – and never sit.

Ep. 11.103

Safronius, you look so meek and mild
I can't imagine how you got your child.

Ep. 12.13

The rich know anger helps the cost of living:
Hating's more economical than giving.

Ep. 12.30

Aper's teetotal. So what? I commend
Sobriety in a butler, not a friend.

DOROTHEA WENDER (1934–)

Classical scholar and teacher, who was born in Ohio and educated at
Radcliffe College and the Universities of Minnesota and Harvard.
She has held various teaching and research positions, and was, until
very recently, chair of the Department of Classics at Wheaton Col-
lege, Norton, Massachusetts. Her verse translations include a wide
variety of Roman poets and (for Penguin) the Greek poets Hesiod
and Theognis.

From *Roman Poetry: From the Republic to the Silver Age* (1980).

Ep. 1.16

Some lines in here are good, some fair,
And most are frankly rotten;
No other kind of book, Avitus,
Can ever be begotten.

Ep. 1.18

What ails you, Tucca, that you mix
In with your old and fine
Falernian, those musty dregs
Of awful Vatican wine?

Did the priceless wine mistreat you once?
What harm did it ever do
To merit this? Or the other stuff,
Does it have some hold on you?
Forget your Roman guests; it is
A heinous crime to throttle
A Falernian, or give strong poison
To a Campanian – bottle.
No doubt your drinking-friends deserved
To die in deadly pain;
That precious amphora should not
Have been so foully slain.

Ep. 1.37 *To Bassus*

You relieve yourself in a golden urn
(Poor urn!) and think it's fine,
But you drink from glass. I guess your shit
Is dearer than your wine.

Ep. 1.47

Doctor Diaulus has changed his trade:
He now is a mortician,
With the same results he got before
As a practicing physician.

Ep. 2.89

Gaurus, you have a fault for which
I freely pardon you:
You love to drink too much, too late;
That vice was Cato's too.

I'll even praise your scribbling
Verses, instead of prose,
With NO help from the Muses, for
That fault was Cicero's.
You vomit: so did Antony,
You squander: records *may* show
Apicius as your model – now,
Who led you to fellatio?

Ep. 3.68

Madam: my little book, so far,
In its entirety
Up to this point, has been for you;
From now on, it's for me.
The gym, the locker-room, the baths
Are next; you'd better skip
This part and go away, my dear,
The men are going to strip.
Terpsichore is staggering
From all the wine and roses,
She lays aside her shame and starts
Assuming naughty poses,
In no ambiguous terms she names
Quite openly, that Thing
Which haughty Venus welcomes
In the rituals, in spring,
That thing which stands in gardens
Scaring thieves with its great size,
Which virgins peek at modestly
With almost-covered eyes.
I know you, Madam: you were tired
And just about to quit
My lengthy little book: *Now* you'll
Devour all of it!

Ep. 3.87 To Chione

Rumor has it your twat is pure
As snow, and you've never screwed;
But nonetheless when you take a bath
You won't go in the nude.
You're acting very foolish
If you really fear disgrace,
If you're so modest, take your pants
And cover up that face!

Ep. 4.56 To Gargilianus

You want me to call you *generous*
Because you shower gold
On widows, and send costly gifts
To none but the very old?
There's nothing quite so nasty
Or so sordidly unpleasant
As what you do and what you say
When you call a snare a 'present.'
The treacherous hook is 'generous'
To the greedy fishes, too;
Trappers lay bait for stupid beasts —
They're generous just like you.
You want to learn the meaning of
True generosity?
I'll teach you about pure largesse:
Just send your gifts to me!

Ep. 8.76 *To Gallicus*

'Please, Marcus, tell the *truth*,' you say,
'That's all I want to hear!'
If you read a poem or plead a case
You din it in my ear:
'The truth, the honest truth!' you beg,
It's damned hard to deny
Such a request. So here's the truth:
You'd rather have me lie.

Ep. 10.65

Since you, Charmenion, come from Corinth
And I from quite another
Part of the world, from Tagus, tell me
Why do you call me 'brother'?*

You're Greek – my ancestors were Celts
And Spaniards. Do we share
Some physical resemblances?
Well, you have oily hair,

In ringlets – my stiff Spanish locks
Are obstinately straight;
I'm shaggy-legged and bristle-cheeked –
Daily you depilate

Your silky skin. Your voice is light;
You lisp in a charming way –
My voice, as my loins can teste-fy,
Is gruff. And so I'll say:

'*brother*': Latin *frater* was commonly used of one's male homosexual partner

We're less alike than eagles and doves,
Or lions and does, so Mister,
Don't call me 'brother,' or
I'll have to call you 'sister.'

Ep. 11.47

Does Lattara shun the baths where crowds
Of women go? It's true.
And why is he so particular?
– He does not wish to screw.

He never goes to Pompey's Porch
As many others do,
Or Isis' shrine, where whores hang out,
– He does not wish to screw.

Why does he take those long cold baths
Anointed with Spartan goo,
In the waters of the Virgin? Why?
– He does not wish to screw.

If he's so scared of women
(That contaminating crew)
Why is he fond of cunnilingus?
– He does not wish to screw.

Ep. 11.93

Flames have gutted th' abode Pierian
Of the wide renowned poet Theodorus.
Didst thou permit this sacrilege, Apollo?
Where were ye, Muses' Chorus?

Ay me, I fondly sigh, that was a crime,
A wicked deed, a miserable disaster.
Ye Gods are much to blame: ye burnt the house
But failed to singe its master!

Ep. 12.56

Poor Polycharmus, you're always sick,
Ten times a year, or more,
It hurts us more than it does you
In fact, it's an awful bore
Always giving you get-well gifts,
Now, here's what should be done:
We're sick of your sicknesses, my friend,
Let this be your *final* one.

TONY HARRISON (1937–)

English poet, playwright and translator, born and educated both at
school and university in Leeds. For much of the sixties he was away
from England in West Africa and Czechoslovakia, returning to
become the inaugural Northern Arts Literary Fellow in 1967–8, an
appointment he again received nine years later. He is best noted for
his work for the English National Theatre, which has performed his
The Misanthrope (1973), *Phaedra Britannica* (1975), *The Passion* (1977),
Bow Down (1977), *The Oresteia* (1981) and other plays. His extensive
publications in poetry and translation include: *Earthworks* (1964),
Newcastle is Peru (1969), *Palladas: Poems* (1975), *From 'The School of
Eloquence' and Other Poems* (1978), *A Kumquat for John Keats* (1981),
Selected Poems (1984), *A Cold Coming* (1991) and *The Gaze of the
Gorgon* (1992). His English libretto for Smetana's *The Bartered Bride*
was performed by the New York Metropolitan Opera in 1978. The

following 'translations', published in the UK, were composed in the first few days of March 1981 at the Hotel Ansonia in New York.

From *U.S. Martial* (1981).

Ep. 2.36

Not Afro- not crewcut
& no way out new cut
but something betwixt and between.

Avoid looking too hippy
or boondocks Mississippi
& try if you can to keep clean.

Shave so close but no closer
no *eau-de-mimosa*,
be macho, not mucho, enough.

I'm a little bit wary
of hirsute and hairy
& your sort of chestrug's so rough –

EVERYWHERE'S
just a jungle of hairs
your legs, your back, your behind,

but one place nothing sprouts
as all growth 's been plucked out 's,
Mr REDNECK, your mind!

Ep. 2.73

What'mmmIdoin'? slurs Lyris, feigning shock.

I'll tell you what you're doing: YOU
are you doing what you always do,
even when you're sober   SUCKING COCK!

Ep. 3.17

The tart passed round for sweet's so hot
no-one touches it. No-one, but NOT
Sabidius whose greed burns more.
He blows on it 1–2–3–4.
It's cool. Still no-one touches it –

Sabidius's breath turns all to shit.

Ep. 3.32

Screw old women? Sure I do! But YOU
you're one step further on, more corpse, than crone
and necrophilia I'm not into!

Hecuba, Niobe, both of them I'd screw
till one became a bitch, the other stone.

Ep. 3.55 *Scentsong*

You swing past, a pong typhoon,
a *parfumerie* afflatus,
wafts over us and makes us swoon.
What brand do you use to bait us?

Dior? One of *Fabergé's*?
Frogshit (*Chanel* no. 2)!
Maybe your shower or bidet's
been plumbed to pipe out *Patou*.

You don't need *Nina Ricci*
or *Givenchy* creations
I think your perfume's peachy
and just like my Dalmatian's.

Ep. 3.70

You're fucking Aufidia, your ex
who's married to the guy who gave *you* grounds.
Adultery's the one way you get sex.
You only get a hard-on out of bounds.

Ep. 3.71 *Twosum*

Add one and one together and make TWO:
that boy's sore ass + your cock killing you.

Ep. 5.9

A slight cold or a touch of flu,
but when THE SPECIALIST and all his crew
of a 100 students once are through,
and every inch of me's been handled twice
by a hundred medics' hands as cold as ice
the pneumonia I didn't have I DO!

Ep. 6.6 *Paula*

She doesn't feel 3
parts in Comedy
quite do.

4's more & merrier!
She hopes the spear-carrier
comes on too!

Ep. 6.40

Time makes enormous differences
between the past and present tenses,
the long way that I did is from I do.

I *love* Glycera, Lycoris. I love*d* you.

Ep. 6.59 *To Bassara*

She likes the Winter season
when there's lots of ice and snow
because it gives her reason
to hold a fashion show.

She loves the weather when it stinks
and no sooner does it freeze
than out come musquashes and minks
and chic *pendant* and *après-skis*.

I don't flaunt **$$$** on my back
or keep a wardrobe like a zoo,
only one threadbare anorak
the Winter blows right through,

so if you really want to be
more noticed in your clothes
and at the same time fair on me
please stay in when it snows,

but when I can sit out in my shorts
and sip a long iced drink,
then you dress up for Winter sports
and run around in mink.

PETER WHIGHAM (1925–87)

Schoolmaster and poet, who produced distinguished translations of
Dante, Catullus, Meleager, the sixth Dalai Lama, Kan'ami Kiyotsugu
and troubadour *chansons*, and several volumes of his own poetry. A
peripatetic intellectual, he occasionally earned a living tending bar
and selling flowers in Santa Barbara, or lecturing to adult education
classes on Pound. Pound's influence upon him is reflected in one of
his final works, *Homage to Ezra Pound* (San Francisco, 1985). His
selected poems, *Things Common, Properly*, appeared in 1984. Born in
England, he lived in Italy and in the latter part of his life in California.
He died in a motor-vehicle accident on a mountain road at midnight
in 1987. His widely praised translation of Catullus was published by
Penguin in 1966.

From *Letter to Juvenal: 101 Epigrams from Martial* (1985) – except *Spec.*
22/23, *Ep. 6.82, 7.17*, which are from *Epigrams of Martial Englished by*
Divers Hands (1987).

Spec. 1 *Caesar's Ring*

Memphis, forbear anent your *Pyramids*
    nor *Syria* boast your highrise skyline;*
Lax *Ionians*, vaunt not *Dian's* shrine,*
    and may her trophies *Phoebus' Delos* hide;
Pendant in space the *Mausoleum* hangs –
    let modest *Carians* play down the fact:
O'er mankind's monuments towers *Caesar's Ring*,*
    the fame of each proclaimed in that of one.

Spec. 21 *Caspian Tigress*

Tonguing its trusting keeper's hand,
The vaunted *Caspian* Tigress sprang
Mangling with bleak tooth a lion.

Occurrence strange in Time unknown,
Foreign to forest fastnesses.

Come live with us and learn our ways . . .

---

highrise skyline: walls of Babylon
Dian's shrine: her temple at Ephesus
Caesar's Ring: Colosseum

Spec. 26

Cautiously the keeper poked the rhino;
    long it took to rouse the giant beast,
And the crowd's hope of *Mars*, his fray, faded,
    till the old rage – all knew – returned:
The double horn tosses an outsize bear,
    as bulls toss bladders to the stars –
Thrust as sure as young *Carpophorus* makes,
    his stout fist driving the *Noric* shaft.
Flexible neck sporting a brace of bullocks . . .
    fierce bison, buffalo, turning tail . . .
The fleeing lion impaled on ready spears . . .
    Chide, crowd, the drawn-out prologue, still?

Ep. 4.22 *The New Bride*

After her wedding-night, the nymph
    avoiding what she seeks (her husband's touch),
Runs to the bright concealments
    of her pool. But water (like glass) betrays
The hidden woman. *Cleopatra*
    glitters through her cloak of water. So
Ornamental flowers, in glass
    or crystal, shroud themselves in the same cheat-
ing clearness. I joined her there. I
    tore up water kisses. Transparent
Crystal robbed us of the rest.

Ep. 4.55 Loved Places

Lucius Licinianus, friend,
Adornment of our days! securing
For *Gaius*, *Tagus*, poetic
Palms that *Arpi* would pre-empt,
Let *Greeks* of *Thebes*, *Mycenae*, sing –
The wrestling pitches of permissive
Spartans – Rhodes, the world's *Colossus* . . .
Let's not, as *Celtiberians*, laggard
Be in filial verse proclaiming
Our own more homely names, to wit:
Bilbilis, its fell mines outstripping
What *Nerici*, what *Chalybes* boast . . .
Plataea, where smithies ring and steel
Is tempered in *Salò's* waters,
Scant but swift, washing *Plataea's* walls . . .
Ramaxae's Ghost, its choruses . . .
At *Carduae*, the festal gatherings . . .
Peteris, pink with woven roses . . .
Regae's ancestral arena . . .
The *Silai*, deadly with light lance . . .
The *Perusian, Turgontan Lakes* . . .
Small *Tuetonissa's* limpid shoals . . .
Buradon's holy oaks where e'en
The flagging traveller cares to wander . . .
The field on *Vativesca's** slopes
Manlius with stout bullocks furrowed . . .
Names outlandish? Names to smile at,
Sophisticate? Śmile on! They're mine –
Mine more than *Roman* names can be.

Plataea . . . Vativesca: names of places, etc., near Bilbilis

Ep. 4.64 His Namesake's Villa

The modest poles of J. Martial,
Than Gardens of the West *more blest*,
Line Janiculum's *lengthy beam*.

Remote heights command the foothills,
And the top, rolling & smooth lies
Open to serener heavens . . .
Mist covering the curved valleys,
It shines in radiance alone, while
Delicate roofs of the tall house
Soar, tapering, to the unveiled stars.

From here the *Seven Peerless Hills*,
Here all of *Rome* herself – appraise,
The *Tusculan*, the *Alban Hills*,
Cooling Parks fringing the City,
Old *Fidena*, little *Rubra*,
Orchards of the nymph, *Perenna*
(Pleasaunces for lustful ladies).

There *Flaminia*, there *Salernia*,
Soundlessly coach-travellers passing –
Wheels not touching softest slumbers
Boatmen's, bargees' sing-songs touch not,
Though nearby hangs the *Mulvian Bridge*,
With river craft that skim down *Tiber*.

This country lodge – more truly 'seat', –
Its Master yields: you'll feel it's yours,
So lacking meanness, filled with cheer,
The genial welcome spread for you.
You'll dream *Alcinous*' hearth, or be
(Like *Hercules*) *Molorchus*' guest.

If nowadays, such seem small fry,
Exploit *Tivoli* with gangs
Of mattocks! Try cool *Praeneste*!
Rent hillside *Setia* out to farm!
M. V. *shall still more blessèd judge*
The modest poles of J. Martial.

Ep. 5.34 *Erotion*

Fronto, Father; *Flacilla*, Mother, extend
        your protection from the *Stygian* shadows.
The small *Erotion* (my household *Iris*)
        has changed my house for yours. See that the hell-
hound's horrid jaws don't scare her, who was no
        more than six years old (less six days) on the
Winter day she died. She'll play beside you
        gossiping about me in child's language.
Weigh lightly on her small bones, gentle earth,
        as she, when living, lightly trod on you.

Ep. 5.58 *Tomorrow*

You say, *Postumus*,* you'll live 'tomorrow.'
        Postumus, tell me, when comes 'tomorrow'?
Is't far that 'morrow'? Where? In what place found?
        – Not lurking 'mid *Armenians*, *Parthians*?
Their 'morrows' now wear *Priam's*, *Nestor's* years.
        At what cost, tell me, is that 'morrow' bought?
'Tomorrow'? – *Postumus*, today's too late.
        The wise man, *Postumus*, lived yesterday.

Postumus: name given to a male child born after his father's death

Ep. 5.78 *Martial's Menu*
for Margaret at Tuscany Alley

My lack of food is yours to share
Should dining home seem desultory.
A pungent leek, a devilled egg
(With tuna stuffed), iceberg lettuce –
These for antipasto shall be yours.
Served on blackened pewter there'll be
Bright green broccoli fresh from garden,
Piping hot for hasty fingers,
Sausage on polenta, *speck* (pink),
Fave (pallid) . . . For second course,
Pears (labelled '*Syrian*'), raisins,
Chestnuts *Naples* sagely ripened,
Roasting on slow-burning embers.
The wine in drinking you'll make good.
After such fare, should *Bacchus* prick
Hunger further, finest olives
From *Picenian* groves, hot chick-peas,
Simmering lupins shall assuage
Your need. My board is spare. For sure.
But you'll not speak – nor hear – false words,
Nor look false looks, at ease, stretched out . . .
No host declaim his lengthy poems,
No girls from sinful *Gades* grind
(With endless suggestivity) sex-
y thighs in nuances of lust.
Instead, small *Condylus*'ll flute us
Melodies not crass nor precious.
You ask if this is all I offer;
'What more,' I answer, 'would you seek?'

Ep. 5.83 *Contrarities*

I run, you chase; you chase, I run.
I love what's cold: what's hot I shun.

Ep. 6.82

He scanned me closely, *Rufus*, just as
Slaves by trainers are e'er purchased –
Sizing me up with eye & thumb.
Then: 'Are you *Martial*, you the one
Whose lewd wit delights all ears
Excepting those a *Dutchman* wears?'
A faint smile, an inclination,
Acknowledging the imputation.
'Why then,' he said, 'the shabby clothes?'
'It's how a shabby poet goes.'
To shield me, where your poet goes,
Send, *Rufus*, some not shabby clothes.

Ep. 7.17

O library of choice country house,
A place to gaze at *Rome* and browse,
Grant among your sober tomes
Room for my lascivious ones:
A meek nook let my *Thalia* find
Her sev'n slim vols, to you consigned,
Proofed by the pen that gave them birth –
Corrigenda that enhance their worth!
Since, choicest spot, these gifts I bring
Shall round the world your praises sing,
As proofs of heart embosom them,
O library of my *Julius M.*

Ep. 10.2 *Rome's Gift*
for Peter Jay

Slipshod writing, premature publication,
    brought Book X back for pumice work.
Much you'll recognise that's been refashioned;
    more that's new: smile, Reader, equally
On each – Reader, Patron, willed to me by *Rome*
    saying: 'No greater gift! Through him
You'll flee neglectful *Lethe's* stagnant flood –
    the better part of you survive.
Wild-fig rives the marble, heedless muleteers
    deride the busted steeds of bronze.
But verse no decrease knows, time adds to verse,
    deathless alone of monuments.'

Ep. 10.4 *His Poems are of Life*

Read of *Thyestes*, *Oedipus*, dark suns,
    of *Scyllas*, *Medeas* – you read of freaks.
Hylas' rape . . .? *Attis* . . .? *Parthenopaeus* . . .?
    Endymion's dreams changed your life? The *Cretan
Glider** moulting feathers . . .? *Hermaphroditus*? –
    averse to advances of *Salmacian* fount . . .
Why waste time on fantasy annals? Rather
    read my books, where Life cries: 'This is me!'
No *Centaurs* here; you'll meet no *Gorgons*, *Harpies*.
    My page tastes of man. Yet you're incurious
To view your morals, view yourself. Best stick
    to *Callimachus* – the mythic *Origins*.*

Cretan Glider: Daedalus
Origins: the poem *Aetia*

Ep. 10.8 *Marriageable Age*

Paula would wed: I pray to be exempted.
She's old. Were she but older, I'd be tempted.

Ep. 10.47 *Means to Attain . . .*

>   *My carefree Namesake, this the art*
>   *Shall lead thee to life's happier part:*

A competence inherited, not won,
Productive acres & a constant home;

No courts, few formal days, your mind stable,
A native vigor in a healthy frame;

A tact in candor, friendships on a par,
Convivial courtesies, a plain table;

A night, not drunken, yet shall banish care;
A bed, not frigid, yet not one of shame;
A sleep that makes the dark hours shorter:

Prefer your state & hanker for none other,
Nor fear, nor seek to meet, your final hour.

Ep. 11.26 *Kisses of Old Falernian*
W.S.L., his shade

Cure of my unquietness
        object of my sighs,
Than whom within my arms
        none now dearer lies,

Yield kisses of *Falernian*,
    shared lip yield to lip
That from the reeking goblet
    Venus forth shall slip,
Then not *Jove* nor *Ganymede*
    shall, as we, enjoy
Themselves my sweetest cock-
    tail shaking wine-cup boy.

Ep. 12.18 *Letter to Juvenal*

While unquiet, *Juvenal*, you haunt
The shrill *Subura*, or loiter
On *Dian's Aventine* . . . while your
Damp toga flaps round great men's doors . . .
While you grow worn with mounting now
The big, the little *Caelian* – I
These winters late, revisiting my
Bilbilis (replete with gold & iron)
Have been accepted . . . countrified.
Here lazily are trips (sweet chores)
To *Plataea, Boterdus*. (Ah,
These *Celtiberian* vocables!)
. . . Indulging in inordinate
Amounts of sleep – past nine or ten.
That's paying myself back, in full,
For thirty years of lack of it.
Togas are unheard of . . . a quilt
From some disused sedan will serve.
Rising, I've a log fire greet me
Fed handsomely from neighboring oak.
My maid drapes it with cooking pots.
The hunting boy comes in – he's one
Some bosky dell would set you lusting.
My steward gives the houseboys food,
Pleads: May he wear his long locks shorter?
These my aids to living, aids to death.

377] EP. 2.33 · J. P. SULLIVAN

J. P. SULLIVAN (1930–93)

Classical scholar, literary historian and critic, born in Liverpool, England, and educated at St John's College, Cambridge. Most of Sullivan's adult life was spent in the USA, where he held professorships at the University of Texas at Austin, SUNY, Buffalo, and the University of California at Santa Barbara. His critical writing and editorial leadership (on the journals *Arion* and *Arethusa*) in the 1960s and 1970s made him one of the most important international figures in Latin literary scholarship. He devoted especial attention to the problems of translation, and translated Petronius' *Satyricon* (1965) and Seneca's *Apocolocyntosis* (1977) for Penguin Classics. Other publications include his *Ezra Pound and Sextus Propertius: A Study in Creative Translation* (London, 1964), which brought the classical world's attention to the importance of Pound as a model for translators, and *Martial, The Unexpected Classic: A Literary and Historical Study* (Cambridge, 1991). The latter is the most distinguished account of Martial to date.

From *Epigrams of Martial Englished by Divers Hands* (1987).

Spec. 37

How damned was the Flavian line by that third heir!
Was it worth the benefits of the earlier pair?

Ep. 2.33

Why no kiss, Phyllis? Your bald head.
Why no kiss, Phyllis? Your skin's red.
Why no kiss, Phyllis? Your one eye.
Kissing you, Phyllis, I'd suck. That's why.

Ep. 2.51

You've got just one coin alone in your box,
As smooth as your asshole, worn down by cocks.
This won't go on bread and it won't go on booze,
But a well-hung young stud will soon pry it loose;
So your poor empty stomach will look on in vain,
As your asshole is feasted again and again.

Ep. 3.72

You want a fuck, Saufeia
But not the hot-tub larks.
Something is very queer.
Is it sagging boobs?
Or is it just stretch marks?
A gaping gash from overuse?
A clitoris that's hanging loose?
None of these. Stripped, you'd turn on guests
And you'd look real cool.
You have a worse fault, though –
You are just a fool.

Ep. 3.96

You lick, you don't fuck my baby doll's puss,
Yet you talk like a macho, a goat.
Let me just catch you, Gargilius,
You'll gargle – Deep Throat!

Ep. 5.17

For rank, descent and title famed,
To gentry Gellia showed her hauteur;
She'd wed only a duke, she claimed –
But then she ran off with a porter.

Ep. 7.30

You'll fuck a Frog, a Kraut, a Jew,
    A Gippo, a Brit, a Pakki too;
Niggers and Russkis all go in your stew –
    But my prick's a Wop – Caelia, fuck you!

Ep. 8.1

Here, little book, is my lord's laurelled hall:
So clean up your language before you go call.
Venus, you're naked: stay away from my page;
Caesar's Pallas Minerva, now you take the stage!

Ep. 8.61

Mr. Charinus is livid, is quite beside
Himself with rage; given to frequent sighs;
Eyes tall trees for future suicide.
        But it's not my reputation; the big literary prize,
        My international distribution, world-wide renown
        That he so strongly resents.
        I have my fans, who give me presents:
        A private car, a summer cottage near town.
Severus, suggest a curse for jealous obsessions.
Of course – the dubious joys of such possessions!

Ep. 9.8

You gave Bithynicus thousands yearly; still
He left you not a penny in his will.
But don't be sad; you really score –
You needn't send him money any more.

Ep. 10.69

You set spies on your husband, while you lead a free life:
That's taking, dear Polla, a husband to wife.

Ep. 11.20

These hot six lines, you blue nose, great Augustus wrote,*
Whereas plain, simple Latin is choking in your throat:
Antony is fucking Glaphyra, so Fulvia brings suit –
Now I have to fuck her, and for her I don't give a hoot.
What, I fuck Fulvia? Suppose that Manius begged for my tool,
Would I bugger him? No, never! I don't think I'm quite such a
    fool.
'Fuck or fight!' she demands, but always dearer than breath
To me is my prick. Ho, trumpets, let's fight to the death.
Spicy little books, Augustus, I swear you'd never correct,
For you too could handle your Latin, however blunt and
    direct.

Augustus wrote: The context of this epigram attributed to Augustus is his siege
in 41 BCE of the Umbrian hill-town of Perusia (modern Perugia) held by Mark
Antony's wife, Fulvia, and his brother, Lucius Antonius.

381] EP. 12.91 · J. P. SULLIVAN

Ep. 11.87

Once you were rich, and a gay life you led;
You took boys, never women, into your bed.
Now you're chasing old ladies, down on your luck,
So poverty finally forced you to fuck.

Ep. 12.77

Mr. Bishop was devoutly religious, but once
Standing up and almost on tiptoe
He farted loudly in St. Paul's Cathedral.
The congregation lost some of its gravity.
But receiving no invitations
To dinner for weeks,
Mr. Bishop took it that God was offended.
Now before attending Sunday services,
Mr. Bishop visits the nearby lavatory,
Farting away ten or twenty times.
But for all his loud precautions,
Mr. Bishop now prays with clenched cheeks.

Ep. 12.91

Your husband's bed you share;
Your husband's boy you share;
    Tell me, Magulla, why
    His cup you'll never try.
Is there something of which you're aware?

Apoph. 119 *A Clay Chamberpot*

I snap my fingers; the slave is slow:
So often a pillow absorbs the flow.

Apoph. 134 *A Brassière*

Go, little bra, confine that swelling breast,
That on it my own hand may smoothly rest.

Apoph. 149 *A Wrap*

Big breasts scare me: on adolescent
Bosoms I make a snowy present.

OLIVE PITT–KETHLEY (1915–)

A graduate of Swansea University (in English and German), who
later worked in Military Intelligence. Since her retirement she has
published light verse in such English journals as the *Spectator* and
New Statesman, and contributed translations of Martial to *Epigrams of
Martial Englished by Divers Hands* (1987) and *Roman Poets of the Early
Empire* (1991).

From *Epigrams of Martial Englished by Divers Hands* (1987).

Ep. 1.37

You've a golden pot for your arse
But you drink your wine from glass –
You value your stink
Far more than your drink.

Ep. 2.1

Three hundred epigrams you might have borne,
But who, my book, would then have borne with you?
I keep books short, I make no readers yawn,
Save paper and the busy copyist too.
He'll run you off within an hour maybe,
I'd say you could be read, too, in no more,
And – last good reason for your brevity –
If bad, a shorter book's a shorter bore.
A guest, five measures at his elbow, will
Skim through before his final cup has cooled.
You're reassured? Oh no, for many still
Will find you much too long, so don't be fooled.

Ep. 2.83

You took a dire revenge, one hears,
On him who stole your wife,
By cutting off his nose and ears –
It's marred his social life.
Still there's one thing you didn't get
And that could cause you trouble yet.

Ep. 3.43

You were a swan, you're now a crow.
Laetinus, why deceive us so,
With borrowed plumage trying?
The Queen of Shades will surely know
When she strips off your mask below –
In Death there's no more dyeing.

Ep. 4.66

Life in the provinces is simple, cheap,
And, Linus, that's the sort of style you keep;
You, once or twice a month, shake out its fold,
And dine out in a toga ten years old.
You've woods with boars, and hares to hand – unbought –
And plump field-hares just asking to be caught,
Fish in your rivers; foreign wines you bar,
And drink rough wine poured from an earthen jar.
You never choose your slaves from dear Greek boys,
But keep a crowd of country hobbledehoys.
If, after too much wine, your passions swell,
Housekeeper, farmers' wives, will do quite well.
You've never had a fire, had fields turn brown
In summer drought, nor had your ship go down
– But then you've never had one – nor lost much,
Playing with knucklebones for nuts and such.
Your greedy mother's million – really gone!
What on earth, Linus, have you spent it on?

Ep. 4.88

My gift was small, but you returned me none,
And now five Saturnalian days are done.
Six silver scruples would have been enough –
Even of Septician plate – or piece of stuff
Given by an ill-pleased guest, or even a jar
Of bleeding tuna-pickle from afar,
Antibes-brand; or Syrian figs though tiny
Would have been *something*, and, yes, even the briny
Wrinkled Picenian olives in a punnet
Would have been welcome – but you've gone and done it!
Others may think your words and smiles mean well,
To me you're just a fake-bag – I can tell!

Ep. 6.47

Nymph of the stream, whose limpid water laves,
As it glides in, my Stella's brilliant halls,
Sent by Egeria from the Trivian caves,
Or a ninth Muse perhaps, now Marcus calls
To make an offering of the pure young sow
Promised in sickness, when he drank by stealth
Your lovely waters. Nymph, absolve him now;
Lend him once more your joys, in perfect health.

Ep. 8.23

I gave the cook a beating, not from spite
Or greed, you bumpkin, but to serve him right.
To whip for such a trifle! said your look;
Isn't it just desserts to baste a cook?

Ep. 9.85

Atilius, when our Paulus ails he tends
To diet – well, not himself but all his friends.
Paulus, you're suddenly unwell, you *say*;
All I know is, my dinner's passed away.

Ep. 11.13

Traveller on the Flaminian Way,
Pause a little here, and stay
On this monument your eyes –
Here the actor, Paris, lies,
Delight of Rome, the wit of Nile,
All joy, all art, all grace, all style,
Of all the Roman theatre chief,
Its former joy and now its grief;
Nor for him only shed your tear –
Love and Desire lie with him here.

Ep. 11.21

Lydia is as wide and slack
As a bronze horse's cul-de-sac,
Or sounding hoop with copper rings,
Or board from which an athlete springs,
Or swollen shoe from muddy puddle,
Or net of thrushes in a huddle,
Or awning that won't stay outspread,
In Pompey's theatre, overhead,
Or bracelet that, at every cough,
From a consumptive poof slips off,

French cushion, where the stuffing leaks,
Poor Breton's knackered, baggy breeks,
Foul pelican-crop, Ravenna-bred!
Now there's a rumour – he who said
I had her in the fish-pond joked;
It was the pond itself I poked.

RICHARD O'CONNELL (1928–)

American poet, translator and professor, born in New York City.
He served in the US Navy during the Korean War, later attending
Temple University, Philadelphia, and Johns Hopkins, where he par-
ticipated in the writing seminars of Elliott Coleman. He taught Eng-
lish literature at Temple University, 1957–93, and since 1971 has
edited the *Poetry Newsletter*. In the early sixties he taught as a Fulbright
Lecturer in Brazil and Spain. He is the author of some dozen books
of poems and has translated Sappho, Lorca, Luxorius, epigrams from
the *Greek Anthology*, *Middle English Poems* and *Irish Monastic Poems*, as
well as producing three volumes of translations from Martial (1976–
91). His poetry has appeared in *The Paris Review*, *New Yorker*, *Atlantic
Monthly* and several anthologies. The following come from his latest
collection of Martial translations.

From *New Epigrams from Martial* (1991).

Ep. 1.27 *Bummer*

Last night when I was carried off with wine
I made you promise to drop by and dine
With me today. Only a fool or turd
Expects a drunken man to keep his word.

Ep. 1.46 *Rhythm Method*

Instead of sighing, 'Hurry up and come,'
Try, 'Slower, darling . . .'
                    Then watch my momentum.

Ep. 2.80 *Mars in Reverse*

Fleeing from the enemy, Fannius fell
On his sword, sliding backward into hell.

Ep. 2.86 *To a Superstar*

Just because I don't pour concrete poems,
Or jiggle word games with computers,
Or xerox the graffiti on shithouse walls,
Or pretend that I'm an oppressed minority,
Doesn't mean I'm not *relevant*, Pubicus.
What this means is that I'm a poet
And not a pandering pimp show biz suck-off.

Ep. 3.12 *Funeral Home*

Fabullus, you serve fabulous perfumes;
With candles burning your whole home's a tomb.
Nothing disturbs the funereal mood;
Nothing, Fabullus, not even food.

Ep. 3.23 *To a Waste-not*

Seeing your guests are given doggie bags,
I'm not surprised to see your wife in rags.

Ep. 4.29 *Precious Little*

Pudens, you're right: I publish far too much
For my own good. I should emulate my peers
Who squeeze out poetry like precious oils:
One tiny volume every twenty years.

Ep. 6.91 *Affirmative Suction*

Downwardly mobile Zoilus sucks
With equal gusto cunts and cocks.

Ep. 6.93 *T.O.*

Worse than a fuller's crock full of stale piss
Smashed in the gutter by the slaughterhouse;
Worse than a he-goat straight from rut, and worse
Than a lion's breath or chicken when it rots
In an aborted egg, or hide a dog
Dragged from the Tiber, or a two-eared jar
Of poisonous fish sauce – so Thais smells
Of Thais, when she steps fresh from the bath.

Ep. 7.25 *Critique*

A drop of venom, a little bit of gall.
Lacking these, my friend, your epigrams lack all.

Ep. 7.65 *To a Court Rat*

Gargilianus, you practically live in court,
Carrying on a crazy twenty-year law suit.
Considering how your costs keep mounting up,
Wouldn't it be more economical to lose?

Ep. 8.12 *In the Saddle*

Because I like the superior position,
I won't marry the daughter of a patrician.

Ep. 8.13 *Short-changed*

You said he was a well-hung idiot.
I want my money back:
                          He's literate.

Ep. 9.81 *From the Kitchen*

Everyone enjoys my delightful books
Except a certain poet who objects.
I aim to please my guests, not other cooks.

Ep. 11.60 *Either | Or*

Bassa's a beauty. Phyllis has an itch,
A lecherous itch that could stretch Priam's tool.
If only strait-laced Bassa had that itch
Or Phyllis could be half as beautiful!

Ep. 11.88 *Decommissioned*

Lupus dry-docks his derriere.
Why?
        Diarrhea.

Ep. 12.42 *To a Facade*

The beard and pubic lips complete the front.
Now you resemble what you are: a cunt.

Ep. 12.43 *Tall Cocktail Story*

You tell us they extracted a martini glass stuck up his ass.
Sabellus, tell us this: Did they get the olive?

Ep. 12.80 *Leveller*

To cheat authentic talent of acclaim
Callisto praises everyone the same.

FIONA PITT-KETHLEY (1954–)

A British journalist and writer who lives in London, where she has worked as a columnist for several English newspapers, including *The Times* and the *Guardian*, focusing on sex and the arts. Shortly after graduating from the Chelsea School of Art, she devoted herself full-time to writing, supported at first by film extra work. Her publications include the travel books, *Journeys to the Underworld* (1988) and *The Pan Principle* (1994), the novels, *The Misfortunes of Nigel* (1991) and *The Maiden's Progress* (1992), and some eight books of poetry, including *Sky Ray Lolly* (1986), *Private Parts* (1987), *The Perfect Man* (1989) and *Dogs* (1993). Recently she produced the prose and verse anthology, *The Literary Companion to Sex* (1992); her *The Literary Companion to Low Life* was forthcoming in 1995. She is the daughter of Olive Pitt-Kethley (see p. 382).

From *Epigrams of Martial Englished by Divers Hands* (1987) and *The Literary Companion to Sex* (1992).

Ep. 2.6

You bid me publish pamphlets now, go on!
    You've hardly read the first two pages when
You, Severus, turn to the colophon
    Yawning. These verses, which, read out again
By me, you used to snatch and copy out
    Upon Vitellian tablets.* These, of old,
You took to dos and theatres round about,
    Tucked away singly in your toga's fold –

Vitellian tablets: small tablets suitable for private (love) messages

These ones, or better ones as yet untold.
        If you must take three days to read it through,
What good's a book, thin as a rod, to me?
        Never was dilettante slacker. You
Give up so soon, a tired traveller. You'd be
        For changing at Camenae if you'd gone
To Bovillae upon some business, too.
        You bid me publish pamphlets now, go on!

Ep. 2.33 *To Philaenis*

Why don't I kiss you? You're as bald as a coot . . .
Why don't I kiss you? You're bright red to boot . . .
Why don't I kiss you? You've only one eye . . .
Kissing you'd be just a blow job, that's why.

Ep. 4.30

Fisher, I warn, from Baiae's lake fly far,
Lest you with guilt depart. These waters swim
With sacred fish who know their lord and are
Obedient to his call. They come to him
And suck that hand, than which there can be none
More great on earth. Each fish is named and they
Swim to their master's voice. Here, some time gone,
An impious Libyan pulling in his prey
From depths, his line quivering, was robbed of sight
And couldn't see the fish; deprived of light,
Loathing his sacrilegious hooks, he sits
And begs by Baiae's lake. At any rate,
Go while you can, still guiltless. Throw plain bits
Of food. The dainty fishes, venerate.

Ep. 4.50

Why, Thais, do you call me an old man?
Where blow jobs are concerned, even old men can.

Ep. 4.84

No man among the people, or in all Rome can show
That he's fucked Thais – many'd like and many've asked,
        you know.
'Is Thais then so chaste?' I said.
'By no means. She sucks pricks instead.'

Ep. 5.41

You've less balls than the loose eunuch; you're more
Unmanly than that Phrygian boy-whore
Cried by the ecstatic Mother's gelded priests,
Yet you talk theatres, places, the Ides' feasts,
Clasps, ceremonial robes, property, and
Point out the needy with your pumiced hand.
If you can use a knight's seat at the play,
I'll see, Dindymus; a husband's though – no way!

Ep. 6.36

His tool was large and so was his nose,
Papylus could smell it whenever it rose.

Ep. 7.72

Paulus, may December bring
You all the best of everything;
Hand-towels, short-weight frankincense,
Useless three-leafed tablets – hence!
No! gifts from friends or from the great,
Antique goblets, massy plate,
Or – which perhaps may please you more –
Novius or Publius to outscore
At Pawns and Robbers; or withstand
Polybus of the swift left-hand
When stripped for play – great praise to earn
From seasoned athletes. In return
Defend me with your voice of might
When I'm maligned as black with spite,
And shout till all the welkin rings;
'My Martial never wrote such things.'

Ep. 7.92

'When there is need, you do not have to plead!'
You say, Baccara, twice or thrice a day.
When hard Secundus whines to me to pay:
You hear, Baccara, and don't know my need.
I'm dunned before you in a public way:
You hear, Baccara, and don't know my need.
When I complain of my threadbare array:
You hear, Baccara, and don't know my need.
My need's some blow of fate, so you won't say
Your piece again, Baccara, 'When there's need . . .'

Ep. 9.4

Galla'll be fucked for two pieces of gold.
She'll do something more, for two more, I am told.
Aeschylus, why does she have ten from you?
Her blow jobs come cheaper. What then? Silence, too?

Ep. 9.69

When you fuck, Polycharmus, you end by shitting,
When poked, Polycharmus, what'll be fitting?

Ep. 11.62

Lesbia swears she's never screwed for free.
That's true, for when she's fucked, she pays the fee.

Ep. 12.23

You're not ashamed to use the teeth and hair you buy.
What'll you do, Laelia? One can't buy an eye.

ENGLISH TEXTS USED
IN THIS ANTHOLOGY

I. TUDOR ENGLAND TO THE RESTORATION: 1540–1660

Henry Howard, Earl of Surrey, *Tottel's Miscellany* (London, 1557, 1st edn, 5 June).

Timothe Kendall, *Flovvers of Epigrammes, out of Sundrie the Moste Singular Authours Selected, as well Auncient as Late Writers* (London, 1577).

Thomas Bastard, *Chrestoleros. Seuen Bookes of Epigrames written by T. B.* (London, 1598).

John Marston, *The Metamorphosis of Pigmalions Image and Certaine Satyres* (London, 1598).

Anon. (sixteenth century), British Library Egerton MS 2982.

Francis Davison, *A Poetical Rapsody Containing Diverse Sonnets, Odes, Elegies, Madrigalls, and Other Poesies, both in Rime, and Measured Verse* (London, 1602).

Sir John Harington, *The Most Elegant and Witty Epigrams of Sir Iohn Harington, Knight, Digested into Foure Bookes* (London, 1618).

John Donne, *Poems, by J. D. with Elegies on the Authors Death* (London, 1633).

Ben Jonson, *The Workes of Beniamin Ionson* (London, 1616); *Ben Jonson*, ed. C. H. Herford, P. & E. Simpson, vol. viii (Oxford, 1947).

Thomas May, *Selected Epigramms of Martial Englished* (London, 1629).

Robert Herrick, *Hesperides: Or, The Works Both Humane & Divine of Robert Herrick Esq.* (London, 1648).

Sir Richard Fanshawe, *Il Pastor Fido, The Faithfull Shepheard, with An Addition of Divers Other Poems, Concluding with a Short Discourse of the Long Civil Warres of Rome* (London, 1648).

William Cartwright, *Comedies, Tragi-Comedies, with Other Poems* (London, 1651).

Richard Crashaw, *Steps to the Temple, Sacred Poems, with the Delights of the Muses* (London, 1648).

Sir Edward Sherburne, *Poems and Translations* or (alternative title) *Salmacis,*

Lyrian & Sylvia, Forsaken Lydia, The Rape of Helen, A Comment thereon, with Severall Other Poems and Translations (London, 1651).

Robert Fletcher, *Ex Otio Negotium. Or Martiall His Epigrams Translated. With Sundry Poems and Fancies* (London, 1656).

Thomas Pecke, *Parnassi Puerperium . . . Six Hundred of Owen's Epigrams, Martial de Spectaculis, Sir Thomas More; Libellus de Spectaculis: Or, an Account of the Most Memorable Monuments of the Romane Glory* (London, 1659).

II. THE RESTORATION TO THE AUGUSTANS: 1660–*c.*1700

James Wright, *Sales Epigrammaton: Being the Choicest Disticks of Martials Fourteen Books of Epigrams; And of All the Chief Latine Poets that have Writ in These Two Last Centuries. Together with Cato's Morality. Made English* (London, 1663).

Abraham Cowley, *The Works of Mr Abraham Cowley, Consisting of Those which were Formerly Printed and Those which He Design'd for the Press, Now Published out of the Authors Original Copies* (London, 1668); *Poems* (London, 1656).

Sir John Denham, *Poems and Translations, with the Sophy* (London, 1668).

John Wilmot, Earl of Rochester, *Poems on Several Occasions, by the Right Honourable, The Earl of R—* (Antwerp [= London], 1680: Huntington edition); *The Complete Poems of John Wilmot, Earl of Rochester*, ed. D. M. Vieth (New Haven and London, 1968).

John Dryden, *Absalom and Achitophel. A Poem* (London, 1681); *The Poems of John Dryden*, ed. J. Kinsley, 4 vols. (Oxford, 1958).

John Oldham, *Poems and Translations* (London, 1683).

Charles Cotton, *The Essays of Michael Seigneur de Montaigne, Translated into English* (7th edn, London, 1759).

Thomas Heyrick, *Miscellany Poems* (Cambridge, 1691).

Henry Killigrew, *Epigrams of Martial Englished. With Some Other Pieces, Ancient and Modern* (London, 1695).

Thomas Brown, *A Collection of Miscellany Poems, Letters, &c. by Mr. Brown, to which is Added, A Character of a Latitudinarian* (London, 1699); *The Fourth and Last Volume of the Works of Mr. Thomas Brown, Containing many Miscellaneous Discourses in Prose and Verse* (7th edn, London, 1730).

Sir Charles Sedley, *The Miscellaneous Works of the Honourable Sir Charles Sedley, Bart., Containing Satyrs, Epigrams, Court-Characters, Transla-*

tions, Essays, and Speeches in Parliament . . . Published by Capt. Ayloffe (London, 1702).

Anon. (seventeenth century), British Library MS Add. 27343.

III. THE EIGHTEENTH CENTURY: AUGUSTANS AND NEOCLASSICISTS

Matthew Prior, *The Literary Works of Matthew Prior*, ed. H. Bunker Wright and M. K. Spears (Oxford, 1959; rev. ed., 1971).

Joseph Addison, *The Works of the Right Honourable Joseph Addison, Esq.* (London, 1721); *The Spectator*, ed. D. F. Bond (Oxford, 1965).

Sir Richard Steele, *The Occasional Verse of Richard Steele*, ed. R. Blanchard (Oxford, 1952); *The Spectator*, ed. D. F. Bond (Oxford, 1965).

Aaron Hill, *The Works of the Late Aaron Hill, Esq; in Four Volumes, Consisting of Letters on Various Subjects, And of Original Poems, Moral and Facetious* (London, 1753).

Alexander Pope, *The Works of Alexander Pope Esq., in Nine Volumes Complete, With his Last Corrections, Additions and Improvements, as They were Delivered to the Editor a Little before His death: Together with the Commentaries and Notes of Mr. Warburton* (London, 1751); *Additions to the Works of Alexander Pope, Esq., Together with Many Original Poems and Letters of Contemporary Writers, Never Before Published, in Two Volumes* (London, 1776).

Jonathan Swift, *The Poems of Jonathan Swift*, ed. H. Williams (Oxford, 1937); *The Epigrams of Martial*, ed. H. Bohn (London, 1860).

William Hay, *Select Epigrams of Martial Translated and Imitated. With an Appendix of Some by Cowley and Other Hands* (London, 1755).

Samuel Johnson, *The Poems of Samuel Johnson*, ed. D. Nichol Smith and E. L. McAdam (Oxford, 1974); *Epigrams of Martial Englished*, ed. J. P. Sullivan and P. Whigham (Berkeley/Los Angeles, 1987).

Revd William Scott, *Epigrams of Martial, &c. with Mottos from Horace, &c. Translated, Imitated, Adapted, and Addrest to the Nobility, Clergy and Gentry, with Notes Moral, Historical, Explanatory and Humorous* (London, 1773).

James Elphinston, *The Epigrams of M. Val. Martial, in Twelve Books: with a Comment* (London, 1782).

Nathaniel Brassey Halhed, *Imitations of Some of the Epigrams of Martial*, Parts I & II (London, 1793).

IV. THE ROMANTICS TO POUND: 1800–*c*.1950

Samuel Taylor Coleridge, *The Complete Poetical Works of Samuel Taylor Coleridge*, ed. E. H. Coleridge (Oxford, 1912).

Walter Savage Landor, *The Works and Life of Walter Savage Landor*, ed. J. Forster, 8 vols. (London, 1874–6); *Complete Works of Walter Savage Landor*, ed. T. E. Welby and S. Wheeler, 16 vols. (London, 1927–36).

George Lamb, *The Poems of Caius Valerius Catullus Translated with a Preface and Notes*, 2 vols. (London, 1821).

George Gordon, Lord Byron, *Lord Byron: The Complete Poetical Works*, ed. J. J. McGann, 7 vols. (Oxford, 1980–93).

Leigh Hunt, *The Poetical Works of Leigh Hunt, Now Finally Collected, Revised by Himself* (London, 1860).

George Augustus Sala, *The Index Expurgatorius of Martial, Literally Translated, Comprising All the Epigrams Hitherto Omitted by English Translators, to Which is Added an Original Metrical Version and Copious Explanatory Notes* (London, 1868).

Robert Louis Stevenson, *Collected Poems*, ed J. Adam Smith (London, 1950).

Goldwin Smith, *Bay of Leaves: Translations from the Latin Poets* (New York and London, 1893).

Anon. (nineteenth century), *The Epigrams of Martial*, ed. H. Bohn (London, 1860).

An Eton Master, *Fifty Epigrams from the First Book of Martial, Translated into English Verse* (London, 1900).

A. E. Street, *Martial, 120 Selected Epigrams Metrically Rendered in English* (Eton, Berks., 1907).

Paul Nixon, *A Roman Wit, Epigrams of Martial Rendered into English* (Boston and New York, 1911).

W. J. Courthope, *Selections from the Epigrams of M. Valerius Martialis. Translated or Imitated in English Verse* (London, 1914).

J. A. Pott and F. A. Wright, *Martial, The Twelve Books of Epigrams* (London and New York, 1925).

A. L. Francis and H. F. Tatum, *Martial's Epigrams: Translations and Imitations* (Cambridge, 1924).

Ezra Pound, *Personae: The Collected Poems of Ezra Pound* (London, 1926); *Imagi* 5.2 (1950).

V. THE MODERN WORLD: THE LATE TWENTIETH CENTURY

Rolfe Humphries, *Selected Epigrams of Martial* (Bloomington, 1963).

Dudley Fitts, *Sixty Poems of Martial in Translation* (New York, 1967).

Philip Murray, *Poems after Martial* (Middletown, Conn., 1967).

J. V. Cunningham, *The Collected Poems and Epigrams of J. V. Cunningham* (London, 1971).

Donald C. Goertz, *Select Epigrams of Martial* (New York, 1971).

Peter Porter, *After Martial* (London, 1972).

Brian Hill, *An Eye for Ganymede, Forty Epigrams of Marcus Valerius Martialis* (London, 1972).

James Michie, *Martial: The Epigrams* (Harmondsworth, 1978).

Dorothea Wender, *Roman Poetry: From the Republic to the Silver Age* (Carbondale, Ill., 1980).

Tony Harrison, *U.S. Martial* (Newcastle-upon-Tyne, 1981).

Peter Whigham, *Letter to Juvenal: 101 Epigrams from Martial* (London, 1985); *Epigrams of Martial Englished by Divers Hands*, ed. J. P. Sullivan and P. Whigham (Berkeley, Los Angeles and London, 1987).

J. P. Sullivan, *Epigrams of Martial Englished by Divers Hands* (ibid.).

Olive Pitt-Kethley: *Epigrams of Martial Englished by Divers Hands* (ibid.).

Richard O'Connell, *New Epigrams from Martial* (Boca Raton, 1991).

Fiona Pitt-Kethley, *Epigrams of Martial Englished by Divers Hands* (op. cit.); *The Literary Companion to Sex* (London, 1992).

OTHER ENGLISH TRANSLATIONS OF MARTIAL

Anon., Cambridge University Library Donington Ms. d. 58.

—, *M. Val. Martialis Spectaculorum Liber Paraphrais'd* (London, 1674).

—, *Thalia or the Spritely Muse*, by a Nobleman of 15 [Charles Ba—e] (London, 1705).

Ashmore, John, *Certain Selected Odes of Horace . . . New Epigrams* (London, 1621).

Barth, R. L., *Earthenware: XLVI Epigrams from Martial* (Havertown, Penn., 1988).

Bohn, Henry George (ed.), *The Epigrams of Martial, Translated into English Prose, Each Accompanied by One or More Verse Translations from the Works of English Poets, and Various Other Sources* (London, 1860).

Booth, Revd John, *Epigrams, Ancient and Modern* (London, 1863).

Bovie, Palmer, *Epigrams of Martial* (New York, 1970).

Boyle, A. J., and Sullivan, J. P. (eds.), *Roman Poets of the Early Empire* (Harmondsworth, 1991).

Buck, Mitchell S., *Martial. Epigrams in 15 Books. Completely Translated for the First Time* (Boston, 1921).

Carrington, A. G., *Aspects of Martial's Epigrams* (Eton, Berks., 1960).

Dodd, H. P., *The Epigrammatists* (London, 1870).

Duggan, Laurie, *Epigrams from Martial* (Melbourne, 1988).

Eliot, John, *Poems: Consisting of Epistles and Epigrams* (London, 1658).

Ellis, H. D., *English Verse Translations of Selections from Odes of Horace, Epigrams of Martial and Other Writers* (London, 1920).

Grant, Michael, *Latin Literature: An Anthology* (Harmondsworth, 1979).

Grundy, G. B., *Ancient Gems in Modern Settings* (Oxford, 1913).

Hill, Brian, *Ganymede in Rome: Twenty-Eight Epigrams of Martial* (London, 1971).

Hughes, J., *Miscellanies in Verse and Prose* (London, 1737).

Ker, W. C. A., *Martial: Epigrams* (Cambridge, Mass., 1925).

Lind, L. R. (ed.): *Latin Poetry in Verse Translation* (Boston, 1957).

Marcellino, Ralph, *The Pensive and the Antic Muse: Translations from Martial* (West Hempstead, New York, 1963).

—, *Martial: Selected Epigrams* (Indianapolis, 1968).

Mills, Barriss, *Epigrams from Martial: A Verse Translation* (Lafayette, Indiana, 1969).

O'Connell, Richard, *Epigrams from Martial* (Philadelphia, 1976).

—, *More Epigrams from Martial* (Philadelphia, 1981).

Pestell, Thomas, *The Poems of Thomas Pestell*, ed. Hannah Buchan (Oxford, 1940).

Randolph, Thomas, *Poems, With the Muses Looking-glasse and Amyntas* (Oxford, 1638).

—, *Poems*, ed. G. Thorn-Drury (London, 1929).

Raymond, Oliver, *To Be Plain: Translations from Greek, Latin, French and German* (Florence, Kentucky, n.d.).

Rieu, E. V., *A Book of Latin Poetry* (London, 1925).

Shackleton Bailey, D. R., *Martial: Epigrams*, 3 vols. (Cambridge, Mass., 1993).

Shaw, William Francis, *Juvenal, Persius, Martial, and Catullus: An Experiment in Translation* (London, 1882).

Stanley, Thomas, *Poems*, ed. Brydges (London, 1814–15).

Stoneman, Richard, *Daphne into Laurel: Translations of Classical Poetry from Chaucer to the Present* (London, 1982).

Sullivan, J. P. and Whigham, Peter (eds.), *Epigrams of Martial Englished by Divers Hands* (Berkeley, Los Angeles and London, 1987).

Tomlinson, Charles (ed.), *The Oxford Book of Verse in Translation* (Oxford, 1980).

Webb, W. T., *Select Epigrams from Martial for English Readers* (London, 1879).

West, Alfred Slater, *Wit and Wisdom from Martial Contained in 150 of His Epigrams Chosen and Done into English with Introduction and Notes* (London, 1912).

Westcott, J. H., *One Hundred and Twenty Epigrams of Martial* (Boston, 1894).

FURTHER READING

Garthwaite, J., 'The Panegyrics of Domitian in Martial Book 9', *Ramus* 22 (1993), 78–102.

Holzberg, N., *Martial* (Heidelberg, 1988).

Hooley, D. M., *The Classics in Paraphrase: Ezra Pound and Modern Translators of Latin Poetry* (London and Toronto, 1988).

Love, H. (ed.), *The Penguin Book of Restoration Verse* (Harmondsworth, 1968).

Mason, H. A., 'Is Martial a Classic?', *Cambridge Quarterly* 17 (1988), 297–368.

Nixon, P., *Martial and the Modern Epigram* (New York, 1927).

Norbrook, D., and Woudhuysen, H. R. (eds.), *The Penguin Book of Renaissance Verse 1509–1659* (Harmondsworth, 1993).

Stoneman, R. (ed.), *Daphne into Laurel: Translations of Classical Poetry from Chaucer to the Present* (London, 1982).

Sullivan, J. P. (ed.), *Martial* (New York and London, 1993).

—, *Martial: The Unexpected Classic. A Literary and Historical Study* (Cambridge, 1991).

— and Whigham, P. (eds.), *The Epigrams of Martial Englished by Divers Hands* (Berkeley, Los Angeles and London, 1987).

GLOSSARY OF SELECTED
ANCIENT NAMES

This glossary lists the names of the major historical and mythological figures referred to in the epigrams. Many of the names in Martial's verses are of friends, enemies and other contemporaries about whom little or nothing is known. Except for a handful of Martial's closest friends their names are not included here.

ACHILLES Greatest of the Greek warriors in the Trojan war and hero of Homer's *Iliad*; son of Peleus, king of Thessaly, and of Thetis, a sea nymph. His love for his friend and attendant Patroclus, who went to his death wearing Achilles' armour, was famous.

AEACUS A judge of the dead.

AEGEAN ('Egean') Sea between the east coast of Greece and Asia.

AEGLE One of the Hesperides.

AENEID Virgil's great foundation epic of Rome.

AESOP ('Esop') Author of fables, especially animal fables, who lived as a slave or ex-slave on the island of Samos in the sixth century BCE.

AGRIPPA Marcus Vipsanius; victorious admiral at Actium (31 BCE) and major minister of the first emperor, Augustus. He was responsible for a large building programme in Rome (especially in the Campus Martius) during the 20s BCE.

ALBAN Name of the hills in which Alba Longa is situated just south of Rome.

ALBIUS Tibullus; Roman writer of the love elegy in the Augustan period (d. 19 BCE).

ALCIDES Patronym of Hercules, from his family connection with Alcaeus, father of Amphitryon, husband of Hercules' mother Alcmene.

ALCINOUS King of the mythical Phaeacians, who received Odysseus as a guest during his wanderings and entertained him generously. Alcinous' gardens, lavishly described in *Odyssey* 7, were much celebrated by the poets.

ALGIDO Mountainous area to the south of Tusculum.

ANACREON Greek lyric poet of the sixth century BCE.

ANDROMACHE Trojan heroine, wife of the warrior Hector, daughter-in-law of Priam and Hecuba, mother of Astyanax.

ANTAEUS Giant from Libya, wrestled to his death by Hercules.

ANTONY ('Anthony', 'Antonius') Marcus Antonius ('Mark Antony'), c.82–30 BCE; Julius Caesar's chief lieutenant in the civil war with Pompey. He was a notorious womanizer. After sharing the Roman world with him, he was defeated by Octavian (later the first emperor Augustus) at Actium in 31 BCE.

ANXUR Ancient coastal town of southern Latium; modern Terracina.

AONIA ('Aon') Area of Boeotia containing Mount Helicon, home of the Muses.

APICIUS ('Appicius') Celebrated gourmet of the early first century CE.

APOLLO God of music, poetry, prophecy, healing, and archery; son of Jupiter and Latona, brother of Diana. He was sometimes identified with the sun. Also called Phoebus.

APOLLODORUS Obscure Egyptian writer.

APONUS A warm mineral spring six miles from Patavium (modern Padua), where Livy was born.

APPIAN WAY Arterial road running south from Rome to Brundisium (modern Brindisi); first of Rome's great roads.

APPIUS Claudius Caecus; censor in 312 BCE, builder of Rome's first aqueduct and first great road, the *Via Appia* or Appian Way.

ARES Greek god of war (= Roman Mars).

ARGO ('Argus') Speech-endowed ship that carried the Argonauts on the voyage (often represented as the first of all voyages) to regain the Golden Fleece.

ARICIA Ancient town in Latium near Alba Longa.

ARMENIA Mountainous country of Asia, east of the Euphrates.

ARPI Town in southern Italy, used by Martial as a substitute for Arpinum, birthplace of the great Roman orator Cicero.

ARRIA Aristocratic Roman wife of Caecina Paetus. A professed Stoic, when her husband was condemned by the emperor Claudius for his role in a conspiracy against him, she stabbed herself and handed Paetus the dagger, saying, 'Paetus, it does not hurt.'

ATLAS A Titan who bore the sky upon his shoulders (also the guardian of the pillars of heaven); symbol of immense strength.

ATTICA Area of Greece in which Athens is situated; adj. 'Attic', generally = 'Athenian'.

ATTIS ('Atys') Emasculated devotee (or consort) of the goddess, the Great Mother, Cybele.

AUGUSTUS The name taken by the first emperor of Rome (27 BCE–14 CE), and, like the name 'Caesar', used by subsequent emperors; most often = Domitian.

AVENTINE One of Rome's seven hills, on which was an ancient temple to Diana.

BABYLON Famed capital of Babylonia, a kingdom in the Middle East on both sides of the Euphrates.

BACCHUS Son of Jupiter and Semele; god of vegetation, wine, poets and inspiration. He forcibly imposed his cult on Thebes.

BAETIS ('Betis') River of southern Spain, now called Guadalquivir; adj. 'Baetic' or 'Betick'.

BAIAE ('Baia', 'Baja') Seaside pleasure resort in Campania near Naples, popular because of its warm baths and scenic beauty; adj. 'Baian'.

BELLONA Native Roman war goddess, who was later assimilated to, or associated with, Cybele. Her devotees, like those of Cybele, were self-castrated.

BILBILIS Ancient Spanish hill town in modern Aragón, overlooking the river Salo (modern Jalón). It was the birthplace of Martial.

BOTERDUS Sacred forest close to Bilbilis.

BOVILLAE Town on the Appian Way twelve miles south of Rome.

BRISEIS Captive and concubine of Achilles at Troy. She was taken from Achilles by Agamemnon and later restored (in Homer's *Iliad*).

BRUTUS (1) Lucius Junius, liberator of Rome and first consul (509 BCE), and husband of Lucretia, paradigm of wifely chastity – see *Lucretia*; (2) Marcus Junius, assassin of Julius Caesar, defeated by Mark Antony and Octavian at Philippi (42 BCE).

CAECUBAN ('Cæcub') Wine from the prized area of southern Latium.

CAELIAN One of Rome's seven hills, which actually contained two hills, the Caelian and the little Caelian (*Caeliolus*).

CAESAR Family name of Julius Caesar (100–44 BCE), and the normal appellation of the emperor, beginning with the first emperor Augustus; in Martial it generally refers to Domitian.

CALLIMACHUS Influential Alexandrian poet (*c*.305–240 BCE), grammarian and critic, whose works include *Aetia* ('Origins'), a long poem on the origins of places, names and rituals.

CALYDON Settlement in Aetolia, north-west Greece; centre of a famous boar hunt.

CAMENAE Italian nymphs, who became the Italian goddesses of song. They had a temple just outside one of the main gates of Rome, the Porta Capena.

CAMPANIA Area of western central Italy bounded by the Apennines and the Tyrrhenian Sea (Mediterranean), and by Latium and the Sorrento peninsula. Its towns included Capua, Naples, Baiae, Pompeii and Puteoli.

CAMPUS MARTIUS Field of Mars, a large area on the bank of the Tiber originally used for military training but studded in imperial times with temples, colonnades, theatres, gymnasia and running tracks. A popular meeting place for business, athletics and religious and social gatherings.

CANIUS Rufus; historian, poet and close friend of Martial from Spain.

CAPITOL Most important of Rome's seven hills. Built on it was a citadel and temple of Jupiter.

CARIA Province in Asia Minor south of Lydia.

CARTHAGE City of north Africa founded and ruled in legend by Dido; major military power with Rome, and its chief rival in the Mediterranean in the third century BCE. The most devastating of the wars between Rome and Carthage was the second Punic War (218–201 BCE).

CASTALIA Nymph of the Castalian spring (of poetic inspiration) at the foot of Mount Parnassus. The fountain was sacred to Apollo and the Muses.

CASTOR One of the Gemini or Heavenly Twins, whose temple stood prominently in the Roman forum.

CATILINE ('Catilin') Lucius Sergius (d. 62 BCE); aristocrat with frustrated political ambitions who took up the cause of the people and attempted a revolution against the state during Cicero's consulship (63 BCE). His forces were defeated and he himself killed.

CATO Marcus Porcius, the younger (95–46 BCE); staunch and moralistic republican who committed suicide rather than surrender to Julius Caesar in the civil war. He became a symbol of puritanical conservatism.

CATULLUS Gaius Valerius, c.84–54 BCE; Roman lyric poet, notorious for his liaison with Lesbia.

CATULUS Quintus Lutatius; Roman aristocrat, son of the consul of 102 BCE, himself consul in 78 BCE, who restored the temple of Jupiter on the Capitol in the most lavish way, dedicating it in 69 BCE.

CAUCASUS Range of mountains between the Black and Caspian Seas; scene of the punishment of Prometheus.

CECROPS Ancient king of Attica/Athens; 'Cecropia' = 'Athens'; adj. 'Cecropian' = 'Athenian' or 'Attic'.

CELTIBERIA North-east Spain, where lived the 'Celtiberians', a racial combination of Celts and native Iberians.

CENTAUR One of a race of half-equine, half-human creatures who lived in the wooded mountains of Thessaly; known for their unbridled passions.

CERBERUS Monstrous three-headed dog that guarded the entrance to the underworld.

CHALYBES Black Sea people famous for metal production.

CHARON Ferryman of the underworld, who conveyed the shades of the dead across the river Styx.

CICERO ('Tully') Marcus Tullius, 106–43 BCE; Roman orator and statesman who revolutionized Roman prose. His speeches against Mark Antony, *Philippics*, led to his proscription and execution. He also wrote poetry which was widely derided, among which was an epic on his own consulship.

CLAUDIUS Roman emperor 41–54 CE.

CLEOPATRA VII; Queen of Egypt, lover of Julius Caesar and Mark Antony, whom she aided in his struggle against Octavian (later, the first emperor, Augustus). After their defeat at Actium, her hopes disappointed, she committed suicide (30 BCE).

COLCHIS Kingdom east of the Black Sea, home of Medea; adj. 'Colchian'.

COLOSSUS ('Coloss') (1) Colossal statue of Nero (with the head altered to resemble that of the sun god) situated at the entrance to the Sacred Way (the 'Colosseum' derived its name from proximity to this statue); (2) The Colossus of Rhodes, a gigantic statue of Helios/Sol, the sun god.

CONCORD Roman goddess with a major temple in the Roman Forum.

CORDUBA Modern Cordova, city in southern Spain, from which the family of the Annaei (the two Senecas, Lucan) originated.

CORINNA (Fictive?) woman in Ovid's love poetry; often regarded as Ovid's girlfriend.

CORNELIA Aristocratic Roman lady of the second century BCE; daughter of Scipio Africanus, wife of Titus Sempronius Gracchus, and mother of the revolutionary tribunes, Tiberius and Gaius Gracchus; renowned as the 'mother of the Gracchi', she was also famous for her morality and intelligence.

CORYBANT Priest of Cybele, the Great Mother goddess.

CRASSUS Marcus Licinius, d. 53 BCE; Roman general and financier of enormous wealth.

CROESUS ('Cresus') Last king of Lydia (sixth century BCE), whose wealth was proverbial. He was overthrown by the Persian king, Cyrus.

CUPID Son of Venus; usually represented as a smiling winged infant armed with a bow and arrows, which when shot inspire love and desire.

CURIUS ('Curio') Third-century-BCE general and censor; example of traditional Roman virtue.

CYANEAN See *Symplegades*.

CYBELE The Great Mother, an orgiastic Anatolian mother-goddess, associated with Phrygia. Her cult was introduced into Rome *c*.205 BCE, where she had a temple on the Palatine. Her consort was Attis.

CYNTHIA (1) The goddess Diana; (2) Name of the (fictive?) woman loved and often addressed by the poet in Propertius' elegies.

CYPRIA Another name for Venus, derived from her famous cult at Paphos on Cyprus; adj. 'Cyprian'.

DAEDALUS ('Dedalus') Mythical architect of the Cretan labyrinth, who constructed wings for himself and his son Icarus to fly to freedom from Crete. When Icarus flew too near the sun, the wax securing the wings melted and he fell to his death.

DAPHNE Nymph who was turned into a laurel as she fled Apollo's erotic pursuit.

DECIANUS Stoic writer and friend of Martial from Emerita in Spain.

DELOS Small island in the Aegean, birthplace of Apollo and Diana and site of famous sanctuaries to them.

DEUCALION Survivor (with his wife Pyrrha) of the great flood sent by Jupiter. He and his wife regenerated the human race by throwing stones behind them.

DIANA Goddess of the hunt, the moon, and childbirth; daughter of Jupiter and Latona and sister of Apollo. There was a famous temple to her at Ephesus in Ionia/Asia Minor.

DIRCE Queen of Thebes, killed by Amphion and Zethus. She was either thrown into or became the famous spring near Thebes which bears her name.

DOMITIAN Son of the emperor Vespasian (69–79 CE), brother of the emperor Titus (79–81 CE), and last of the Flavian dynasty. *Epigrams*, Books 1–9 and the first version of Book 10 were written during his period as Roman emperor (81–96 CE). Among the titles Domitian assumed were 'censor perpetual' and the notorious 'master and god'. He was assassinated before reaching the age of forty-five, and condemned to oblivion by the Roman Senate, who hated him.

DRYAD Wood nymph.

EARINUS ('Earinos') Domitian's young favourite and castrated catamite; he was a freedman from Pergamum in Asia Minor. His name ironically means 'Vernal' or 'Springboy', and is the source of much wordplay among the Flavian poets.

EGEAN See *Aegean*.

EGERIA One of four prophetic Italian nymphs, the Camenae (later the Italian Muses); honoured as the 'wife' and advisor of Numa.

EMERITA City of south-west Spain; modern Merida.

ENDYMION Beautiful youth, loved by Diana and granted eternal sleep by Jupiter.

ENNIUS Quintus, 239–169 BCE; revered Roman tragedian and epic poet, whose *Annals* chronicled the rise of Rome and influenced Virgil's *Aeneid*.

EPHESUS City on the west coast of Anatolia, famed for its temple to Diana; adj. 'Ephesian'.

EPIMETHEUS Literally 'After-Thinker', Prometheus' less intelligent brother, who ignored Prometheus' advice and married Pandora.

EROTION Loved and lamented slave-girl of Martial, who died before her sixth birthday.

ERYTHRAEAN From the Red Sea, *mare Erythrum*.

EUROPA Daughter of the king of Tyre; she was raped by Jupiter in the guise of a bull and taken to Crete.

FABRICIUS ('Fabricio') Roman general of the third century BCE and example of traditional Roman virtue.

FALERNIAN Among the best of Roman wines, from vineyards in northern Campania.

FATES Three sisters who determined the length of a person's life, conceived of as a thread of varying length.

FAUN Minor rural god associated with Satyrs.

FIDENAE ('Fidena') Town just five miles north of Rome.

FLACCUS (1) Rich friend of Martial addressed in many epigrams; (2) Horace, the lyric poet (see *Horace*).

FLACILLA Mother of Martial or of Erotion.

FLAMINIAN WAY Arterial road leading from Rome to northern Italy.

FLAVIAN Pertaining to the imperial family of the Flavii, viz. Vespasian, Titus and Domitian.

FLORA Italian goddess of flowers; her festival, the Floralia (28 April–3 May), was a licentious holiday celebrating the rites of spring. Games, stage shows and exhibitions of naked prostitutes were featured.

FRONTO Name of Martial's father or of the father of Erotion.

FULVIA Strong-minded wife of Mark Antony in the late forties BCE.

GADES Important port city in southern Spain; modern Cadiz.

GAIUS Mountain in north-east Spain.

GALAESUS ('Galesus') River near Tarentum, south-east Italy; adj. 'Gal(a)esian'.

GALATEA Name of a beautiful sea nymph; more generally, a beautiful woman.

GALLUS Gaius Cornelius (c.69–26 BCE); soldier, political figure and elegiac poet of the late republic, who committed suicide after falling from favour with Augustus. Often credited as the founder of Roman love elegy.

GANYMEDE ('Ganimed') Handsome son of Laomedon who was carried by Jupiter's eagle from Mt Ida to heaven to serve as cup-bearer (and catamite) to Jupiter.

GORGONS Three mythical monsters, girded with snakes and having wings, brazen claws and enormous teeth. The most famous was Medusa.

GRACCHUS See *Cornelia*.

HAEMUS Mountain range in northern Thrace.

HANNIBAL Leading Carthaginian general in the second Punic War (218–201 BCE); after bringing his army across the Alps with the aid of elephants, he defeated Rome in many battles in Italy before being defeated himself at Zama near Carthage.

HARPIES Fierce, winged monsters, with faces of women and the bodies of vultures. They left a stench, and snatched and defiled the food of their victims.

HECTOR Son of Priam and Hecuba, husband of Andromache, and the greatest warrior among the Trojans in Homer's *Iliad*. He was slain by Achilles, who dragged his corpse three times around Troy.

HECUBA Wife of Priam, king of Troy, and mother of numerous Trojan heroes and heroines; in her grief over Greek brutality and the loss of her children, she was turned first into a barking dog and then into a rock known as the 'Dog's Tomb' (Cynossema).

HELEN Wife of the Spartan king Menelaus, whose abduction by the Trojan prince Paris (promised the most beautiful woman in the world) precipitated the Trojan war. She came to symbolize female beauty and infidelity.

HELLESPONT Modern name, the Dardanelles.

HERCULES Son of Jupiter and Alcmene, a hero of incredible strength who even strangled two serpents in his cradle. His Twelve Labours were performed either out of duty to Eurystheus of Argos or as a penance imposed on him by Delphi to expiate the killing of his own children in a fit of madness. He was deified for his achievements. His boy attendant and lover was Hylas, who was taken from him during the voyage of the Argonauts.

HERMAPHRODITUS Beautiful youth, offspring of Venus and Mercury, who was enticed into her fount by the nymph Salmacis. The two fused into a single being, both male and female.

HERO See *Leander*.

HESPERIDES Keepers of the legendary golden apples in the far west.

HIPPOCRENE Fount of the Muses on Mount Helicon, created by a blow from the hoof of the winged horse Pegasus.

HOMER Greek epic poet of the eighth century BCE, author of the *Iliad* and *Odyssey*, who is regarded as the founder of the European epic tradition. He was reputed to have been blind and to have been born in Chios or on the Ionian mainland.

HORACE Quintus Horatius Flaccus, Roman lyric poet (65–8 BCE), author of *Satires*, *Odes* and *Epistles*.

HYACINTHUS Spartan boy beloved of Apollo, by whom he was accidentally killed with a discus.

HYDRA Nine-headed water-serpent killed by Hercules as one of the Twelve Labours.

HYLAS See *Hercules*.

HYMEN Roman god of marriage.

IDUMAEA Country south of Palestine; adj. 'Idumaean' generally = 'Palestinian'.

ILIAD Homer's epic on the wrath of Achilles and the Trojan war.

IONIA Central west coast of Asia Minor (modern Turkey); colonized around the eighth century BCE by Athens and other Greek cities, it developed a high degree of culture, despite pressure from its neighbours.

IRIS Goddess of the rainbow and messenger of the gods.

IRUS Beggar in Homer *Odyssey* 18, whom Odysseus (Ulysses) fights and defeats.

ISIS Egyptian goddess worshipped at Rome in a temple in the Campus Martius.

IULUS Son of Aeneas; ancestor of the Julian imperial family and (more generally) of Rome.

JANICULUM Hill in Rome on the west bank of the Tiber.

JASON Leader of the Argonautic expedition which, through the magic of Medea, recovered the Golden Fleece; he married Medea and rejected her (with tragic consequences) in Corinth. See *Medea*.

JOVE See *Jupiter*.

JULIA (1) Daughter of Julius Caesar and wife of Pompey the Great; (2) Niece of Domitian, with whom it was rumoured that the emperor had an incestuous and adulterous affair, causing her premature death through abortion.

JUNO Daughter of Saturn, wife of Jupiter and queen of heaven.

JUPITER (or Jove) Roman sky god, king of the Olympian deities; father of Apollo, Bacchus, Hercules, etc. His Olympian wife was Juno.

JUVENAL Roman satirist and poet of the early empire, writing under the emperors Trajan and Hadrian (98–138 CE).

LABICI ('Labicum') Small town in the vicinity of Rome, to the south-east.

LACEDAEMON Sparta, important Greek state in the southern Peloponnese, famous for its martial qualities. It had a famous temple to Venus.

LACHESIS One of the Fates, who decided on the length of life for each individual.

LAIS Name of two celebrated courtesans of Corinth, one in the fifth, one in the fourth centuries BCE. They were paradigms of the expensive, high-class prostitute, and subjects of various anecdotes.

LAR Household god that provided the centre of Roman family worship; generally depicted as a young man dancing. Tutelary deity, often of a house. Most often used in the plural, *Lares*.

LATINUS ('Latine') Famous comic actor, a favourite and spy of Domitian.

LATIUM Region of Italy in which Rome is situated; adjs. 'Latin', 'Latian'. The inhabitants of the area, the *Latini*, gave their name to the Latin language.

LAUREOLUS Notorious robber who was punished with crucifixion and dismemberment by wild beasts. The incident became the subject of a mime under Caligula, and was re-enacted 'for real' in the arena of the Flavian amphitheatre with a criminal 'playing' Laureolus.

LEANDER Famous lover, who used to swim the Hellespont nightly to visit his beloved Hero, a priestess of Venus.

LESBIA The married mistress of Catullus in his love lyrics, often identified with Clodia Metelli, an aristocratic *femme fatale* of the sixties and fifties BCE. Two of Catullus' poems (nos. 2 and 3) are concerned with Lesbia's pet sparrow.

LIBER (1) Another name for Bacchus; (2) Charioteer friend of Martial.

LIBYA ('Lybia') Coastal district of north Africa, west of Egypt, often used for north Africa generally.

LICINIANUS Compatriot of Martial from Bilbilis; orator and senator.

LIGURIA Area of northern Italy and southern France, stretching from the Rhône to the Arno and inland to the south of the river Po.

LIVY ('Livie') Roman historian (*c*.59 BCE–17 CE) during the reign of the first emperor Augustus. His monumental history of Rome from its foundations was the longest work in the Latin language (142 books).

LONGINUS Author of the literary treatise *On the Sublime*.

LUCAN Marcus Annaeus (39–65 CE); Roman epic poet of the Neronian era, author of the civil war poem *Civil War* or *Pharsalia* (incomplete in nine and a half books). Involved in a conspiracy to kill Nero, he was forced to commit suicide.

LUCRETIA ('Lucrece') Legendary Roman heroine, wife of Brutus the Liberator; her rape by Sextus Tarquin and subsequent suicide led to the expulsion of the Etruscan kings from Rome and the establishment of Rome as a republic (509 BCE). She became a symbol of old-fashioned Roman chastity.

LUCRETIUS Famous Roman poet of the late republic, author of the Epicurean didactic epic *On the Nature of Things*.

LUCRINE ('Lucrin') Lagoon (now Lago Lucrino) near Baiae, renowned for its oysters.

LYCORIS Name of the woman addressed as the beloved in Gallus' elegies. Often identified with the actress Cytheris.

LYDIA Region of western Asia Minor, ruled by King Croesus in the sixth century BCE.

LYSIPPUS Renowned Greek sculptor of the fourth century BCE.

MAECENAS ('Mecenas') Important minister of the first emperor Augustus and patron of literature. Among those he supported were Horace and Virgil.

MANTUA City of northern Italy and traditional birthplace of Virgil, who was actually born at the nearby village of Andes in 70 BCE.

MARCELLA Wealthy patroness of Martial in Bilbilis after his retirement there. She gave the poet a small country estate.

MARCIA Great aqueduct near Martial's house in Rome.

MARO See *Virgil*.

MARS God of war and father of the founder of Rome, Romulus.

MARSUS Marcus Domitius; Augustan epic poet and epigrammatist.

MARTIAL The name not only of the epigrammatist (Marcus), but of his closest friend during the thirty-four years he lived in Rome, the lawyer Julius Martialis.

MASSILIA Modern Marseilles; an early and prosperous mercantile town on the coast of southern Gaul, long allied with Rome.

MAUSOLEUM Great tomb of Mausolus, king of Caria (d. 353 BCE), built by his wife Artemisia. It ranked among the seven wonders of the ancient world.

MEDEA Tragic and epic heroine, who, for love, helped the Argonaut Jason in his quest for the Golden Fleece. When he rejected her for a princess of Corinth, she killed both the princess and her own children (by Jason) in revenge.

MEGARA Wife of Hercules, killed by him in a fit of madness.

MELIOR Marcus Atedius, wealthy patron of Martial and Statius, who dedicated Book 2 of *Silvae* to him.

MEMPHIS Main city in Egypt after Alexandria; centre of Lower Egypt.

MENTOR Fourth-century-BCE engraver.

MERCURY God of travellers, boundaries, unexpected treasure trove, merchants and thieves; the guide of the souls to the underworld.

MINERVA Virgin goddess of arts and wisdom, and so of schoolboys, who paid their fees on or around the festival of Minerva (19 March); identified with the Greek goddess Pallas Athena, patron goddess of Athens, protectress of civilized life and goddess of war, wisdom and agriculture, especially the cultivation of the olive; Domitian's adopted patron goddess.

MINOS Legendary king of Crete, husband of Pasiphaë, and (in the underworld) one of the judges of the dead. See *Pasiphaë*.

MITHRIDATES ('Mithridate') VI King of Pontus (120–63 BCE), who waged war successfully against the Romans, but was finally defeated by Pompey. Immune to poison because of his prophylactic precautions (or 'mithridates'), he had himself killed by a guard's sword.

MOLORCHUS Poor man who entertained Hercules before the latter slew the Nemean lion.

MULVIAN BRIDGE Bridge over the Tiber just north of Rome, famous later as the site in 312 CE of the defeat of Maxentius by Constantine the Great.

MYCENAE Prehistoric town in the Argive plain of the Peloponnese; centre of Mycenaean civilization.

NARNIA ('Narni') Town in central Italy forty miles north of Rome.

NAUSICAA Unmarried daughter (in Homer's *Odyssey*) of Alcinous, king of Phaeacia, who directs Ulysses to her father's palace.

NEMESIS Name of one of the women addressed as the beloved by the poet in Tibullus' elegies.

NEMI Lake area in the Alban hills south-east of Rome.

NEPTUNE Olympian god, ruler of the sea, sharing universal power with his brothers, Jupiter and Pluto. His symbol was the trident.

NEREID Sea nymph, born of Doris and Nereus.

NEREUS A god of the sea, father of the Nereids.

NERO Roman emperor, born 37 CE, who reigned 54–68 CE; famous for his interest in the arts, persecution of Christians, lavish building pro-gramme (most especially the 'Golden House') and autocratic style. The civil war and instability which followed his death were ended by Vespasian, first of the Flavian emperors (69–79 CE).

NESTOR Mythical king of Pylos in the Peloponnese, who contributed his experience and his sons to the Trojan war; celebrated among the heroes of Troy for his wisdom, eloquence and longevity.

NIOBE Daughter of Tantalus; she had twelve children by Amphion and compared herself favourably with Leto, mother of Apollo and Diana (Greek Artemis). The two gods killed the children for her presump-tion. Niobe, who wept inconsolably, was turned into a rock and her tears into a waterfall.

NOMENTUM Town thirteen miles north-east of Rome, near which Martial's 'poor' villa was situated.

NORICUM Roman province in the area of modern Austria, famous for its metal production; adj. 'Noric'.

NUMA Second king of Rome (715–673 BCE), a lawmaker, who taught the values of peace; a standard model of old-time virtue, especially 'piety'.

NYSA ('Nisa') Place in India where according to legend Bacchus was reared by local nymphs.

ODRYSIAN Thracian and more generally northern, from 'Odrysae', a Thracian people.

ODYSSEY Homer's epic on the wanderings and return of Ulysses (Greek Odysseus) after the end of the Trojan war.

OEBALUS King of Sparta; adj. 'Oebalian' = 'Spartan'.

OEDIPUS King of Thebes, who unwittingly killed his father and married his mother, by whom he produced two sons and two daughters. When the truth was revealed, he put out his eyes and abdicated the throne.

OPIMIAN Wine produced in the consulship of Opimius (121 BCE), a famous vintage year; more generally, the finest quality wine.

ORESTES Son of Agamemnon and Clytemnestra, who slew his mother to avenge her murder of his father.

ORPHEUS Famed singer and musician of Thrace who, after the death of his wife Eurydice, went to the underworld, where he so charmed Pluto with his singing that she was allowed to leave. However, he lost her on turning to look back just before arriving in the upper world. In extreme grief he ignored the women of Thrace, who, furious at his neglect, tore him to pieces and scattered his body over the fields.

OVID Roman elegiac, erotic and epic poet (43 BCE–*c*.17 CE); his works include *Amores*, *Heroides*, *Art of Love*, *Metamorphoses*, *Fasti* and *Tristia*.

PAELIGNI ('Peligni') Inhabitants of the area of central Italy east of Rome, the chief town of which was Sulmo (modern Sulmona), where Ovid was born.

PAESTUM Town on the Italian west coast, renowned for roses.

PAETUS ('Paeto', 'Poetus', 'Petus') See *Arria*.

PALATINE One of the seven hills of Rome. It overlooked the Roman Forum and was the site of the main imperial residence (hence 'palace') from Augustus onwards. Also on the Palatine were the temple of Apollo and its libraries, the house of Romulus, and the temple of Magna Mater, the Great Mother.

PALESTRINA See *Praeneste*.

PALLAS A title of the Roman goddess Minerva, taken from her Greek counterpart Athena. See *Minerva*.

PAN God of woods and shepherds, protector of sheep, inventor of the shepherd's pipe, consisting of several reeds of different lengths.

PANDORA First woman, created as a punishment for men; she possessed 'all gifts', which she kept in a jar or 'box', from which all the evils of the world were let out.

PARIS Celebrated pantomime (actor-dancer) of the Roman stage with an immense following; executed by Domitian.

PARMA Northern Italian town.

PAROS Aegean island famous for the brilliance of its marble.

PARTHENIUS Domitian's chamberlain, who participated in his assassination.

PARTHENOPAEUS Arcadian warrior; the youngest and most handsome of the 'Seven' heroes who attacked Thebes in the war between the sons of Oedipus.

PARTHIA Unconquered kingdom on the Roman frontiers in the east; perceived as a constant military threat, the Parthians figured frequently in Roman poetry.

PASIPHAE Wife of Minos, king of Crete, mother of Ariadne and Phaedra; she achieved notoriety through the consummation of her passion for the bull sent by Neptune to her husband for sacrifice. This 'monstrous passion' gave birth to the Minotaur (half-man, half-bull).

PATROCLUS Greek hero, companion, attendant and close friend of Achilles in Homer's *Iliad*.

PEDO Albinovanus; Augustan epic poet and epigrammatist, friend of Ovid.

PENATES Gods of the inner reaches of the house, technically of the storecupboard; used by metonymy for the house itself.

PENELOPE Wife of Ulysses, for whom she waited for twenty years; model of wifely chastity and devotion.

PERENNA Anna; a native Italian goddess, whose festival on the Ides of March involved the singing of licentious songs by women.

PERSEPHONE See *Proserpina*.

PHAETHON Hero who was permitted to drive the chariot of his father, the Sun, but was unable to control the reins, and, struck by Jupiter's thunderbolt, fell to his death in the river Po.

PHIDIAS Major Athenian sculptor of the fifth century BCE.

PHILOMELA ('Philomel') See *Tereus*.

PHINEUS ('Phineas') Blind prophet from Thrace.

PHOEBUS See *Apollo*.

PHRIXUS ('Phryxus') Son of Athamas and Nephele, who escaped on a ram with a golden fleece to Colchis. The recovery of this golden fleece was the object of the Argonautic expedition.

PHRYGIA Region of north-western Asia Minor, often identified with Troy; adj. 'Phrygian'.

PICENUM Fertile region of east-central Italy; adj. 'Picenan' or 'Picenian'.

PIERIAN Sacred to the Muses (the 'Pierides'); poetic.

PINDAR Distinguished Greek lyric poet of Thebes, who flourished during the first half of the fifth century BCE.

PLATEA ('Plataea') Place near Bilbilis.

PLUTO Brother of Jupiter and ruler of the underworld.

POETUS See *Paetus*.

POLLA Argentaria; widow of the poet Lucan.

POLYPHEMUS ('Polyphem') One-eyed Cyclops, son of Neptune, who herded sheep. He was blinded by Ulysses.

POMPEY Roman general, known as 'the Great' (106–48 BCE); defeated by Julius Caesar at Pharsalus (48 BCE), he fled to Egypt where he was assassinated by Pothinus, decapitated and burnt on the Egyptian coast. His two sons, Gnaeus and Sextus, were killed in Spain and Asia respectively. He was responsible for building the first stone theatre in Rome (55 BCE), known as 'Pompey's Theatre', which the elder Pliny claimed seated 40,000 spectators. Many prefer a figure of 10,000. Adjoining the theatre was Pompey's portico, built at the same time.

PORCIA ('Portia') Daughter of Cato the younger and wife (from 45 BCE) of Brutus (2).

PORSEN(N)A Lars, Etruscan king of Clusium, who besieged Rome in a failed attempt to restore the exiled king, Tarquin the Proud. See *Scaevola*.

PORTIA See *Porcia*.

PRAENESTE Modern Palestrina; town in the Alban hills twenty miles east of Rome.

PRIAM Famed king of Troy during its war with the Greeks and father of numerous Trojan heroes and heroines including Hector and Paris; his wife was Hecuba. He was a symbol of longevity and, because of the fall of Troy and death of all his children, of personal tragedy.

PRIAPUS Ithyphallic god of sexuality and fertility, whose symbols were the erect phallus and the sickle. He was the protector of gardens, in which his statue, normally of wood, was placed to ward off thieves.

PROMETHEUS A Titan who created mankind out of clay and defied Jupiter by stealing fire from heaven and giving it to man. He was punished by being chained to a crag in the Caucasus, where a vulture daily devoured his liver.

PROPERTIUS Sextus; Roman elegiac poet of the Augustan period.

PROSERPINA ('Proserpine') Daughter of Ceres and Jupiter, wife of Pluto, queen of the underworld (= Greek Persephone).

PYLADES Friend and constant companion of Orestes.

PYRAMUS Ovidian hero who falls in love with his neighbour's daughter, Thisbe, and communicates with her through a chink in the party wall of the houses. When they at last arrange a rendezvous, Pyramus commits suicide thinking Thisbe to be dead. Thisbe finds his body and does likewise.

QUINTILIAN Marcus Fabius; noted rhetorician of the second half of the first century CE; author of *Institutio Oratoria* and the first 'professor' to be given an imperial salary. He came from Spain.

RABIRIUS Perhaps the foremost architect of the Flavian building programme; designer of the great palace of Domitian on the Palatine in Rome.

RAVENNA Important harbour city on the north-east coast of Italy south of the Po.

REGULUS Marcus Aquilius; feared advocate under Nero and Domitian, notorious for his prosecutions for treason; patron of Martial.

RHODES Large island off the south-west coast of Asia Minor, famous for its pure air, seafaring, rhetoric and the Colossus.

RUBRAE ('Rubra', 'Rubre') Place just north of Rome on the Via Flaminia.

SABINE ('Sabin') People just north-east of Rome who were the first to be absorbed into the Roman state, their women being taken forcibly as wives by the men of Rome ('the Sabine Rape'). The women became symbols of old-fashioned hardiness and chastity.

SALARIAN WAY *Via Salaria* (*Salernia* in Whigham), 'Salt Way'; main road leading north-east from Rome through Reati (modern Rieti).

SALERNIA See *Salarian Way*.

SALMACIS A nymph – see *Hermaphroditus*; adj. 'Salmacian'.

SALO River of Bilbilis.

SAPPHO Famous Greek lyric poetess of the sixth century BCE from Mytilene on the island of Lesbos.

SASSINA ('Sassinum') Umbrian town.

SATURN ('Saturne') Mythical king of Italy, then an early Italian god of agriculture, who was later identified with the Greek Kronos (hence the father of Jupiter and Juno). He ruled in Italy during the Golden Age (= 'Saturn's Age').

SATURNALIA Cheerful winter festival celebrated 17–19 December, when it was customary to give gifts.

SATYR Rustic demigod, bestial in nature and appearance (part-goat or part-horse), associated with Bacchus.

SCAEVOLA Mucius; legendary Roman hero, who, failing to assassinate Porsenna, the Etruscan king besieging Rome, held his left hand in a fire to prove Roman endurance.

SCIPIOS Important Roman family in the third and second centuries BCE; Scipio Africanus the Elder defeated Hannibal at the battle of Zama (202 BCE).

SCYLLA Daughter of the king of Megara who killed her father for love of Minos, king of Crete.

SCYTHIA Area in northern Europe and Asia stretching from the Black Sea and inhabited by nomadic tribes.

SEMELE Daughter of Cadmus, founder of Thebes, and mother of Bacchus by Jupiter, who in response to Semele's request to visit her in all his might entered her as a thunderbolt and killed her. The fatal intercourse was contrived by Juno.

SENECA (1) Lucius Annaeus, the Elder (c.55 BCE–c.40 CE), author of a lost history of Rome and a surviving (but badly mutilated) work on Roman declamation, *Controuersiae* and *Suasoriae*; (2) Lucius Annaeus, the Younger (c.1 BCE–65 CE), second son of (1), tutor and chief minister of the emperor Nero, eclectic Stoic philosopher and Roman tragedian.

SEPTICIAN A less valuable kind of silver.

SETIA Hill town some forty to fifty miles south-east of Rome; modern Sezze.

SILIUS Italicus; Flavian poet, author of *Punica*, a seventeen-book epic on the second war between Rome and Carthage (218–201 BCE).

SIRENS ('Syrens') Birds with the faces of virgins, who dwelt on the south-east coast of Italy. With their sweet songs they lured ashore those who sailed by and then killed them.

SISYPHUS Infamous sinner, condemned in the underworld to the eternal torment of pushing a large rock uphill only to have it roll down again.

SPARTA See *Lacedaemon*.

STELLA Lucius Arruntius; praetor in 93 CE and consul in 102 CE; important, congenial and generous patron of Martial. Like many Roman aristocrats, he also wrote verse.

STOICISM Influential philosophy among the Roman aristocracy, advocating reason, virtue, endurance, self-sufficiency and a submission to the divine will (= fate), and condemning the false values of wealth and power.

STYX Chief river of the underworld; by it the gods swore their 'greatest and most dread oath'; adj. 'Stygian'.

SUBURA Commercial and red light district between the Esquiline and the Viminal hills; the social centre of Rome.

SYMPLEGADES The Clashing or Cyanean Rocks, famous as the passage taken by the Argonauts on their journey to Colchis to seize the Golden Fleece.

SYREN See *Sirens*.

TACITUS Roman historian (born *c.*56 CE), who began writing after the death of Domitian; author of the *Histories* and *Annals*.

TAGUS River in Spain famous for its gold deposits; modern Tajo.

TANTALUS Son of Jupiter, condemned to eternal hunger and thirst for serving his son Pelops to the gods at a feast. Water and hanging fruit would withdraw from his grasp as he reached for them.

TARTARUS Bottommost pit of hell; the underworld's grimmest part, where the wicked were consigned for punishment. Generally, the underworld.

TATIUS Sabine king at the time of the Rape and subsequent co-ruler of Rome with Romulus; another standard model of old-fashioned virtue. See *Sabine*.

TELLUS Mother Earth.

TEREUS Mythical Thracian king, married to Philomela, who raped his sister-in-law Procne and cut out her tongue to prevent her from denouncing him. Philomela's revenge consisted in serving their son, Itys, as a meal to Tereus. The sisters fled and were turned into birds, Philomela into a nightingale, Procne into a swallow. Tereus was turned into a hoopoe. (In the Greek version Philomela was the sister and swallow, Procne the wife and nightingale.)

TETHYS Sea goddess, wife of Oceanus; in general, the sea.

THAIS Originally the name of a famous Athenian courtesan, it was regularly used as a 'street-name' by prostitutes.

THALES Early sixth century BCE Greek philosopher; one of the Seven Sages. He believed that the universe originated from water.

THALIA Muse of comedy, pastoral and 'small scale' poetry such as epigram.

THEBES Greek city, capital of Bocotia, founded by Cadmus and associated with the Oedipus saga.

THETIS Sea goddess, daughter of Nereus and mother of Achilles.

THISBE See *Pyramus*.

THRACE Territory stretching from the Danube to the Hellespont (Dardanelles) and from Byzantium (Istanbul) to the Strymon; its tribes were regarded as wild and primitive.

THYESTES Former tyrant of Mycenae who was given his sons to eat by his brother Atreus. The story was regularly treated in Roman tragedy.

THYMELE Comic actress in Roman mimes (obscene vaudeville).

TIBER River that flows through the city of Rome.

TIBUR Ancient hill-town of Latium, on the Via Valeria fifteen miles east of Rome, a favourite retreat from the hot Roman summers.

TIRYNTHIAN Hercules, native son of Tiryns.

TITUS Born in 39 CE, son of Vespasian, brother of Domitian, and second of the three Flavian emperors; conqueror of Judaea (70 CE). During his short reign (79–81 CE) occurred the volcanic eruption of Vesuvius and the destruction of Pompeii and Herculaneum in the Bay of Naples.

TIVOLI See *Tibur*.

TRITON Minor sea deity attending Neptune.

TROY Celebrated city in north-western Asia Minor plundered and destroyed by the Greeks at the end of the ten-year 'Trojan War'; adj. 'Trojan'.

TULLY See *Cicero*.

TUSCULUM Ancient town of Latium, in the Alban hills fifteen miles south-east of Rome, near modern Frascati; adj. 'Tusculan'.

TYRE Major maritime and commercial city of Phoenicia, famous for finely woven fabrics of silk or linen and for a purple dye; adj. 'Tyrian'.

ULYSSES ('Ulisses') King of Ithaca, who was pre-eminent among the Greeks at Troy for his cunning and eloquence. Through the device of the Wooden Horse he contrived Troy's fall. He wandered the Mediterranean for ten years before reaching Ithaca, where his wife Penelope and son Telemachus awaited him.

UMBRIA Region of central Italy north of Rome.

VARIUS Lucius Varius Rufus, Augustan poet and tragedian; author of the *Thyestes* performed at the triumphal games of 29 BCE. He was a friend of Virgil and his literary executor. He and Tucca edited the *Aeneid* after Virgil's death.

VENUS Roman goddess of sexual love (corresponding to the Greek Aphrodite), mother of Aeneas and Cupid.

VERGIL See *Virgil*.

VERONA Northern Italian city, famous as the birthplace of Catullus.

VESPASIAN Father of Titus and Domitian, and founder of the Flavian dynasty of Roman emperors. Born in 9 CE, he reigned 69–79 CE.

VESTA Roman goddess of the hearth and of the city; her cult, with the care of the undying flame, was served by the Vestal virgins. Vesta's temple and house, in which the Vestals resided, were in the Roman Forum.

VESTAL See *Vesta*.

VESUVIUS ('Vesuvio') Famous volcano in Campania near the bay of Naples that erupted on 24 August 79 CE, burying Pompeii, Herculaneum and Stabiae.

VIPSANIAN Built by Marcus Vipsanius Agrippa. See *Agrippa*.

VIRGIL ('Vergil') Publius Vergilius Maro, most renowned of Roman poets (70–19 BCE), who lived through the great political and social changes of the first century BCE, when Rome moved from a senatorial republic to the virtual monarchy of the empire; author of *Eclogues*, *Georgics* and the great foundation epic of the Roman state, the *Aeneid*.

VITELLIAN Name of small writing tablets.

VULCAN God of fire and technology; married to Venus and cuckolded by Mars.

LIST OF EPIGRAMS
TRANSLATED

LIST OF ENGLISH POEMS

INDEX OF POETS

READ MORE IN PENGUIN

In every corner of the world, on every subject under the sun, Penguin represents quality and variety – the very best in publishing today.

For complete information about books available from Penguin – including Puffins, Penguin Classics and Arkana – and how to order them, write to us at the appropriate address below. Please note that for copyright reasons the selection of books varies from country to country.

In the United Kingdom: Please write to *Dept. EP, Penguin Books Ltd, Bath Road, Harmondsworth, West Drayton, Middlesex UB7 ODA*

In the United States: Please write to *Consumer Sales, Penguin USA, P.O. Box 999, Dept. 17109, Bergenfield, New Jersey 07621-0120*. VISA and MasterCard holders call 1-800-253-6476 to order Penguin titles

In Canada: Please write to *Penguin Books Canada Ltd, 10 Alcorn Avenue, Suite 300, Toronto, Ontario M4V 3B2*

In Australia: Please write to *Penguin Books Australia Ltd, P.O. Box 257, Ringwood, Victoria 3134*

In New Zealand: Please write to *Penguin Books (NZ) Ltd, Private Bag 102902, North Shore Mail Centre, Auckland 10*

In India: Please write to *Penguin Books India Pvt Ltd, 706 Eros Apartments, 56 Nehru Place, New Delhi 110 019*

In the Netherlands: Please write to *Penguin Books Netherlands bv, Postbus 3507, NL-1001 AH Amsterdam*

In Germany: Please write to *Penguin Books Deutschland GmbH, Metzlerstrasse 26, 60594 Frankfurt am Main*

In Spain: Please write to *Penguin Books S. A., Bravo Murillo 19, 1° B, 28015 Madrid*

In Italy: Please write to *Penguin Italia s.r.l., Via Felice Casati 20, I-20124 Milano*

In France: Please write to *Penguin France S. A., 17 rue Lejeune, F-31000 Toulouse*

In Japan: Please write to *Penguin Books Japan, Ishikiribashi Building, 2-5-4, Suido, Bunkyo-ku, Tokyo 112*

In Greece: Please write to *Penguin Hellas Ltd, Dimocritou 3, GR-106 71 Athens*

In South Africa: Please write to *Longman Penguin Southern Africa (Pty) Ltd, Private Bag X08, Bertsham 2013*

READ MORE IN PENGUIN

A CHOICE OF CLASSICS